A Burden of Ice and Bone

Kyra Whitton

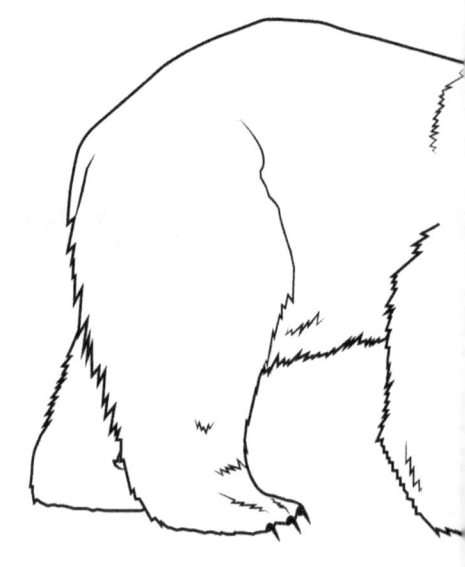

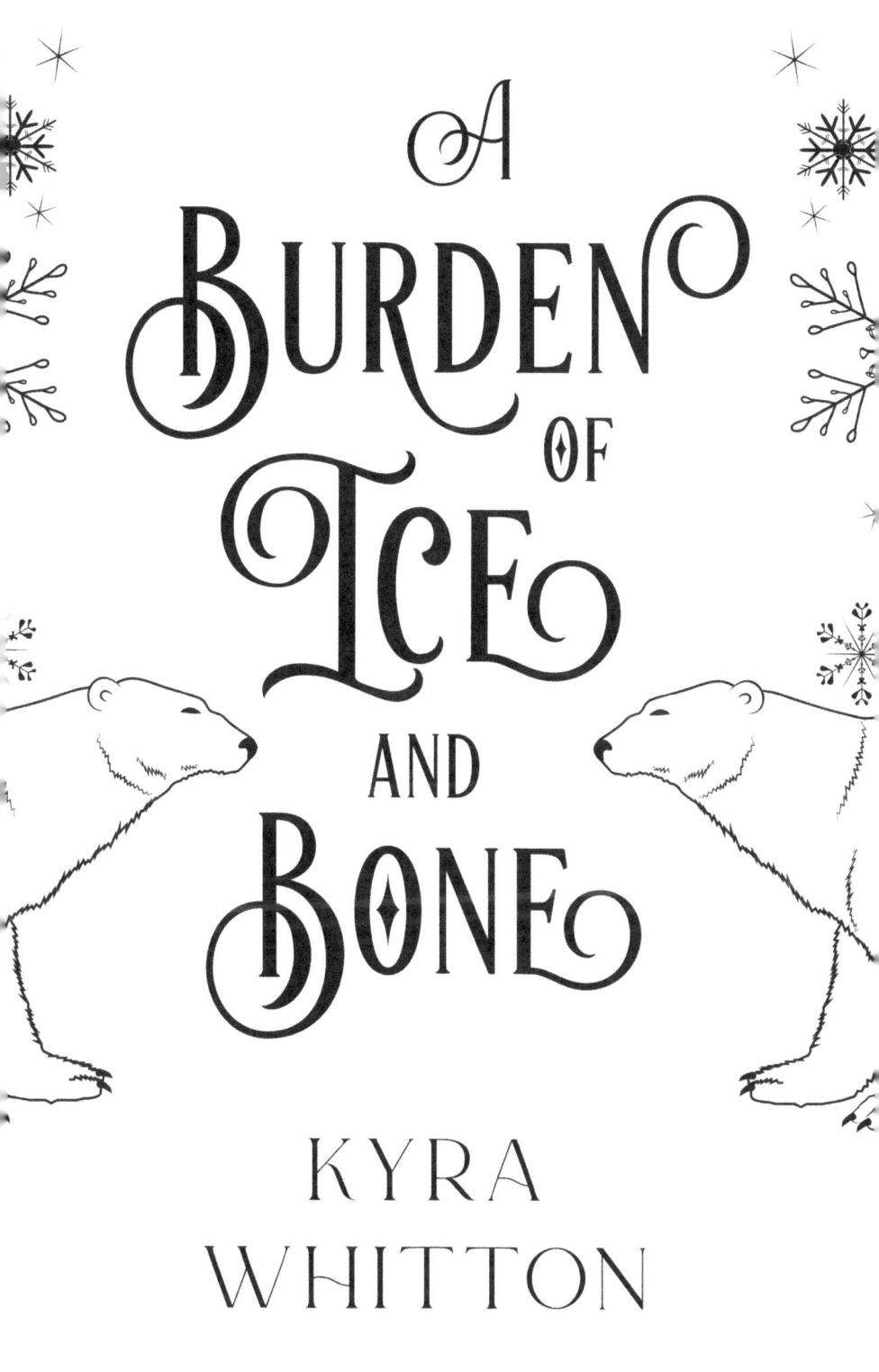

A Burden of Ice and Bone

Kyra Whitton

In Memory of my brother, David.
I know you never would have read this because no one is brutally murdered by axe or man dressed like bat, but I still like to think you had something to do with it becoming a book.

CHAPTER 1

Autumn is the most dangerous time of year in Willoughby.

Both bay and sea lap against the long stretches of shoreline near our little town, the winter ice not yet solid enough to walk across. In a matter of days, great, frozen sheets will cover the bay and the edges of the sea, tempting the polar bears away from our settlement. But until then, the bears roam the shallow waters, rolling dunes, and sunken tide pools. Hungry. Starving. Hunting for food on a land with little to offer them. And in that stretch before the ice fully forms, those cooling days of autumn, the bears turn their attention to Willoughby and the scents of meat rising from our storehouses.

Granny Grin sees it as an opportunity. Not for herself, but for me. She says I'll be the one to change Willoughby.

My great-grandmother's assertions usually come with a gentle hand on my hair or a soft squeeze to my shoulder. Sometimes she makes them off-handedly when I visit every week, matter-of-factly, like commenting on the weather. Others it's more pointed; she murmurs the words softly as she pours me a cup of tea made from leaves we gather together inland, usually when she sees my role as Dira Cloon, the Great Disappointment, pressing down on me like the weight of winter's ice. A nice sentiment, meant to placate me, to soften the blow of being the youngest in my family, the aimless, a survivor of our only enemy: the bears. As if it can erase the scars I already left on our town. But she never fails to say it. Just as I never fail to hope she's right.

Because changing twenty years of perception is a heavy burden.

My breath puffs out like fog rolling in over the bay as I stare up at a fading harvest moon with burning eyes. Sleep eluded me most of last night. I knew I would be waking far earlier than I am used to, and so, naturally, my brain refused to quiet. It ran through every possibility, every early morning patrol scenario. When Mama shook me awake in the still-dark hours, adrenaline coursed through my veins like the crashing waves of a summer storm. Even now, my heart flutters nervously.

The sun hasn't yet brightened the sky, but the edges glow a soft, murky purple. It won't be long before dawn stretches into morning, and I itch to get on with it, to take to the muddy streets. Making the rounds won't make the shift go by any faster, but standing here only plucks at my nerves, the buildings' walls closing in, blocking out the wide-open spaces of the wilds that call to me.

What's taking him so long?

The flurry-tipped winds tug at the hood of my parka as I wait outside the patrol office for my partner. Willoughby seems fresh and new, like the first day of winter come early, and I long to be traipsing through the wilds despite the hard, damp wind and the scent of ice in the air.

The whine of unoiled hinges drags my attention to the patrol office's front door, and my fluttering nervousness ebbs, replaced by the same hopelessness I felt the first time my older brother handed me a rifle.

It comes every shift, the pull of emotions in every possible direction. Anxiousness always, but also fear. Doubt. Melancholy.

Autumn is the most dangerous time of year in Willoughby.

For people and polar bears.

Every day, I long to set down my rifle. But despite the wrenching in my soul, I reluctantly pick it up and prepare to save one by stepping between both.

"Moore and Linka encountered a large male last night near the Crevitt house." The door bangs closed behind my eldest brother, Landry, as he sidles up beside me. I'm not sure who's being punished by being paired together this morning, him or me. Since I joined the patrol last year, I've always done my rounds with one of the older members, like my uncle Thesper or cousin Joles. If my twin hadn't decided to get engaged yesterday, I wouldn't be out here at all. Instead, I'd be still snugly cocooned under my blankets at home. I certainly wouldn't be spending the whole morning with the last person I want in charge of me: the same guy who shoved his dirty socks under my nose and dug his knuckles into my scalp when we were children.

Landry pulls his parka's fur-lined hood over an old knit cap and buttons his collar up to his chin. "He was aggressive, took out three of Dorin's reindeer before trying to break into the town market."

Not much would be left in the market house after hours. During the day, villagers lay out crab and fish and whale blubber to trade for wool and cheese, ox milk, fresh honey, and venison. All of it is gone now, but the smells remain, stinking up the wood. And three reindeer out of a herd of a thousand isn't significant, yet people tend to forget simple arithmetic when it's livestock.

3

I lean forward to stare down the street where the market stands in the morning shadows, half-expecting to see the bear there now. But there's no sign of it, not even a paw print in the mud.

But in Willoughby, the people believe the bear will come back again and again once he knows where to find an easy meal. That he'll strike out at children next, and then the elderly. After that, it will only be a matter of time before the bear rips through everyone else, bloodthirsty and eager for a kill. And they think if one catches our scent, others will too.

It's happened before. Not recently. Not since I was seven, and that was a misunderstanding, an anomaly that hadn't happened in a hundred years and never repeated itself. But it happened, and once is enough for the people of Willoughby.

"Did either of them recognize it?" I try to hide the rush of anxiety marching through my blood at the thought of one of *my* bears. I've named the ones I watch from a distance, even though I've been told for years I shouldn't. But after that day more than a decade ago, I snuck around the curve of the shore to catch sight of them, my notebook and a pencil tucked under my arm to jot down everything I could observe. Hidden in the willow shrubs or high up in the trees, I could see what no one else even bothered to look for: their beauty, their majesty, their power.

Over the years, I uncovered patterns, not just in how the bears behaved, but which ones summered along the uninhabited beaches outside of town. I have a few favorites, though I haven't seen most of them this season. Big Boy likes to lie in the willow shrubs with his belly toward the sky and his nose twitching in the wind. Bear Paws is missing a nail on the front left paw, so when he strolls through the first snowfalls, he's easy to track. And Head Case; I've always liked him best, ever since Linka and I found him with his head caught in an old, broken crab trap on the bay side beach. I've never been sure how he got it off, yet the rip in his right ear might be a clue. But I haven't found the young cub with the pink freckle on his nose or the giant scarred male again. Maybe one day I will.

Patrolling the late afternoon shift has always been my preference because it gives me plenty of time to hike into the wilds in the mornings or evenings to watch the bears along the coast. But more importantly, the bears are least active when the sun is the highest and as it falls to the horizon in a thousand hues of gold and blue and plum. During my year on the patrol, I've never encountered a bear in town or along the outskirts.

And that's how I like it.

Because any bear that wanders through our invisible borders is swiftly and violently dispatched. And I can't bear to be a part of it.

Landry must sense my eagerness to know the bear's identity because his eyes narrow, and his mouth thins beneath the fringe of his mustache as he nudges me forward. "Come on, Whelp. Let's not spoil your first morning shift by romanticizing the monsters that want to rip your face off."

I start to protest, but clear my throat instead. He expects me to argue with him. He knows why I take the warmest hours of the day, even though they come with the least pay. And he doesn't understand why, not after what we both saw that day thirteen years ago. "They didn't take him down?"

Landry steers me west toward the bay side of town, and I readjust my rifle onto the opposite shoulder so it doesn't knock into his.

"No."

"Why not?" I ask with as much innocence as I can muster.

He shoots a suspicious look down at me. I may be taller than most of the townspeople, but he still towers over me. Us Cloons are a mountainous lot.

"It was dark. They didn't want to risk a stray shot."

I nod sagely, but a smile threatens to take control of my lips. Who could the bear be? Perhaps a new one for my journal. I've recorded hundreds of bears as they flock to the coastlines when the ice melts away, and I'm always glad to find a new one. It's one step closer to finding the bear from my childhood.

"Moore said they tracked him east but lost him in the surf. Dad thinks he might try to come back now that he's caught the scent of food."

"Think he's still out there?" I stare down Main Street toward the shoreline, half expecting the bear to wander into my line of sight. But there's nothing there that shouldn't be.

"Probably. But we can't go jumping off our route without any sign of it. Yet." Landry turns his steel gray gaze on me and reaches up to pull on an escaped curl just over my ear.

He thinks he knows me so well. After all, it was Landry who usually caught me sneaking off when I was younger. Following instructions has never been my strength, and because of him, I had to become sneakier. I think he still suspects I spend time picking my way through the wilds alone, but he never says anything about it anymore.

I swat his hand away. "I wouldn't do that." And I mean it. Lately, I've been careful to toe the line, to do everything my father asks, within reason. His frustration with me is thinly veiled, especially after my last expedition took me further around the bay than I intended, and I spent a night camping in the wilds alone. My parents worried their nightmares of me being mauled finally came true. Now my father watches me with more intensity than a red-tailed hawk, waiting for one more missed shot. One more claim of near-sightedness, and I fear he might disown me. Then the stars as my only blankets might become a reality.

Landry snorts and adjusts the rifle strap hanging off his shoulder.

"I know you better than you think, Whelp. At this very moment, the gears are spinning in that overly large head of yours, trying to come up with a way to distract me from the task at hand." He lifts a shaggy eyebrow and his lips quirk into a knowing smirk beneath his scruff of tawny facial hair. "It isn't going to work."

Fine. Let him think whatever he wants. Adding a bounce to my step, I take the lead. "We have to start on the west side of town, anyway." Eight of us are on patrol right now, and we all move in overlapping circles through Willoughby's narrow lanes and outer perimeter. If a bear were to slip into the streets, one of us would come across it. The process works. At least that's what my father, the patrol chief, would have everyone in town and on the governing council believe. Because no one has been attacked inside the Willoughby boundary lines, not since the patrols were set up a hundred years ago. We kill the bears before they can even enter.

"Good. Now, just stick to normal plans and procedures, all right? I promised Calla I wouldn't let you do anything stupid, and I'm a man of my word."

"Yeah, but if you were a smart man, you wouldn't promise anything."

"If I hadn't been assigned to you, she wouldn't have asked." He glares pointedly down at me. Landry's wife, Calla, always finds something to be anxious over, and most days, I think it's me. I should put her fears to rest. But it's a lot more fun stoking them.

"Just don't do anything we'll both regret. Please, Dira," Landry warns as he swings his gaze back toward the bay's shore.

But something in his voice changes, and I lean around him to follow his gaze.

A white speck against the gray morning sky.

I lift my binoculars.

Lumbering along the edge of town, a large bear, male by the size of him, lifts his nose into the air. Coming in from the ocean side, the wind ruffles the plaits woven tightly against my scalp, pulling strands free before it drives across the narrow stretch of land toward Willoughby Bay. The wind carries the scent of me, of Landry, the whole town, toward the bear.

He's well outside the town boundaries, off the circular path we're supposed to follow. He should be safe.

My heart rate kicks up as I lower the lenses and Landry murmurs, "There he is" from beside me. Excitement colors his voice. "Let me call it in."

I turn to glance up at him as a sick feeling settles into my stomach. "Why? He's way over there. He's a safe distance away."

My protest falls on deaf ears as Landry unhooks the radio from his belt and trudges forward, his long strides eating up the mud. "Come on."

I drop the binoculars so they swing down from the strap looped over my neck and rest my hand on the butt of the rifle. We shouldn't be going forward. "But what about the route?" I call after him.

Ahead of me, Landry cranks the two-way radio, the gears whirring as he powers it up. Ignoring me.

My pulse beating wildly in my throat, I trot forward, my boots slapping in the mud. If I can get ahead of the situation, I can control it. Yes, that's exactly what I'll do. Landry might be my lead, but he's distracted.

My pace slows as I reach the last few clapboard houses huddled at the edge of town. If we get too close too quickly, the bear might see it as a sign of aggression and charge us. They can run faster than any human, and once we step onto the open beach, there will be no place for us to duck and hide. I don't want him to charge—that will be a sure, swift death for him. It'll have to be. But maybe if he sees me, he'll wander off, find an easy meal rather than something he has to fight for.

The bear lifts his head as I approach, unconcerned by the firearm at my back. He's huge, one of the largest I've seen, well over half a ton, with thick, sturdy front legs and a twitching black nose. A scar gashes his left cheek, just missing one of the obsidian eyes staring back at me.

I stop, my feet spread apart as our gazes clash. The scar on his cheek is the same as the one that's sped into my dreams since I was seven. I've watched for him every day since, waiting until I might see him again.

My pulse pounds in my neck. It can't be the same bear. And yet it has to be. His gaze bores into me, seeing me as I see him, recognizing something that only two spirits linked as we are can. Every fiber of my being wants to rejoice, and yet I stand there, rooted, not a muscle twitching.

Landry's boots crunch on the gravelly shore behind me.

"I don't care where it is. Take it out. Is that clear?" crackles our father's voice over the little radio. He's been patrol chief since before I was born. No one has dealt with more polar bears than Dad. And because of it, he thinks he knows how they move, where they go, what they think, how to deal with them. Everyone sees him as the authority.

But he's wrong. They're wrong.

And this is my chance to prove it.

"Perfectly," Landry rumbles back as he comes to stand beside me. He lowers the radio to his hip, sliding it back into a pouch hanging from his leather belt, and heaves a heavy sigh. "I'll do it. Put your rifle away." He glances down at me. "I know you don't have the stomach for any of this—shit!"

My gaze flies to my brother and then follows his unblinking stare. Just down the shore, a lone boat rows up onto the sand. The air knocks out of my lungs as I take in the familiar vessel, the pile of crab traps, and my best friend's dark hair.

"Beren!" I scream, but the wind slaps his name back into my face.

The bear lifts his nose into the wind, then follows it toward Beren's fresh haul of crabs.

But Beren doesn't notice, his back to us as he splashes into the shallows and grabs hold of the boat's sides to drag it out of the water. Between the distance and the crashing waves, he doesn't hear my screams as the bear trots closer.

Landry swings his rifle around, checks his ammunition, and thumbs off the safety.

No. I want to holler it until my throat scratches in pain, to distract my brother, to scare the bear. But as my heart thunders erratically, I can no longer find the air. I swing my gaze back to Beren. If I don't do something, my best friend could be gone in an instant. My gaze bounces between the two of them, and my pulse screams in my ears, echoing the words I can't say—won't say.

Don't shoot him now that I've found him!

In all my days on the patrol, I've made sure I've never seen another bear get shot. Today won't be the day. This won't be the bear.

But Beren— If we don't do something, circumstance will take another Metz from us—the last one. The bear could be on him in seconds, toss him like a ragdoll, snap his neck, rip his face from his skull.

A thirteen-year-old memory of the first flurries of winter, the sound of crashing waves, and sand covered in the deep red of blood blots out the scene in front of me. I can't let that happen again.

I have to choose.

The bear.

Or Beren.

And I have to make a decision before my brother makes the choice for me.

Time slows as I firmly press the rifle into my shoulder and take the bear into my sights.

CHAPTER 2

From the outside looking in, autumn's beauty is almost enough to make anyone forget the danger that comes with it. The clouds roll in thick as the cooler months push over our little town, and the bonfires billow outside long into the evening as the fishermen, hunters, and gatherers bring in their catches. That leaves the children with the run of the town, and they take advantage of every last moment of sunlight before winter sets in when they are ushered inside until the ice melts.

Thirteen years ago, I was one of those children, and it was the last time my parents knowingly let me out of their sights once the polar bears landed on solid ground. They thought my older brother and the fires would keep me safe.

But I skipped ahead of Landry, my braids flopping up and down in front of my face, and he didn't call me back; he was too distracted by Calla. I wouldn't go far, I told myself. Just over the dunes and toward the slender creek that ran between the willow shrubs south of town. The water was clear and cold, run-off from the glacier that sat heavy over the land and dipped into the sea.

It was rare that I got to go about exploring alone. Usually, Beren and my twin, Linka, were with me. Just the three of us, as inseparable

as if we were roped together around our hips. But after they got caught fist fighting in the mud outside the patrol office—I *may* have instigated their argument, hitting each of them in the back of the head with tiny pebbles and then blaming it on the other—both were forced to help gut fish with Beren's parents as punishment.

Alone without the two of them, I squatted down next to the rushing water. I reached for a small, round shell. It fit easily in the palm of my hand and the swirl was tight and well-pronounced, but when I turned it over, the dark gray flesh of a snail shined up at me. My fingers always tingled when I plunged them into the fresh water to pick out round, black snail shells from the shallow bed. If they were empty, I shoved them deep into my pockets to take home, but I always left those that had a blobby gray creature inside.

I dropped it and reached for another just as a fat snowflake drifted toward the water.

It was still early for the first snow, and I glanced up to watch as more flakes winked against the blue-gray clouds like stars. I loved when the first snows arrived. It meant that in only a few weeks, the ice would form over the water and stretch out as far as the eye could see. The freezing forms of the waves would scrape and scratch against the shore, piling up into bright white sculptures as the water buckled the thick sheets from beneath. The white and calm would then blanket our house in quiet, and my father would spend more time at home and less time at the patrol office.

I reached up to catch one of the fluffy flakes, and just as the icy edges landed on my fingertips, the willow shrub's branches crackled. I jerked my hand back as a polar bear cub stumbled out of it toward the water.

I felt frozen, and from the look of the bear cub, so did he. He was small, not much bigger than one of the dogs Mama raised. In the winter, when their full coats came in, they were as stocky and fluffy as the cub, strong and agile enough to pull her sled over the snow. They could bite, but never did. The bear could probably bite too. But I didn't think he would hurt me. He was just a baby.

Babies were gentle.

We stared at each other, his black eyes piercing into mine and his nose twitching in the wind, just like the wisps of pure white fur on the tips of his ears. I'd never been that close to one of the bears before; the patrol kept them well outside the village perimeter.

But we weren't near the village. We were perched in the wilds, out of earshot of our parents.

My heart pounded against my chest, but I stretched my hand forward. My lips parted in wonder as the bear extended his nose. Black but for three small pink dots, a tiny constellation of freckles. My breath held. Our flesh touched for only an instant, and then the cub scrambled backward with a jump.

A giggle escaped me as he fell back on his rump.

He leaped back toward me, his paws outstretched to press against my chest, and I fell back onto the damp, sandy soil, more giggles bubbling up from my throat. He jumped off me, bounding away like a puppy before bouncing back. I scrambled up onto my knees and launched myself at him, burying my nose in his soft fur as we tumbled to the ground.

The bear let out a little cry of surprise, but hopped up and clambered inland, keeping to the edges of the little stream before diving into the willows.

I couldn't let my new playmate go. I had so few moments that I could play, and so few playmates to enjoy. I was already planning where the bear cub would sleep at the foot of my bed when I splashed through the water after it; the branches reaching out to scratch at my bare hands and face and pull at my jacket. We trudged up the small incline of the dunes, farther down the shore from my brother and the others, and then I slid down through the loose soil toward the water.

The cub turned and pawed at me, his foot as big as my face. I pressed my palm to its thick, black center. His fur was soft, softer than the fox hair that lined my winter parka, his body warm like one of the puppies who snuggled with me while Mama trained with the big dogs.

"Dira!"

My name rose over the tossing of the waves against the shore. But I didn't turn toward the sound, my attention too focused on keeping up with the cub as it bounded down the beach. When I brought him home, I could hide him under my bed, saving scraps of dinner to feed him. Maybe I could even train him like Mama trained the dogs, and I could have a best friend all my own, one I didn't have to share with Linka.

"Dira! Dira!"

The voices neared, more than just my brother's and Calla's. But the bear cub was getting away, and I wanted to catch it. Once my father saw how well I could train him, he'd have to let me keep him.

The cub raced toward the old beached whale skeleton. It was a local landmark, and we were all told never to go near it lest we get trapped as the water rose, and certainly never go past it into the never-ending stretch of the wilds where we'd be lost forever. My parents would be furious if they knew I got this close, but they wouldn't ever find out.

My new friend ran between the exposed, bleached white ribs of the long-dead animal, and I followed, clambering over the vertebrae.

The old bones were wet and slippery with seaweed. It smelled of fresh sea, of the barnacles nesting on the waterside lengths of bone. The skeleton had marred the seascape since long before I was born, but it still drew in the bears and seagulls, small fish and crabs. The skeleton offered a haven in high tide, but once the water pulled back away from shore, many creatures were trapped in its ribcage, a feast for land animals.

I hopped down from the spine to the ocean side, the cub right in front of me. It rushed forward, splashing into the water with a high-pitched cry, and paddled out into the sea. Confusion froze me in place as loud chuffs echoed over the waves, and I searched the surface, my eyes falling on the bobbing head of a polar bear treading water near the whale's tail end.

Everything around me froze, the edges of the world darkening until all I could see was that mother bear. It was huge, its head nearly the same size as the small cub I hoped to snag. And big heads housed big teeth. Teeth that could bite right through me.

My mind raced with conflicting thoughts. Run. Don't run. Scream. Don't scream. I couldn't choose, couldn't remember any of the instructions my father gave me about how to escape when escape was an option. But even if I could, I probably broke most of his rules when I played with the cub. What was I supposed to do? What *could* I do?

My body reacted on instinct, not allowing my brain enough time to come up with an answer.

I sprinted through the bones, my boots slipping and sliding on the thick layer of algae growing over the rocks and ivory. I caught myself before I could fall flat on my face, my hand landing in the slime and slipping through it with a splat. But I kept running, even when I realized what I thought was the pounding of my heart was the sound of bear paws thumping against the sand. I was fast, but she was faster. When would she catch up? In ten steps? Five? Three?

I bounded toward the willow shrubs, my chest aching with the terrified screams erupting from my throat. I was an arm's length away from the safety of the willows when a streak of white raced across my vision. Large, white legs stood between me and the mother bear, the scent of fish and seawater and dirt clinging to the damp fur. I could have reached out a hand and touched it. It was so close.

A ferocious cry deafened my ears to anything but its angry roar as the new bear lunged forward, crashing into the mother.

The two bears danced, their teeth bared and paws swiping. On the other side of the sparring adults, the cub mewed, prancing back and forth in the snow flurries. His mother peeled her lips back over her teeth as she positioned her mouth over the much bigger bear's jugular, but he pivoted and shoved her away.

He was easily twice her size, and a dark scar marred his cheek. His jaws looked powerful enough to crush her, and yet he made no move to use them, instead growling loudly and shoving her to back down.

She lunged forward again, and they pushed at each other with their thick paws, her mouth open to target the other's throat.

The baby continued to pace, the tiny cries coming faster and faster, escaping his mouth not unlike the ones made by Dorrin's reindeer calves.

"Dira!"

I turned at the sound of Mella's voice. Beren's mother was almost as precious to me as my own, and she bounded across the sand unevenly, her braid threaded deeply with gray, jostling against her shoulder.

Everything about me froze as she drew nearer to the fighting bears, her fish knife clutched in her hand.

Behind her, others spilled over the dunes. My father, his rifle in hand; Linka, his face pale but for two bright red spots where the wind chapped his cheeks. Even Calla. My gaze bounced between them and Mella as my father raised the rifle and took aim.

I stretched out a hand and screamed, "No!"

The bang of the rifle cracked through the air louder than thunder.

The bears broke apart and scrambled, the mother bear and her cub diving for one another before sprinting toward the gray-green waves.

But the giant male made no move to escape. He turned a wide circle, putting himself between me and Mella.

Another shot cracked through the air, burying itself in the massive bear's shoulder. He let out a roar and rose on his back feet to tower over Mella. She raised her fish knife high as he fell forward, bringing it down into his shoulder as he tumbled into hers.

She crumpled like the hollow husk of a log in a fire.

Another shot rang out, the bullet burying itself in the sand just to the right of the scarred bear.

It turned and ran, skirting the whale's carcass before diving into the water like the other two.

I slowly rose to my feet. My knees wobbled as I approached Mella. A dark pool of blood spread out beneath her, and her neck was cocked oddly to the side. Her dark eyes, so like Beren's, stared sightlessly up into the heavy clouds as fat flakes collected on her cheeks before melting under her warmth. I expected her to blink. To groan and push herself into a seated position. But she did neither.

She did nothing.

My eyes flicked up toward the waves. Just beyond the white-crested waves, the mother and her baby paddled into the dark water. I couldn't find the male.

It wasn't until my father pressed my face into his shoulder, his hand heavy on the back of my head and the scent of gunpowder still hanging in the air, that I realized Mella Metz was dead. I tried to push away, to wriggle out of his hold, but he held fast as his voice boomed over the cries ripping through my throat.

My best friend's mother was dead. If she'd just stayed away, nothing would have happened to her. If my father hadn't shot, he wouldn't have startled the bears. If they'd just left us alone, no one would have gotten hurt.

"Take her home," he commanded and shoved me toward my oldest brother. Landry, his face pale and eyes wide, left Calla's side to gather me into his arms, but he wasn't as strong as Dad, and one swift kick below the belt was all it took for me to break free.

I hit the ground with a jolt and sprinted toward the tide, following the wounded bear's trail of bright red blood where it stained the new dusting of snow.

Flakes like wool fluff hung in the air, suspended on the whipping coastal winds, like a curtain pulled across the bay. They obscured my vision and grayed out the horizon and the tumulus waves. I waded into the surf until it lapped at my ankles, my breath catching on each sob as I pulled the frigid air in through chapped lips. But there was no longer a sign of the bears.

"Careful, Dira." Landry grabbed me by the upper arm and dragged me from the water. He held tight, anchoring me to him and the beaches of Willoughby Bay.

But I kept my gaze on the ocean, watching, waiting for the soft, white ears of the mother bear and her cub to pop up over one of the waves. There was no sign of the male, and sadness I should have felt for Mella weighed me down.

Because he saved me that day.

Not Mella Metz. Not my father's rifle.

But they would never believe that.

He saved me, and he didn't deserve to die too.

CHAPTER 3

The rifle jerks into my shoulder as I squeeze the trigger, and a spray of sand erupts into the air around the bear, flying up in a beige cloud. The wind catches it and scatters it out to sea as the polar bear flees. He angles into the water, diving beneath the waves and disappearing into an ocean as dark and gray as the coming winter.

In less than a second, it was like he was never there. The sea undulates just as it always has, and the crack of the rifle no longer echoes around us, swallowed by the rolling waves and hurried wind.

Beren turns and stumbles backward, the only indication that the bear had come close, that I squeezed the trigger, that danger lurked on the beach. His thighs knock into the boat, and he sprawls against the crab traps, his feet flying up into the air. If Beren hadn't rowed onto the beach, I never would have hesitated to warn the bear away. My heart would never have made it into my throat. I wouldn't be holding my breath.

I don't drop the rifle as I pull relief into my lungs, the breath salty and cold with morning air. It stretches me from the inside and eases the rapid pounding of my heart in my chest. The butt of the rifle still presses into my shoulder, my hands shaking enough I'm afraid I might drop the gun if I relax my muscles even just a pinch.

"Dammit, Dira." Landry whirls on me as he lowers his own rifle. "That wasn't your shot to take."

Thirteen years of feeling defensive rise up. "I thought I had him." It's a lie. One I will tell others, maybe even myself, when this all sinks in. I had to take the shot. It had to be me. If it wasn't... Landry would have hit the bear, and instead of staring off into a cloudy morning seascape, dawn would have been ruined by the animal's bright red blood pooling on the beach. My hands shake as I finally lower the rifle, the adrenaline ebbing as my heart rate slows.

He is still alive. The bear who saved me all those years ago is still alive. Exactly as I remembered him. Large and powerful and scarred. I found him. Finally. The bullet Dad put in his shoulder now was just a bad memory.

"You weren't supposed to shoot at all." Landry's cheeks flame beneath his unruly facial hair as he reaches for the radio hanging from his belt. "I had the orders, not you. Dammit, Dira."

I shoulder the rifle strap and hold my binoculars over my eyes as I scan the low, ice-crested waves. White ears pop up out of the frigid water, and then the rest of his head skims the surface as he heads to the west. "He's leaving."

"Dira, he's dangerous. He could come back and—"

"Then you'll have another chance at him," I say, even though my conscience rears up in protest.

He throws an arm up into the air, pointing toward the waves. "And Beren? Think he'll feel the same way about the bear who almost ate him getting away?"

Guilt squeezes my chest as I realize I never really made a choice.

In the rhythm of one heartbeat, I looked between a polar bear and my best friend—and I chose to hope that a missed shot would be enough to save them both. I clench my teeth together and meet my brother's gaze. The backs of my eyes prickle with the familiar burn of tears. They always come when emotion becomes too much to bear: happy tears spilling down my face, angry ones bubbling up, sad ones when the weight of life feels too heavy. Mom calls me an emotional crier, and I hate every single tear, every evidence of my weakness. But I refuse to acknowledge them now, just as I refuse to justify my missed shot to my brother.

Landry just shakes his head, his breath puffing out like he's trying to fog up a mirror, and he begins to wind up the radio as he turns to give me his back.

Beren is back on his feet when my attention returns to him. I tap my fingers against my thighs and sniff the tears away. They wet my lashes but evaporate before they can slide down my cheeks.

As my father's voice crackles over the radio, I step down the dunes toward my friend, the one person who knows me better, perhaps, than my own twin. We tell each other everything, which is even more precious than my connection with Linka. It takes more strength to put voice to words and knowing Linka is effortless. It just is. But Beren is a choice, and we always choose each other.

Except for today.

His hands tremble as he rights the fallen crab traps, and his deeply bronzed skin has taken on a rather green undertone.

"You all right?" I ask as I reach for the other end of one of the fallen traps. Together, we lift it back into the narrow boat. The dinghy had been his father's before he died. When we were children, it was painted a bright green like the Metz's house, but years of use in the salt water have stripped away most of the paint, and what's left stretches in long lines that peel around the edges.

Beren jerks his hand away and swears under his breath as he kicks the little wooden vessel's stern.

He shoves his finger into his mouth and then pulls it out to shake out the pain of a crab's pinch.

Now probably wouldn't be the time to point out it could have been worse. Much worse.

"I was almost mauled by a damned bear, Dira."

My stomach flops over and I wince. Apparently, he noticed. "Good thing you weren't, though, right?"

He side-eyes me and sinks down into the sand, his knees bent and the bottoms of his boots flat on the ground. "I should have known that when my worst nightmare came to pass, you'd be cracking jokes."

I toe the ground and refuse to look at him. I'm afraid if I do, I'll see more emotion on his face than I know what to do with. My own reaction is one I am familiar with. I am unable to do anything but act like everything was just as it was thirteen years ago. My parents sat me down and told me to be careful around Beren. To not talk about it. And I'm afraid that's stuck through the years.

When Mella died, everyone treated him like a fragile trinket, sure he'd break if he knew the full extent of what happened. Which meant he knew almost every minute detail, even at seven. Whenever the bears came up, I would gulp down my own sadness and turn the course of the conversation. Silence was a tactic I learned to use to my advantage, and Beren seemed to appreciate that. Mella wasn't killed by a bear if we didn't talk about it. I wasn't saved by one if the conversation never came up. Only my father kept the argument alive, but I gave up trying to convince him it was all just an accident, a horrible misunderstanding.

But my father continues to use what happened that day to support his platform that the only good bear is a dead bear. To him, we are their targets, and Mella's death was some sort of premeditated murder. It doesn't matter what evidence I provide to the contrary. His reaction will be the same every single time: kill the bear.

When I was younger and still being sent to the town hall for school, I'd use what we read in the village's few books as some sort of leverage for my agenda. I'd pour through all six tomes, saved from a time long past and locked in a cabinet for everyone to share, my finger pressed in the spaces beneath the black letters like I could root out proof there was another way. But not even my application of the lessons found in *Romeo and Juliet* and *The Art of War* could be used to sway him. I argued, so his reaction was to hand me a rifle. I begged him to see it my way, so he forced me onto the patrol.

As if forcing me to stand against the bears would change my mind somehow.

"I scared him away, though." It's a hollow sentiment, and Beren must know it.

He barks a short, cynical laugh and drops his face into his hands. "I almost wish you hadn't."

I frown. He seems particularly dour today. "Don't say that."

"Why not? Who would miss me?"

"I would." But it seems like an empty assurance, especially after I placed the bear's well-being over his.

My stomach turns over with guilt, and I glance over my shoulder. Landry still paces around the top of the dunes, the radio pressed to his face and his empty hand waving in the air as he recounts my stupidity. He'll be a few minutes more, embellishing every one of my shortcomings. But the rest of the patrol teams will have already adjusted to cover our absence. No one will miss me if I spend a minute here.

With a heavy sigh, I lay the rifle on the ground and sink down next to Beren. I lean my head onto his shoulder, and his wavy black hair flutters across my face, tickling my nose. "What are you doing over here, anyway?"

"Boat sprang a leak."

"I keep telling you, you need a new one."

"You can't just wish for a new boat, Dira. I need something to trade for one, and with this stupid thing always falling apart, it's a wonder I even bring in enough to eat." He bangs his fist into the hull.

"You know you're always welcome at our house. My parents would love to have you there."

Beren's been alone since his father died three years ago. And really, he was alone long before that, as Vashar drank himself into a stupor every night after Mella's death. My parents tried to convince Beren to move in with us. Landry had already married Calla at that point, much to my constant annoyance, and Beren could have easily bunked with Linka. There had been a longing on his face when my mother offered, her hands pressed to his cheeks and her eyes sincere.

But he refused. Instead, he dismantled his parents' house piece by piece and hauled the boards and beams and stones to the other side of town where he rebuilt on the ocean shore. He painted a sedate white over the bright green, a blank canvas against the backdrop of our colorful village.

"Your house is too crowded."

He isn't wrong. Even though Landry and both of my sisters moved out when they married, they still manage to shove themselves back in for most evening meals. When Linka brings Liddet home, dinner sees a dozen people around our table, jostling for space.

And now that Linka and Liddet are engaged, that will be most nights. But Beren belongs at our table, and one day he'll be there, sitting beside me.

"At least tonight is the Night Magic Ball." I nudge him with my arm.

It's the biggest gathering of the season, a celebration of the harvest and the coming winter. The whole town assembles in the meeting hall with an overabundance of food and drinks and music and dancing. I've always loved the celebration and the new season it signals. The one that sees the bears disappearing from our shores and traveling to distant lands all their own.

"What do you think I'm crabbing this early for?" Beren drops his head back. "I don't think I'm going. Don't feel much like celebrating."

I make a face. "Pfft. You have to go. Everyone goes." I don't want to be there alone. Every year Beren and I huddle in a corner, judging others and drinking too much of Granny Grin's berry brandy.

"I was nearly attacked by a bear. And Linka—never mind. I'm just not in the mood."

I start to ask him what he means about Linka when Landry's voice drifts over the splashing of the waves.

"Dira. Dira!"

I look up to find him striding toward us, his mouth pinched and eyebrows pulled low in a grim expression.

That can only mean one thing: I'm about to get a lecture.

Annoyance settles in as I push myself up. Can I have just one week go by without someone complaining that I don't stack up? I didn't even want to be on the patrol in the first place, much less this shift.

What will the lecture be about this time? There are endless options, and I've just about memorized all of them. Will Dad fall back on the "you need to grow up" speech or insist I don't take dangerous situations seriously? That I should have listened to my lead and not shot at all? Or that I don't spend enough time practicing my shooting?

I mentally roll my eyes at the last thought. They don't know that I'm a damn good shot. Better than all of them. I practice daily out in the wilds where no one can see or hear what I'm up to. You'd think they would realize that even a bad shot hits their target sometimes, and I'm always, *always* just off the mark.

If my father had been off the mark thirteen years ago, Mella would probably still be alive.

I brush off my backside and offer a hand to Beren to haul him up to his feet. Toe-to-toe, we stand at exactly the same height, though I have a tendency to slouch for his benefit.

Landry scowls at me, his winged brows furled together and his mouth a straight, unyielding line. "Dad wants you back in the office."

My chin inches up. "Why?"

"Don't do this, Dira. You know why."

Tears tickle the back of my throat again. Of course, I know why. I can't do anything right, and when I try, when I *do* the right thing, all they see is that it isn't what they *wanted* me to do. Beren and the bear are both still alive, and it's all because of me. But they'll never see that. Instead they'll focus on death and maimings and "why can't you just do as you're told, Dira?"

"You're my brother." My chin wobbles, and not just because he's throwing me out to sea without a line.

I don't expect to see sympathy cross his face, but it still hurts when there is none. "And you're my sister."

I swallow painfully and look at Beren. "I told Beren I'd help him."

Both of Beren's eyebrows bounce up in surprise, but he's the one person who would never rat me out. He runs a hand through his unruly hair. "Uh, yeah, boat sprang a leak."

I hold on to my relief that he caught on. Bless him.

"Dira, Dad wants you back at the—"

I sweep up my rifle and loop the strap over my head so it drops across my back, the barrel pointing toward the ground. "I can't just leave him out here, can I? Isn't that the patrol's whole reason for existing? To protect? What if the bear comes back while Beren's out here alone?"

Landry shifts his gaze away as he mulls over my words.

They were exactly what he needed to hear.

He nods once. "Fine. But once you get it patched, you need to get back to the office."

My chin bobs. "Understood."

With a sigh, my brother turns and leaves us on the beach.

Once he is out of earshot, Beren turns to me. "You're not going back to the office, are you?"

I pick at a blister on my thumb as Beren hammers the last nail into his patch job. The sun is now high though thin, ashen clouds obscure it from view, and it shines through them like a lantern breaking through fog. My shift will be over soon, and if Beren takes long enough to

29

get the dinghy back in the water, I can avoid going into the patrol office. The lecture waiting for me isn't one I am particularly eager to participate in, and preparing for the ball tonight is an excellent excuse for why I couldn't make it back to the office.

"Still working on that?" I call over the side of the boat from my place on the sand.

"I'd be done and halfway home by now if you'd bothered to help."

"You know that's a bad idea. I'd probably only make the holes worse. Remember that time you asked me to help with your roof? It rained in your bedroom for three days straight. And it was a dry spring." I wave my hand absently. "Besides, I've been protecting you from additional polar bear attacks."

"You'd be a lot more convincing if you hadn't been staring at the toe of your boot the whole time."

Hmm, he has me there. I push myself up and look down into the hull. I don't know if his patch job made the thing seaworthy, but it might be enough to get him home.

He drops the hammer and steps out of the boat. I expect him to start reloading his catch, but instead he wipes his hands down the thighs of his walrus-skin coveralls and runs a hand through his hair.

"You know, I've been thinking. With Linka and Liddett getting married and everything..." He shoves his hand into the chest pocket of his parka, and when he brings it out, a slender black leather thread nestles in the palm of his hand, the ends strung through three white beads carved into snowflakes. He used to carry it around when we were younger and wrapped it around his wrist like a bracelet as we grew. But I haven't seen it since his father died and he threw himself into building a house and fishing the coast.

He rubs the middle one between his thumb and forefinger, and reaches forward to snag my hand. "It was my mother's," he says sheepishly as he drops it into my palm.

I stare down at the necklace, and then back into his face. My heart pounds against my chest as realization slams into me like a winter gale, and my mouth forms a little "o."

He's going to ask me to marry him.

And I'm going to say yes. Because I've known for years, it was the only way anyone would ever allow me to make up for my part in what happened to him. But it isn't a bad thing. I've resigned myself to it. We'll make a good couple. We hardly ever fight. I know all his bad habits, and there isn't any room for misunderstandings between us; we've completely figured each other out. When my sister, Dara, first got married a few years ago, she was barging through the back door at all hours of the day so she could shout about Moore and the ridiculous things he did like leaving his socks in the middle of the floor and slurping his morning tea. She hated the way he wore his boots around the house instead of taking them off by the door and that he turned on the lights when he got up to go hunting before the sun rose. I won't have any of those surprises with Beren. And he won't have any of those surprises with me.

We'll be happy, I tell myself.

I wrap my hand around the beads, letting them press into my palm, and the edges cut into my skin. What will it be like to be engaged? Will he kiss me? Hold my hand? Will there be… will there be more? Linka and Liddett seem to be all over each other all the time, so there must be something that will change.

"It's just that, well, maybe…" He runs his hand through his hair.

"Beren!" Linka's voice cuts through the tossing of the waves behind us.

Beren immediately perks up to his full height—barely an inch shorter than mine—and glances toward town. His lips parted and his eyes wide. But he quickly shutters, his features pressing into a near-frown.

My twin jogs toward us, his rifle already in hand for his shift—*my* shift—and my own face creases into something that must mirror Beren's.

Linka stops next to us, his cheeks red from running or the cold or both, and his breath puffs out like the smoke of a fire made from wet wood. "I thought you were still on patrol."

I meet his gaze. "I am. Although I shouldn't be." The only reason I was out there this morning is because of Linka; because he wanted something that didn't belong to him and took it.

He deflates. "You know I need the afternoon shift."

"No, I don't *know* that because you never said anything to me. You just showed up at dinner and demanded it without even asking me first."

Linka rolls his eyes, drops his head back, and stares up at the sky. "Come on, Dira, is it really going to kill you to take the morning shift?"

"Could it have killed you to ask?"

"You would have said no."

I cross my arms over my chest. "Well, I guess we'll never know, now, will we?"

"Can you two just stop for a second?" Beren presses the pad of one thumb into his forehead and closes his eyes.

I raise my eyebrows at my brother, but he turns his full attention on Beren.

"Can we talk for a minute?" Linka asks quietly.

Beren continues to glare at him. "We were kind of in the middle of something."

I grip the snowflake beads tighter, hiding them from my brother's view; I'm not ready to tell anyone about Beren's proposal, especially since it hasn't happened yet.

"Yeah, I know. That's what I wanted to talk to you about."

Beren sighs heavily. "Now's not a good time. I have a lot to do before tonight." He moves the crab traps back into the bow, stacking them precariously on top of one another.

Linka deflates, his shoulders hunching forward and his chin dipping toward his chest. The wind catches the tips of his hair so they flutter around his face. He's always kept it relatively short, ever since Landry pretended he couldn't tell the two of us apart. That was the same year Linka tried and failed to grow a full beard or mustache and I took to stuffing my shirts with rolled up socks.

I start to ask him what's wrong, but I'm still mad at him. Letting him stew a bit longer won't hurt either of us.

"Dira, could you get the other end?" Beren calls.

I shrug and hold my hands up. "Better get to that shift you wanted so badly," I say to my twin as I walk past him.

Linka huffs and spins away, his boots grinding in the sand as he heads back toward town.

Now that he's gone, will Beren get down on one knee and ask me to marry him? Does he have a whole speech prepared? Written and shoved in his pocket? No, that would be ridiculous. He had no idea he would see me today, much less here on the beach.

But he remains silent even after we have the boat repacked and pushed back into the chunky slush. Soon, the freeze will be complete, and no one will be using a boat, much less collecting crab traps. The spark of anticipation building inside me fizzles out, leaving behind something hovering between disappointment and relief.

"We better get this back before it gets stuck in a floe." I laugh at my own poor joke.

But Beren doesn't even crack a smile. "I've got it from here. I'll see you tonight." He presses off the beach and launches himself into the boat, leaving me on the shore, the necklace still pressed into my palm.

CHAPTER 4

Hours later, Liddet loops her arm through mine as we approach the meeting hall, her hand resting on the brilliant blue brocade of my sleeve, and the pearl my brother gave her sitting brightly on her slim third finger. A twisting of polished silver surrounds the pearl, the curves and curls like the edges of fat, fluffy white clouds that sit overhead in summer.

"Your brother is such a romantic. Did he tell you he plucked it from an oyster just for me?" Her cheeks round out into apples as she smiles, her white teeth flashing against her dark complexion. They must ache by now from the grinning and giggling she's done all afternoon. That finger must be tired too. She keeps holding it up, hand stretched out so she can admire the pearl, ignoring me as she disappears into her own thoughts.

My gaze catches on it and I suppress a frown. Does she know it was Beren who found it, in the shallows of the seaside two years ago, not Linka? He was there to make a living, wading into the low tide with a bucket for collecting jagged-edged oysters from the reef. Linka excitedly chattered about his new position on the polar bear patrol from his perch on a rock, and I mourned mine while sprawled out in the sand, my hair flying around my face and the warmth of the sun kissing my nose.

"You should join us. Dad will give you a shift if you just ask," Linka said.

Beren didn't respond as he reached down into the water and pulled up another gray shell. He tapped it once, and it snapped shut. He tossed it in the bucket. "I don't think I'm cut out for it."

I knew I wasn't, and yet that didn't matter. My father wanted me as firmly under his thumb as he could get me, and the patrol was his perfect solution. And since I couldn't name a viable alternate career—wildlife observer was swiftly vetoed and apprentice to Granny Grin got me nothing more than a narrow stare—the patrol was where I stayed.

"But you're cut out for this?" Linka waved absently toward the lapping waves of low tide.

"There's nothing wrong with fishing. Both my parents were fishers."

"I didn't say there was anything wrong with it. But don't you want more than this? Don't you want to be able to support your family? Give them a good life?"

"I don't know if you know this, but I don't have a family anymore." Beren's icy tone cut the conversation short, silencing Linka.

I glanced between them. Linka wasn't usually so pushy. He tended to go with the flow, floating through life like an autumn leaf on the wind. But he pouted as he stared down at his overly large boots and twisted his fingers together.

Beren released the tension in his shoulders, and his chest collapsed in a sigh. "I like fishing," he said. "It's quiet—usually." He leaned down to pluck another oyster from the water. "And every once in a while, I find something beautiful." With quick fingers, he reached between the two halves of the oyster and plucked out a glistening, white pearl.

It wasn't the first one he had found. He often collected them in his pocket, taking them to the market to trade. But they were usually small, no bigger around than a pebble.

But that pearl was large and milky, its diameter almost as big as a ripe berry. He held it up toward the sun between his thumb and index finger before rolling it into his palm and stretching it out toward Linka. "For you."

Linka frowned as he took it. "You don't want to keep it?"

Beren pressed the pearl into my brother's palm and shook his head. "No. It's for you." He tapped the oyster and when it closed, he dropped it into the bucket with the rest, then quietly reached for another.

My brother turned the pearl over in his hand before carefully slipping it into the front pocket of his shirt.

I didn't even know he kept it until I arrived on Liddet's doorstep to see it flashing on her finger. It shouldn't fill me with annoyance, but he didn't tell me he was going to ask her to marry him. And though the news didn't surprise me, grumpiness still plagues me I wasn't the first to know—or even the *only one* to know—he intended to ask. But he told all of us over the dinner table last night, nonchalantly, like he was commenting on the weather, and then turned to Dad and made his argument for my shift.

"I need the afternoon patrol hours, Dad. Cal Tuppet said he could use a guide, and my cut will be fifteen percent of the haul. If I'm going to build a house and support a wife, I need to take advantage of every opportunity."

Dad leaned back in his chair, his pleased smile still hanging from his lips. "Schedule's been set for some time. I can't just go upending—"

"Give me Dira's shift. We'll switch, and then no one else is put out." Linka didn't even bother looking at me.

I nearly choked on my potato as disbelief slammed into me. I didn't want to change shifts. I didn't want to be on the patrol at all, but definitely not at a time when I was more likely to be put in front of the bear that saved me. "But I don't—"

"All right. Done." Dad avoided my slack-jawed stare as he speared a piece of carrot with his fork. "You have the dawn shift from now on, Dira."

"No. I don't want to change." I dropped my fork, so it clattered on my plate.

"This isn't up for negotiation. When you have someone to take care of, you'll understand. Think of someone other than yourself for a change."

A full day later, the conversation stings like it just happened.

None of that was Liddet's fault. She would probably be horrified if I told her Linka acted that way. She has always been so kind and thoughtful, quiet and fair. I shouldn't let my brother's moodiness and secrecy goad me into taking away her joy.

"It must be because I'm engaged this time," she says beside me.

"What?" I blink back to the present and look down at her. The top of her head barely skims my shoulder, but her black hair, twisted into two perfect cones to look like the ears of a fawn, adds a few inches to her height.

She tilts them back to shine her sun-bright smile at me. "The ball. It feels different this year, doesn't it?"

If she means it somehow feels insignificant, then yes, I suppose I agree.

Usually, it's my favorite celebration of the year. I spent months bringing payments to Pinky Palvo for this year's dress, a deep blue wool embroidered with glinting silver stars. I don't do the rich blue justice, my skin just a touch too pale and the muscles in my arms and shoulders pulling at the sleeves. The tightness prevents my arms from raising above my head, and I haven't taken a full breath since Liddet pulled the laces tight as we readied ourselves together, but it makes me feel like one of the queens in Granny Grin's fairy stories.

Pinky told me she traded for it at one of the summer festivals to the south. I've never gone to one of the meets with those who gather for trade and gossip over a full week when the sun is longest in the sky. My family is always needed to keep up the patrols. Yet many of the artisans and traders like Pinky make the trek, and she always comes back with an eclectic collection of knickknacks and baubles and fabrics. But a full dress was unusual. The moment I saw it in the market as I helped Beren unload his catch, I knew I had to have it, even though it was worn along the hem and slightly too small. The workmanship was exceptional, each cut even and finished like the gowns Granny Grin says were once made by machines. Calla would only find something wrong with it—or me being the one to wear it.

As we near the hall, the rich, ringing notes of ice instruments bleed out through open doors. The ice plays a beautiful and haunting song, but combined with the walrus skin drums and pipes made from dune reeds, it's a sound made only for this time of year.

We enter the meeting hall, already half full with partygoers. The chairs that normally ring the center for council meetings have been pushed to the walls, and the town's elderly lounge there, tapping their toes to the beat and watching as the early dancers take to the polished planks. I look for Granny Grin among them, but her steel-gray hair and weathered face are absent. She didn't come last year, either, saying her old bones didn't like walking after dark, but the rest of my family already crowds into the far corner opposite the musicians. Dad bellows his laughter with the other patrollers, Mom smiling with contentment at his side. I quickly turn my back in case he looks over. I don't want him to see me. Any interaction with him will come with The Look of Disapproval, and I don't want the night ruined.

"I don't see Linka," Liddet murmurs beside me. "Do you?"

I haven't seen him since this morning, and I'm not sure I want to.

I shake my head and scan once more. Pine boughs and brightly twinkling lights powered by the windmills above wrap around wide support posts. Larger ones drape from the ceiling, and as the wind whips outside, the windmill blades whir faintly over the music and conversation. Leaning forward, I peek around the columns, my gaze sweeping from one side of the hall to the other.

But Linka is nowhere to be seen. I don't lay eyes on Beren, either. "He's probably around here somewhere with Beren."

Liddet pouts prettily, but as she catches sight of her aunt and sisters, it quickly disappears and she glides toward them without another word to me.

Landry breaks free from the other patrollers, and, skirting the perimeter of the room, approaches me. Hand raised; he bows softly. "May I have this dance?"

I wrinkle my nose. "No."

He chuckles and turns to look out at the dance floor, his arm brushing against my shoulder. Most dress up in costume for the evening, but all Landry has done is add a pair of felt wolf ears to the top of his head and a matching tail clipped to the back of his pants.

I run my eyes over both and lift an eyebrow. "Calla's losing her touch."

"She's been occupied with other things. Putting together costumes wasn't high on her list of priorities."

Rolling my eyes, I make a disgusted sound in the back of my throat. "Isn't she the one who said that if you don't make an effort, you shouldn't bother coming?"

"I don't remember that."

"I do." She sneered at me and said those exact words last year when I came as a rainbow, each piece of my costume a different color. The scraps came from dresses past, either too small to fit me anymore or torn and full of holes from too many attempts at repurposing. I can't imagine she'll have many nice things to say about my night sky gown, either.

I should drop the subject. Landry doesn't care what I think, and he'd defend Calla even if his wife held a knife to my throat. "Have you seen Linka? Liddet was looking for him."

He shakes his head. "He went looking for you and Beren when you didn't show up at the patrol office. Haven't seen him since. But while we're on the subject of family… Where have you been? You were supposed to help Beren and then come back."

I glance over my shoulder to the corner where my parents stand, and my father stares back, The Look firmly in place. Gazing up at him is like seeing into Landry's future, disapproval and all. But where Landry's forehead is only starting to show the subtle creasing and fading of adulthood, Dad's is like a well-used leather satchel, sagging into wrinkles around the middle. I snap my head back around. "Getting ready. Liddet invited me to prepare with her."

"You've been there all day?"

My gaze drifts over to Liddet, where she preens in front of her aunt. "Haven't you seen Liddet? That kind of beauty isn't achieved in ten minutes."

Landry's lips settle into a straight line. "This isn't a joke, Dira."

"I know. No one wants to come to the best party of the year looking like they tangled with a moose on the way here."

"I'm serious."

I smile blandly and flutter my lashes. "I am too."

He flicks his gaze away, and a muscle ticks in his jaw. "I know you were young, but you do remember what happened, right?"

"Of course I remember. I was the one in trouble, not you." I don't want to have this conversation, so I decide to go in for the kill. "If you'd been focused on keeping me out of trouble, instead of flirting, none of it would have happened."

I yank my hand away and storm off the dance floor. I'm not even sure if I'm talking about that evening thirteen years ago or this morning. But the look of utter defeat on his face was enough to give me a flash of satisfaction. Landry received his punishment for not keeping a closer eye on me, but it ended years ago. He hasn't had to live with the disappointment every single day since like I have.

I weave through the growing crowd to the refreshment tables. He calls after me hoarsely, but I don't turn around. My stomach is too nervous for food, so I accept a glass of brandy from one of the older women working the table.

I throw the liquid back and hold the glass out for more. It's quickly refilled. This is a night of revelry, and no one will deny me copious amounts of alcohol. The second helping is quickly gone, and the third I take with me.

Warmth spreads through my veins, coursing through my fingers and pooling in my stomach. It pulls my lips into a smile and dulls the anger and sadness and defeat I carry every day. I need tonight to block out this morning, especially if I'm going to relive it all over again tomorrow.

The best dance partners are the men around my father's age. Old enough they've attended scores of dances. Old enough, they don't care if they look foolish. But still spry, still able to perform each step. And strong enough they can lift me up for the whirly parts.

I love the whirly parts.

Calla may be an irrational harpy, but her father is one of the best dancers on the floor, and he twirls me around as if I weigh nothing. I love him for that. Arm-in-arm, we step and kick, twirl and kick. Then he turns, grasping one hand and placing the other around my waist. As the flutes peak and the drums beat, he spins me in a quick circle, slips the other hand around my waist, and up I go in an arc, just like the girls who don't skim six feet.

By the time the musicians stop playing, I can barely catch my breath. But my smile won't go away, and when Calla's father kisses both of my cheeks, the giggle that escapes my throat sounds high-pitched and silly even to my own ears.

As I smothered my worry away with dancing, the crowd swelled to stifling, and I wend my way through it to find the drinks table again. Sipping the cooled brandy, I scan the partygoers. My breath catches and my heart skips a beat.

Across the room, the unmistakable white fur of a polar bear wades through the crowd. And yet no one steps back, no one runs away. Not a scream rings through the throng.

Rooted to the floor, I watch as he steps out from behind a partygoer and turns toward me. No long black nose twitches in my direction, and the lights are too dim for me to make out his features, but the fur wrapped around the man's shoulders and draped over his head is, without a doubt, that of a polar bear.

Who outside of the patrol would have taken down a polar bear? My people may shoot to kill, but they would never dream of keeping their enemy's pelt to wear to a party. The people of Wilhoughby are a superstitious lot, and to keep the hide of an enemy is to invite its spirit to live amongst us. When a bear is put down, every part of it is traded away to those outside the town, the meat to the reindeer herders for milk and cheese, the bones to artisans to make buttons and beads, the pelts to those in the south who have far less opportunity to obtain heavy furs for the winter months.

That must be it. He must not be one of us. An outsider. A newcomer, or a trader perhaps? Someone visiting? My interest piques and I resist the urge to run toward him. We haven't had anyone new in town in years, but surely I would have heard news of him.

"Dara," I say, catching my sister's arm as she walks past me. "Who is that?"

Dara turns to follow my stare, brushing against me. The older of my two sisters, she's always been a rule follower and a bit bossy. I can tell from the pinched set of her mouth she's as annoyed with me as the rest of the patrol. Though she isn't on it herself, her husband, Moore, serves and she's on the town council. I steel myself for a quick rebuff or even a scolding, but she doesn't turn her back on me. "Who?"

"There. In the polar bear fur."

She weaves a bit on her toes and shakes her head. "I don't know. Must be one of Dorin's new sons-in-law."

"No one told me his daughters were married."

She shrugged. "I just found out myself."

I frown and continue to stare long after she leaves. A reindeer herder, Dorin, sees far more of our world than most of the town's people. While we prepare to hunker down for the winter, he and his large family prepare to take their herd inland, breaking up the numbers into smaller groups and spreading out to find food for the reindeer. He brings news from the dozen or so settlements that dot the terrain inland and to the south.

His middle daughters aren't much younger than Linka and me, and in the summers, we used to play along the shore together. I hadn't heard anything about marriages, but that isn't particularly surprising. The reindeer herders, even those who summer near Willoughby, usually find their mates among others of their kind. Us town folk are far too stationary for their tastes.

The stranger turns to stare back at me, but the shadow cast by the hood continues to obscure his face.

I've been caught. My heart jumps into my throat, and I quickly look away, pretending to be focused on something just over his shoulder. Yes, nothing has ever been as interesting as the thick, wavy glass in the windows. The way it bubbles and catches the light.

But my heart races as I try not to look back at him.

And where is Beren? We need to talk.

I reach up to finger the beads displayed across my collarbones and hope I do them justice. Maybe seeing me wear them will prompt Beren to pull me off into a corner and finish what he started earlier. Liddett asked me about them as I offered her both ends to tie behind my neck. I wanted to tell her she wasn't the only one with a fancy new piece of jewelry, but all I could manage was, "Beren gave it to me."

But I don't see any sign of Beren, and when I shift my gaze back, the man dressed in polar bear furs still watches me.

My throat goes dry.

Who is he? And why is he staring at me, of all people?

"Dira, come dance with me." Dasha's husband, Dunnal, steps between us, his grizzly face split into an alcohol-fueled grin. He doesn't seem perturbed by this morning's events. Of my brothers-in-law, he's the more reserved and least likely to get involved in family squabbles. Perhaps if I am congenial enough, he'll put in a good word with the rest of the patrol. Yes. He might be my ticket back into everyone's good graces, and the promise of a new husband on my arm could seal the deal.

"Lead the way," I say and drop my hand into his. But the hairs on the back of my neck stand on end, and my mind prickles with unease.

CHAPTER 5

Dunnal passes me to Dara's husband Moore, and from Moore I find myself in the arms of Cal Tumpet, Moore's brother. He whirls me around as the song's final notes play, and we laugh together when he stamps down on my foot again. At barely sixteen, he's all gangly limbs and floppy feet. He wants to join the patrol in the coming spring, and I bite my tongue to keep from telling him he can have my spot. The words almost tumble out, anyway, brute strength keeping too many cups of berry brandy from loosening my lips. Would Dad even let me quit if I found myself a replacement?

His awkward bow is met by my coquettish curtsy, and I turn to scan for Beren once more, only to run straight into the person standing directly behind me. A reflexive apology dies on my lips as I look up and find myself staring into the shadowed face of the man draped in polar bear fur.

He quickly steps out of the glow of the twinkling lights, lowering his head so the hood of his cloak fully casts his face into darkness. I've never had to look up at a man I wasn't related to before, and I search out his features, but come away with nothing but shadow.

"Who—"

He lifts his hands, cutting me off as he brings up a crown of golden holly leaves, laying it atop my head. The barbs cut into my hair, catching on the strands Liddet so painstakingly wove and pinned, a thousand points poking into my tender scalp.

And without a word, he turns away to brush past another partygoer. I reach out a hand, but he escapes swiftly, and the tips of my fingers barely graze the soft fur.

"Who was that?"

I flinch at Liddet's voice from where it comes beside me.

"I—I don't know. Dara thought he might be one of Dorin's sons-in-law."

She shakes her head. "No, I met them both just a few minutes ago. But that—I have no idea who that is." Her eyes glance up at the top of my head. "It is a lovely crown, though."

Reaching up, I finger the leaves. Thick and waxy like holly, yet I've never seen holly this color. Why would a complete stranger gift me with such a thing? "Who is he, then?" I ask.

"From over there, I thought he was Landry."

I shook my head. "Calla has him dressed up like a dog or something." Why is no one else questioning the man's presence? My hand drops from the leaves and skims the necklace. I need to find Beren. "Did you ever find Linka? Was Beren with him?"

She shakes her head, but I almost miss it as I strain my neck to follow the stranger's trajectory through the crowd.

"I spoke with Linka for just a minute. He's acting really strange. But Beren wasn't with him. I told Linka you were looking for Beren, but he said he didn't know when he was coming. Or if he'd even be here. I'm sorry, Dira," she says as her expression turns to one of sympathy. "It

48

looks like you won't have a date after all. Maybe you should go after the stranger if you want to make sure you get a kiss at dawn." She giggles, her breath thick with berry brandy.

"Date?" Beren and I never planned to come together, and though the dawn kiss is a tradition, I hadn't anticipated sharing one with Beren, engagement or not.

"Oh. I—I'm sorry. I just thought since he gave you the necklace and you two are always together… I'm sorry. My mistake."

"It's fine. I'll be right back." I search out the flash of white once more. I spot him just as he disappears into the night and I shove past her. The musicians have begun the next song, and dancers move in to sweep me up in the crush of their reel.

Weaving through the masses of partiers, I make for the door. It stands open to let the frigid air from outside cool the stuffy hall, and I stumble out into the fat flakes of snow falling from low-hanging clouds. My gaze sweeps from one side of the street to the other as it begins its transformation from the dull brown of mud and autumn to the frosted delicacy of winter. Snow collects in the eaves, along windowsills, and in the ruts crisscrossing the main thoroughfare.

But the man draped in polar bear fur is nowhere to be seen.

Frowning, I step across the boardwalk. It's already slick with ice, and my heels nearly slide out from beneath me as I round the corner of the building to stare down the shadows. The narrow alley between the meeting hall and market building swallows up light, devouring even the feather light snow.

I find no flash of white there, either, but voices echo against the wood siding.

Voices I know.

I step off the boards and into the soft mud. Soundlessly, I approach the rear of both buildings, slowing as the lights shining from across the back street highlight Beren's silhouette.

"You can't ask me to do that." The second figure turns, giving me a perfect side view of my twin.

My feet root to the ground.

"I can. I can beg you every single day for the rest of my life. And I would if I thought there would ever be any chance to change your mind," Beren responds angrily. "But you can't marry her and say it's so you can have children, but demand I remain alone. I don't want to live the rest of my life hoping for scraps of you and dying from loneliness. Either choose me or let me find happiness some other way. Dira and I can make it work if I try hard enough."

"You think you can do that? Even after what we have?" Desperation bounces off the walls in the form of Linka's voice.

"You think you can with Liddet?" For every ounce of Linka's desperation, Beren matches it with anger.

"That's different and you know it. I—I love Liddet."

"And I love Dira."

He loves me? Of course, he loves me. Just like I love him. I start to step forward, to call out his name, but Linka's voice stops me before I can even twitch a muscle.

"No, not like that. You love Dira like I do. She's a sister to us both. You can't—you can't really think you can make it work with her."

My chest squeezes. Why would Linka be so cruel? Beren and I might not have the kind of love story Granny Grin talks about, but—

"And you and Liddet have something different?"

"Of course we do." But Linka doesn't sound so sure. "How will you

50

be able to wake up to her every morning after she killed your mother?"

Everything stops. The flurrying of snow, the whip of the wind, my own breathing as the sting of betrayal stabs through my heart. I know they all think it, but no one has ever said those words aloud, at least not in front of me. They don't know I'm here, and yet my twin's accusation cuts to the quick, stealing my tears before I have a chance to sniff them away.

"She didn't—"

"She didn't what? She didn't do exactly what she was told not to do? We were all the same age, Beren. We didn't go running off into the willows after bears because *we knew better*. She does whatever she wants whenever she wants, and she doesn't care who she hurts. You think she saved you today? Come on, Beren. You know her better than that. We all do. We've all just been too careful to keep from saying it so the council doesn't throw her out alone into the wilds."

Beren shook his head. "She scared it away. She may have missed, but—"

"She didn't *miss. Dira doesn't miss.* She spared one of the monsters that destroyed your family. How can you live with that?"

I shouldn't be here. I shouldn't be listening to them. What was I thinking coming outside? I should be inside with the rest of the town, dancing the last hours before sunlight away. But my feet won't move. They won't propel me backward, help me flee.

"If you really believe that, then don't let me. Fight for me. Save me. *Choose* me." Beren's voice breaks.

I stare toward them, my lips parting.

Linka drags in a ragged breath and leans into the outside wall of the meeting house, his chin dropping to his chest and his breath puffing out in a silver cloud. "Don't make me choose," Linka begs.

Choose? Why does he have to choose?

"You have to." Beren lunges forward.

A sharply indrawn breath catches in my throat but holds.

Beren pulls my brother's lips down to his, and the pair melt into each other. Steam from their mingling heat rises into the darkness as their moans and sighs join it.

But it's dull compared to the sound of my world breaking.

I stagger back in stunned silence.

Does everyone know? Do they really all suspect I chose the life of a bear over my best friend's? Am I really only one misstep from exile?

My whole life has been a lie, my father's well-sculpted illusion, and now it shatters, blotting out all other sounds. I just want to find my mother, fall into her arms, and let her take me home. I want to bury my face in the crook of her neck and let her rub my back and tell me everything is fine like she did thirteen years ago. I want her to say it will all work out, that I was a child before, and I have a good heart now. I want her to say all those things even if I'm not sure I can believe them, and I don't even care that my father will be at her side, his stern gaze judging me.

Just as Linka has. And Beren didn't deny it either. Is that why they kept this secret from me? Because I wasn't worth confiding in? And for how long? Everyone led me to believe it would be us one day—even Linka, with his girlfriend and proposals and talk of building a house.

Did anyone else know? Could it really be the inability to have children that made them keep it a secret? The council did put a hefty emphasis on repopulation, on having the numbers to fish and herd and hunt. But I never thought it applied to us. Our business is the patrols and raising dogs. But why keep it from me? Was I not worth confiding in?

I reach for the necklace pressing into my throat, my fingers wrapping around it until the string cuts into my palm. He gave it to me hours after Linka gave the pearl to Liddet. Was the necklace just some sort of revenge to hurt my brother?

I should yank it off and toss it away, but I can't. My fingers loosen as I stumble toward the boardwalk.

Why did I come out here? Why did I ruin tonight? Why couldn't I just stay where I am supposed to stay and do what I am supposed to do?

I have to get out of here. But what do I do? Where do I go?

My heart squeezes, wringing out tears as I splash through the mud into the center of Main Street. Music wafts through the open windows of the meeting house, but the crush of bodies blocks out most of the light. I am alone in the darkness.

"There you are, Dira."

Chapter 6

My head snaps up as Granny Grin hobbles across the boardwalk, her shoulders hunched over the smooth wooden cane she only uses when she leaves her cottage. Sparrow, the ragged, one-eyed raven who is her constant companion, perches above one of her bony clavicles, his wings stretching out and then pulling back in for balance with every one of her small steps. He bobs and flinches, talons digging into the black fur of her shawl.

I swipe under my eyes, brushing away any evidence of moisture clinging to my eyelashes, and sniff away the signs of any residual emotion. "What are you doing here alone, Granny?"

She offers a smile and her face scrunches up like boots that no longer hold their shape and slouch at the ankles as she shuffles forward. Her feet barely lift off the ground as she nears me, her arms open for a hug. Silvery hair is pulled back from her face in a low bun, glinting like moonlight and holding the scent of smoked meat, caribou cream, and herbs.

I hesitate, but bend down to wrap my arms around her, careful to avoid knocking Sparrow from her shoulder. She smells exactly as I expect, but with the sharp, cold scent of ice also clinging to her.

She rarely leaves the small cottage at the other end of the faded ribbon of land curving between the Willoughby Bay and the choppy ocean. Only Granny Grin's small stone cottage occupies the spit, two small windmills—one with a sun painted on it, the other a moon—spinning from the roof's apex. It's a long trek for a woman as bent and gnarled as she, especially after dusk falls.

"I came for the ball. Why else would I be here at this time of night?"

"It's so late. I didn't think you'd come." She hadn't last year or the year before. "I would have fetched you this evening if you'd asked."

She wags a gnarled finger in my direction, nearly upsetting the one-eyed bird. "I could have asked if you'd come as you normally do."

She is right. Usually I make the trek to her cottage every day, but it's been several since I traveled down the narrow strip of land to bring her news of the town, to tell her about the polar bears I witnessed rolling around in the willow shrubs, or to escort her inland to pick leaves for her tea mixtures.

"I'm sorry, Granny." But I don't say any more. I don't want her to see my faults like everyone else has. She'll only try to regale me with one of her stories, to try to make me feel better, and that's the last thing I want right now.

She snorts. "Dear girl, are you feeling quite all right?"

I just blink at her. Words escape me, but I don't want to talk, anyway.

A gust of wind swoops through the town, and the rickety windmills teetering on top of the roofs spin wildly, rattling overhead.

She takes a deep breath, her chest heaving, and her expression softening into one of somber contemplation. "Winter's come early this year. The bay's already freezing over, and the sea isn't far behind." She stares off into the dark distance.

I've never known her to be wrong, but it seems too soon. Just this morning, the ocean still churned with unfrozen water. "Why do you say that?"

"Don't you listen to the wind, Dira? See the signs written in the sky? Smell the scent of the ice on the water and hear the crystals as they hit the sand? It's all there." She points a bony finger in my direction. "I taught you, girl, and if you took a moment to look up, you'd see this season will be different. Now's your chance."

It sounds crazy. And most people *think* she's crazy. They don't trust that she would rather remain alone on the Spit, her cottage a solitary gem on a crooked finger of land. It's a dangerous world, and she confronts it like no other: defenseless. The strange mumblings and theories don't exactly help.

She's right, though. I haven't been paying attention. I've been focused on my brother, destroying everything I thought was true about my life in two quick strokes. But I've never known Granny Grin to be wrong.

She slips a hand through my arm. "Now help me over to that bench. I need to sit."

I glance over my shoulder, half-expecting to see Beren and Linka around the corner, hand-in-hand. I've never been able to hide my emotions from either of them, and the fear of having to face them fills every corner of my soul. But the darkness between the buildings is empty, and though my heart pounds against my ribs and my hands shake, I jerk my chin up and down in an impression of a nod. She leans her weight into me, and together we cross the slippery wood to one of the low benches stretching out along the meeting house walls.

"You're quiet, Dira." She peers up at me from her seat as I straighten, and Sparrow mimics her stare.

What do I tell her? That I didn't shoot a bear this morning, and it could have killed my best friend? Do I tell her I expected to marry him, but instead I found him professing his love for my brother? My *engaged to someone else* brother? Do I tell her everything is falling apart around me and the only thing that makes sense is not killing the polar bear this morning?

I settle on saying nothing. If I speak, my voice will break and the tears hovering just behind my eyes will spill down my cheeks, because I can never *not* cry.

"Is it about the bear?"

"You—you heard?" Who would have told her?

"Mmm."

"I missed the shot." The confession doesn't pull any of the weight off my shoulders. I hoped it would, but it only settles more heavily. "I scared it off."

"Of course you did. No one would believe otherwise." She snorts and settles back, her cane balancing under her hand. Sparrow cackles as he sways from side to side, his beak pointed toward me. "Well, not anyone with half a brain."

I should have proved them wrong. I should have shot the bear. If I had, none of this would be happening. I wouldn't be avoiding my father, my brother wouldn't be mad at me because his wife is a constant thorn in his side, Beren never would have been in danger, and my whole future wouldn't be as slippery as the mud stuck to the bottom of my shoes.

But the bear who saved me all those years ago would be dead.

And I would have been the one to kill him.

"The people of Willoughby think they have every reason to be scared of the bears. But their fear comes from the misplaced belief that they can control everything, even nature. People see themselves in competition with nature itself, and they create villains when sometimes there are none." Granny Grin's gaze moves to the crown on my head. The wind pulls at it, the sharp ends catching on my hair as wisps tangle over them. Her eyes narrow, but the edges of her lips turn up. "Did I ever tell you the story of the polar bear king?"

"No." I frown. I've clung to every tale she weaves of a near-forgotten past, of glittering cities and daring princes who save those who can't save themselves, and I've heard many of them more than once. But I have always loved the polar bears. I would have remembered one of the polar bear kings.

She must have kept the story to herself for a reason, just as she does all the others. Ripe to pluck at just the right moment, to teach, to coax, to admonish. This was clearly one of those moments, and I would be wise to listen well.

Granny Grin doesn't deal in fairy tales, only distant truths, but a king among bears? They are solitary creatures. With the exception of mothers and their cubs, I've never witnessed more than a few together at a time, and they always disperse to go their separate ways. But there's always been a ring of truth to her stories, even if the tone is soft and sometimes easily overlooked.

She pats the empty stretch of bench next to her and waits until I settle to speak. "When the polar bears first swam into these waters, it was as the people fled the great ice floes. Those who lived through the storms and survived journeyed south, and only a few remained here, pledging themselves as the first defense against the great white north. But the bears were comfortable in their expanded territory. They became kings. Conquerors. Once, the bears were pushed to the edge of extinction, but not anymore. They were warriors of the snow, and not even the guns of man could stop them. They raided the storehouses, killed the livestock, even maimed a few of the first Willoughby citizens. They grew strong, and so did their numbers.

"A young leader from the village began the first patrols. Any bear seen would be shot on sight. But despite his best efforts, there was little the people could do against the thousands of bears flooding the bay in autumn. The people were starving, already ignorant in the ways of the cold, of farming, of animal husbandry. Each year brought greater cold and devastation. And more bears.

"Desperate, the young leader went to the local wise woman and begged for her help. If their people were to survive, he needed the strength to end the bears' reign. She saw the fear in his heart and the arrogance in his request, but still she bestowed upon him a simple spell to right the balance and told him to use it the next time he put himself at risk against a polar bear.

"That night, he went seeking the strongest of the bears, and when he stood in the shadow of the great one, he did as he was instructed. There was a skirmish, and the villagers lost sight of him. All they could hear were the young leader's cries, first those of a warrior, and then those of a broken man. And the next day, when they went looking for their leader, there was no sign of him. The great bear was victorious. And the young man was never seen again.

"Some say the bear took the spell for himself and became the most powerful polar bear to roam the ice. That perhaps he still does, seeking out a worthy opponent amongst the townspeople. A polar bear king, for there was no one who could defeat him. Others think a stupid young man thought himself above the laws of nature and paid the price."

"Why are you telling me this?" The question comes out as a whisper.

"The real question is, why do *you* think I am telling it?"

I frowned as I skimmed through the images that rose in my mind. Where was the seed of truth? "Do you think the bear from this morning is the polar bear king?"

She reaches out her hand and Sparrow hops from his perch to her lap. Slender fingers slip into ebony feathers, and she scratches the top of his head. "Could be. How should I know?"

Disappointment hits like a heavy stone and sinks to the bottom of my gut. "But Granny—"

One bony finger rises. "Life comes with tough choices, and you will only ever be judged by how you act, no matter how much care went into making the decision. Some things aren't always as black and white as they seem, and we can't always trust our own perspective." The finger joined the rest where they rested over the head of her cane, and she leaned back. "There will come a time when you have to choose, just like the young leader, and you'll be remembered by that choice. But will you have the ability to see beyond yourself and your cause? Because in the end, it could mean the difference between dying a headstrong child and ensuring the rise of a polar bear king."

CHAPTER 7

None of Granny's tales seeped into my mind and stuck there like this one. It dug in its claws, refusing to let go. It made me uncertain. Unsteady.

Why did no one ever talk of this polar bear king? And to which side did I owe my sympathy? A young man trying to save his people from starvation? Or the bears who simply followed their own nature?

The answer seems impossible, and yet I am asked to make it every day. Choose Willoughby, choose survival. But we aren't starving. We are thriving.

And the bears haven't changed at all. They're only bears.

Everyone wants me to choose Willoughby, but when has it ever chosen me?

The soft crooning of ice music stops abruptly as I leave Granny Grin to step back into the quiet meeting house. She says she wants to stay and listen to the wind, to feel the ice on the gusts. Did she come for the party? Or did she come for me?

I don't know, but I just want to get lost in the music and pretend like this day hasn't happened.

But a new song doesn't start up, and no one inside says a word.

Instead, all attention looks to my father at the far end of the room. He towers over my cousin, Merritt, as she leans up to speak to him. She's dressed in her parka, her rifle strap looped over her shoulder and binoculars over her neck.

Though most of the town is here in the meeting hall, a few volunteered to patrol the streets in shifts. Merritt has volunteered the last few years, mostly because she hates parties and dislikes dressing up even more.

The cold air blusters up behind me, and an uneasiness settles over the attendees.

The jovial air is gone. The mood has turned somber. My father nods once and takes a single step forward, but stops as he sees me.

The entire room pivots to take me in.

I blink. Why are they all looking at me? What did I do now?

The whispers begin then. Starting off like the hush of a breeze and building into a full-forced gale. They sweep through the villagers, people I have known my entire life. My aunts and uncles, my cousins, my sisters-in-law, my neighbors, and friends.

Is it the crown they stare at? The silent offering from a man no one seems to know? The draft from outside tugs at my hair, the circle of holly tangling with the loose strands. It settles into my scalp almost painfully, and I lift my hand to adjust it.

Dad steps forward, his boots heavy on the floor. He's never dressed up, not in all the years I have been allowed to attend the ball. He wears the same clothes he might wear to the patrol office, one of the radios clipped to his belt loop, and always proclaims he will attend as the patrol chief. Mom usually rolls her eyes, but it's always with a smile. As if he's still funny after all their years together, even though she's heard the same jokes for years.

But even she looks at me with a slight pucker to her brow and down-turned lips, not the usual quiet acceptance she casts my way.

"We need to talk," he says as he wraps a hand around my arm.

"About what?" I shift my gaze away from him and glance around the room. The gust of rumors has settled as the others look on curiously. But by the shake of a few heads and the deep frowns of others, I fear they already know the meat of it.

"Let's go to the office. We can discuss this there."

My heart pounds against my chest, the beats so loud they ring in my ears. I swallow. He's angry about the bear. He knows I missed on purpose. That's what this has to be about. He doesn't want to say it in front of Beren, but Beren—

My vision shimmers with tears again. Why must I be like this? Why can't I stand up for myself without dissolving into a puddle of sobs and snot? Why does any range of emotion beyond neutral send me to tears? I hate appearing weak, but I can't help it. "Is this about the bear this morning?" I meant to whisper my questions, but my voice refuses, breaking, growing louder.

Everyone seems to press closer.

"Dira."

"Did it come back?" I shift so I can see around him, my gaze finding Merritt. "Did you kill it?" I ask her.

My breath hitches as my imagination runs wild. My father probably gave the order. When she called it in, did he take great pleasure in giving her permission to shoot? He's always been thirsty for the blood of the polar bears that come too close, even when I suggested there could be other ways to protect our people. All we have to do is scare them away. Move them along, convince them wandering into Willoughby is a danger too great to risk. Just like this morning, I've seen the way they avoid the loud cracks of rifle shots.

But he has too. And he doesn't seem to care.

He thinks someday I will understand. That if I spend long enough on the patrols, I'll become like him. That the work will eventually mold me into the perfect Willoughbier, and I will somehow forget the scarred polar bear and what he did for me that day.

"It was just a missed shot," I insist. "You know I have terrible aim. I shouldn't even be on the patrol. Uncle Thesper has better marksmanship, and he can't see ten feet in front of his face without his glasses." I sound giddy. Irrational. The words tumble out of my mouth. "But the bear went away, didn't it? You didn't have to go after it. It fled. Like they all do. And Beren is *fine*. Really, he is."

But he's not. He's in love with Linka. He's going to ask me to marry him, but only because he doesn't want to be alone. Not because he loves me or actually *wants* me or thinks we will be good for each other. But because he has no other choice, because Linka's marrying Liddet. Liddet, who's so sweet and kind. Liddet, who would never hurt anyone. Unlike me.

I hurt everyone. Linka said it himself, and Beren didn't disagree, not really. I shouldn't even be here. I should have run home the moment I stumbled upon their secret. I could have screamed it and this horrible day into my pillows, fallen asleep, and woken up to get through another brutal day all over again.

My life. A series of events I want no part of. I wish I could just disappear into the wilds and live with the polar bears. It would be best for everyone.

"Let's not talk about this here, Dira." Dad tries to steer me out the door.

"You're kicking me off the patrol, aren't you?" A glimmer of hope rises. No more shifts. No more pretending. I can be free of it.

"I'm not kicking you off."

"But why not?"

Murmuring begins anew. They all agree. The whole damn town. They know I don't measure up. I'm *dangerous.*

"Because three people are dead, Dira. Three people were mauled by that monster, all because you can't follow directions. You not only put Beren in danger, you *killed* the Leigs. And now you're going to clean up your mess. Now let's go."

The meeting house erupts into a roar of gossip and rumor as we leave, my upper arm still in the powerful vice of my father's grip, and my mind speeding across the landscape as if riding on the back of one of the dog sleds. Are they discussing what should be done with me? Demanding the counsel expel me from the village?

I can't stop on any one point and just speed along, trying to outrun the words: three dead. *You killed them.* The patrol office door squeals on uncoiled hinges and then bangs shut behind us.

"Where have you been all day?" Dad releases his grip on my arm to pace from one end of the long room to the other through the darkness. He makes no move to turn on any of the lamps.

"I stayed with Beren while he fixed his boat and then I went to Liddet's to get ready for the party."

"Avoiding your responsibilities. As always. Dammit, Dira, when you pull stunts like this, letting dangerous animals escape so they can return, you put all our lives on the line."

The radio at his hip crackles, and he gives me his back as he answers. He holds it up to his ear, balancing his opposite fist on his hip.

Suddenly, I am a seven-year-old girl again, standing in the middle of the wreckage of my best friend's world as everyone talked around me. As my father talked around me.

He took charge that day, proving himself to be the leader Willoughby thought they needed in their fight against the polar bears. He doubled the patrols on the spot, using his radio to call in anyone not already making the looping rounds through the village.

I stood looking out to sea, hoping to find any sign the bear who saved me didn't drown as he succumbed to his bullet wound, as my father plotted his revenge and gave Landry the verbal thrashing that turned my carefree older brother into the stick-in-the-mud he is today.

"What were you thinking?" Dad demanded that day, his voice rising above the crash of the incoming tide, over the hushed murmurs of frightened teenagers unable to look away as one of their own was dressed down before them. "You were given a responsibility. Your sister could have been killed. Do you understand that? She could have died all because you—I don't even want to know what you were doing." He took a long, ragged sigh and paced across the sand just like he paces across the wooden floor of the patrol office now. "A woman is dead because you didn't take responsibility. Now, for once in your life, do as you're told and get her out of here."

I didn't fight Landry. I let him wrap my hand in his and drag me back over the dunes, through the willow shrubs, to home.

Dad has given me variations of the same speech over the years. Usually, he tells me I am a danger to myself, and that because of my actions, I will get myself killed and break my mother's heart. I can almost recite the words verbatim; he hasn't rewritten his speech in quite some time.

I wait for it, knowing I deserve it, even though every ounce of me will fight against it. I don't want to believe the bear could have done this. Not the bear I saw on the beach. Not the bear that saved me all those years ago. I refuse to believe it. I *won't* believe it.

And yet with each breath, the gaping hole in my chest grows. Because, just like what happened to Mella, they will all think it was my fault.

I bite down on the insides of my cheeks to prepare for his lecture.

But when he turns around, all he says is, "If that bear had been killed when I ordered it, three people would still be alive right now. You're coming out to the homestead with me. You'll prepare their bodies for the pyre. You'll set the fire. You did this, Dira. And if this doesn't make you understand, so help me, you won't stay in this town and continue to endanger us all."

CHAPTER 8

Yosef Leig is only a few years older than Landry, and when he met a young woman at a trade fair one summer in the south, he brought her back to our shorelines for a small, romantic wedding ceremony cast in a berry-colored sunset. At least that's the way my sister, Dasha, told it when she came home with the news, her teenaged eyes wistful with the prospect of romance, even someone else's.

When Yosef set up his own household, it wasn't near his father's bright blue house in the center of town, but on the edge of the bay outside the patrol's boundaries. He and his wife are far enough away. We often forget they even live there until he arrives with a fresh haul of fish on the odd market day or comes to our house to buy a sled dog puppy from Mom. A few years ago, his wife, a quiet woman from a village where they keep and shear sheep, from a people even further removed from the rumor of civilization than Willoughby, gave birth to a son, and they kept to themselves even more.

I don't know how anyone would even know they were dead until I see the faint orange glow of a dying fire spreading through the black husks of their house's frame. Gray smoke curls up toward the sky to the tune of a faint crackling. Ash spreads out, mixing with the snow,

the dull gray flakes dirtying the pristine sparkle of the coming winter.

They died in a fire. How is that the bears' fault?

Throwing off the furs piled over my legs, I unfold myself from the dog sled and follow my father to where a handful of others look over the quiet scene.

Snow blankets the ground in fluffy tufts that spread out over the shoreline like goose down. I stare at the ruins that were once the Leigs' home. How did a polar bear kill them and set their house ablaze? Something doesn't add up, and yet my father voices no skepticism. Blaming the bears is easier than entertaining other options.

"Yosef's over here." Merritt escorts Dad away from the dogs and toward one of the lumps laying across the ground. She settles back on her haunches and lifts a wool blanket, most of the snow covering it tumbling to the ground. Some of the flakes stick to it, a bright white against the fabric's dark dye. "Connell saw the blaze from the north side of town and came out to investigate. We think Yosef set the house on fire accidentally while trying to get the bear away. He still has the torch in his hand."

I creep closer, peering over the blanket at the only vaguely familiar face. A deep slash bisects his cheek, but only one. Wouldn't a polar bear's claws do more damage? Wouldn't there be more claw marks? More injuries? The puncture marks of teeth? "How do you know a polar bear did this?"

Merritt turns her gaze up to me as she readjusts her position. "There are bear tracks all around the house, and the barn door has claw marks in it. The bear didn't get in, but it tried."

I frown down at the dead man's face, and my stomach pitches as I realize the deep cut reveals the bone beneath. I press the back of my hand against my mouth and swallow down the bile rising up the back of my throat. "But this doesn't look like a bear—"

"Seen many bear attacks?" she asks with ice on her tongue.

"Have you?" I shoot back.

"Dira," Dad cuts in. "You know what you need to do."

I glare at him and turn on my heel.

He didn't give me time to go home and change, just shoved me out the door as soon as Mom brought the team around, so I slog through the soft ground in my delicate shoes and ball gown. The hem dusts against the fresh snow, collecting a thin layer of flakes. It will be impossible to find dry wood all the way out here unless the family kept some in the barn; anything else they had clearly went up in the fire.

I pass by others—my brother-in-law, Dunnal, his best friend, and my cousin, Joles. They stare at me with a mix of sympathy and anger crossing their faces, but I refuse to be cowed and stare right back. Only Dunnal gives me a nod of sympathy.

There are no sounds of excited goats bleating as I undo the latch to the barn door and push it open, nor a flurry of chicken feathers like I expected. It's well-cared for, the hay fresh on the ground, and the smell of oats wafting up from the buckets. Where did the animals go?

In the corner next to the sled dog harnesses is a pile of wood, and I gather as much as I can carry and bring it out. Three or four pieces of split wood at a time. I build a small pyre, spreading the wood out over ice-covered sand. Once that task is done, with shaking, chapped hands, I spread dry hay from the barn over it to act as kindling.

Granny Grin once told me that people used to bury their dead. They would use their shovels to dig a hole as deep as my father is tall and carefully lower the body into it, then stand back as they filled it up.

The animals couldn't get to them that far down, she said, and markers would be placed over their graves so mourners could come back and visit.

"Why?" I remember asking as I leaned my chin onto my hand, where it rested on her knee.

She laid her hand on the top of my head, just like she does when she knows I need comfort. "So people could become one with the earth again. So they could feed the roots and become part of nature like they are supposed to be. Men try to tame the world, but in the end, it used to consume them, anyway."

"Why did they stop?"

She threaded her knobby fingers through my hair, combing out the knots the wind must have put in it. "When the world froze, they had no other choice. They broke the earth, and they had to pay for it in ways they never imagined. Instead of becoming part of it, they were destined to leave it forever."

What happens to us now that we can't go back to nature? Granny Grin didn't know then, and the answer doesn't come to me now.

I brush my hands off and stand back to appraise my work. The pyre appears decent enough, though not nearly as well-built as those I've seen in the past.

I hug my middle and look back at the others. They just stand near the dogs and the sleds, watching as I work. Ensuring I learn my lesson: kill the bears so they don't kill people. So they don't kill *us*.

I stare across the charred earth, and tears prickle at my eyes for the dead. I should feel a deeper sadness, but it's frustration that bubbles. My conscience rebels, demanding a better explanation.

Your bear didn't do this. My own voice lashes out through my mind.

This was something else. Someone else. It has to be. He wouldn't do this. But I have no better explanation. And arguing's never gotten me anywhere in the past—why should it start now?

My muscles ache from the work, heat building beneath my skin despite the cold kiss of winter blowing in from the north. No one makes a move to help me as I cross to the first blanketed body left on the beach. I sink down and draw the wool back to reveal the woman's face.

She could be sleeping. Her lips part slightly in the middle, chapped yet plump. Her eyes are closed against her ashy skin, lashes resting against her cheeks, and she looks peaceful, even though blood colors the corners of her mouth.

I toss the blanket away. Dark red stains her abdomen. I stare at her wound as I try to imagine a bear ripping through her, but I just can't see how claws or teeth could leave such a clean entry. I expected to find tatters and ribbons of flesh, but there are none.

Glancing up, I plead with someone to help me.

Dunnal starts to move forward, but my father stretches out a hand to stop him.

"She has to learn," he says and then folds his arms back over the barrel of his chest.

"I'm sorry," I whisper to the woman whose name I never knew and fit my hands under her armpits. Leaning back, I drag her dead weight across the sand to the low pyre. My hands brush against the cooling wetness of her blood as I wrap my arms around her to haul her up over the wood, and then, with heavy legs, I move for the smallest blanketed mound on the shore.

I can't bring myself to throw back the wool this time, instead wrapping my arms around the whole bundle to cradle it against my chest. It's small and weighs less than I expected. My chin wobbles as I push away images of the younger children in the village. The image of Linka when we were kids. Beren as he wept over his mother's body. I deposit the small bundle next to his mother, cradled in her limp arms.

By the time I stand over Yosef, tears stream down my cheeks, hot and frozen all at once. They collect in my lashes, weighing them down, even as I use the brilliant blue of my sleeve to blot them away. I try to drag him as I dragged his wife, but his body won't budge, and as my feet slip out from under me, a sob rents through the air around me.

I didn't ask for this. I didn't ask for any of it. I just wanted the killing to stop. I wanted the bears, so beautiful and solitary, to get to live just as we do. And I wanted to repay the favor.

A life for a life.

But I didn't ask to build pyres for the dead. I didn't ask to do it alone. I didn't ask to be a disappointment, a daughter my father doesn't want to claim.

I didn't ask to be the outcast. And I don't want to be.

But no one will ever look at me the same.

Dunnal comes to my rescue as my sobs become hysterical, my tears falling over a dead man like a pouring rain in summer. He pushes away my father's hand when he tries to stay him a second time and marches toward me. "Get his feet," he says in his gentle-giant of a voice as he approaches.

At that moment, I understand why my sister, Dasha, finds happiness in him. In his kindness and his strength.

I press my hands into the snow and push myself up, my mouth hanging open as my cries drown out everything else around me.

"You can do this," he says. "And then it will all be over."

Together, we carry the man's body to lie with the rest of his family's, and as Dunnal passes, he hands me a small box of matches. "Sometimes, the hardest step is the one most needed."

CHAPTER 9

In a burning trail, a tear falls. It skids down my cheek, and the wind wickedly licks it away.

The hay catches fire easily, and the bright flames fan out, thick plumes of black smoke licking at the low-hanging clouds above. I step back as the fire consumes the Leigs and any evidence of their existence. For the six of us at their homestead, the place where they took their last breaths, this will be the way we remember them forever. They will be smoke and ash on the last night of autumn, a memory no longer of this earth.

Tears still fall from my eyes. They stream down my already wet cheeks, each gust of wind drying them into a stinging burn. But I feel nothing but emptiness.

The flames roar around their bodies, and yet I feel like the one who's no longer alive. I should be cold, but I am numb. My life no longer belongs to me. Nor does anything I can control. But was it stolen, or did I give it up freely? Was one decision all it took to destroy my future?

Or did I never really have one here in Willoughby?

Heat builds, stretching out toward me, and I close my eyes as it

plays over my skin, the flickering creating dancing silhouettes on the backs of my lids. Was this really my fault? Would they still be here, huddled in their beds or dancing in the meeting hall, if I had only aimed true?

A different life plays through my mind. A life where I never wandered away from Landry. One where I stuck to his side and watched as he pressed fumbling hands to Calla's shoulders and a wet kiss on her lips. I kicked at the sand and complained of boredom until he took me home. In that life, Mella still hummed lullabies as she cleaned fish by the harbor, her hair caught up in a kerchief. Beren would bring in a large haul with his father, and she would cluck her tongue at them both as she cut and pulled, cut and pulled. I would take any patrol offered to me, my father at my side, brimming with pride as I lifted my rifle and—

I cut the fantasy off abruptly, and I open my eyes. How quickly my deepest desires turn to my darkest nightmares. I don't want to choose the people who would destroy the bears and burn their dead instead of putting them back in the ground to be one with the earth. I don't want to choose brute strength over kindness or lies over honesty. I don't want an enemy. I want to save us both.

Just like the bear saved me that day.

I stare at the other patrol members. They are a sad congregation of mourners, but there is no other way—we would expect the same treatment if it was any one of us. The scent of the dead could bring animals in search of an easy meal, who would then rip apart their bodies until there was little left to burn. We never let our dead rest. The risk of attack by the polar bears is Dad's greatest concern.

My shoulders droop; it will never be any different. I can miss every single shot I take, and it will never be enough. Thoughts of the bears consume Dad, but it isn't their beauty or majesty that captivates him; it's the fear they instill. He will never be happy until he has destroyed them all, and I refuse to be a part of it.

My father wants me to be someone I'm not, and he'll use any opportunity to force me to change. But I don't want to be on the patrol. I don't want to be punished for refusing to kill.

I back away from the pyre, turning on my heel and marching away from the fire I was forced to set for a family whose deaths my father wants to blame me for.

Despite my aching muscles and the blister rubbing on my heel, my legs churn as I put distance between us.

The glimmering skirts tangle around my knees and I trip. The ground reaches up to meet me, my nose within inches of the sand and gravel as I catch myself. Sharp rocks dig into my palms, the gritty sand squishing through my fingers. I pause, waiting for a sob, even a tear, to erupt, but all I can do is swallow around the dry patch in my throat.

Cold wetness seeps into the fabric, and no amount of washing will get the streaks of blood out of the soft, delicate fiber. The most beautiful thing I own, the thing I earned through my own skill and cleverness. Gone. Unsalvageable. Ruined.

I sniff as I steady myself on wobbly feet.

I don't want my father's blame. I refuse it. I didn't kill these people, and neither did a bear.

I continue my walk up the bay's shoreline, sweeping toward the west, hoping to find some control where there is none. No one follows me. No one calls my name. I glance over my shoulder.

They've all moved away from the pyre, a few marching toward the barn, likely to collect anything useable to bring back to the village, and the others seeing to the dogs. Not even Dunnal looks for me.

I'm alone.

Ice stretches out over the water. The thin discs latch to create solid sheets, locking together and smoothing out. No longer do the waves crash against the shore in an echo of a thousand bells. Winter did come early, and it came in a few short hours, just like Granny Grin predicted. It came, and the polar bears will leave, disappearing back to wherever they go when they aren't haunting the boundaries of Willoughby.

Do they return to some far away kingdom? Do they reunite with their polar bear king?

It should sound stupid, but all of a sudden it doesn't. They go somewhere, abandoning Willoughby's shorelines until spring. Why not go to the halls of their king's castle? Could he be the truth to Granny Grin's story? Could he still be out there?

If he was, perhaps he'd accept a truce.

If I can end this pull and tug between men and bears, maybe I can still have a life in Willoughby.

My skin prickles back to life, my heart thumping in my chest.

I search out Granny Grin's cottage on the dark strip of land over the bay, but can make out only a dark outline against the white ice where it should be. No lights shine from the little house caught between the eastern sun and western moon. I point myself in its direction. She'll let me curl up in her loft for the night, and then, in the morning, I'll make a plan over a mug of tea.

As I get farther away from the Liegs' homestead, the wind picks up, and without the buildings to break the gusts, snow slaps me in the face, the thick flakes like daggers. My cheeks sting, flesh so cold it burns hot, and my toes ache in the flimsy shoes.

I stare down at my feet. Snow collects in the unmistakable shapes of polar bear paws, but they point toward the bay, not the homestead. I kneel to trace one, sliding my finger around the edges. But there is something else there, too.

Boot prints.

My eyes follow them in the silvery moonlight. A cloud of white air puffs out in front of me as I exhale.

And when it clears, on the edge of the shore, something moves.

White like the ice.

A man.

My breath catches as I take in the white polar bear fur pulled over his head, around his shoulders.

He turns his head toward me, his features bathed in darkness beneath the hood. I can't move, his hold powerful and unbreaking, and for a long moment he doesn't either. Slowly, a single hand stretches out toward me.

Who is he?

Reaching up, my fingers brush the crown. It's slipped down the side of my head and sits crookedly over my temple, the spines digging into my skin. Why did he give it to me? And where is he going?

I drag the crown from my head and run my fingers over prickly at the end of the leaves.

But when I glance up, he no longer stands on the shore.

Instead, a lone polar bears lopes onto the ice.

I squeeze my eyes shut. Too much dancing, too much work, too much to drink. Not enough food. When was the last time I ate? I can't remember, but it was early in the evening, when the first haul of fish fry arrived in the meeting hall. And I'd only picked at it then.

I must be seeing things.

But when I open my eyes, I find the backside of a polar bear again just before it disappears into a curtain of snow.

Hand dropping to my side, and the crown dropping to the path at my feet, I gather up the skirts in my fist and stride forward. One step. Two. Four.

My shoe slides on the ice. No crack fractures it, no creak slicing through both air and ice. My other foot joins it, and I walk out onto the ice. The soft soles skid, and I redistribute my weight to lean forward.

I look up and ahead.

He waits for me, turned back to watch as I shuffle forward. His nose raises, twitches in the air, and with a clouded huff, he turns and chuffs softly before trudging forward to lead me away from Willoughby. And everything I have ever known.

Perhaps I haven't reached the end of my journey.

I don't have to turn back.

Dunnal was right. Sometimes the hardest step is the one most needed.

CHAPTER 10

Willoughby is gone.

Beneath my feet, the new ice shifts and wobbles, but I remain steady.

Turning back is no longer an option. I don't know in which direction I travel, the wind-whipped snow a fickle curtain.

But I don't want to turn back, either. Without a truce, what is left for me there?

Forward.

It's the only way.

Forward.

To the land of the polar bear king, wherever it may be.

My teeth chatter; my lips, cracked and dry, sting with each breath.

Forward may have been a bit optimistic. My whole plan may be a bit optimistic. But stories aren't just based on fancies, there has to be a root of truth to them, and I am determined to find this one.

The burn in my fingers becomes unbearable, and I shove them under my arms, curling the tips into my palms. The movement aches in the bone, pulls at the skin.

No longer do my muscles shake uncontrollably. In fact, they barely

move at all.

I drop to my knees, but no pain shoots up into my thighs, just a jolt of surprise.

Ahead, the polar bear stops and glances over his shoulder.

Helplessly, I sink farther into the snow and ice. Exhaustion or cold, one of them grips me, but it doesn't matter which. Here, I will surely freeze. I'm going to die out here, alone in the snow. It should terrify me, and yet all I can think about is that at least I will go back to the earth instead of up in smoke.

I shudder. I just need a moment to warm up, and then I'll be able to continue.

Curling up into myself, I picture a fire. But not just any fire. One roaring in Granny Grin's hearth. She putters around me, bringing me tea and blankets, tucking the corners around my legs. The heat from bright orange flames licks my face.

My eyes shoot open.

A large black nose hovers inches away.

I can only blink as my heart pounds against my chest.

The nose nudges my cheek.

I let my eyes focus. Not only on the nose, but on the face attached to it. Sheer white, with a curving scar slicing through one cheek. My gaze returns to one of the dark eyes over me.

This is my polar bear. The one who put himself between me and the mother bear. The one who ran across the shore for Beren. I hold my breath. Did he also end the lives of the Leigs? Will it now be the end of mine?

I don't believe it. I *won't* believe it.

He nudges more insistently, wedging his large head under my arm.

Stiffly, unsteadily, I push myself back to my feet, my hands in the snow. It stings my already red fingers, the pain both numbing and sharp. I weave on tingling legs, and he bumps into me again, lowering his shoulder.

My fingers dive into his fluffy fur.

I've felt fur like this before.

Closing my eyes, I lean into it. The warmth underneath, the softness.

I am a little girl again. Seven years old and with a wild spirit that drags me toward the shallow creek bed. I wrap my arms around a warm, wiggling weight and heft it into myself before we both tumble over. The soft fur, lighter than the down feathers Mom stuffs into our pillows, tickles my cheek.

"Dira!"

My father's voice cuts through my mind like a newly sharpened cleaver.

"Take her home," he says sternly. I know he is talking to Landry. But Landry isn't there. Neither of them are.

I jolt.

A snowflake catches on my eyelash, and I blink it away just before a hot tear drips into his fur.

I lean into him, the soft hairs brushing my cheeks, and my eyes close again. When he makes no growl of disapproval, I swing my leg over his back and wrap my arms around his neck.

He stands and carries me into the storm.

Warm.

So warm.

No. Hot.

Stifling heat wraps around my legs, sweat gathering in the creases at the backs of my knees.

It plucks and pulls at every inch of my skin, a growing inferno coming from the outside in. Or the inside out. I can't tell which, only that it roasts every part of me, like the bright flames of the pyre dancing amid fat snowflakes.

And I have to find relief.

Kicking wildly, I dislodge the heavy white furs and quilts, and then, hiking up the cumbersome wool skirts of my ball gown, I strip off the wool stockings I'd tied over my knees that afternoon. They bunch around my ankles, and I breathe deeply as cool air slaps my calves. My skin prickles into gooseflesh, but I lay there unmoving as the heat billows away.

As panic subsides, I tongue my cracked, chapped lips and open my eyes.

Gray light streams through a bank of tall, slender windows, catching dust as it floats like foam over a calm sea. I stare at them, at the light. Why do they look so different? So strange? My single window in my room is far smaller than any of these, the glass in it far thicker, wavier. Here it's smooth and uniform. Perfect. Almost like the seams of my dress.

I blink and shift my gaze to the ceiling. Cracked white plaster, shades of brown and yellow blooming along the bubbled edges, stares back.

That's not my ceiling.

I shoot up, muscles screaming in outrage and aching right down to the bone. Scrambling on the pile of fur and blankets, I find my feet, the dull wood floors creaking as I spin.

This isn't my room.

That isn't my bed.

If you can even call a pile of blankets and musty furs a bed.

My chest heaves as a choked sob threatens to escape.

Where am I?

And how the hell did I get here?

The soles of my stockings catch on the scarred floorboards as I lunge for the nearest window.

A white world stretches out toward a darkening sky, a ripe apple sunset tinting the edges. Buildings sprinkle the landscape below, their roofs heavy with snow, a thick wall standing guard a thousand meters away.

I stare out at nothing familiar. Not the shape of the buildings, nor their size. I've never seen any quite so large. Not even the meeting hall or the marketplace stretches out with quite the same impressiveness. Some are no more than crumbling ruins, their roofs caved in, and there's no sign of a windmill to power their lights anywhere.

My stomach knots.

How did I get here?

Pressing my forehead against the windowpane, I peer out to one side. The high wall surrounds whatever tower I'm in, stretching out in both directions. It overlooks a frozen ocean, a sight not unfamiliar to me. Once the ice sets in around Willoughby, the sea and bay look much the same. How many times have I stared across both and wondered what was on the other side?

Still looking out, I glance down; the ground sinks far below. Much farther than any of the trees I climbed to spy on the bears.

The distance sends a shiver of fear up my spine, and I back away.

Turning around, I take in the room with fresh, assessing eyes. The pile of blankets where I slept slump together in a corner, and the only other furniture in the room is a wooden chair settled next to them. No table, no lamp, no rug to warm the floors. And my ruined shoes lay on their sides, one closer to the middle of the room than the other.

My teeth clack together, and I realize my breath puffs out in clouds in front of me.

Is this a prison?

The notion curls up in my stomach like a scared house cat, the hair on the back of my neck rising just the same.

Stooping, I draw one of the furs over my shoulders and tug it tight over my chest. It falls over the dark blue skirts, now streaked with dirt and fraying along the hem. Toeing the closest shoe upright, I shove my foot in, not bothering to readjust my stocking, where a hole allows my toe to peek out. The other shoe receives the same treatment.

I hold my breath as I test the doorknob. Will it open? Or am I trapped here?

A sigh of relief ruffles the dark curl hanging over my eyes as the knob whines loudly. The hinges soundlessly give way, and the door swings into a long, shadowed hall.

Not a prison.

Or at least this room isn't my cell.

I lean out through the doorjamb.

More doors line the corridor, all identical, and at the end of the hall, a large hole surrounded by rotting wood looks out over the frozen plains. Snow flutters through it, collecting on the jagged-edged floor that juts out into nothing. The snow covers the wood like a thick sheen of dust, those flecks still flying, fluttering toward me.

Inching away from the doorjamb, I slip down the hallway in the opposite direction of the gaping hole, my shoes echoing ominously with each soft tap of the little heels. The shadows grow longer as the corridor comes to an end, another door capping it.

It opens easily, revealing a cold stairwell lit only by the fading dusk pouring in from smooth-glassed windows.

My hand grips the rust-covered handrail as I creep down the stairs, my muscles protesting with every step. The temperature drops steadily as I descend, and when I hit the bottom floor, my breath puffs out in great white clouds. I strengthen my hold on the thick fur, pulling it tightly over my shoulders as I push through the single door at the bottom.

Another hall, almost identical to the one above, greets me. More debris litters the floor, piled up where lightly colored tiles butt up against the walls. Wide cracks and slender fractures course through them, and most of the doors hang askew, one laying on the floor.

My teeth chatter, the thick streams of my breath rising through cracked lips and chapped nostrils to mingle with cobwebs.

I peer into the first room. Empty.

The second, as well.

Furniture stuffs the third. Chairs and tables stacked and pushed against the back corner, fencing in a row of empty shelves. The earthy scent of mildew wafts through the air, and I duck back out.

When I reach the end of the hall, I find something resembling a kitchen. I don't recognize much, but even the sight of metal countertops, bowls, large mixing spoons, and wide pots twists my stomach with hunger.

Cylinders wrapped in faded pictures dominate shelves on the opposite wall. I cross to them, reach for one, and turn it over, testing the weight. The colored illustrations peel around the edges, their scenes unfamiliar, the script illegible. I carefully add it back to the stack and pull on the handle of a large cabinet. The heavy door sticks at first, but I pull harder. Only the sick, putrid smell of death clings inside, and I shove it closed as my stomach revolts. I gag, my insides turning in painful knots, and move back into fresher air.

Maybe one of the other rooms contains something edible. Looking around, a hearth in which to cook it is noticeably absent.

I worry about the edge of my thumbnail with my index finger. If I can't find anything to eat here, I'll have to find something to hunt with.

A swell of unease expands in my chest. The thought of killing something is nearly enough to squash the rumblings in my belly.

A growl grumbles from my stomach, ripping through the quiet.

Nearly.

I've never hunted before because I haven't needed to. Each week, everyone in town brings a portion of their own stores to the patrol office as payment for our services. It's divided up between all of us, and Dad, as the chief, always has the largest share. Fish, meat, eggs, game, produce, wood, fabric… all of it can be found in our baskets and can be traded for other services or goods. Most of mine went toward my ruined dress. And it assured me I would never have to kill with my own hands to eat because someone else had already done it for me.

But there is no one else here, so if I don't want to starve, I have no other choice.

I'll need warmer clothes and something to protect my eyes from the reflection of the light on the snow if I'm to hunt. And a harpoon or spear, though a rifle would be better. I went with my brothers and Moore as they fished out on the ice when I was younger, with Beren when I grew older. I can replicate what they did. Probably.

Nervous flutters play deep in my belly, and I turn my thoughts from my best friend to finding something useful in the fortress.

I don't find anything but ice and snow, dust and debris. Many of the windowpanes sprawl in sharp pieces on the floor. What light lays beyond them is nearly lost.

As the temperature continues to dip, I give up. I won't find anything in the dark.

The climb back up the stairs starts slowly, my bones protesting with each step. At least there, my breath was only a whisper of mist, not a full storm cloud. And I have a better chance to stay warm buried under that pile of furs.

As I reach the final landing, the door below bangs open, heavy wood connecting with the wall, the whistle of wind accompanying it. It rushes up the staircase, and my dress flutters around my legs.

I don't move. Hold my breath. Listen.

I got here somehow. How did I not question how?

CHAPTER 11

Without taking a breath, I rush down the top corridor, through the door I came out of, and hide under the pile of furs.

Heavy steps thud purposefully on the wood floors. Each thud louder than the next, they echo down the hall in an even tattoo, muffled only by the closed door.

Remaining under the covers, I breathe through my mouth to better hear each movement, hoping the footsteps walk right by the room.

Instead, they stop and three knocks sound on the door.

I freeze. What do I do? Should I answer?

My mouth forms an "o," but no sound comes out. Only my own hot breath hitting the coverings and wafting back to hit me in the face. I lick my cracked lips.

Two more knocks.

"H-hello?" I manage.

The mechanisms in the doorknob squeal, and I hold my breath, listening for the soft sigh of quiet hinges.

"I thought you might be hungry," a deep, masculine voice murmurs into the room, the edges gruff, just short of gravelly.

He is right. It feels like days since I last ate. Lifting the edge of one of the furs, I peek out.

An inky silhouette crosses the distance between my corner and the door. From my vantage point, he appears tall, nearly as tall as Landry. I drop my gaze to the boot inches away from my nose, but it doesn't move as he kneels between me and the window, blacking out the deep charcoal of twilight.

Pure energy twitches through my veins, my fingers shaking uncontrollably.

A metal plate rattles as he places it between us, the rich scent of roasted seal wafting under my nose.

My mouth waters.

Slinging back the blankets, I dive for the food, not bothering with any sort of manners as I sink my teeth into the seared, fatty flesh. Rich, greasy juice drips over my lips, down my chin, and I barely chew the first bite before sinking my teeth in for another. Mom would be horrified.

It's a good thing she's not here.

I knew I was hungry, but not how ferocious my appetite could make me. Chewing becomes a reflex, a hurried action performed only to the barest minimum, and I struggle to swallow. A cough and a sputter erupt as the too-large bite works its way painfully into my stomach.

My companion chuckles and sets a cup next to the plate before straightening. With two steps, he drops himself heavily in the chair next to the makeshift bed, the wood groaning under his weight.

I reach for the cup, my hands wrapping around the cold glass, and I look up at him, eyes wide. "It isn't poisoned, is it?" I probably should have considered that possibility before devouring half the meat on the plate.

The shadow of the man shifts, leaning forward to balance his elbows on his knees. "Why would I do that when you've gone through all the trouble just to get here?"

I raise the rim to my lips and gulp the cool water. Only it isn't water, but something far harder. The liquid stings the back of my throat, and tears spring to my eyes. I sputter again. "What is this?"

"Whisky." A hum of a chuckle sounds deep in his chest.

I wrinkle my nose and sip it again. It tastes terrible. Nothing like the sweet honey meads or the berry brandy made in Willoughby. Dad keeps a bottle of whisky he traded for at one of the summer festivals in his sock drawer. Linka found it once, but he was the first—and only—to try it. No way was I putting it in my own mouth after I saw the face he made.

I can't imagine Dad's bottle could taste any worse than this.

"Why are you here?"

"Why am I—" I cough again and hiss out a breath as the stinging subsides. I wipe my mouth dry with the back of my hand. "Why would anyone choose to drink this? And who *are* you?"

"Because it'll make you forget the cold."

I doubt that. Gingerly, I set the cup down and push it away.

"I am Valemon. And who are you?"

What an odd name. So formal and… stuffy. Neither of which fit a grumbling shadow. "I'm Dira." I wipe my palm down the already ruined front of my dress and stick it out between us. "Dira Cloon. Of Willoughby."

"Mmm." He shifts and the wooden chair groans, but he doesn't reach out to grasp my hand. "Willoughby," he muses softly.

I shrug and reach for the meat with the hand he ignored. Anything to get that wretched taste off my tongue. Plate in hand, I fall back into a sitting position and fold my legs in front of me. "Is there a light in here?" I ask as I pull a morsel of meat from the larger portion to plop into my mouth.

"No. No lights." He pauses. "Why did you come here?"

I chew thoughtfully. That really is an excellent question, and one I would like an answer to myself. The last thing I remember is snow smacking me in the face, and I was so turned around, I couldn't tell north from south. More threads through that memory, but I can't quite piece out what was real and what was a hallucination. "I really don't know. I woke up here."

"You woke up here." The words may sound like a statement, but a question lingers there, hidden in the soft burr of his voice.

Do I detect amusement? A smile?

I pop the morsel onto my tongue and nod. "Yup. Walked out onto the ice to chase a polar bear wearing nothing but…" I glance down at my dress, barely able to make out any of the shimmering threads embroidered across the skirt. I must sound ridiculous. I feel ridiculous. Especially sitting here, talking to someone I don't know in the dark. "Are you sure there isn't something for light? A lamp? Candles?"

"No."

"It's just that it's impossible to see you. Are there others here? Is your village nearby?"

Silence is his only response.

I shrug and take another bite. He may be a featureless stranger, but he fed me. And if he's a stranger to me, I am just as much a stranger to him. He knows nothing of me, my skills, my past, the polar bear patrols, my brother and—

No. Best not to go there.

"Why would you follow a polar bear out on the ice? Were you trying to get killed?"

Despite the fact that it is totally wasted on him in the dark, I roll my eyes. He sounds just like my father. My brothers. Everyone. The familiar heat of anger rises, and my hand twists into a tight fist. "I don't know," I say through gritted teeth. I don't owe him anything, least of all an explanation. "It seemed like a good idea at the time. I was... upset. Where am I, by the way? I can't imagine I made it very far from Willoughby, but I don't recognize anything outside."

"Monroe." The name erupts, more like a grunt than an actual answer. "And you should stay put for a while. A storm's coming in, and even if you dress in ten layers, you'll freeze to death trying to get back to that side of the bay."

I frown. The other side of the bay? How far did I walk? No one goes around the bay unless they're hunting. There isn't anything to the north of Willoughby; we're the last stop, the very hem of civilization. My eyes narrow on him. "How did you know I was here?"

"I brought you here."

"You brought me here." I worry my thumbnail as the uneasy feeling that should have been sending up warning signals finally flares. "From where?"

"From out there."

"Where is out there?" My voice comes out high and thin.

His dark silhouette shifts in what I can only assume is a shrug.

"Where did you find me?" My voice still isn't quite my own and my pulse is so rapid, my head swims.

"Out on the ice."

On the ice. The memory of the man with the polar bear fur and golden crown resurfaces. Of him stepping away from the shore near what was once the Leigs' house, turning only to offer his hand. It seems so long ago. Like a hazy memory or a story, I told myself. "It was you, wasn't it?"

"Who found you on the ice? Yes. I thought that was already established." Amusement drips from his tongue.

"Yes. I mean, no. I mean, you were the one at the Night Magic Ball." Everything becomes clearer, the fog lifting from my brain, and a heat settles over my cheeks. Did he know I noticed him? That his presence made my pulse quicken and my curiosity spike?

I wait for a response but receive none.

"You were there, weren't you? You wore the polar bear fur, and I thought you were one of Dorin's new sons-in-law, but no one knew who you were. You gave me a crown of leaves. I went after you..." The image of Yosef's face and his wife's abdomen swims up, and I shake my head to rid myself of it. "You went onto the ice, and you held your hand out to me."

Everything about those moments muddles my brain. There was a man, yes, but then there was a bear. I followed the bear into the storm. He warmed me when I was ready to give up. Carried me on his back. I could feel the beat of his heart and the thickness of his fur.

"A polar bear brought you here?" he asks, more than a little disbelief dripping from his tongue.

I didn't realize I had spoken aloud, and my head snaps up as I refocus on him. "What?"

"You said you rode a polar bear here. That just seems rather... fantastical, don't you think? A polar bear would be more likely to maul you and eat your insides than carry you like a white steed."

"A what?"

"Steed? Like a horse? An animal you ride on?"

"Mm." What is a horse? The only animals anyone rides in Willoughby are the reindeer Dorin and his family raise. Are horses something I should know? Best not to reveal any weaknesses like a lack of knowledge. "I don't see why it's so implausible. Polar bears are only a threat to people if we get between them and their cubs. Or maybe their food. But seeing as how I did neither, I was perfectly safe." I cross my arms over my chest before remembering I don't have anything to prove to this man, even if his voice does strange things to my insides. He doesn't know me. I don't know him. And though I seem to have arrived here—wherever Monroe is—how safe am I really?

Another prickle of fear settles between my shoulders. I have no weapon with me, no protective clothing. I ventured out on the ice in a ballgown with a fifteen-hundred-pound wild animal. How am I even alive? Or was it all a dream?

I press my fingers into the corners of my eyes and will the first twinges of a headache away.

"You don't think maybe you give the bears more credit than they deserve?"

"Maybe you don't give them enough," I snap, dropping the hand back down to my lap.

"Maybe you're right."

Three beats of my rapidly pounding heart pass, and abruptly he stands, the joints of the wooden chair sighing with relief and the darkness of him shifting into something taller. "There are clothes in the next room over. In the footlocker by the bed. They're probably too big, but you're tall, so something might work. There're some old boots there too. I'll do what I can to get you enough food to keep the fat on your bones, but until then… dress in layers."

His boots pound on the floor as he strides across it for the door.

"Wait. You're leaving?" I don't even know him. I barely have a name for him. But loneliness latches onto my soul, dragging it into despair. The weight of yesterday presses down on me, the loneliness quickly following. I've felt it before, especially when I traipsed out into the wilds. But it was nothing like this. Nothing like darkness and cold.

He stops just inside the doorway. "It's been a long time since anyone else has been here."

"Wait—there's no one else here? It's just the two of us?" My nail slips and digs into the flesh on the side of my thumb. I barely feel the scratch.

My interruption fazes him little. "I can't have you freezing to death before we get to know each other, now can I?" He knocks on the wall twice and leaves, pulling the door shut.

Only a small hunk of meat remains on the metal plate, but I push it away and curl up on the furs, tucking them over my shoulder and resting my cheek in the crook of my arm.

He's here? Alone? All the questions I should have asked come flooding into my mind like the first ice chunks of winter crashing into the shore. How is he surviving out here without others? And where is here, exactly?

No one else knows where I am. No one will come for me.

It's just the two of us here in a ruin across the frozen bay.

I should be terrified. But, instead, I'm oddly free.

CHAPTER 12

My knock goes unanswered.

I ease the door open slowly and poke my head inside. Not much sets it apart from the one I slept in. The size, flooring, even the water-splotched walls are identical.

Large windows dominate the far wall, and a bed backs into one corner, a chest resting at its foot. The mattress collapses through one of the frame's corners, lying half on the floor. High ceilings collapse inward, giving me a narrow, unobscured view of the sky, revealing light gray clouds full of snow. The scent of snow wafts through the hole, even if no flakes fall. A metal bin rests below it, black soot staining the edges of both the hole and the wall leading up to it.

"Valemon?"

Only the soft hiss of wind hitting the wood above answers. I didn't expect anything else.

"Valemon?" I call one more time for good measure before pressing into the room.

A shiver runs through me as I cross to the chest, the draft from above wrapping around me as it whips through the room and out the opened door.

The make is unlike anything I have ever seen before. Long and low, the black substance isn't wood, and it's so smooth, it feels like glass. I rub my thumb across it. I would expect it to be colder, if it were glass. Harder. This has an almost soft quality to it, though there is no give. Rusted metal clips lock the lid in place, the first one sticking as I pry it up with a harsh whine. The second takes less effort.

The heavy scent of cedar pours out from inside, masking the underlying must of disuse. It reminds me of the chest Mom keeps the furs in during the summer months. Of the little pieces of wood she tucks into the drawers containing our clothes and quilts.

I kneel down as I drag out the first item in a pile of carefully folded cloth. With a shake, the top bundle unfurls.

Pants in a stiff, brown-and-green pattern. Three sets. A little worn at the knees and along the seams, but free of moth holes.

The next in the pile are matching jackets. Below it are long-sleeved brown shirts with round, stretchy collars, and made of a thin fabric not unlike the cotton shirts traders like Pinky bring back to Willoughby for summer wear. But this has no wrinkles. I pull one once. Twice. It springs back to its original shape. How strange.

I glance down at all of them and my nose wrinkles. The smell isn't terrible, but the clothes… They aren't attractive. And they don't appear to be particularly warm either. I won't be able to wear them out in the elements for more than a few minutes if I don't want to freeze to death.

Were these the clothes he meant? I catch my lip between my teeth and do another sweep of the room.

They must be. There isn't anything else here.

With a deflated sigh, I drop the clothes on the floor next to me and dive in for a pair of old boots, several sets of green socks rolled into their shafts, and the single, heavily quilted coat, also made from the same brown-green material.

"I guess this will have to do." With a glance over my shoulder to make sure he isn't standing in the doorway, I reach around my back and pull at the laces binding the once beautiful dress to me. They instantly loosen, falling apart after being so tightly bound. The fabric slips down my shoulders and hangs from my waist. As I stand, the skirts pool around my ankles in a dark blue puddle.

There likely isn't much worth saving. Even if I can scrub the dirt and grime from the fabric, the frayed hem can't be repaired without drastically shortening the skirt, and small holes have rubbed through at the elbows. Patches would look ridiculous. What would I need it for, anyway, out here in the wilderness? There won't be any balls with only the two of us.

With a sigh, I step away.

The camisole I wore beneath sticks to my skin. I pinch it between my fingers and pull it away from my waist. Fresh air hits my flesh. There was nothing in the chest to replace it with. Or my underwear, either. I catch my bottom lip between my teeth. I want them off, the scent of my own sweat clinging to them, but I also don't want to go without, and I've seen no sign of a bath anywhere.

"Dammit." I leave both.

The brown shirt pulls easily over my head. Baggy around the shoulders and chest, it hangs off me, tightening near the hips. It only falls over them because the neck slides off my shoulders, and the hem skims the very top of my thighs.

Using my heels, I remove the equally destroyed shoes and toe off the wool stockings before pulling on the dull green socks. Thick as the ones Mom makes, they stretch over my calves all the way up to my knees. The pants fit snugly over my hips and I have to strain to push the buttons through the holes, but the legs fall well past my ankles.

If these are his clothes, he must be at least as tall as Landry. Maybe even slightly taller.

Once dressed, the pant legs shoved into the boots, and the layers of jackets and coats buttoned tight, I almost remember what it feels like to be something close to warm. My bones still ache with cold, but my muscles no longer quake, and the pain in the tips of my fingers subsides. I investigate the hole. Flurries drift through it, rocking and swaying as they come to rest in the bin. The inside of the bin is dark with char and the blackened husks of wooden boards. Gingerly, I press my fingertips to the outside and a hum rises up in the back of my throat. It's still warm.

My host must be around here somewhere.

But the building is eerily quiet. I peel myself away from the waning heat and lean over the deep sill to look out the window. Thin veils of snow turn the world gray, but below, the shadow of tracks in the drift are unmistakable.

I start to pull away but catch sight of my own reflection in one of the panes. My dark hair sticks out in fuzzy, wild curls, flying away from the perfect plaits Liddet wove at her house. Hastily, I pull the pins out, dropping them onto the sill, and run my fingers through my hair. The carefully measured, even loops loosen, and my hair droops over my shoulders. I gather and twist it into a tight bun on top of my head, and vanity winning out, grasp the coat's hood, and yank it over my head.

I don't know why I care how he views me, but I hope he can see past the lumpy, too large clothes, wild hair, and skin that hasn't seen a bath in two days.

Making as much noise as I can, I clomp down the stairs, the boots booming in the stairwell. Too big, they easily flop on my feet, making more noise than they would if they fit.

Maybe I should have stuffed an extra pair of socks in each of the toes.

"Valemon?" I call as I reach the bottom floor. Are you down here?"

Shadows darken the hallway.

"Valemon?"

The wind rattles the main doors insistently.

Right. The footprints. He must have been leaving, not coming back.

Steeling myself for the cold, I take a deep breath before shoving my way outside. Wind instantly attacks, seeking out any weakness or gaps. It seeps in through the sides of the hood, up the sleeves of the coat, and under the wrists of the jacket. It prickles my skin and tightens my muscles. I shove my hands in my pockets and search out the shallow divots made from Valemon's boots.

They aren't there. The smoothed-out curve in the snow, swept there by tossing wind, wiped them away.

Dammit.

My boots crunch in the thick covering as I carefully balance down the three steps leading away from the building before turning to stare up at it. Five rows of glass windows, half of them broken or boarded over, the rest in even red bricks, each cut nearly identical to the last, the variation in shade their only difference. The roof caves in at one end, and on the other, a small hole stands out against the backdrop of snow.

I've never seen anything like this place before.

It must have been magnificent once, the way it reaches up to touch the sky. Do clouds swirl around its peak on overcast days? From the roof, could people once reach up and skim the underbelly of a passing storm? The tallest house in Willoughby is three stories, and that's only because it houses the light that guides fishers back to shore during the night. I was never allowed up in it, but it seemed to offer no more of a vantage than my own second-story window.

A hoarse, gravelly caw snags my attention. It echoes against the red walls, bouncing off and back to me in a muted copy. I whirl to stare out toward the high wall encircling my building and the others surrounding it. A large raven perches there, its eye on me as it leans forward, wings held out slightly for balance.

"Sparrow?"

He answers by bending his knees and launching into the air, wings spread wide as he glides down to land a few feet in front of me. He hops forward in the snow.

"What are you doing here?" I sink down on my haunches. Talking to Granny's pet is probably just about the most useless thing I can do right now, but seeing a friendly face—even a mangled, one-eyed raven face—makes this place seem less empty.

He caws and fluffs his feathers up until he resembles a large black ball and then smooths them back down.

"I don't know what that means."

He cants his head to one side and peers up at me with his one glassy eye.

"Did Granny Grin send you to find me?"

His head tilts in the other direction.

I take it as an affirmative. "Well, you can tell her I'm not coming

103

back. Not yet, at least." Even if I can make it back across the ice, I need to prove myself first. Until I do, I might as well stay here forever; they were going to throw me out, anyway.

Sparrow bobs up and down twice before launching himself into the air, his wings beating the air. He soars over the wall, disappearing into the gray curtains of snow in the distance.

Is she the only one worried about me? Have they even noticed my absence? After all the things Linka said about me, I wonder if they might decide to skip the council meeting and sigh in relief that they don't have to deal with me anymore. How much of the last thirteen years has been an act? The hugs when I had a bad day, the well wishes on Linka's and my birthday? The laughing and teasing around the dinner table? A tickle rises in the back of my nose, but I sniff it away and drop my gaze to the wall.

From the window, the wall appeared much shorter. Not as thick and looming. But from here, the top of the wall is easily two stories high.

Is it meant to keep something out?

Or to keep something in?

Trudging through the snow, I approach. Much of the barrier is earthen, a sheer face of dirt and dry grass and brown moss. Small patches of red brick the same color as the building behind me peek through, but it crumbles along the edges, the mortar between each perfectly spaced line chipped away or marked by holes.

I reach up to fit my fingers into one of those holes to pull myself up.

But the brick comes loose and smashes to the ground, narrowly missing my foot.

Definitely won't be going over it.

So how did we get in here? There must be a way around. Or a door or gate or something.

Maybe a wall is the solution to all of Willoughby's problems. I snort. If I were to suggest it, Dad would have a thousand reasons why it would be a terrible idea. Maybe that's a bug to put in someone else's ear. Linka's, maybe? If it came from him, Dad would almost certainly accept it.

But I don't want to talk to Linka. Not now. Maybe not ever. We were supposed to be a pair, tell each other everything. How could he not tell me he was going to propose to Liddett? How could he ask Dad for my shift and not me? Why didn't he tell me he was in love with Beren?

I shove my hands into the coat's pockets, balling them into fists for warmth. Or maybe anger.

First things first: learn the terrain. If I'm to stay alive, I need to know my surroundings. My food sources. Any possible danger.

I glance back at the buildings. They are so large, so dominating. Like the stories Granny Grin used to tell of soaring castles filled with beautiful people without a care in the world. They had others who brought them food, clothes, and had little trinkets dropped at their doorsteps. They never needed to leave their palaces. Endless days of leisure and luxury.

As I hike away from Valemon's building, I observe the wall to my left, the damage done to the other buildings becoming more visible. Glass panes missing entirely, doors sagging inside, roofs caved. What did they look like before? How impressive were they?

I reach the end of the wall.

It angles sharply, jutting in a new direction, but in the distance, more wall stretches out in the same way I travel.

I thought it would run in a circle, maybe a square. But the odd angles and corners will demand more time out here than my frozen appendages can handle. Already my toes burn with cold.

I don't want to go back, but I can't risk wandering around aimlessly; I'll freeze to death before I find any food. I'll pick up where I left off and try to get a better lay of the land from the windows inside.

Halfway back to the building, large tracks break up the snow. These weren't made by my own feet, and Valemon didn't make them either. They came from a four-legged animal.

And judging by the bright red spots bordering them, it's hurt. Or it's hurt something else.

CHAPTER 13

My gaze follows the blood spots up to the front doors of the building, and the hairs on the back of my neck stand on end.

There, next to the two double doors, stands a large polar bear.

Blood stains his face, crimson streaking the fur around his mouth and across his cheeks. It highlights the scar slashing just under his eye.

The mangled corpse of a seal hangs from his teeth.

Our eyes meet and he steps forward, his large paws smearing the blood on the snow into pink blotches. One step. Two steps.

I hold my ground.

He has food. He doesn't need me. And I'm making no play for it. I'm no threat.

But my heart pounds wildly, and Dad's voice tickles the back of my brain, warning me.

I don't have any reason to think the bear will attack me.

With a huff, the bear drops the meat on the bottom step. His nose raises into the air, as if he is pointing it straight at me, and then he turns to lumber away.

I don't move. I don't even breathe until he disappears around the opposite corner of the building.

I didn't imagine it. A bear really did bring me here. A giant white bear with a scar across his cheek standing on the ice near the Leig homestead. I rode into the snowstorm on his back.

Not a dream.

Not a delirious fantasy.

But real.

My breath stutters out through my lips, and my gaze drops to the nearly unrecognizable hunk of seal.

"What are you doing in here?"

I whirl around, my arm knocking into a large metal bowl. It clangs as it bounces on the floor, rolling in a circle until it settles.

"You scared the crap out of me." My hand clutching the front of the jacket relaxes as I take in Valemon's dark silhouette. He swallows up what little light filters through the doorway, and it casts his face in deep shadows.

My heart does a little flip in my chest, and I reach up to smooth my hair behind my ear. I must look an absolute mess; something deep down inside me wants to impress him.

"I sure hope not. That would be rather messy, and I don't have that many sets of spare clothes hanging about." He leans against the doorjamb, and I realize how much of it he takes up. I've never known anyone taller than Landry, but this man may have succeeded. What would it be like to stand next to him and feel small?

"What?" My pulse slows, but the sick, shaky feeling of fleeing adrenaline remains. As it clears, understanding dawns, and I glare at him. "Ha. Ha. Very funny."

Stooping, I grab the empty bowl from the floor and deposit it back on the countertop. "I'm trying to figure out how to make a fire. This is an oven, right?" I point to the box set inside the nearest wall. "I don't see where the wood goes."

He chuckles. "That's because it uses electricity."

I perk up. "Electricity? I didn't see any windmills. Are there—"

"No, there aren't any. So, it won't work. But there is a gas stove and a few tanks if you insist on cooking in here. I'll hook one up, but you'll want to use it sparingly. There won't be any more once the tanks are gone."

"Gas?" I echo, but he's already left through the door, disappearing into darker shadows.

The sun set not long ago, and the remaining glow of early evening filters through high, narrow windows. But it won't last much longer, and my eyes will once again have to adjust to a devouring dark. I'll have to ask him if the lamps here run on this gas as well, because I can't imagine spending half the day feeling my way around.

When he returns, he balances a large white cylinder on his shoulder. I squint to make out any of his features, and though what little light remains highlights a curtain of light-colored hair falling out from under his hood, I still can't see the planes and angles of his face. "Does that thing work on the lights, too?"

He kneels and lowers the cylinder gently to the floor, the metal thudding softly. "No. This building is old and…" He straightens with a heavy breath. "The technology used to power it no longer works."

I glance up at the ceiling, my gaze running from one darkened corner to the next. "Candles, then? A lantern?"

"I've never found any." He reaches around one of the metal cabinets and pulls a cord from behind it. With quick movements, he connects it to the cylinder and turns a knob on the side, the dark silhouettes all I can make out. He straightens, and a clicking noise echoes through the room before a whoosh ends it.

He steps away and a round, blue flame sits just below a black grate.

"How did you do that?" I rush forward to bend down and examine it, welcoming the heat on my face.

"Just my own special kind of magic," he says wryly.

I snort. "Seems like it would have been easier to install windmills and a wood-burning stove." I can't imagine why anyone would want to make things more complicated for themselves.

"You probably aren't wrong there."

I turn to sort through the pile of pots and pans I emptied onto the countertop to find one suitable for the slab of seal meat. I already cut what I could use into more manageable pieces, slicing away the fatty bits the bear left. Which wasn't much. Most of the people I know prefer the thick outer layer of blubber, feasting on it raw, but I've never been able to stomach it, and will use what I trimmed off as cooking grease. Eating cooked meat feels less like eating something that once lived.

"Does your magic include other useful tricks? Like cooking?" I ask. Maybe something akin to Granny Grin's talents. She always seemed to conjure up something delicious from nothing but a few dried leaves and a lot of mumbling. "Because it's not a skill I possess."

"I'm afraid not. Basic survival aside, I'm terrible in the kitchen."

I wish I could see his face, because I'm sure he speaks with a smile. "What about what you brought me last night? That was really good." It may have been the best meal I've ever eaten. My mouth waters at the memory of the flavors as they washed over my tongue.

"I'm afraid you were just hungry. It tasted more like the pine wood I cooked it over than the meat itself. Whatever you have planned now will no doubt put last night's meal to shame."

Sighing heavily, I yank out a small, shallow pan. I hold it up to my face and sniff it. Seems clean enough. It clangs against the grate as I lay it over the flame. "Then I think we're both up for considerable disappointment."

"Don't trouble yourself over me."

"And why not? I have all this food. Someone might as well take advantage of it since it landed in my lap."

"How did you come by it?"

I grab one of the hunks of meat I cut with a dull cleaver and toss it into the pan fatty side down. It hisses and sizzles, the sounds doubling when I throw another sizable hunk in. "By what?"

"The meat. Where did you get it?"

Metal clangs against metal as I sift through the box of utensils on the second shelf of the center workstation. I hold two up to gauge their general shape and toss the spoon back into the bin. "What makes you think I didn't go out on the ice and kill it myself?"

He leans back against the metal workstation where most of the pots are still piled, dipping deeper into the shadows. "Did you?"

My lips twitch to one side. "No."

"And?"

"My… friend brought it to me." I turn back to the pan and flip the meat over with the spatula. It doesn't sizzle like it did initially; the bottom must be filled with grease and juice. Is it odd to call the bear my friend? We've only come face-to-face a handful of times, but none of them have ended in a quick, painful death. For either of us. And yet,

I feel an odd sort of connection to him. And if he feels comfortable leaving food for me, there must be something on his side as well.

I can't help the smile that pulls my lips up a fraction. I knew the bears never meant us any harm.

"A friend." Valemon doesn't say it like a question, but more like something he already knows. A joke shared between two people who have known each other far longer than we have, and despite our short acquaintance, there is a familiarity already hanging over us.

"Do I know this friend?"

"How am I supposed to know? We haven't exactly been running around in the same circles." I search through the shelves and cabinets for some plates but come up empty-handed.

"Here."

I reach out as he passes me dishes, glass or maybe porcelain, not metal like I expected. He carefully avoids what little light the circle of flame gives off, stepping quickly away.

"I suppose you have to be friendly with him. At least a little. Why else would he bring me to you? Drop dinner on your front step?" I flip one of the slabs onto a plate and hand it back to him. "I've thought about it, and it's the only thing that makes sense."

He doesn't take the offered food. "I'm really not hungry."

I shove it at him more insistently. "Well, try. And pretend to enjoy it." I sound a lot like Mom on the nights we complained about a meal we didn't particularly like. "I like it when my ego is stroked."

He chuckles, and I find myself grinning back in the darkness. It's easy to tease him, this man I can't even see. This man I've known less than a full day. Why is that? The only other people I've had such a natural rapport with are those who've known me my whole life.

But then, in a place like Willoughby, who haven't I known my whole life?

This is a fresh start. And here, I can be myself without judgement.

He finally takes the plate.

"Do you find the need to have your ego stroked often?" He gently sets the plate down.

"Of course." There were just intolerably few to stroke it back in Willoughby. I put the rest of the meat on the second plate. "But I'm afraid I'm going to have to put that on hold, because I have no idea how to extinguish this."

"Let me." He leaves his meal on the prep surface and slips by me, his face tucked away as he kneels beside the cylinder.

"So, are you? Friendly with anyone? Or anything?" I pick up our last bit of real conversation as I use my fingertips to pull apart the meat. Heat burns them, and I drop the morsel back onto the plate to cool.

"Didn't you know? I'm a hermit. Wanting and needing no one." The soft whoosh of the fire ceases with a click.

I don't need to see him to know sadness lurks there, despite the levity in his voice.

"What do you do all day? I went exploring and—"

"You shouldn't do that. It isn't safe."

My hackles rise. "I can take care of myself."

"I'm sure you can. But these buildings are ancient and falling down. The cellars beneath are crumbling, and they could collapse at any moment. And that's just the infrastructure. The animals—"

"I told you. I can take care of myself."

"This isn't Willoughby. We're out here all alone, and you need to have your wits about you at all times." Exasperation lurks just below the surface of his words, and I'm reminded of the way my father's voice becomes clipped whenever I question his instructions.

I stare down into the darkness where my plate resides, annoyance seething through me. Why does everyone assume I'm wrong about everything, that I am going to get myself or someone else killed just because my way of doing things is different from theirs? I've been poking through the wilds alone for nearly a decade and have come out alive every single time.

Whatever hunger plucked at my stomach trickles away, and I shove the plate just out of reach. Half of my serving still remains, and the few bites I did manage sit heavy in my stomach.

Valemon picks it up, adding it to his own. "I'll clean up. Go and rest."

"I'm not tired." I sound like a petulant child even to myself. Closing my eyes doesn't soothe my mind back into submission, and I push away from the metal surface to pace along its edge. "I need to get out of here to *do* something. I won't just lie around upstairs staring out into the snow because you think it's too dangerous."

"This place isn't kind even during the warmest of summers."

As if to prove his point, the wind howls, whistling through the windowpanes at the far end of the room until the glass rattles.

I wrinkle my nose and lean back over the table, my forehead pressed to the edge of the cold metal. "I didn't ask to come to your rundown castle." My words come out muffled against the high collar of the coat and jacket still buttoned tightly around my neck. I don't know what I expected when I decided to abandon Willoughby so I could find answers, but it wasn't this.

"My what?"

Lifting my head, I find his silhouette in the dark. "If I wanted to be talked down to all day, I could have stayed at home. There were plenty of takers—I don't need a stranger to do it for me. So, you can either help me or get out of my way."

He doesn't say anything but moves around the kitchen, the plates clanging when he drops them into the metal sink. I wait for the rhythmic sound of a pump to bring water over the dishes, but it never comes. As cold as it is, the pump is probably already frozen, and we'll be drinking and cleaning with melted snow. Collecting it in the darkest hours when our own well-water was unavailable was a chore left to Linka and me when we were children. And since we were the youngest, it continued to be our job since everyone else got married and left.

It seems I won't be dodging the task any time soon.

"Why *are* you here?" he asks after a moment.

"They were probably going to throw me out. I was merely speeding up the process." I don't add that I intend to integrate myself right back in.

"That's an answer for why you wanted to leave Willoughby. You could have gone south where there are a lot more places better suited to… surviving. But why go out the ice? Why come north?"

"It's complicated."

"I have plenty of time."

With a groan, I drop my face into my palms. What part of my story is the least likely to get me thrown out on my own? He might be a stranger, but he has a roof and four walls that I desperately need. "Look, I just… I needed to get away to sort things out."

"But why travel into the *wilds?*"

I glare through the darkness in his general direction. "To prove them wrong."

He taps his fingers on the metal surface twice and then sighs. "Right."

"What is that supposed to mean? I'm not speaking to my family. Any of them. *Including* my twin after... After I found him..." I squeeze my eyes shut and shake the image out of my head. How can the embarrassment of not knowing still sting so intensely? "I just need a little time so when I go back... So they'll have a reason to..." *Respect me*, I want to say.

But I can't finish the sentence. My lower lip wobbles, and tears spring to the corners of my eyes. I sniff, immediately giving my emotions away.

His warm hand covers mine, fingers wrapping under my palms.

The tears spill. I don't want him to hear me this way. To think I'm weak.

"You don't understand," I whisper when my voice doesn't fully work. "I feel like I'm just someone they all have to put up with."

"I'm sure that's not true—"

"It is." I jerk my hand away and swipe it across my nose. With a clearing of my throat, I get my voice back. "Look, I understand if you don't want me here, either. I'll leave. I can go back and stay with Granny. She won't be happy about me sleeping in her loft, and I'll basically be admitting defeat, but—"

"You think you can make it back to Willoughby? Dira, winter is here. Crossing the bay can be treacherous during the thaw, but now? Alone? You won't make it a hundred meters out on the ice in those clothes. Five miles will be impossible. I don't think you'll be leaving anytime soon."

116

My stomach knots, and my first instinct is to argue with him. "So, what? Now you're going to force me to stay here?"

"No. No one is keeping you here." He pulls away and heads for the door. "Go and die out on the ice for all I care."

Panic grips me. He'll leave, and I'll be alone. Sure, I made the rash decision to abandon home and disappear into the wilderness, but that doesn't mean I want to be alone. "Wait!"

He stops but doesn't turn around. He hangs in the doorway, one hand resting on the doorjamb.

"I'm sorry. You wanted to know why I came here? It's stupid, I know. But I… I thought this would be temporary. I thought I could find the polar bear king and prove to everyone that what I did wasn't a terrible thing. I think we can change things in Willoughby, so we don't have to kill the bears. And then I would go home, and they would believe me and…"

I shake my head and release the tension from my muscles.

"Polar bear king?"

I wince. It sounds a lot more ridiculous when he says it. "Yeah. It's… a story Granny told me. Of a young man who thought he could save his people if he killed the strongest of polar bears with a spell given to him by a witch. But the polar bear killed him instead and used the spell to become the polar bear king. And instead of saving his people, the young man's deed only made the townspeople more scared and violent. Best to kill rather than be killed, you know? That's their philosophy, anyway."

"And finding this… king of polar bears? What do you think that will accomplish?"

I was afraid he was going to ask that. "Will you think I'm crazy if

I tell you I think I already found him?"

"I already think you're crazy. Polar bear king or no."

"Hey!" A chuckle escapes from under the indignation, and I grin into the darkness.

"You asked." By the light tone in his voice, I think he might be smiling too.

"There was a bear who showed up in town a few years ago. More than a few years ago, actually. I was just a kid, and I got caught between a mother and her cub. And he… saved me. I've been looking for him ever since, and I found him a few days ago. He wandered into town and—" I stop myself; he doesn't need to know I gambled with my best friend's life to save the bear.

"A bear did all this?" Could he sound more interested than skeptical?

"Yes, I swear."

"And so that makes him this king of bears?"

I cross my arms and lean back against the table. "Now you're just making fun of me."

"No, no, I am genuinely interested."

"It's just… a guess." A wish. A feeling at best. "I think Granny knew, which is why she told me the story when she did. But I saw him again today. He brought the seal."

"Mm."

"Fine, think I'm crazy. I don't care. I just want to prove to my father I'm right. That they don't purposefully hunt people, so we don't have to kill them. That's all."

"Well, my home is yours. You can come and go as you please, just… be careful. And stay out of the other buildings. Once the ice melts this spring, I'll help you get back to Willoughby."

"Spring." That will be at least six months from now. I'll miss the solstice, the light festival, and the bears arriving back onto shore. My stomach twists in a knot, and I wish I hadn't eaten. "I'll miss Linka's wedding." The words bubble over my lips like the crash of seawater on rocks.

Linka's wedding.

The other half of me pledging himself to be the other half of someone else. My heart aches at the thought of missing it, even though it never seemed real before.

When he told us he'd gotten engaged, I wasn't able to move. My mouth hung open and my mind went blank as I tried to make sense of him not even telling me he was considering it. We told each other everything, and he was one of the only people to indulge me when I talked about the bears. Congratulations didn't even make it from between my lips before he asked Dad for my shift.

An image flashes through my mind of everyone gathered around him and Liddet as they make their vows to one another. My family will huddle around them, welcoming Liddet into the brood after hours of cooking and baking and decorating. The house will be as busy as it was when Dasha got married two springs ago. We'd all woven flowers through our hair and danced on the beach long after the sun went down.

Will Linka have a wedding, though? Is Liddet even now crying into her pillows, heart breaking, as her aunt and sisters comfort her? Or is my whole family gathered around the large table, planning for a spring celebration as if nothing happened? As if her fiancé wasn't kissing someone else in the alley behind the meeting hall?

Would I even be able to watch their wedding knowing what I know?

"Winter here won't be easy."

My attention snaps back to Valemon. "I never asked for easy."

"I'm sure you can find something to do. Go to the library, find some books to read. Take up drawing or…"

"Read? Draw?" I squeak.

"You do know how—"

"Of course I know how to read. I just can't imagine spending my whole day cooped up in here doing nothing but reading *Romeo and Juliet* and *The Art of War* for the fifteenth time. I have things to do."

"And what would you be doing if you were back in Willoughby?"

He has me there. In truth, there is very little to do in Willoughby in the winter and reading two of the town's handful of books again would likely be one of those few things.

Once the polar bears leave, the patrol becomes a skeleton crew. Mom does most of the dog upkeep at home, and I might help feed them, but they aren't my responsibility. When I was a kid, I had my studies, but once I turned eighteen, I was done with those and there was nothing else anyone could offer me in the dark months. "I'd… spend a lot of time with Granny at her house. She likes the company and I… I'm sure she'd have something for me to do."

Last winter she taught me how to knit. Or she tried to, anyway. Everything I attempted was lopsided or had a giant hole where there shouldn't be one. I must have been a test to her patience, but she just ripped my terrible crafts apart and suggested I start over again. Said that I would improve with practice.

Well, I didn't want to improve with practice then, and now, knitting seems about as useful as sitting in the dark room upstairs reading about star-crossed lovers and battle strategy. Especially since I don't have any of the materials, anyway.

"You sound like you've never spent a winter in Willoughby before," he says.

"Of course I have. I grew up there. But usually— Wait, what will you be doing all day?"

He straightens, the black shape of him growing taller in the darkness. "It's…. it's late. You should take the room in the corner. It's easier to warm. I'll bring some kindling for a fire up to you."

"But then, where will you sleep?"

"I have some things to do. I'll take the other room for now. Don't worry about me." He ducks out of the kitchen, and it's hours later before I realize how much I revealed about myself, how good it felt, and…

And how little I know about him.

CHAPTER 14

Three days.

I haven't been outside for three days, cooped up on the building's top floor as a storm raged, wind slinging snow through the hole in the ceiling. I shivered through three nights. Curled up on the floor next to the fire I stoked every evening, furs piled over me, and flakes clinging to my hair each morning when I awoke.

Alone.

Always alone. Valemon disappears all day and most of the night, reappearing only long enough to offer me more wood and to wish me a good night. I stopped preparing him any of the leftover seal meat. It stayed fairly fresh, pressed up against a block of ice in one of the large metal bowls I found beneath the prep surface in the kitchen, and I ate it alone sitting next to the metal can as flames grew toward its rusted edge.

But I finished it last night.

There isn't any more. And if I want to feed myself, I need to figure out how to get to the other side of the wall.

I stare out toward it from the front door. At the rounded top covered with snow. The gray stone face.

For three days, I thought the storm would never end.

Well, it finally has. Snow no longer falls. The wind is but a light breeze, and gray sunlight filters through the smooth glass panes.

Now's my chance.

Bundled up in every stitch of clothing Valemon offered me, I trudge into the first heavy drift. My leg sinks to the knee, snow slipping down between the shaft of the boot and the ugly green-brown pant leg.

Getting to the wall proves difficult, but the snow isn't as deep along its edges, and I lean into the stone as I hike to the spot where I left off the other day.

Long ribbons of steam puff out from my lips, each indrawn breath like a dagger against a bone-dry throat.

Yet I trudge on. A gate must exist somewhere. And beyond it… Well, I don't know. The ice. Food. Polar bears.

I should have asked Valemon how he comes and goes, but every time the thought pops into my head, I remember his hollow invitation for me to leave and die on the ice, and I don't think he would actually tell me. If I've learned anything in my twenty years, it's that asking permission always comes with more challenges than simply doing whatever I want. I'll just figure it out myself.

The wind picks up, and the clouds cover the sun. My toes tingle with cold, and my fingers turn red. When each step becomes a stiff challenge, I turn.

Valemon's building looms in the distance, only the roof and the small black hole visible around the conical trees and ramshackle buildings. I need to give myself time to warm up before I try the walk back.

I look toward another building. A dozen meters away instead of hundreds. I could step inside the walls long enough to escape the winds and give my hands and toes a chance to warm before I trek back to my room empty-handed again.

A large sweeping staircase leads up a full story to the main door, and I drag myself up by the slick railing, my feet slipping and sliding out from under me on the slippery steps. The front porch silently sags as I inch across it to the door, shadows cast by the balcony overhead. Icicles thick as my wrists hang down, threatening reminders that I should keep out. Valemon may have warned me away from the other structures, but I'll be careful. I have plenty of experience climbing trees and up the faces of river gorges. An old castle like this one is nothing to worry about.

Stripped of all but a few scraps of white paint, the wood siding is dark with rot and weathered by salt. It was probably impressive once. Perhaps not in the same way our red brick building is, but this one has an air of importance.

The door doesn't budge at first. When I throw my shoulder into it, it swings inward with a crunch.

My eyes quickly adjust to the gloom.

Doors flank the main entrance on either side, a hall leading straight back, and a curving staircase, the first two steps, collapsed, dominates the left side. Walls gray with age sag under ceilings browned by moisture. Shadows rest too deep to see farther.

I remove the socks I drew up to my elbows in place of mittens and exhale heavily into my hands to warm them.

The door to the left opens easily, and more light pours in through jagged blades of broken glass, ice hanging from the sills like the metal bars placed over storehouse windows, and snow piles along the floor.

A moldy rug takes up most of the floor, blotches of brown and black covering whatever design once decorated it.

I step across the hall to the other door. It falls off its hinges with a bang and a flurry of dust at only the touch of my hand to the knob. The window's glass remains intact, and the wet scent of mildew doesn't carry through this room. A large fireplace dominates its center, a dusty table set before it.

It's all so plain. Just a large, cold, unused version of my parent's house. I can't look at the long table without imagining a family like mine sitting around it, loud and jostling for space, laughter ringing as often as raucous arguments.

I shake my head, back out, and set my sights on the staircase.

Apart from the missing steps, it appears sturdy enough. Maybe I can see a way through the wall from one of the higher floors.

Gripping the banister and the railing set into the wall, I test both.

Neither gives, and I hoist myself up to the third step. It creaks under my weight but holds firm. My heartbeat skips into a trot as I stare into the shadows above. When I was young, Dara would try to scare me away from her things with stories of ghosts who traveled through mirrors and creatures that dwelled in the dark, their claws long and their teeth longer. She collected pretty little trinkets—shells from the oceanside beach or bits of glass from between the smooth rocks near the bay—and I liked to paw through them when she wasn't around to shove me away. Her tales never scared me, though, mostly because I knew Dara was all bluster even from a young age, and if she didn't think she was in charge of everyone around her, she might just explode into flames. But if malevolent ghosts and sharp-teethed beasts really existed, surely, they would dwell in an abandoned place like this.

I hesitate. It would be easy to hurry back down the stairs and just wait until my fingers and toes were warm enough to make it back to the room with the hole in the ceiling. I don't need to find my way through the wall, not if it means coming face-to-face with some sort of goblin or evil spirit.

But when have I ever shied away from danger?

Never. The wilds are my playground, peril a challenge. I can do this.

Slowly, carefully, I climb into the dark and then back into a pool of light as the stairs curve around to the third floor.

Giant, sweeping windows covered in a thick film of dust flood the landing with dim sunlight. I turn as I take in the molding at the top of each wall and the scuffed, dust-covered wood floors. Furniture sits against the walls, and I slowly inch toward a threadbare sofa huddled under a framed landscape, carefully testing the floorboards before allowing them to take my full weight. My fingers glide over the fabric. So smooth. So fine. The stitching is so tight and neat, I can barely make it out.

Continuing down the wide hallway, I turn into the first doorway. A table sits in the middle, a chair behind it, and a wall of books.

We have only a few like these in town, all of them kept in the back room of the meeting hall, like something sacred. They are allowed to be looked over, but never taken out of the building, and I don't know anyone who has actually taken the time to pour over each one. Aside from the few stories I nearly know by heart, I only attempted to read the others, never finishing. Barely making it part way. The language was long and complicated, the subject matter dry. I flipped through the rest, but they were the same: verbose discussions of matter and gravity and chemical reactions. It was so bland my eyes crossed, and a headache formed from trying to translate it into anything I understood. I vowed never to look at them again. And so it was only *Romeo and Juliet* and *The Art of War* for me.

But I reach for one now. The floorboards groan as my weight shifts to pull down one from the top, a thick, heavy tome with a thin sheath of brittle paper wrapped around it. Cradling it in both hands, I turn it over to stare at the cover. A few large block letters grace the dark red paper, a symbol a little like a flower at the center. I rub my thumb over them; their edges stand up in relief.

Inside, the ink is faded, and most of the letters can't be made out. Reading it will be impossible.

But the paper is so smooth and fine, the fibers small enough, I have to raise the book right up to my nose to make them out.

I'm no stranger to paper. I've traded for small notebooks created with the leftover wood scraps. The pulp is soaked in water and then spread out over screens to dry. Bert Rifkins then cuts the edges so they are even and binds them between soft leather covers. My notebooks make the trek into the wilds with me to be filled with notes and observations and sketches.

I wish I had one with me now.

I clap the book shut and a cloud of dust bursts from the pages. I raise it to the shelf.

But I can't bring myself to slip it back into place. Its weight presses down into my palm, and I stare at it hovering just over my forehead. It belonged to someone once, precious enough to keep on a shelf, not tear apart and use for kindling.

It could become important to someone again.

It could become important to me.

I unbutton the coat and slip the book into my waistband. It fits snugly over my hip; the corners pressing the brown shirt into the skin just below my ribs.

The other rooms are far less interesting. Most have tables and chairs, some with little pieces of artwork on the surfaces, others with pictures tacked to the wall. But that one has the only books and the biggest windows.

In a back corner, I find another set of stairs, narrow and dark, steep enough to cause my weary, aching muscles to strain. They lead straight up, no curve like the ones below, into a dim fourth floor attic.

The ceiling hangs low, slanted up into a peak. No giant holes puncture it, none like the ones in Valemon's ceiling, but tiny shafts of light peak through, like stars speckling a clear night sky. What's left of it, anyway. It slopes down toward the floor, dormers stretching out toward the windows, making it possible to walk upright.

I carefully make my way to one with the glass still intact and look out over the snow and ice. It stretches forever, but something dark sits on the very edge of the horizon.

Could it be Willoughby?

It would be ridiculous to believe it is, but does it hurt to pretend? To imagine the people there can look out and see the speck of me as well? Something glints in the distance. A spyglass?

At the fear of being spotted, I back away.

A crack rents the air, and my foot presses against nothing.

Weightlessness overtakes me as the floorboards splinter and fly around me, the low ceiling vaulting upward as I fall.

It happens so slowly, as if time suspends in stagnant water. I float through it, my arms and legs not my own, my mind unable to catch up to my body, screaming silently, yet blank. I should say something, do *something*.

I crash into the floor below, my hip hitting first, the edges of the book spearing into my torso, but the same splintering crack of wood breaking shrieks in my ear. I squirm and crawl, desperate to get away, but my legs slide out behind me to dangle over the gaping edge.

My arms strain to keep me from plummeting down again, but my palms scream as my weight drags them across the boards and my legs kick wildly, every movement sending a shock of pain through my bruised hip. But with every frantic movement, I only manage to slip farther.

The ceiling height between the first and second floor is much taller. Grander. I fight the urge to glance behind me and see just how far I will plummet.

I choke on a sob. "Valemon. Valemon!" Is that my voice? Begging? Pleading?

My palms slip farther, an ear curdling screech erupting between my flesh and the smooth wood.

This is it. This is how I will die. Not from an accidental gunshot wound. Not from drowning after slipping beneath the ice. Not from the polar bear attack my family is sure will befall me. But from falling through four stories of an abandoned building.

I laugh, but it comes out like a strangled sob, ripping through my chest pitifully, and I glance over my shoulder. It's so far down.

"Help!"

With a grunt, I swing my leg up, but get nowhere near the broken splinters of the floor.

Instead, I slip.

My breath refuses to catch, and a scream echoes around me as I plunge to what will surely be my death.

CHAPTER 15

My scream crescendos like the high note of the reed flutes played during the Night Magic Ball.

Long and sharp and piercing.

My voice feels like it belongs to someone else, the sound foreign to my own ears, even as it rips from my throat.

The air knocks from my chest, pressed out by the crunching of my ribs against bone and fur and warmth.

I stare up at my rescuer. The white fur glistening with the gold of the late afternoon through the open door. The large black nose.

My mouth hangs open, but no noise comes out. My muscles bunch, freezing up, but not from the cold.

He steps back for balance, and I scramble away, hitting the floor with a thud.

But it doesn't crack. It doesn't break, plunging us both into the cellar below.

The prickle of relief quickly abandons me, and with jerky movements, I shuffle away, my backside bouncing against the floor until my spine butts up against a wall. I shove myself into it, my feet flat on the floor as my eyes blow wide just as the pain in my tailbone

registers. It's far less important than the giant beast standing at least three yards tall above me.

"I-I-I." I swallow as awe or fear or both bloom, and I fail to form the right words. "You're... you're my polar bear," I breathe, my stare stuck on the scar slashing across his face.

He falls to all fours and stalks forward, his paws bigger than my head, turned inward, nails dragging against the wood. That nose, blacker than any midnight sky, nears mine and his mouth opens.

My heart swells, ready to burst. The beat never comes, stuck, trying to press through. When his jaws clamp down on the coat's hood hanging over my shoulder, the cycle completes, and my pulse erupts against my chest as it sprints into a panicked tattoo.

With a jerk, he flings me onto my back, my shoulders smacking into the floor. Only a grunt escapes before the coat's collar rams into my throat as he drags me across the floor by the rough brown and green fabric.

Reaching up, I shove my fingers between the collar and my skin to yank it away from my windpipe. "Hey," I protest before my butt bumps down the first step.

"Ow!" I howl.

Snow cushions the next, but the third one down sees my tailbone connect with the edge.

"Dammit, let me go."

Only when I lay sprawled out on the ground at the foot of the stairs does the tension on the hood release.

I roll onto my hands and knees, coughing, my bare hands sinking into the thick snow. It melts around the heat of my body, seeping into the knees of the too-big pants.

The bear circles me once, and then paces around in the opposite direction, nose pointed toward mine, dark eyes assessing. A heavy growl reverberates from his throat, but his mouth remains closed, the massive teeth inside hidden.

His pacing ceases, and he leans into me.

We stare at each other, breaths held on both sides. His eyes bore into mine, flashing. I search them for something. Anything. Sympathy, understanding, even hatred. But none of those things flash back. Only an emotion I don't recognize.

He barks a steamy breath into my face and turns to lumber away.

It isn't until he disappears around the corner that I can breathe again.

Purple marks stretch across my waist and onto my hips, a particularly dark one spreading just below my rib cage. They bloom and bleed into darker shades around the edges, and soon, each will probably link to another, the spaces between them already darkening into an angry red. The colors remind me of a sunset, the sweep of them expanding like blood mixing into water.

I grit my teeth as I press the worst of them with the pad of my index finger. An aching pain radiates from each one.

"Damn."

I toss the book away, and it bounces once on the uneven mattress before flopping onto its front cover.

If only I'd left the stupid thing there. What did I think I was going to do with it, anyway?

The bang of the front door echoes up the stairwell, and I drop the shirt hem. It flutters loosely back down over my hips, and I pull the jacket closed as I step into the hallway.

Valemon's heavy boots echo up from below, the even, slow rhythm of someone exhausted from a long day. Those first few weeks on the patrol last year, Linka climbed the stairs to our room with the same lethargy, a slight shuffle at the end of each step before his toes butted up against the wood backing.

"Finally decided to come back, hmm?" I cross my arms over my chest as he steps into the hallway.

He doesn't lift his gaze to meet mine, and the hood continues to conceal his face. "I wasn't aware I needed to check in with you."

I shift, uncomfortable. He's right. He doesn't need to check in with me. And yet, I want him to. Am I really that lonely?

Yes. Here, the nights are quiet. There is no soft echo of Linka's snoring in the next room over or the faint barking of the dogs begging for their breakfast as the sun rises in the morning. Only the whistle of wind and crackling of fire as I drift off to sleep.

"Well, um, no," I say. "But… where do you go all day?" *And why weren't you close enough to hear me scream your name?*

I know better than to put that burden on him. We are barely more than strangers, and yet he's my only lifeline here. He makes me feel safe.

"Fishing." He brushes past me to the far room.

Only a wall separates us, but at night, in the darkness, it feels like farther. I don't want him to leave. I want him to stay, keep me company. We could talk. And I could forget the pain radiating through every inch of my body, but mostly my bruised and battered torso, my aching tailbone. I just want someone to talk to like Beren or Granny

Grin. Someone nearby.

I turn just in time to see him stop and turn back to look at me. Straining to see his face does me no good, but I try every time. He has become an expert at hiding in the shadows, keeping me from seeing even the line of his lips or the cut of his jaw.

I tighten my arms against my chest. "Just fishing? But you never bring anything back."

"I do. I left some black cod down in the kitchen for you. It's on ice. When I didn't see your fire burning, I figured you must be asleep."

"Oh." I stare down toward where my feet must be. The darkness is too thick to see the layers of socks keeping my toes reasonably warm. It's nice to know he thought of me, though. That he looked up to see if I was still here. Maybe he enjoys my company? Just a little? A soft smile twitches my lips upward.

"Did you need something?" The question is so polite, so distant. It instantly chills the warmth blooming behind my smile. Why should it be anything more? We don't know each other, and though I crave interaction, he can't seem to get away from me fast enough.

I bite my lip as my fingernails dig into my biceps. "No. No. Not anymore… I needed your help earlier. I called, but… I guess you were too far away to hear me."

"Oh." The shape of him leans against the wall. "And what was it you needed?" He still sounds distant, not at all concerned, and maybe mildly interested at most.

"Oh, nothing. Really, it's nothing." He warned me away from the other buildings, and I didn't listen. Admitting it will only lead to… Well, if my past experiences are any indication, it won't be pleasant. Best to just avoid it.

Maybe I should have learned that lesson sooner. I might not be here if I had.

"Right." He straightens. "Well, in that case, I'm glad I didn't come running." His door opens quietly, and he shuts it firmly with a click.

I don't turn for my own room. Instead, I stare at the space he just occupied. If all he did was fish all day, why didn't he take me? Or invite me? I could have helped, or at least kept him company.

Perhaps he didn't want me there.

I back away before turning and feeling my way through the darkness down to the kitchen.

Sure enough, a fish awaits, packed in a thick layer of snow.

I saw no sign of water on this side of the wall. No place to fish.

I've been going about this all wrong. I shouldn't be wasting my time following the lines of the walls. If I want to find a way through the wall, I just need to follow Valemon.

CHAPTER 16

My back aches and my neck cracks as I stretch, every square inch of my body protesting with a myriad of pains. A groan escapes as I push myself away from the window I slept leaning against and swipe my fist across my drool-covered chin. The mattress, though lumpy and still hanging askew, looks so tempting, the furs spread over it warm.

I could crawl over and bury myself below their weight, letting my muscles relax and burning eyes rest. Sleep will come fast, and following Valemon can wait for some other morning. Warmth and peace are just a few yards away.

I inch toward it but stop.

Going back to sleep would be a waste of an uncomfortable night. A missed opportunity to look for the bears. Besides, the more time I have to study them, to figure out how to fix what the young leader in Granny Grin's story couldn't, the better.

Sitting back, I rub my fingers into the corners of my eyes and yawn without covering my mouth.

Mom would be so disappointed.

The heat emanating from the metal bin cooled significantly overnight, and only a soft orange glow hums from beneath the broken, blackened husks of wood. I stare at it, forcing my pupils to adjust to the light so I won't be tempted to close them again.

Unfolding to stand takes more effort than I thought it would, and I raise inch by inch, my back straightening slowly with enough cracks and creaks to rival Granny Grin's old bones. Outside, the sky lightens around the edges of heavy clouds hanging low over the ice. Fat and soft, by the looks of them, they will drop more snow before the morning is done.

I add another scrap of wood to the fire and dress as quickly as my muscles will allow, my movements halting and bruises aching. Two layers of heavy pants and tops make my motions stiff and awkward, but they'll keep me warm on the ice. I hope. I leave only one of the brown shirts out, wrapping it over my hair and using the arms to tie it around my head before pulling the coat's hood down over my forehead. It won't be as warm as fur or even a musk ox wool cap, but it will offer better protection than nothing.

As the wood catches, it cracks and hisses, a thin ribbon of smoke curling toward the hole in the ceiling. It grows thicker and more robust as I hunch over to tie the too-big boots, and I watch the wisps rise, counting the belches and sighs as I wait for activity from the room next door.

An achingly long whine whimpers from Valemon's doorknob, muffled enough by the walls that I almost don't hear it. But then the soft echo of heels on floorboards follows, and I shoot to my feet. Waiting until Valemon passes, I inch toward my own door and ease it open.

His silhouette passes through the doorway to the stairwell, and I quietly count each of his steps as he descends. Once he hits the first landing, I follow on my toes. Careful not to let the heavy, thick heels of the old boots touch the floor, I hug the walls, sticking to the darkest of shadows as he does, my teeth gritted against the painful jolt of each step.

I reach the stairs before his feet find the second landing and I hang back. The echo in the stairwell booms even with the lightest of steps, and though I am practiced at sneaking in and out of my own home without anyone noticing, I don't know how finely tuned his ears are.

Once he reaches the bottom floor, I swiftly tiptoe down, breathing through my nose to keep from drowning out the surrounding sounds. I expect him to take the main door, but he strides past it down to the opposite end near the kitchen where a side entrance nestles. I hang back at the bottom stairs, concealed by the doorjamb as he yanks open the heavy metal with a foul squeal of hinges and strides out into a shaft of creamy morning light.

As the door bangs behind him, I slip out from my hiding place and race down the hall, not caring that my boots thump loudly on the floor and my breath puffs out noisily.

Inching the door open without a sound comes at the cost of great patience, a skill I tend to under exercise, and I peer out into the morning.

The ice and snow sparkle in the last shimmers of moonlight. Like the sun catching the ripples of small swells during sunrise, it gleams. A blanket of fresh white, untouched by human feet.

I don't think for a second Valemon goes to hunt and fish every day. He always comes back with too little—or nothing at all. This is the time of year the hunters and fishers in Willoughby are most busy. They are the least at risk of polar bear attacks close to the shorelines, and with the water freezing over, they can set their nets and snare enough fish to last them the whole of winter when the ice becomes too thick to saw through. The elk fatten and slow; the seals come to rest on the solid surfaces. Not every hunter has the luck to find their meal on every outing, but one fish in nearly a week? If it weren't for the seal meat the bear brought, I would be close to starving, and yet Valemon, who is far bigger than me, doesn't seem to ever eat.

Either Valemon has terrible survival skills, which I don't believe for a minute, especially living out here alone, or he's up to something else.

My gaze swings around.

Where are Valemon's footprints? He just left. They should sink into the drifts just beyond the short stone steps, but other than the few tracks made by the treads of his boots, there is nothing to indicate he was ever here.

I frown as I assess the sunken trail of a lemming tunneling beneath the surface.

The shallow footsteps of a fox. The heavy indentations of a polar bear's paw.

But nothing on two legs.

A polar bear.

My eyes clap back on the large paw prints meandering along a soft slope.

My polar bear's tracks.

They must be.

They dip right into the drifts at the bottom of the stairs, ambling directly toward the wall.

I stare at them for a long moment and then slip out from behind the protection of the door and bound down the stairs. Each of my jogging steps fits into one already made, and I trudge through the snow with more ease than I did yesterday thanks to the tracks, following the line of the wall. They lead me right past the section I explored before, around to the left. And there, right in front of the building responsible for all of my more colorful bumps and bruises, gapes a hole.

"You have to be kidding me," I grumble under my breath. It was there the whole time, right in front of me. If I had just turned once, glanced over my shoulder, looked out one of the dusty windows, I would have seen it. An expletive hanging on my lips, I slip into the dark tunnel.

Gravel and slush line the side, the center a solid sheet of ice. Dampness hangs in the air like a wet rag, chilling my skin down to the bone. But at least the walls offer a reprieve from the wind.

At the other end, shadowed movement crosses the light. Valemon. It has to be. He must have used the tracks to get here just as I did. And why wouldn't he?

How could I be so stupid as to think he just disappeared?

I follow, hanging back as I approach the opening. If he spotted me, he would have turned around. Confronted me. Yelled at me to turn back, just like all the other men in my life. The women too, come to think of it. Granny Grin is the only one who hasn't admonished me for seeking adventure.

Leaning into the curved wall at the end of the tunnel, I peer out over the landscape.

A slender bridge juts out toward the frozen sea, but it crumbles away after only a few meters. Slopes of snow rise to meet it on either side, lumps and clumps marring the smoothness where animals have traveled.

I swing my head from one side to the other, looking for a dark spot against a world of white, but there is no sign of Valemon.

A bear shuffles across a narrow strip of land separating the first ice-covered river from a vast, frozen sea. He glides across it with more grace than any dancer at the Night Magic Ball, the first spindles of sun reaching out to caress him, casting long shadows where chunks of glacier ice have frozen in the once choppy waves.

He skates across it and then disappears behind a towering ice hummock.

I may have found my bear, but where is Valemon?

Leaning far enough out of the tunnel for the winds coming off the frozen water to slap me in the face, I search the landscape for any sign of him. My hood billows and flaps, the edge whipping against my cheek. I grab it between my sock-covered fingers, holding it in place. Even scanning for a second time, Valemon doesn't materialize.

But the bear is still out there.

The bear has tracks I can follow.

And if he's the polar bear king, he could lead me to the others.

Before I can talk myself out of it, I slide down the embankment, leaning back over my heels as the snow piles up under the boots' soles. They hit the ice and I skid at first but gain my balance easily. When I was younger, we would play along the frozen beaches where the ice met the sand. Landry taught me how to lean slightly over my toes and stick my butt out, so I didn't land flat on it. We'd slip and slide and giggle and glide.

It all stopped when Mella died, and he became serious.

Guilt twitches through me.

He used to be so fun. So carefree. And after that day, he just…

wasn't.

He would hate every second of being on this thin strip of ice, if only because Calla would rage at him for the danger, I think as I follow the bear's footprints up a steep bank of snow.

At the crest, the ice spreads out in every direction. Clean and white and snow-covered, it meets the ashen sky.

The bear steps out from behind a field of ice hummocks, loping across the frozen bay without a backward glance.

Gingerly, I step onto the ice, expecting it to move or sway as new ice often does, tossing me as the water bounces beneath. But it holds firm.

I don't live my life out on the ice, not like the fishers and hunters. But I know enough to know that stepping out onto it is dangerous. It's never just one solid, even sheet, and some places are thinner than others. Most use long rods to poke at the ice, testing its sound and feel. They tap it, press into it, and if they don't like what they see or hear, they turn back. Because one wrong step could cause it to break. Shatter. Fine for a polar bear, but I could plunge beneath the surface and be swept away.

It'll be fine. I'll be fine. I'll go slow, test it with the toe of my boot. An axe would be better. A spear. Something to check the thickness like the fishers. But not even a pointy stick stretches out across the snow. I'll just be more careful than I was yesterday.

The second step is less precarious, and I keep my eyes down, following the tracks. If the ice was sturdy enough for a fifteen-hundred-pound bear, it'll be strong enough for me. But I still point my toe, testing first, listening, before I take the next step.

Out here, the wind whips harder, whistling in my ears, and driving up any loose snow. It swirls in gusts and motes. I tighten my hold on the hood, pulling it tighter over my face.

When the crack comes, I barely hear it. Every muscle in my body freezes, my breath catching as I strain to hear over the incoming storm. The splintering snaps only inches from my toe, and the ice jolts beneath my feet.

Balance immediately thrown off, my arms stretch out to regain it. But the ice rocks dangerously forward with enough force to drive me close to the edge where dark, icy water splashes up.

Another crack and my sliver of ice bumps in the opposite direction, bobbing and tipping.

I fall back, banging my already sore hip on the ice. My boot slips precariously close to slurping water. I yank my foot back, but with my weight so close to the edge, I'm at risk of sliding right into the depths.

I scramble up the slanting ice, only to slip back down. A sock-covered hand snakes up to hook around a jagged, jutting shard, latching on with as much strength as I can muster. My fingers scream as I flex, clawing my way up the newly broken floe until it tips in the other direction, evening out, a splash of water smacking me in the face.

The cold burns as hot as fire, the wind on my wet cheeks instantly chilling to the bones beneath. It's all the motivation I need.

Muscles wailing in agony, I launch myself toward land, knees cracking against the ice and shards sharp as glass digging through the socks and into my palms.

Scrambling on all fours, I push until I can climb up the slender ridge of land and sink into it.

Swiping at the crystals on my cheeks, I stare toward the horizon.

The bear is gone. Far enough away, I can't see it. Or perfectly camouflaged.

A sigh of relief or maybe frustration escapes into the frigid air, thick as the clouds above.

And the first few snowflakes of the day begin to fall.

I lost the bear. I lost Valemon. I almost killed myself. Again. And if I remain out here any longer, I will freeze to death.

Picking up my weary body, I turn back for the hole in the wall.

Perhaps I'll have better luck tomorrow.

CHAPTER 17

Hauling a giant pot of snow up three flights of stairs was the last thing I wanted to do, but the splash of warm water on my face makes it almost worth it. My hands sting as I dip them into the streaming pot, heated by a fire fed by some of the last scraps of wood Valemon left me.

It doesn't immediately quiet the shivering, but slowly the uncontrollable vibrations subside, and I quickly wipe away the grime and stickiness of the last week. For a moment, the water soothes the aches and bruises, but as it cools and the only steam comes from my own breath, it loses its novelty, and I search out a new source of warmth.

I drape the clothes I wore over the door in a sad attempt to dry them. Glowering at them doesn't seem to make the wet spots disappear any faster. The hems crunch, still frozen, the knees and elbows and torso damp. Maybe I shouldn't have so diligently layered, because now my only option is to wait in a single brown undershirt and a pile of furs.

Red, skinned knees and hands chapped from cold punctuate the bruises painting most of my body. With nothing better to do, I take up the space between one of the windows and the fire, balancing the book I extracted against my thighs, perhaps the only flesh not riddled

with marks.

Ragged pages easily fall open, the ink inside faded to gray on yellowed paper. Each letter curves and swirls elaborately, far more decorative than the straight, jagged script I write. Curling further into myself, the gray furs rising to tickle the tops of my ears, my nose sinks toward the words.

One of the middle words is one of the few that is easily recognizable. *Be.*

Easy enough. But not terribly telling.

The first word starts with a *Chr, but the rest blends in with a smudge.* The next words are barely more than a shadow. *Won't.*

I move along the line, catching the visible letters and trying to fill in the rest. But they are too soft, too faded.

My head hurts before I even make it to the first period.

Why did I bother with this stupid thing?

If only I had paper of my own. Something to write with. I could take down notes like I used to at home. No one has observed the polar bears outside of Willoughby. Contact with them is sporadic and not usually recorded. I'm the only one who goes out looking for them, observing them, and I've never made it more than a few miles down either of the beaches, and only in the summer and fall before they disappear again.

What would I even write?

Leaning my temple against the cold glass, I stare out toward the ice.

Bear rescues damsel in distress? No. No one would believe that. Landry would laugh at me; Dad would give me The Look. The one where his mouth tightens beneath his mustache, and his eyes narrow just a fraction. Disapproval. Annoyance. Exasperation.

I don't think any of my siblings know that look. Not like I do, anyway.

Embarrassment and shame swell in the pit of my stomach. Just like they do every time I think of that look. The one that will forever make me feel fifteen.

That's how old I was when he first turned it on me in connection with the bears. We all sat around the table. Dasha with Dunnal, Landry with Calla, Dara with Moore. Only Linka and I sat without a significant other at our side, and that was only because Liddet was visiting her mother's family inland on one of the reindeer farms. It was years ago, and yet I remember the small details with intense clarity. Mom served flat cakes with berry compote, pickled root vegetables, and fresh goose. It was once one of my favorite meals.

Fall was just around the corner, and the bears lazily spent their days strolling up and down the beaches of Willoughby Bay. Studies were suspended until the cold months set in for good. Most of the kids my age still needed to help on farms, to gather wood, fish, go on the hunt. Our days with the books wouldn't start until the birds headed south, and the flurries started in earnest.

By fifteen, I had the run of the world so long as I came home when expected. Landry had been on the patrol for several summers. Dara had been married nearly two of them and lived on the other side of town near Moore's family. Not that it stopped her from spending most of her days at our house. Dasha had only become engaged earlier that spring. And though Linka still had as much schooling left as I did, he helped Dad out in the patrol office most mornings.

At the time, I thought no one knew where I went. Maybe I was wrong, but I'd been sneaking off for years, covering my tracks to avoid a scolding. That was the first summer I went beyond screaming distance, letting the warmth of summer tempt me to the outer fringes of the mapped landscape around Willoughby. It was there I found the bears. They lazily loped in the willow shrubs, dined on the dead crabs or the occasional whale carcass that washed ashore. I filled three notebooks with drawings and observations that summer. Of the way they ate, diving below the surface to snack on the whale meat kept fresh by the water. How they hugged the shoreline to wallow in the cool tides. The way the males challenged each other in the shallows, playing roughly but never drawing real injuries.

It was Dad who brought up the polar bears at the table that night. I've run through that dinner more times than I care to remember, the humiliation spreading like a fire through dry wood each time.

"Several males have been seen on the bayside." Dad looked at Landry when he said it.

I sat up straight. I'd been observing them for weeks, cradled in the crook of a tree with nothing but a canteen, my notebook, and a pen. "They're all collecting around the creek side," I piped up. "It's hot, and they don't stray far from the water. I think they practice sparring to—"

"You shouldn't be out there." He stabbed his dinner with the fork, the metal tines scraping as they speared a piece of goose.

My face heated and my heart pounded. I wanted to prove I was careful. Mature. That I could be a part of the adult world and not just the conversation. "I didn't get too close. And they didn't care about me. They were all in the water and—"

He banged a fist on the table, plates and cups rattling. "Dammit, Dira. Do you not remember Mella Metz, or are you just too selfish to care?

Stay away from them."

"But Dad—"

"We're done talking about it." He turned The Look on me for only a second, but it burned through me.

I swallowed down all the words I wanted to hurl back at him, never even thinking of uttering them again.

In a few quick words, he severed my desire to share that part of myself with him or anyone else. After that, I hid it and kept it hidden.

His attention snapped back to Dara, everything about him softening. He never looked at me the way he looked at Dara. With me, he was tense and short. With her, soft and sympathetic. I never got his attention like that. "How was your first hunt?" he all but crooned.

My stomach squeezes at the memory, and I jolt back to the present, blinking my scratchy, dry eyes to clear them of exhaustion. I squeeze them shut again.

Nodding off wasn't on my agenda, and when I drag my eyes back open, the sky darkens around the eastern edge. But the memory doesn't abandon me. Not yet.

"It was so exciting," Dara said. "We neared the walruses, and a polar bear came right up around them. He was so close I could have reached out and touched him."

Dad hung on her every word. Asked her questions. Seemed genuinely interested in what she had to say. Not once did he admonish her for getting too close. He didn't berate her for not remembering that day when Beren's mother died, didn't accuse her of not heeding his every single directive, of being careless. He didn't insinuate that she didn't care about anyone but herself.

She never got The Look.

Was it because Moore was at her side the whole time?

Maybe. But more likely he never gives her The Look because she isn't me.

I didn't eat much at that meal, despite it being one of my favorites. Mom passed me the compote, even spooned some on the cakes when I failed to do it myself, but I just pushed my food around the plate with my fork.

My stomach growls now. Since being here in Monroe, meals have been sporadic at best. I should probably head down to the kitchen and collect the last of the fish out of the icy bowls. The fire burns hot enough I could cook it in minutes and then snuggle back into the furs for the rest of the night.

But just as I straighten, movement from the corner of my eye stops me.

I turn my attention toward the outer wall as a yawn pulls my jaw open. My lungs fill and then fog up the glass, but I quickly wipe it away.

It isn't Valemon but the large, lumbering bear who lopes around the corner of the next building over, his thick paws dragging through the snow. I lean forward, watching him through the small, broken fragments of the window. He passes through a dark shadow cast by the waning light.

But he never emerges on the other side.

Instead, the unmistakable silhouette of Valemon trudges through the drifts toward our building.

Chapter 18

I come screeching to a halt in the main entry, my socks skidding on the smooth floors as the door opens to an evening painted a deep, misty plum.

"What are you doing?" Valemon releases the door, and it slams shut behind him, casting us both in shadow. His outline is strange, abnormal, a bulk slung over his shoulder.

I tighten my hold on the furs pulled over my shoulders. I feel like an idiot standing in nothing but socks, a shirt, and a musty elk pelt.

"You're the bear." I didn't mean for it to come out like that. I was going to ease into it. Ask him. Not blurt it out, putting him on the spot.

He stops abruptly, and I hold my breath.

"Bear?"

I didn't expect that answer.

But what did I think he would say? Nerves hammer my insides, but why? I'm not afraid of him. I'm not afraid of anything. I walked across a frozen bay—well, most of it—and stood in the shadows of polar bears. I can handle an adult man.

Except I may be a little afraid of being alone, especially in this place. I'm not going to push him away, am I? Push him to leave me here in the cold and the darkness without food?

No, he wouldn't do that.

But do I know him that well? No. I don't. And whatever ease I feel with him, it could mean nothing. It could be completely one-sided.

I square my shoulders. "Yes. You're the bear. The bear that brought me here. Were you the same one on the beach in Willoughby? That day when I got too close to the bear cub?"

"I don't know what you're—"

"I saw you!"

My own shrill, desperate cry rings through the halls, deafening my ears, but he doesn't say anything.

Silence spreads between us.

He doesn't move.

And I'm reluctant to.

A great shadow of a man, he tries to keep his secrets hidden, and I just revealed he did a poor job.

Maybe I should rethink that whole fear thing.

I draw in a breath, ready to launch into more accusations or even an explanation, but he speaks first.

"You saw me?" Soft and unsure, his voice rumbles through my center, plucking up guilt.

My gaze drops to the floor. Maybe I shouldn't have said anything. I could have let him believe his secret was still safe. "Yes, I saw you change from—from a bear back into…" Without looking up, I gesture at him with my hand.

"I don't know what you think you saw, but I was out hunting." He turns on his heel and strides toward the kitchen.

My hesitation doesn't last long, and I trot after him, balancing on my toes. The socks offer little protection from the cold, and it seeps up through the cloth. "I know. I followed you this morning. I thought you just walked through the bear's tracks because it was easier. I went right out onto the ice, but—" Admitting I nearly fell through it seems like a bad idea. "I, uh. I returned and saw you walk into the shadows as a bear and come back… Come back out, a man."

His heavy sigh is the only confirmation I need. It floats back to me as he turns into the kitchen, the shadows deepening. Could it be that… he concedes?

I follow him in. "I knew it. I have so many questions. Have you always been like this? How does it happen? And why didn't you tell me?"

He drops his burden with a thud. "Tell you? How do you tell something like that to someone? That you are an animal?"

I shrug, even though he can't see me. It doesn't make any sense, and yet it makes perfect sense. Granny Grin has been telling me tales of beasts who turn to men and girls who fall under spells since I was a small child. It never occurred to me that I might experience one first-hand. And that they could be… Well, it is delightful. "Honestly, I prefer animals to people."

His head whips around, the hood covering his hair dislodging to expose the light wisps. Fine. Nearly white. Like snow in the night.

Like polar bear fur.

I gulp. Clearly, my joke didn't land on receptive ears. "Look, I—I don't know, but I would have understood."

With a yank of his hand, the hood pulls back down over his hair. "No. It's too dangerous. I didn't want it to be this way. I thought—You know what, never mind. This was a bad idea. I'll find a way to get you back to Willoughby."

"But I don't want to go back." At least not yet. What is there for me there? More scorn and derision, no trust, no respect. Every tragedy is somehow my fault, and I am never allowed to forget it. Someday, I might be able to go back, to prove them all wrong. But it won't be now. "I decided to leave. That I got to come here and see the—"

Shit. The polar bears.

I thought I was out here observing the polar bears. Making a case I could bring back to my father. I thought I could see how they really were, and that it wasn't in their nature to deliberately hunt people. But nothing I have seen in the last days is useful, is it? Nothing about a bear protecting me could be used to make my case. Because I was observing a man. A man with man thoughts, not bear thoughts.

I can fix this, maybe even come out stronger. I haven't been out here that long. And there is still time to find the polar bears. The *real* polar bears. And he can help me. I *need* him to help me.

I spread my hands out in front of me and take a deep breath. "I don't want to go back. I *can't* go back until I have something to take back with me. But you brought me here, and I think it's only fair that you explain it to me. All of it. You owe me that much, right?"

"Dira, I told you, it's dangerous."

"Dangerous? How is it dangerous?" A laugh that isn't a laugh at all bubbles up from inside me. "You wouldn't hurt me—that much I know. You carried me here. Gave me your room, your clothes. You made sure I was fed and warm—well, *warmer*. And I'm still alive, so…"

He leans back against the metal worktable. "You knowing is dangerous for us both."

"Then tell me *why*." I reach for his hand, wrapping it in both of mine. Begging with a touch.

Warmth spreads out from beneath the mitten's worn leather, but he yanks it away and rounds the work surface.

My hand tingles from the contact, and I stare at it as if it doesn't belong to me. I shake my head to clear it.

Stay the course.

If I'm anything, it's persistent. And stubborn. But I shouldn't have to beg him for an explanation. He brought me here. And maybe I consented when I walked out on that ice without any sort of plan, but he owes me this.

My fingers curl into a fist, and the desire to ram it into something, anything, nearly overpowers me. Instead, I turn on my heel and head for the door. By the time I reach the room upstairs, maybe the urge will be gone. And if it isn't, the mattress is always available.

"When I was a boy, the world was overflowing with people."

I stop, but don't turn. Not yet.

He sounds so innocent. Wistful.

"We lived near a large city with millions of others. Not hundreds, like you know. Not thousands. But millions. Only they were wrong. The world couldn't die." The meat he brought in slides across the metal, and with a deafening crack, a cleaver slices through the muscle, fracturing bone. "But we could."

The soft sadness in his voice loosens the tension in my hand. Pinky says almost a thousand people come to the festivals in the south to trade, and they travel from all over. But she's never mentioned a place that could have millions. How long ago was this? Where did he grow up? I don't dare interrupt him, though. I want him to continue.

"Winters there were cold, but not like now. Snow and ice were rare. And summers were warm enough we could swim in the waters. It wasn't until I was sixteen that the weather turned strange. That year, winter never really came. And summer didn't, either. We'd been warned for decades the world was dying. That if we didn't change things, we would be next."

The slide of metal-on-metal splits the air as he rummages through the pots and pans.

I turn, hoping he will see me. Hoping he will say more. Explain more.

I've never known a summer warm enough I could swim in the water. Even in the hot months, the water can quickly kill a person who stays in too long. Their lips and nail beds go purple, and they shiver violently until they eventually stop.

When we were fourteen, I dared Linka to see who could stand it longer. That summer, the sun beat down harder than usual and fewer clouds swept across the sky. We'd stripped out of our jackets and rolled up our pant legs to wade in the surf near Granny Grin's cottage as sweat trickled down our backs and temples.

He was reluctant at first, but I pressed him, and soon we were both wading in up to our knees and then our waists.

The cold was a shock with every lapping wave, and my teeth quickly began to chatter.

I won out, Linka scrambling back up the beach with a curse so loud, Mom came running out of Granny's house with a panicked look on her face. We both received a scolding and extra chores that night.

I've heard stories of southern waters where the ice sheets never form, and water powers the lamps instead of wind. "If you could swim in the water, are you from the south?"

"No. When I was a boy, *this* was the south."

"I don't understand. It's always been like this—"

"It was long ago. And the change came quickly. It's difficult to understand. I don't think I truly comprehend what happened."

"Try?" I prop my chin in my hand as I leane forward against the table. "Tell me what you do know? I like stories."

He is quiet for a long moment, and when he speaks, his voice is soft. "The floods came first. And then the storms. They covered the surface, blotting out the sun. Temperatures dropped, and the places that barely saw the cold were frozen over. Billions died. And then millions more. Those who didn't drown died from the cold. Those who survived the cold died from hunger. Crops couldn't grow, or they were lost to the frosts. Livestock died faster than the people. The food shortages caused mass chaos while everything else burned to the ground." He leaves the prep surface for the stove, turning the knob on top of the cylinder before bringing a blue flame to life.

There were food shortages when I was younger. The frosts came early and killed the few crops that grow this far north, and a rainier-than-normal summer meant fewer people traveled to trade at the festival. The town council collected all the food and evenly distributed it between everyone. Most of our meals were meager, the portions small and made up almost entirely of meat. Mom's stockpiled her grains ever since.

My stomach has growled with want for food, but there is always something to stave off true hunger. Even here, I've not had what I am used to. But imagining not having any food to even share seems impossible.

"I joined my country's military, just like my parents did when they were my age. But when they joined, it was about protecting the greater good and our way of life. When I joined, it was about surviving. We were the bridge between what was left of the government and the people—we brought water and fuel, rescued people from floods and fire. I was well trained. Well educated too. And so, I was better equipped to survive than the poor wretches on the ground."

I slowly inch back toward him, but I don't think he notices. He is somewhere else, lost in the memory of a place I can't even picture. "How did you end up here, then?"

One of the pans joins the flame.

"Once our country was no more, we were on our own. I landed here, with others from my battalion, and we set up an encampment about five miles south on a strip of beach known as Willoughby. We all agreed we would help who we could. We would keep an outpost. Make sure those who found us would, too. Others followed, and we learned to survive. Together. Those who knew how to fish taught the others. Those who knew how to hunt taught the rest. We built homes, and then the northerners came. They were the few who thought they could survive any cold pushed their way, but even the winter that arrived in the coldest climes was more than they could handle. The winter coming was one that would never end."

Emotion clogs his words, and he clears his throat. "They agreed to stay. To help. We needed it too." He brings the cleaver down again and saws through the sinew that didn't snap under the blade's pressure.

"One woman with them saw more than most. She seemed almost happy that so many people were succumbing to the world's revenge." He pauses. "Happy might not be the right word… she was content with it, I suppose. She kept to herself, but she always seemed to know a bit more than the rest of us, looked for things others missed. Desperate people often went to her looking for answers, and though she never said what she meant—or maybe she didn't mean what she said—she did always help in some small way." The cleaver comes down again and again, each hit harder than the last, a punctuation to his hardening voice.

I lean down against the surface. Far enough away I won't be in the line of his knife or the spray of blood and mutilated muscle.

On the stove, the meat sizzles. Seal. He brought seal. The smell is distinct, pervasive. Gamey and fishy all at once.

"I can't tell if you appreciated her or hated her," I say.

He snorts. "She knew something bigger was coming but could—would—never tell us what."

"Do you think she hid it?"

"I don't know. Maybe. Maybe she didn't really know, either, but wanted us all to believe she knew more than we did. It wasn't until her second summer with us that the polar bears came, and by then, I think we'd all given up on taking her seriously. She never confirmed they were her warning, but she never denied it, either. And when they swam onto our shores, she refused to prophesize more. They broke into our food stores, attacked the livestock. They drove the other animals off the beaches we fished and hunted on, tore through our homes, ate our clothes straight off the drying lines. We struggled to survive on so little through the winter, and then they returned the next summer. And by the third, we were starving and unable to keep them away. I knew we couldn't survive another year sharing the land with them, so I suggested setting up a guard. We would rotate, someone always on duty. Just like we had done before to protect the supplies from pillagers."

My heart pounds against my chest. I don't need him to continue to know what he's going to say next. But I don't stop him. I need to hear it. Want to hear it. And he seems to need to say it.

"Polar bears are strong creatures. And there were just as many of them as us. More, even. They were better suited to the climate and conditions. They weren't the ones starving. They weren't the ones trying to learn subsistence, the ones leaning on old technology just to survive.

"Guards weren't enough. I was stupid to believe they would be, and Alex… well, one of my fellow officers was mauled by a bear tearing into one of the storehouses. We lost half our supplies, and Alex was barely hanging on by the time we found him. He was pieced together by the last of our thread and dirty bandages, and everyone in our camp was looking to me to make things right. Not just for him, but for all of us. Every single person in that village wanted me to come up with the solution." His words are clipped, emotion punctuating every sentence.

"I went to the woman and asked for her help. I wanted to take them on. I wanted to make them pay. And if I was going to be able to do that, I needed to be able to think like one. To have their strength. Their knowledge. She promised she could give me all of that—and a way to bring the struggle between our two sides to an end. I thought she meant it would help me kill them. But she didn't mean that at all.

"That night, I went after the bear who got fat on our supplies and maimed Alex. I drank her disgusting tea and said the words she told me to say under the moonlight. And I prepared to rip that bear to shreds with my own two hands. But I never got the chance. Because she turned me into one of those damn things.

"Alex died that night. I watched from afar as they burned his body.

She robbed me of the opportunity to be by his side as he took his last breath, or to say goodbye as he left this world. And every morning at dawn, I lose half of myself to become one of those beasts, and there's nothing I can do to stop it. I've wandered this land for lifetimes, failing to make it all come to an end. It took me a long time to realize she didn't want one of us to win. It was never about winning. It's always been about learning to live with each other.

"So, the bears keep coming, and the patrols in Willoughby keep trying to fight them off. I come back to Willoughby hoping to see some change and I never have. Not until that day I saw you, a child who grew up in a community of people who wanted to destroy the polar bears, playing with one. You gave me hope that someday I might be rid of this curse."

Chapter 19

Words of comfort don't come. They are lost somewhere in the hollow pit of my stomach or stuck in the back of my throat. Something kind or sympathetic should bubble up. Words like my mother always manages to find. *Things always seem worst right before they get better* or *sometimes obstacles are set before us so we can find a way to grow around them.* But I can't produce them. They would only sound empty and insincere coming from me, anyway.

"But I was a child. I wasn't even eight years old. How could you have possibly known I wouldn't change someday? Hate you just as much as everyone else did after Mella died?" I finally choke out. I could have. I should have. Everyone else did, and Beren was my best friend, Mella as dear to me as the rest of my family.

"I wasn't sure until you deliberately missed me that day on the beach, too. You found something to appreciate in the beasts enough to miss one. And I never thought I would see that from someone in Willoughby. I thought I was doomed to live a thousand more lifetimes."

"But I'm nothing but a disappointment," I mumble. "Everyone knows it—they don't even try to hide it anymore. You shouldn't hope for anything from me. I only make everything worse."

"You can't possibly believe that."

After the tale he told me, I should be consoling him, not the other way around. I turn my eyes up to his, finding only the light of the small flame reflecting back at me. What color would I find there in the light? Deepest black? Brightest blue?

"Dira, I've lived lifetimes trying to find a single person who sees something worthwhile in those animals. And I failed every time. People only became worse. I was ready to give up, and then there you were, running after a bear cub like it was a lost kitten. You are proof a person can see the bears differently. And you stood up for that belief."

A twinkle of pride suspends somewhere in my chest, growing into a soft glow. I've craved such easy acceptance and understanding from my family for more than a decade, and yet here it is, right in front of me, coming from a near stranger.

I drop my gaze down to my socked feet as the glow sputters out, but it's too dark to lay eyes on them. "Yeah, but I'm only one person. And no one listens to me. They don't even want me around."

He sighs deeply and shifts away. "You give up too easily."

My hackles instantly rise, self-doubt melting away. "You don't know me very well. I've spent years trying to make them see you weren't a danger to me."

Silence pulses between us as a flurry of flames flies up toward the ceiling like bright orange stars in a clear sky.

"You put me in an impossible position last week. Why were you going to attack Beren?"

"The boy with the boat? I was testing you."

"That's a pretty shitty thing to do. What if I did nothing? Would you have ripped his face off?"

"What do you think?" Genuine surprise colors his voice.

No, I don't think he would have. But what would he have done? I'm not sure the answer matters. My eyes narrow, mouth puckering as my gaze follows the darkness of him across the kitchen. He sounds so smug, so self-assured. "I wasn't the only one there. And my brother never misses. None of the Cloons do, in fact."

Plates rattle as he lifts them down to place on the countertops. "Your *brother* was scared."

Landry? Scared? He must not know as much as he thinks he does from whatever observing he's done. Landry hasn't been scared of anything except Calla since he first went sweet on her. But what else has Valemon seen and not pieced together? Does he somehow know I spent my summers traipsing through the wilds? Does he know Granny Grin's house is my refuge? Or that I thought the most important person in my life would be Beren? Did he orchestrate me finding Linka and Beren embracing in the shadows? I swallow. "And the night of the ball? Why were you there?"

"I wanted to see you. And it was the only opportunity I had to get up close without someone pointing a rifle at my hide or recognizing I'm an outsider. Which you did immediately."

The sizzling on the stovetop ceases abruptly, and a plate rattles as the meat hits it.

"Am I supposed to be impressed that you stalked me?"

"I didn't stalk you any more than you stalked me." Light teasing lilts from his voice just before a plate lands in front of me.

He makes a fair point, and some of my ire melts away, replaced by something that makes my pulse quicken. I gather up the pelt in one hand and use the other to pick at the meat he served me. He even cut it up into smaller pieces. But they are still too hot, burning my fingertips. Dropping the meat, I shove my finger into my mouth, sucking away the sting. "I just wanted to see where the polar—where you go every day."

"No, I meant that night on the beach. I left, and yet you followed me."

"You... intrigued me. I wanted to know where you got the bear pelt."

He doesn't answer. I try the meat again, this time plopping it onto my tongue. It would be better with a little more salt, a little onion, maybe a sprig of juniper. But it's far superior to anything I could ever cook. "You wanted me to follow you."

"Well... I didn't discourage you, if that's what you mean."

"You held your hand out to me," I say around a mouth full of food.

He grunts a noncommittal answer.

"Why?"

"Why?"

"Why did you hold out your hand?"

"Because I need a way out, and that way out has to be you," he says.

"You could have told me, you know. Or just asked. You didn't have to keep it a secret."

"It would have been easier if you had never pieced it together. You knowing for certain will create some challenges."

I stare down at the plate. Wherever it is in the dark. Picking through the meat, I chew slowly. "You say you need my help to make them accept the bears. If they do, your spell is broken? Is that right?"

Again, I get no answer. I must be onto something.

"There's just one problem." I fumble for the last piece of meat on my plate before pushing it away.

"Oh? And what's that?"

"I need to convince everyone in Willoughby that polar bears aren't out to get them. But the only one I have been able to observe—*really* observe—is you. And you're not really a polar bear, now, are you?"

The pans clatter as he clears them away, and I stare into the dark, my head cradled in my folded arms atop the newly cleaned work surface.

"Can't we find some lights somewhere? I could help you make some windmills. I've repaired ours more than once, so I have a general idea of how it's done. Plus, we wouldn't have to be in the dark all the time."

"No."

"Fine. Candles?"

"No wax."

"I could use tallow. Use the oil from a seal—although I think whale is supposed to be better. You could catch one and—"

"No."

"No? That seems awfully final. Do you *like* the dark?"

"Yes." He rounds the table for the door, standing in it as he waits for me to pick myself up from my lounging position and follow.

"Well, I don't." I humph as I pass him into the hall, each one of my muscles aching with the movement. The sun made its full descent, and only the moon's silvery glow lights the way down the hall. It isn't much, but on a clear night like this, with the winds quieting and the snow fresh, it reflects with enough brilliance to see by. My eyes easily adjust, and I glance over my shoulders.

Of course, Valemon still hides his face.

I sigh. Tonight might be clear, but we won't have many clear days, not this winter. It already stinks of snow in the air, and once the storms come through, there are few opportunities for them to let up.

I enjoy a cozy fire in the darkness of winter or the candles Granny Grin prefers in the late evening, and the deep blackness of the building most nights will only deepen as winter descends. How will I continue an entire season with only the small glow of a fire to warm my soul? How will I survive in the cold?

I'll have to think of something because he sure hasn't in… however many years it's been.

We climb the stairs silently, him at my back, nothing but loneliness to my front. I'll enter my room, shut the door between us, and long for a conversation. Or even just the sound of someone else's breathing.

I reach my door but whirl around to catch Valemon before he can stride past. "Will you stay with me tonight? I—I'm lonely." Admitting it comes with the heavy burden of the truth. I *am* lonely. And maybe I have been for far longer than I would like to admit. I may have pushed my family away with a stray shot and a stroll onto the ice, but most of them let me down long ago, and the rest…

Well, the gaping wound left by Linka's words and Beren keeping the truth from me about him and my brother will take a long time to heal.

Valemon leans against the wall, only a few steps in front of me. The moonlight from an open door down the hall catches the line of his boots, the hem of his coat. I stare at them because it's easier than trying to make out his face.

"You? The fiercest woman I've ever met? Lonely?" He chuckles.

"Why is that so surprising? I grew up with four siblings. And it's so... quiet here."

"I thought two of them were married and moved out of your parents' house."

"Three. And how would you know that?"

"I've observed."

"Hmm." I shift the pelt from one hand to the other, and a sigh escapes me. "Linka will be gone in the spring, too. So, I suppose it will just be me if I go back."

"If? Planning your failure already?"

Why not? I've yet to succeed elsewhere. But I only shrug. No use dragging him down with me. "There is a certain amount of danger here, isn't there? I could freeze to death. Or starve. Like the people you once knew." I shiver. Death at Mother Nature's hand has always been a possibility, but one cast nebulously. A bad harvest or poor fishing season or extremely bad weather are always a risk. And yet, I never felt like I was in danger.

Until now.

"Will you tell me about them?" I plead, desperate to keep him with me.

He turns away and says nothing. Did he not hear me? I start to ask again, but he clears his throat.

"Why don't you go in and warm your fire? I've got some things to do, but... I'll come back."

I open my mouth to protest, but he turns from me, walking down the hall to the next door. What could he possibly need to do? The door shuts behind him, and I have no choice but to do as he suggested.

Only three pieces of wood remain. I'll have to find more later. Maybe pull up more floor boards from one of the other rooms if I can't find any stored elsewhere. I toss them into the fire, and it roars from sad orange to brilliant yellow. A small circle of light casts down onto the floorboards. What would it take for me to get him to sit there so I can see his face?

I sink into my blankets and furs and pull them up over my legs. My muscles go all soft and liquid. I didn't realize how tired I was. I nestle down, curling into myself and pulling the warm furs up around my ears. The cold doesn't simmer away, but the warmth promises it will overcome the chill. Melting into the darkness behind my eyes, I barely hear the door when the knob whines.

"You'll stay with me, right?" I murmur. I don't want him to leave, don't want this closeness to go away. When he doesn't answer: "Please?"

"All right," he whispers. The floorboards creak as he lowers himself down beside me. I turn into the warmth between us, my nose hovering in the space of our shared heat. I want to burrow closer, but I don't dare, and then the fog of sleep descends.

In what seems like only minutes, the coverings shift, and the floor creaks.

"You're leaving?" I scramble for his hand. Cold air slaps my bare skin, but my fingers wrap around the heavy fabric of his jacket and hold tight. I squint into the darkness only to find it lightening at the edges.

Squeezing them closed again is reflexive. "Don't go."

"Yes." He clears his throat. "I only have a few minutes before... before."

"You could stay." What would it hurt? I know he's the bear. And that he won't hurt me. We could sleep the morning and the cold away.

"I can't. I shouldn't. It's—I need to be out on the ice. The urge is too great to ignore, especially first thing in the morning. I can try to fight it, but it usually does no good. I'll be back later."

I shake my head and crack an eye open. "I could come with you."

"No. It's too dangerous. The ice is still thin in places, and I don't come across other bears often, but it's always a risk. You aren't their preferred meal, but you'd do for an old, slow one. And they aren't the only predators out there."

"I need something to do," I whine as he gently pulls my fingers from his jacket sleeve. I curl back into myself and squeeze my eyes shut. I don't remember much about him coming in last night, but I remember being warm—truly warm—for the first time since I arrived in Monroe.

"I'm sure you will find something to occupy your time. Just stay out of the other buildings. We don't need another incident, do we?"

I stick my tongue out at him, but bury myself in the furs once more. I won't make any promises.

Chapter 20

My muscles ache, but at least the floor is clean.

I stare at the freshly swept room. Little has changed about it, yet nothing is as it was when I finally rolled awake.

No longer does the bed sag in one corner, thanks to a box of rusty tools I found in one of the rooms downstairs. With the help of some floorboards I pried up from an unused closet on the first floor, I was able to fix the bed so the mattress lays flat. And each of the screws was also tightened, so it doesn't shift when I sit on the edge to pull on my boots.

I bounce on it, testing its strength. The mattress is thin, but mostly goose down. Soft and warm. I imagine Valemon setting up shelters for the geese like my mother does each spring. The birds prefer their nests to be hidden from view, and they line them with their own down feathers. When they move on in the fall, Mom goes through and pulls the feathers from the nests, cleaning them and using them to stuff our pillows and mattresses, quilts, and parkas.

Yes, the bed is much better. The mattress could use more stuffing, but it's softer than the floorboards. And with the added furs and quilts…

Pride pulls my lips into a smile, even though no one is there to see it. My skills at keeping house likely rank somewhere right around my ability to cook, and I've avoided it at every turn, leaving that to my sisters and Mom. But seeing everything so clean, the cobwebs brushed away from the corners and the glass wiped clean of a thick layer of dust and soot, instills an odd sense of accomplishment in me.

Humming an old work tune under my breath, I slap my thighs and stand to collect the tools. I dump them into an equally rusty toolbox, shove it under the bed, and swipe my palms down my hips.

There has to be more in this drafty old place I can use. And if I am going to live here for the next who-knows-how-long, I am going to need more than a bed, a metal can for a fire, and a hole in the roof. Especially to survive the winter. By the darkest night of the year, breath can freeze on one's upper lip. Mustaches turn to icicles, and the wind chaps the skin right off exposed cheeks.

And even if I do manage to get this place warm enough for the winter, what am I going to *do* with myself? There is only so much to clean, and I may have already reached my limit there.

Best to leave on a high note, right?

Valemon will only worry or try to talk me out of it if he knows I'm traipsing around the wilderness looking for the real bears, so I have to convince him I will never leave the building. I'll give myself a few days, let him believe I am staying put, and then explore more once he's satisfied I will stay right where I am.

It's the same tried-and-true method I used every summer to find my way to the shoreline alone. Let them think I was busy doing something else or helping Beren and then sneak off.

Was that when Linka and Beren became so intimate with one

another? While I disappeared into the wilds? I used Beren as my alibi so many times, letting everyone believe I helped him with traps or fishing nets.

But if Linka was with him, even only some of the time, that means my twin knows I wasn't.

Shit.

I squeeze my eyes shut and press my fingertips into the corners until bright white spots appear behind the blackness of my lids. A month or so back, the weather was foul, and I didn't journey too far on account of the rain. The temperatures were already dropping, and the first ice crystals were forming on top of the freshwater streams, which meant the salt water would freeze over a few weeks behind it as it got even colder. Getting stuck out in the rain like ice daggers was something I wanted to avoid, even if it meant missing an opportunity to watch how the bears acted in the storm.

But as I did every time my plans changed, I walked the long, narrow rut toward Beren's house, and plopped myself down at his tiny table as he repaired knots in his fishing nets.

He only flicked his gaze up at me and lifted a single black eyebrow. "If you'd come earlier, you could have gone with me to check the crab traps."

I wrinkled my nose. "I don't know if you noticed, but it's been raining all day."

"Rain doesn't change the fact that I have to eat."

"You can always come to our house. Mom would feed you every meal if you let her."

He didn't say anything, and I sat forward, reaching for the net. The fibers were coarse and stiff, some of the ends fraying. I plucked at a loosening knot and worked it tight.

Moments later, Linka burst in through the same door I had used.

"Dira," he said with surprise.

I glanced at him over my shoulder. "Linka," I said with a mocking lilt.

He shifted from one foot to the other. "I didn't realize you'd be here."

"I'm here a lot, you know." I pulled another knot tight and reached for a fraying edge of rope that had come undone completely. I did come by almost every day, but usually in the morning to bring Beren some of the tea leaves I gathered with Granny the day before or a loaf of bread Dasha left with me for him. After that, my notebook and I trudged into the thickets for the abandoned coastlines.

"Oh."

I glanced at Beren, who looked up at Linka, but he didn't say anything.

"I, uh, I guess I can come back later," Linka mumbled.

I drop my hands now and sigh. He must have been there to see Beren. Well, not see Beren, but *be* with Beren. Warmth spreads over my face as their kiss plays out in my memory. Every time I lied and said I was with my best friend, Linka must have taken my place there.

What else didn't I see?

An ache spreads through my chest. One I don't want; one I don't accept.

Throwing my shoulder into one of the doors on the opposite side of the hall, I burst inside. Frosted sunlight pours in from a hole in the roof far larger than the one in my room. But a broken table and pair of intact chairs stoop in a dry corner.

The chairs look sturdy enough. I wiggle one. It could use an extra nail, maybe.

Grabbing both by the backs, I haul them across the hall and into my room, situating them against the wall.

The table is heavier, despite having a missing leg; it lies on the floor, splintered at the center. The remaining three legs scrape and screech against the wood floor. Getting it out the door presents a problem. Tipping it over on one side, it has to be wedged out one way and back through my door another. I set it upright and go back for the broken leg.

Woodworking isn't one of my better skills, but I've helped make household repairs when needed. Dad was always at the patrol office, and once Landry was old enough to be there, he was, too. Dara and Dasha prefer to be inside making clothes, baking, or doing any of the butchering that needs done. I don't think Dara stepped outside for longer than the ten-minute walk to the market before she married Moore and he encouraged her to go on hunts with him. He yanks her out of her comfort zone, but I'm not sure how much she enjoys taking on the outside air.

And Mom has the dogs. Once Dasha and Dara took on most of the indoor chores, she spent more and more time with them. I would have liked to learn at her side, but she preferred things a certain way, and I rarely did them to her exacting standards. I never understood why it mattered if I played with the puppies before taking them to run or fed them last.

So when it came time to do things like fix the roof after a hard winter or repair a broken windmill, Linka and I were the ones to take it up. Functionality over craftsmanship is my motto, much to my twin's chagrin. I was usually relegated to passing him tools and nails while he did all the actual work.

But as I sit down with the table leg, I imagine how he might go about fixing it. He'd sand down the rough edges, reinforce it with screws. I catch my lower lip between my teeth and pull the toolbox back out from under the bed.

When Valemon returns, it's to find me huddled close to the fire, a screwdriver in hand as I tighten the last of the little metal bits holding the leg into the tabletop. It isn't a perfect fix. Fragile still. But it can withstand some light writing and a meal.

"What's all this?"

I toss a glance over my shoulder. He is but a dark silhouette in a room of more darkness, the little fire's light not reaching his face. "All of this?" My mouth twitches up into a sarcastic smile.

"You've… changed things."

"I needed something to do. And since you wouldn't let me come with you… well." I shrug and drop the screwdriver into the toolbox. "Why don't you keep your rooms downstairs? Closer to the kitchen?"

"I can't see Willoughby from there."

I perk up. "You can see Willoughby?" Is it the dark spot I saw the other day?

He hovers in the doorway, not stepping in, but not turning away either. "If you know where and how to look. Also, few animals climb all the stairs to get up here."

Pushing to my feet, I cross over to the window and stare out across the icy sea. Is that a yellow light? Smoke curling up from a chimney? I squint and then blink when my vision goes fuzzy.

"It's probably too dark now. But in the morning, you might be able to make out the rose house on the edge of town."

"That's my parents' house."

"Mmm."

Does he know? Suspect? I throw a glance over my shoulder, but he hasn't moved from his place in the doorway.

"Well, it's the brightest on the edge, so it's easier to see on a clear day. And with a spy glass."

"Do you have one of those?" I turn to fully face him, perking up. Going home isn't an option. I don't want to be there. The weather's only bound to get worse, making it impossible to reach by foot, and there isn't anything left for me until I can prove myself, anyway. Yet if I could just see it, see how life is without me, I could know I am exactly where I need to be.

He finally moves from his spot and crosses the floor to lean over the table, his fingertips tracing the edge. Head bent forward, the hood obscures his face even as the warm light of the fire catches the edges of the fur. The orange glow highlights his edges, and for the first time, he appears more than a large, dark shadow.

Height is one of his advantages. And breadth. I've never been considered small, and yet he dwarfs me. How much of that is the bear in him? Or was he always big boned and thickly muscled in the arms? Does it make him the larger-than-most polar bear he becomes?

"This might be the nicest thing anyone has ever done for me," he murmurs, his attention still glued to the table.

I snort and shake my head. Discomfort always appears when others express their gratitude, and I do everything in my power to dissuade them. "Done for you? This was all for me. I am the youngest of five. I learned at a young age that if I wanted something, I had to do it myself." I look up and the bluster falters. "But maybe it was a little for you, too."

"No one has ever done anything nice for you? I find that hard to believe."

My gaze shifts to somewhere far off as I remember the gifts others have given me over the years. Socks, hats, hand-me-down clothes. I've never wanted for anything, but I can't say anything was heartfelt. I reach up and twirl my finger through the leather lace looped around my neck.

"Who are they?"

"What?"

"Whoever you're thinking about."

"Oh." I drop my hand and lower it to my lap. "Beren. The one on the beach. He's my... best friend." I sound just as confused as I feel. Was he my best friend? If I didn't know him as well as I thought I did, could I still call him that?

"Just a friend?" he teases lightly.

"Yes." I gnaw on my lip as heat creeps up my cheeks. For once in the last week, they are warm. Truly warm. But not because of Beren. "I, uh, I thought we would get married someday, but..." I don't want him to think I have someone waiting for me back in Willoughby.

"But? I imagine you usually get what you want when you want it." He snorts with incredulity.

I roll my eyes. "Oh, how very little you know me. No, it just seemed convenient. And like I owed it to him since his mother... Well, his mother was the one..." I wait for the resentment to rise, to cause me to pull back. But even though I know the man in front of me is also the bear who once saved me and killed her, I can't seem to merge the two. "You know. All those years ago with the bear cub."

"I don't know what you mean."

I frown. "That day. When you saved me. You—his mother came to my rescue with a knife and…"

"And?"

Does he really not know? I run through those moments again. The bear rising on his rear legs, the gunshot, him falling, and then turning tail toward the water. Maybe he really didn't know.

"She died that day. When my father shot you, you fell. And… her neck. It broke." How is it so hard to recount something that happened so long ago?

He pulls the chair out from the table and sits heavily. "I had no idea."

Silence stretches between us until it becomes uncomfortable. I fidget, picking at a hangnail.

"So why won't you be able to swoop in and save—what was his name? Beren?"

I slump back against the wall. "I found him with… I saw him… He was kissing my twin."

"Oh."

"Yes. Oh."

"I'm… sorry?"

"I don't know why I didn't know—I should have. I know everything about Linka. And Beren always tells me everything. But I guess I was wrong. I don't even know if I will see either of them again, but if I do, I don't know how I will face them."

He doesn't say anything, and the silence between us drags on. It feels hollow and empty, and I can't not fill it.

"And what about you?"

"I've never kissed your twin. He's not really my type."

A laugh escapes my chest, a small surprised one. It feels good. "Oh? And what's your type?"

"I've always been more interested in women." His voice drops an octave. "Tall ones who are brave and self-assured. Ones who are probably a lot smarter than me, even if they let their impulsivity get in the way."

My face flames, and I duck my head to stare down at my hands. I'm not used to people saying nice things to me, even with a backhanded compliment, and yet hearing him say them, someone who knows so much more than I do, has *seen* so much more than I've seen, seems strange and impossible. Everything feels off balance, and I don't know how to react. "It probably helps when you haven't seen one in, what? A hundred years?"

"More. But that's beside the point."

I snort. "You're probably so relieved to see a female, you don't care that she hasn't bathed with soap in a week and smells like a rotting fish."

"Maybe I like the smell of rotting fish."

"And that's how I know you're desperate for company." But my heart still pounds, and my stomach flutters wildly. I want him to say more nice things about me, to like me, to want to be close, but I don't know how to encourage it.

"Have you eaten?"

I shake my head, cheeks still warm.

"Good. I caught you something special."

"Special? That sounds ominous."

"You rest here. I'll bring it up."

"I can—"

"You'll ruin my surprise."

I nod and sit back down. Nerves swirl around my stomach, so overwhelming I worry I might get sick. Something has changed between us. And though it makes me feel anxious and a bit giddy, I think I like it.

Valemon returns not with dinner, but with two buckets of steaming water.

"Hold on," he says and turns back through the door.

He rolls a half-barrel through, tipping it over onto its base in the center of the room.

"I have no soap to offer, but here is some salt." He sets a bowl down on the floor. "Just rub it in, and it will—"

"You brought me a bath?"

"It seemed important to you."

I blink. "I—thank you."

"I'll go fix that dinner now." He pulls the door closed behind him.

Once the sound of his footsteps disappears down the hall, I rip at the clothes, yanking buttons from their holes and dragging shirts over my head until I stand naked in front of the small basin. Whatever I clean from myself will just get soiled again when I put the clothes back on, but for a few blissful moments, I won't be dirty.

The water barely fills half the barrel, but I climb in anyway, sinking down so as much of my body slides into the warmth as possible. My knees come nearly to my chin and my stomach folds in on itself like a book. Cramming myself into such a small vessel will likely have consequences, but as the water laps over my chest, I decide I don't care.

Dragging in as much air as my lungs will hold, I rock back and slip down until my hair dips under the water. I dig my fingertips into my hair, and massaging furiously, I work out any dirt or grime caught in and around the roots. My chest burns and I break free of the surface only long enough for another breath.

The salt will dry out my skin, but it's a small exchange to make. I scoop out a handful of the soft granules and furiously scrub them into the exposed skin, working them into the crevices and nooks where extra dirt and sweat hide. Red from the hot water or maybe the salt itself, my skin burns raw, yet clean. After working every available inch, I slip down so only my nose and eyes remain above the surface, most of my legs poking out.

Beren's gift may have been the most thoughtful thing anyone ever gave to me, but this bath is definitely in the running. There was no reason for it—no birthday, no winter solstice, no spring festival. Just a man who noticed I wished for a bath and prepared one for me.

What did Valemon say? A few chairs and a table were the nicest thing anyone had ever done for him.

Maybe a bath was the nicest thing anyone ever did for me.

Maybe the small things are the most important.

The water cools around me. It's only been a few minutes, but the steam no longer rises like a cloud to join the smoke from the fire. In a few more minutes, it will be cold.

I step out, reaching for a now-dry shirt from where it hangs over the door. It makes a decent enough towel, wiping away the beads of water clinging to my reddened skin. Once dry, I flip my head down and wrap the shirt over my hair and then twist it into a knot on top of my head.

It would be nice to come back to a warm room every evening. Not one barely hovering above survival. But truly warm.

As I dress, I stare down at the barrel, yellow flames peeking over the edge.

Did this place ever look like a home?

No. Probably not.

But it will soon.

CHAPTER 21

ira?"

I jump at my name, heart rising to my throat as I whirl around.

The doorway remains empty.

"I'm dressed," I call out and wrap my arms around my waist. Was I so lost in thought I didn't hear him come up the stairs?

He rounds the doorjamb, arms laden with food and head bowed so the soft flickers of light can't play along his face. After depositing the plates on the newly reconstructed table, he turns to me and pulls the chair closest to the fire out from beneath it.

"I, uh, thank you," I mumble as I sit on the edge of the seat, a silent prayer playing through my head. *Please don't break. Please hold me.*

As I stare down at the plate, he takes the chair opposite, tucked into the shadows.

"What is this?" I look down at the steaming meat.

He nudges a fork across the wood. "Ptarmigan."

"Ptarmigan?" Most of the birds flew across the skies for the south at least a month ago, only the heartier birds staying a bit longer. But even they would have found warmer waters before the ice closed up and the first storm hit the sea. "Where did you find them this time of year?"

He picks up his own fork and stabs it into the plump leg resting on his plate. "It was injured. It must have been left behind by its flock."

I can't help it. My lower lip wobbles, and my eyes well up as the meat disappears beneath the darkness cast by his hood.

A sniff follows, and I dash a finger under my eye before a tear can spill over. It feels so stupid to cry over a dinner he made especially for me. He probably would have been happier with something large, like walrus or seal or beluga. That's what bears like, after all. But the curve of the bird, the shape of its body, is so obvious. And for it to be left all alone, scared, without its family, must have been so traumatic.

"Do you not like it?" Valemon murmurs, concern, not hurt, in his voice.

"No." I shake my head furiously. "It's not that. This—this is wonderful. I just—I just feel bad. I know what it's like to feel like a burden. To be left."

A long pause stretches between us before he says, "But you're the one who left."

"You're right. I mean, technically. But… they were going to cast me out. Probably. I am a bird without a flock and… we don't survive well on our own." We are the same, the bird and I. Only it reached its end. Was mine not too far off?

"You have to eat," Valemon murmurs. "You'll never survive the winter if you don't."

"I know. Just… just give me a minute." I bow my head over the plate and squeeze my eyes shut. "I'm sorry," I whisper; perhaps the apology is as much for the bird as it is for me. No one should be a sacrifice for the rest of the flock. And yet that is the way of the world.

When I look up, his hands still balance over the table, the fork in one hand, everything else about him still.

"I've only ever met one other person who sympathized with her food before."

"Oh?" I gingerly flip my portion over so it looks less like a bird. But the bones show through, and I have to cut my gaze away as I pick at it with my fork.

"Mm. In Willoughby. She was strange. She would only eat meat from the earth if she had no other choice." He cuts into more of the meat with the side of the utensil and then scoops it up.

"From the earth?"

The hood bobs in a nod. "She'd eat from the water. Fish and crabs and clams were all fine. But if it shared the land with people, she avoided it."

"And what about birds?" I carefully place a bit on my tongue. Ptarmigan is a gamey fowl, fat and plump like a grouse. I prefer poultry instead of the heavier venison or gritty meat from the wild goat my father likes to bring home from his portion. My stomach rumbles with hunger as I swallow. And Valemon roasted it well. I should forget the rest. Enjoy it.

"No bird spends its whole life in the sky."

I take another bite. This one is easier as my body begs for more. "Some spend most of their lives at sea. For years, you know."

"I'll be sure not to mention it to her when I see her next," he says dryly and digs in with more gusto.

He did this for me. No more seal, which is probably what he is partial to. And he ate with me, not standing off to the side to watch. I must sound so ungrateful.

He stands, strides over to the window, and stares out. There isn't much to see, even on a clear night when the moon's light bounces off the ice to make it sparkle.

I stare at his back, the orange light of the fire highlighting his shoulders and the curve of his backside. My eyes stop there, and as they become dry, I squeeze them shut and shake my head. What am I doing?

I clear my throat and push the rest away. I picked most of the meat off the poor bird, leaving only some stringy bits of skin and the spindly fragments of skeleton.

Valemon abruptly turns and places a small, yet heavy, object on top of the table between our two place settings with a quiet thud. "For you," he murmurs and then reaches for the door. "You should get some sleep."

Shoving my own chair back, I whirl around, nearly sending it toppling over. "Where are you going?"

He melts into the hallway's shadows, his hand still on the doorknob. "I'll just be next door."

"I thought you would stay here." I frown and hug myself, but I refuse to tell him I don't want to be alone. I slept better with him next to me than I have in years, and admitting I liked it seems like some sort of betrayal. To whom, I don't know. Myself? My self-assigned mission? Beren? I should be focused on finding the bears, not on him and his gentle warmth and kind words. My fingernails dig tighter into the outer layer of the green and brown fabric covering my arms. "It's your room, and—and I can go sleep in the other one," I say to cover up my own desires. *But please don't make me*, I plead silently. *Let me stay. Stay with me.*

The door closes a fraction of an inch. "No, you need the fire more than I do. And it's an old bed. I never really fit—"

Nerves and wanting aren't enough to keep my sarcastic mouth shut. "Are you calling my workmanship into question?"

"No, but—"

"Think I sabotaged it on purpose?" I saunter forward with fake bravado until we're close enough I could touch him. I lift an eyebrow as I tilt my head back. I can almost make out the shape of his jawline. My heart pounds in my chest, blood running through my veins so fast I can feel it. My show of confidence doesn't do anything for my nerves, but I refuse to back down. I don't want to be that bird anymore. I don't want to be alone.

He sighs. "Dira, I can't let you sleep on the floor when you put so much work into—"

"Then it's settled. We'll both stay." I swallow to wet my suddenly parched throat.

"There's no way—"

I step aside and point at the bed. "You stayed last night, and it was fine. Stop arguing. Get in the bed."

"Dira."

"Valemon." His name somehow forms in my dry mouth and I straighten my shoulders in a mirror of his confidence. I want to be that girl—no, that woman—he thinks I am. Strong and brave.

But deep down, I feel anything but. I feel young and stupid and in way over my head. And I don't want him to see it.

We stare each other down, my heart pounding and my focus entirely on the shadow of him. He sighs heavily in defeat and pulls the door shut.

I bite down on my lip to keep from sighing in relief and as he climbs into the bed, I tuck myself into his side. He wraps his arm around my shoulder, his fingers softly rubbing my freshly cleaned skin through the fabric as I breathe him in. He smells of moonlight on the ice, of windblown salt, and the warmth of a hearty wood fire.

He smells like home.

Binoculars.

They sit in the middle of the table, just where Valemon left them before I cajoled him into staying with me. I was so intent on keeping him here that I never looked at the gift. In fact, I forgot about it until I rose and saw them there, nestled between the dirty plates I will take down later to clean in a bucket of melted snow.

But I turn the gift over in my hands now, their weight heavier than the ones we use in Willoughby. No smooth, polished birch wood here, but a heavy, hard, black substance. Dust collects around the edges of the curved glass lenses, and I reach under my jacket for the soft shirt underneath and gently wipe it away.

Dawn only just breaks, the sky red around the edges. A storm comes, and likely a heavy one. Snow already whips toward me from below, carried on wailing winds.

Valemon probably woke me as he left, though the moment my eyes flew open, he was gone. The door closed to keep the warm air in.

He'll be making his way out to the ice now, and hopefully back before the storm rolls in. By the whip of the gales, it will be a long one.

I lift the binoculars, but instead of looking for my polar bear down below, I scan the horizon in search of Willoughby.

Granny Grin's cottage comes into focus first. Small, still far away, but unmistakable. The twin windmills whirl, the sun atop the western one flashing gold in the morning light, the moon on the eastern side beaming a bright silver. Someone must have climbed on the roof recently to clean them for her. Last I laid eyes on them, a thin layer of sea salt and dirt had dulled them.

Shifting to the right, I find the rose cottage I grew up in. The house where my things still sit, my family still gathers. Without me.

Without the bears on land anymore, Dad will be at home rather than nestled in the patrol office. By now he must be at the table, a mug of hot tea in one hand, ground oats in the other. Mom might be in with him, but preparing to take food out to the dogs in the back. Once, before I joined the patrol, that had been my job, but I fed my favorite too much. Or played with them for too long. I riled them up when I shouldn't or didn't discipline them correctly. I was often sent off to lessons with a scolding and an exasperated groan from my otherwise mild-mannered mother.

She probably doesn't have anything to sigh about now. No manic movements as she prepares to fix whatever perceived mess I might have made. And Dad likely sits back in his chair, happily reading over reports and making notes about the patrol schedule.

A long column of black smoke catches my attention, slithering up to the sky to meet the blue ribbon beneath a red sash of storm clouds. I shift the lenses to follow it away from the rose cottage and to the nearby beach.

The smoke grows into a belching, swirling cloud erupting from orange flames.

Small specks surround it, huddled and swaying in the wind.

Not specks. A crowd of townspeople. All surrounding the fire on the icy sands.

No. Not a fire. A funeral pyre.

I swallow uncomfortably as I note its proximity to my family's home.

A lump forms in my throat, a hole in my chest.

A funeral and I'm not there.

A funeral for someone in my family.

Who is it?

Linka? My mother? Father? Granny Grin?

The world tilts, its edges going black.

I try to force a breath as I sink down to the floor. But it won't break through, refuses to fill my lungs.

Someone died.

They aren't here anymore.

Never will be again.

They are lost to the sky, no longer a part of this world. Gone like the Leigs. As if never even here.

And I'm not there. I'm not there for them. For any of them.

Because I left.

A sob breaks free of my throat as I drop the binoculars. Ribs heaving, an inhuman sound wails out from between my lips. The ache of loss rips through my chest, yanking it apart at my sternum, dragging it open with clawed fingers of grief.

Who is it? Who is dead? Whose voice will I never hear again? Whose arms will I never again feel around me in a hug?

A stream of sunlight warms my skin.

I sniff back the tears.

The sun shines. The storm might be on the horizon, but it's hours out still.

I can make it across the ice. If I leave now and travel quickly, I can be back home in a matter of hours. Maybe less if I travel fast.

Scrambling for the locker at the end of the bed, I fling open the lid and drag out the clothes I only just folded back inside. The boots hit the floorboards with a thud as I kick them off, and, hands shaking, I drag the extra pants on, shrug on a second and third jacket. I can barely move, stiff with so many layers, and struggle to bend over to retie the boots. The extra socks make them a tight fit, but they might save my toes from frostbite.

Without a backward glance, I scramble down the stairwell, each step echoing, and burst out the side door into the snow. My feet fit into the boot prints Valemon left when he exited not so long ago, and then I leap from paw print to paw print as the prints change to polar bear tracks.

The empty, hollow buildings, crumbling ruins, the tunnel, they all blur past, my mind not seeing them, only a rising column of smoke above brilliant orange flames.

I burst out onto the broken bridge, only to screech to a halt as blinding white light forces my eyes closed. Without shades, the sun's reflection could blind me, but I don't care.

Feeling my way down the embankment, I slide down the snow, and once my boots hit solid ice, I glance up again and right my trajectory.

And I run.

My nose burns in the cold, and I curl my fingers into my palms in the safety of the coat pockets. All the extra socks are on my feet. My hands will have to find another way to stay warm. In only a few hours, I will be home. I can wrap them in fur then. Hold them over the warmth of the stove or the fire in the hearth. I can press into my mother's hug, feel Granny's hand as her fingers brush down my hair. I'll even accept my father's angry words.

At least the clothing's dark colors draw in the sun's heat. The wind cuts through them easily, not like the furs and skins and musk ox wool I am used to. But absorbing the sun's energy will be enough to keep me going. I hope. Because my muscles have already stiffened, working against my bones. And my throat burns dry.

Beneath my feet, the ice bounces and sways over the water. Here it is flimsy. But it doesn't break. It will hold.

It has to hold.

How many miles did Valemon say it was to Willoughby?

Five. Five miles across the water. Five miles across the frozen bay.

I've traveled further into the wilds.

I look up and scan the horizon through slitted eyelids.

And skid to a stop.

A shadow falls over me, blotting out the rising sun.

My gaze rises, sweeping up the polar bear's length. He stands on his hind legs, front paws held in front of him. As our eyes meet, he tosses his head up and growls, large teeth bared.

"Valemon?"

I squint. But there is no slash across his cheek. No scar.

The bear chuffs.

My knees quake.

I have no weapon, and my feet are frozen in place.

He doesn't want to hurt me. He doesn't need to hurt me.

But even I don't believe the words chanting in the back of my mind.

One giant paw rears back, and I close my eyes and draw in a breath to scream. To scare him off with the only weapon I have left. My throat is on fire, my lungs exploding.

But the yell never makes it past my lips.

A fierce growl crackles through the air, and I open my eyes just as a second bear leaps between us. He swipes a paw at the other, and they stand, front legs spread like a pair of dancers. But their lips pull back, baring long white teeth to one another.

Black-lipped mouths parry and retreat, incisors pressing forward like daggers, aiming for a hit.

Large paws land on white shoulders, and the pair spins in a deadly embrace.

I scramble away, mouth hanging open as the slashing scar on the second bear's cheek becomes visible.

Valemon.

My heart pounds as I back away. Valemon swipes at the other bear with one paw and lunges forward with bared teeth. I can escape. I can run until I reach Willoughby and fall into my family's arms and beg for their forgiveness.

But how far will I really get?

How many steps will I put in before the next bear springs up? Or I come across the sharp end of a walrus tusk? Or the ice breaks beneath my feet?

How far will I get before I regret leaving Valemon?

The other bear dodges, its teeth sinking into Valemon's neck, and Valemon lets out a roar of pain. His paw lands on his opponent's jugular, and he thrusts all his weight into the other bear's neck.

Teeth bare again, and they fall to all fours.

The ice shudders and shakes, a hollow thump echoing into the depths below.

But it holds firm.

Crimson falls in vivid drops on the pure white snow, pinkening as the bears spread it with each step. Thump, thump.

Crack.

My hands sink into the snow as they pace, mouths wide, my own feet slipping and sliding on the ice as the snow kicks away. Blood smears across the mouth of the other bear and mars Valemon's white coat.

And yet Valemon advances, feet flying to send the snow jumping into flurries.

The other bear rears back onto his feet, and Valemon does the same. Their dance accelerates, teeth snapping, claws swiping, and rear feet stomping.

The ice creaks again.

With an ear-splitting roar, Valemon sinks his teeth into the other bear's neck.

They both fall to their feet.

Valemon lunges forward, chuffing.

And the other turns tail and runs.

My protector gives chase, the bright red blood staining the ice in a trail behind him.

"Valemon!" I cry after him, my hand stretching out as if to catch him.

He comes to a stop and turns to stare me down. A deep, puffy cloud of steam erupts from his twitching black nose as he snorts into the air. It rises into the blue-black clouds, moving to block the sun.

And the temperature drops as the last rays are squeezed out.

The storm is already here.

I glance between Valemon and the distant shore of Willoughby.

And sink down into the snow with a sob.

 CHAPTER 22

Valemon nudges my arm over his head.

I lean my face into his neck, letting the thick fibers of fur dry away the tears that won't stop flowing. Breathing him in is like breathing in the best scents of snow, of the warmth right before waking. The pounding of my heart slows, and he butts his head into me.

On shaking legs, I stand and lean into him. What adrenaline ran through my veins abandons me, and my muscles weigh heavily on my bones. He takes my weight with ease, and I fist my fingers into his fur as we slowly turn toward Monroe.

Through wet eyes, I stare back at the ruined fortress. I thought I had traveled at least halfway to Willoughby. Each step seemed so fast, the world whizzing by. But Monroe's walls loom within eyesight. I didn't make it far at all. Defeat hangs from my shoulders, my feet dragging as we trudge up the slope toward the tunnel entrance.

Valemon leads me inside, and once the door shuts behind us, I sink down onto the floor, my face hidden in my dry, reddened hands.

Who was it?

Was it Dad? Did he fall through the ice at the edge of the shore when he made his rounds?

Or Landry?

Did someone's shot on a hunt turn wild and bury itself into Dara's chest?

Did Dunnal fall off his parents' roof trying to repair their rickety old windmills?

Maybe it was Calla—

No, the thought of even Calla's sneering face never gracing my vision again brings the tears harder and faster.

I rock back and forth, my forehead dipping to tap the floor.

I'll never make it back to my family. I'll be trapped here. I'll never know who died. And they'll despise me even more. Or worse, not care at all that I wasn't there.

Valemon settles down beside me, and I bury my hand in his fur, my fingers digging deep and holding fast. A deep groan escapes his chest and I hold tighter.

But everything quiets. Slows. The tears dry, and then his voice breaks through the silence.

"Let's go upstairs. We'll get you warm."

Mouth cottony and eyes swollen, I shake my head. To move is to accept it's over. That it's happened.

Valemon covers my hand with his, his fingers wrapping around mine. His thumb dips around mine, loosening the grip I still have on his—

Hair.

I unlace my fingers from the strands, yanking my hand away as if burned.

Released, he hisses in pain and rolls away.

"Sorry," I mutter, embarrassment thick and heavy in my chest.

"It's fine. Come on." His hand finds mine again, and he hauls me to my feet.

Toes tingling and calves asleep, I overcorrect and stumble into him, but he steadies me, an arm around my back. I've never been clumsy, but I've also never felt so weak, and his steadying arm is welcome. It stays there as we take the stairs one at a time, all the way up to the top floor and into the room I've spent so much time repairing.

Cold squeezes me from all sides as he gently presses me down to the edge of the mattress.

"What were you doing?" Anger resides just below the surface of his voice, yet he kneels in front of me to pluck my bootlaces free of their knots. His tone is familiar, one I've experienced every day at home and never accepted.

"I was trying to get home," I mumble as shame washes over me. I probably deserve his ire. "There was a funeral on the beach of Willoughby." I nod to the forgotten binoculars by the window. "At my house. Someone—someone—" My breath hitches as I try to explain.

"Someone is gone," he finishes, his voice softened.

I give a jerky nod. "I just needed to know—I needed to know who it was. And I needed to be there for everyone else. They shouldn't have to suffer while I just… left. I could help." I sniff and swipe at my cheeks again. "I should be there to help."

"Dira…" He wraps his hands around my wrists and brings them down from my face. "No one died."

I sniff and turn my gaze up toward him. He still hides in the cloak of darkness. "But—"

"It's you, Dira." He releases my wrists to squeeze my palms instead. His hands are warm, his palms not nearly as callused as mine. "They were mourning you."

"Me? But I'm not dead. I'm right here." I draw my hands away to wipe my eyes dry and sniff to keep snot from running out of my nose. Worry melts into relief. No one is dead. They think it's me. They mourn *me. Relief quickly turns to dread.*

"They don't know that."

"Well, then I should tell them. I have to go back. Now." I stand, my legs aching, and brush past him. The outer layers of clothing have already thawed, wet splotches soaking through to my skin. I'll just have to make do. "They can't think I'm dead. I only left because I thought they were going to throw me out. And—and I thought I could fix it." I shake my head. "I should go back. You could help me. Protect me. Like you did today. With you guiding me—"

"What exactly did you think they were going to believe when you walked out onto the ice and disappeared?" He stands as well, putting himself between me and the door as I pace from one side of the room to the other.

"Not that I was dead." I've gone out into the wilds before. I thought they'd just think I was there. Or maybe that I was making a statement. I didn't really think about it. But it stings that they think I would go down that easily. That after years of training, of proving I knew what I was doing around wild beasts, they would think I would just wander out into the night and die. I had hoped they would give me more credit than that. But it seems I was wrong about that too.

"Move, Valemon." I come toe-to-toe with him and reach around him for the doorknob.

He bumps my hand out of the way with his hip. "Dira, there's a storm out there. It's too dangerous."

"But—"

"I risked my life for you," he bellows.

I step back as my heart leaps.

"You shouldn't have been out there! You're reckless and stubborn, and you have no idea how your actions affect others." He takes a deep breath but doesn't pursue me farther into the room. Instead, he hangs back in his spot by the door. "And I would do it again," he says with more calm. "But only if I had to. Only if it were life or death. It's too important that we…" Something in his voice changes. "You're safe here."

I frown. What was he going to say? "Too important? Too important that we what?"

"Stay… stay alive." He leans back against the door, sagging into the wood. His shoulder bumps against the jamb as he hisses through his teeth.

"Are you okay?" I step forward. The other bear's mouth had been stained with blood. The snow, as well. Valemon's blood.

And I didn't ask him about it because I was only thinking about myself. Have I always been this selfish?

"It's just a scratch. I'll survive it."

"No, you're hurt." Because of me. I'm a fool. I reach for him, but he jerks away as my hand lands on his shoulder, pushing back the hood always covering his face. The shadows consume his features, and he jerks the hood back up so I can only just make out the deep puncture wound oozing inches from his jugular.

I lean into him, squinting in the dark to see past the wet, sticky blood. It warms my fingers where it soaks through his shirt, and I gnaw on my lower lip. "I'm not good with a needle and thread, but I can try."

He rolls his shoulder away, grunting, his breath fluttering against my cheek. "It's better to leave it. Let the toxins seep out."

"I can help flush it. Or whatever you need. It's the least I can do since—since it's my fault." My voice drops to a whisper. The words feel thick and foreign. They leave a bad taste in my mouth. "You told me to stay here. But I thought…" I thought I could somehow fix it. The burden to repair Willoughby rests squarely on my shoulders because no one else seems to see that it's broken.

"I didn't think." I'm close enough his heat seeps into me… and I like it. The way he makes my pulse leap, but the rest of me feel safe. I step closer, my chest to his, seeking out the same comfort I found with his side pressed into mine as we fell asleep last night. Maybe he takes some comfort from me, too? Is it his heart beating against my chest or is the thumping just my own? He smells wonderfully the same as he did as a bear. Like warmth and snow.

"I should have known you wouldn't listen." His voice rumbles through us both.

Do I sense fondness there? Amusement? My lips tug up at one corner. "I'm sorry I didn't listen." It's only a partial lie. The last thing I want is for him to be hurt, and yet, the call to act always seems to come swiftly, drowning out everything else. It tugs at me even now as my fingertips trail up, brushing his jaw, seeking more of his closeness.

He flinches but doesn't turn away.

I didn't expect his face to be shaved smooth. Not my polar bear king. I lay my palm against his cheek, my thumb brushing over the first rasp of stubble. It passes over a slender, slashing ridge.

The scar I use to tell him apart from the others.

"What happened here?" I raise up to my toes and turn my eyes up, hoping to catch his.

"My first fight with a polar bear." His words whisper against my cheek.

I turn my head, just a fraction of an inch, my breath mingling with his. Our mouths are close and I wonder what it would be like to have him kiss me.

"Dira," he warns as I pause just a hair away.

"Valemon." I've never kissed anyone, and no one's ever kissed me. There are few options in Willoughby. Or maybe I limited my options. There was Troy Aloo when I was twelve who asked me to be his girlfriend, but I was already a foot taller and I felt awkward every time he tried to hold my hand. And there was Neilen Gu when I was thirteen who I followed around like a hungry barn cat, waiting for scraps when his crush, Liddet, turned her eye on Linka. Then, when I was fifteen, as the other girls began pairing off with their first loves, I decided there couldn't be anyone else for me except Beren. But it was probably so I wouldn't feel so self-conscious that no one wanted me. Since Beren didn't make a show of being interested in anyone else, I assumed we were in agreement.

"We shouldn't…"

"I do all kinds of things I shouldn't." I press my lips to his, waiting for him to respond, finding only a warmth spreading through me like sunlight. My every muscle trembles as I give him a piece of myself I've never given anyone else.

And I've never wanted to give it to anyone else.

The realization rocks me. Beren never made me feel this way. Beren never *scared me* like this.

But Valemon remains motionless.

My bravado melts away my body with it. Cool air rushes between us, but he grasps me by the biceps, keeping me from retreating entirely.

"I'm sorry." I fall back on my heels with a jolt. "You must think I'm an idiot."

"Not because of that," he says against my temple.

I cough out a laugh, but a bit of sting remains.

"You have to stop letting your heart rule your every move. You're young, but you have a brilliant mind; listen to it. You don't want to be tangled up with someone like me."

"Of course I do—"

His thumbs rub up my arms and then back down. "Believe me, it can't end well."

The same fire that courses through my veins every time someone tells me I can't do something burns through me now. "Why does everyone insist on telling me what I can and can't want? What I can and can't do?"

He leans his forehead down so it rests against mine. The fur of the hood caught between us. "I will only hurt you."

"I don't care."

"That's the problem. You *should* care. I will use you to rid myself of this curse. I *am* using you. Every second you are here is an opportunity for me. And once it's gone, you'll see I was right."

I should care, but I don't. I should pull away, but instead I lean forward.

"Dira," he whispers, voice strangled as I press into him. "Agree. Please. Tell me I'm right."

My lips fall open with a sigh as my pulse beats anew. "No."

And he drinks it up, his tongue tasting my bottom lip.

A tremble runs through me, my body unsure of what to do other than feel. It's all I can do, the want and need suppressing everything else. The pounding in my ears matches the pounding in my chest, and I can't breathe.

But I don't want to. I want to drown in him. In the soft press of his lips, the taste of him in my mouth.

My hands slip free to twine behind his neck, and I raise myself back onto my toes. We fit together, hip to hip, thigh to thigh, heart to heart.

I break away, drag in a breath, and then capture his mouth again, all the longing I didn't know I possessed overpowering me like the storm outside. I cling to him, my fingers carding through the long strands of his rabbit-soft hair where it drapes over his shoulders.

His hands fall to my waist, resting on my hips. Heavy and quiet, holding me to him. Or perhaps keeping me from pressing myself into him until neither of us can tell where one stops, and the other begins.

Everything dulls but him and me. We are acutely in focus, perfectly in tune. I want him to touch me more, I want to feel him more, to kiss and kiss until...

No part of me doesn't tremble, and I let him support me, swing me around so my back is pressed against the door frame and lifted until my feet no longer touch the ground.

I twine myself around him like a flower climbing up a trellis to reach the sun, his lips the liquid gold of spring, of summer, of the sky.

"Valemon," I whimper against his lips.

They leave mine, glancing off my cheek, settling just below my ear. Soft, warm caresses promising a sweetness I have only imagined. A shiver runs through me, skin sensitive to the slightest touch.

My breath hitches as his grip tightens on my waist.

He pulls away, lowering my toes back to the wood floor before dipping his head and pacing away toward the windows. The glass rattles in the panes from the approaching storm, but our breathing, heavy and quick, drowns out the wind's demands.

The cocoon of warmth we created dribbles away, leaving me cold and aching, the air, once full of electricity, now dead. The sills shudder and settle.

Silence.

It unnerves me.

"Is this the part where you turn back into a handsome prince?" Unsure, I laugh at the poor joke and run my hands through my hair, tucking it behind my ear. Most of it has come out of the braid I wove it into after my bath last night.

"No." The word cracks like the flat of a hand on a cheek.

"How do we break the curse, then?" A single kiss and already I want to save him as he saved me. Visions of a small cottage on the edge of the sea fill my head. Blue, the color of a storm rolling in. With white trim and large windows with a view of the frozen ocean spread out before us. Cozy blankets and warm stone hearths. My imagination paints a vivid picture of me there, with him, but I can't picture his face.

"Curse?"

"Yes, you. As a bear. Every day. You told me you were going to use me to break it. Well, here I am. Use me up."

"I suppose you would think it was that easy." He tugs on the hood again, and all that I could see of his jaw disappears into shadow. When he turns around, he angles his face away from me. "Try to stay out of trouble tomorrow," he mumbles as he passes, yanking the door open.

"Wait! What did I say?" I whirl around, my hand outstretched to snag him, but I miss. His abruptness stings, and I want him to soothe it away. "You're leaving?"

But he doesn't answer, quietly shutting the door between us.

I press trembling fingertips to my lips, reminding myself of the feel of his against mine.

I spent an entire lifetime loving the bears. And an entire lifetime trying to make my family proud. But my heart never ached for either like it does now.

CHAPTER 23

The week creeps by with no sign of Valemon.

Each morning, I find fresh meat waiting for me in the kitchen, and though cooking with the gray light of day streaming through the dusty windows has its advantages, I'd prefer the dark if it meant he would be with me.

What did I do that was so terrible? What did I say? I run our final few moments through my mind over and over so they whir like the spokes of Granny's spinning wheel. I thought he understood I'm on his side. That I want to help. I'll do whatever it is he needs. But I can't pinpoint what I did wrong or how to fix it.

A nervous flutter now lives in my stomach, reminding me of all the moments I dared to imagine us growing closer. Valemon bringing me binoculars so I could see home. Valemon saving me from becoming another bear's meal. Valemon kissing me like he did our last night together. But it also reminds me he may never kiss me like that again.

Or he may never come back.

I press my forehead to the cold glass, and my heavy sigh fogs it in a deep circle. Drafts no longer seep through the window, the panes pulled from the frame, and the wood gently tapped back in place. A pile of stone takes up a wide berth in the corner where I try my best to build a hearth with red rocks collected from a room down the hall. My hands are raw from rearranging them, their sides rough and uneven.

With no sign of my lone companion, I turn back to the job, picking up a stone and turning it over in my hands until I find a place for it. Wedging it next to a similarly sized one, I adjust it until it slides into place, almost like it was carved for the position.

With a metal spoon I took from the storage room, I stir the paste I made from the mud I could scrape from the bottom floor and melted snow. Once it dries, it makes a hard sealant, but now it smells like wet earth and must. I've found a lot of things in those rooms, even an old rifle tucked underneath a floorboard. Splattering a helping of mortar over the newly placed stones, I use the back of the spoon to even it out and then pick through the pile for more rocks, wedging them together.

Patience has never been one of my virtues, and it shows in the shoddy workmanship. Linka would be disappointed. Maybe even a little disgusted. I wanted even, rounded lines, but the rocks stick out at odd angles and the goop I use to bind them isn't close to even. But it's strong and nearly my own height. Soon, I'll have to stand on a chair and then the table to reach the chimney through the hole cut in the roof.

When it's done, I imagine the round hearth will be good not just for heat, but for cooking. No more going down to the cold bottom floor. Everything is right here.

I could live in this room forever. My stomach turns at the thought, and it just keeps turning. I've been rationing the food Valemon leaves for me, stretching the fatty pieces out over a few small meals a day. If things get any more dire, I could die in this room.

The wind howls, reminding me it's a distinct possibility. The winter solstice won't arrive for weeks yet, and the coldest days of winter settle in after it.

Patching up the roof and building the hearth and chimney might be my only chance of survival.

Especially if he decides I'm not worth coming back for.

Stomp. Scrape. Stomp.

My lids fly open over dry eyes, scratchy and swollen from crying.

The thumps and scratches halt outside the door and the floorboards whine.

I sink under the blankets and keep my breaths long and even, despite the rapidly fluttering pulse in my neck.

Who could be outside?

The heavy gait moves unevenly outside in the hall, unfamiliar and nothing like Valemon's purposeful steps.

But who else could it be?

My chest swells with panic.

It could be anyone. It could be someone from the village. Or worse — someplace else. I grew up with stories of the other people like the remote village where Yosef Leig's wife hailed from. Few of them, but still out there. According to Valemon, most headed south when the world fell apart, never heard from again. And there are other pockets of civilization, like Willoughby, scattered across the shorelines and farther inland.

Mama used to tell stories of an uncle who left for the mountains and a settlement there. She spoke of it and him quietly, her voice full of warning. We never thought kindly of the mountain people. They closed themselves off in their hollows and rarely traded goods or exchanged news, but threatened our hunters if they came too far inland.

One of them could have seen the smoke rising from my new chimney and come to investigate. Visions of angry men wielding hatchets and rifles fill my head, and my heart skips into a thundering sprint. Valemon hasn't left me anything in days, so he won't come to my aid, and the newfound rifle isn't within reach. If I want to defend myself, I'll have to come up with something else.

The doorknob squeaks as it turns, and my hand shoots out, fingers wrapping around the handle of the hammer. I ease it off the top of the toolbox, dragging it under the blankets until the cool metal of the heavy head rests against my chest.

The door slowly swings into the room, the shadows of the hallway spreading in like the push of the surf onto the beach. But as the door inches toward the wall, the orange glow of the fire battles the darkness away.

My fingers tighten around the leather-wrapped handle.

"Dira?" The dark shadow speaks my name on a gravelly choke as heavy boots stumble into the room.

I freeze as my mind attempts to riddle out who it belongs to.

The shadow takes another staggering step. "Dira?"

Valemon.

I throw off the blankets and swing my feet over the side of the bed, releasing the hammer just as he tumbles toward me.

The white fur of his hood falls over his face as I catch him, his weight more than I can handle, pinning me to the floor. I manage to shift him onto the bed, and he hisses between his teeth.

"What happened?" I demand.

"Multiple… gunshot…"

"Shot? What? Where?"

I lean over him, pulling at the coat. Cold, sticky liquid coats my fingertips, and I recoil in horror.

"Shoulder. And… and side." He heaves to the side, a groan ripping through his throat as he disentangles his arm from a sleeve.

The fabric covering his top half is stained dark in the middle.

I can only stare at it. "I don't know what to do."

"I think—I think they passed straight through."

"How can I tell?"

He leans forward, a cry escaping as the effort rips through him. "Do you see exit holes?"

"How am I supposed to know? I can't see anything!" I turn, looking for something to bring the light closer to him, but I've never come across so much as a candle here.

He doesn't answer, instead reaching across his chest with his uninjured arm to prod the opposite shoulder. What I can see of the shirt falls in tatters, blood staining the seam.

A hiss escapes from between his teeth, and I push the hand away.

"It just grazed you," I murmur, leaning close to assess the gash as best I can.

"And the other?"

I lean forward, peering over his back. "Blood here too."

"Good. Good." He sighs and sits up, shifting his weight over the edge of the newly repaired framed. "I just need to clean it out."

"You? No. I'm here, let me—" I scramble toward the bucket I found for fresh water and knock over the pile of pots and pans I brought up from the kitchen. I sift through them, metal clanging on metal, bouncing off wood, as I search for a small, deep pot. Water splashes over the side as I pour it, my hands shaking from nerves and worry. The husks of burning floorboards hiss as I shove it into the fire to heat.

"What about bandages? And—and a needle? Thread?"

"Footlocker."

"What?"

"The little box in the bottom of the footlocker. It has everything you need."

I scurry to the edge of the bed and fling open the lid of the long wooden chest. I've emptied it of just about every wearable item, and all that's left is the small box, a second pair of the too-large lace-up boots, and a musty blanket spotted with holes.

With shaking hands, I extract the box and lay it at the foot of the mattress. The lid lifts off, and I fling it to the floor, out of the way, and upend the whole container onto the furs. Everything scatters, brittle packs of paper and a roll of yellowed cloth unrolling across the covers.

"Tell me what to do."

"Stop. Calm down. I can handle it. This isn't—this isn't the first time I've been shot, as you know." He brushes my hands away and picks up one of the packets. He raises it to his teeth and tears through it, flicking out a small white patch from inside. "Please," he says around the packet in his teeth. "The water."

My socked feet slip on the wood as I scramble to get to the pot of heating water quickly, and I nearly fall on my face. I save myself only to burn my hands on the pot handle.

"How did this happen?" I ask as I set it down on the nearby chair.

"I was hunting up near the Buckroe settlement when strangers approached from the west." He dips the corner of the square into the water and then gently wipes the blood from his shoulder. "Their warning shots weren't as well-aimed as yours." He laughs huskily at his joke.

"Buckroe?"

"A village," he says through gritted teeth. "About two miles north of here."

"There are others? To the north?" I always thought Willoughby was the northernmost settlement. We pride ourselves on being the last stop before the world is ruled by wild animals and wilder climates.

"They're the ghosts of the glaciers. They survive on polar bear meat and raiding unprotected homesteads. It's unlikely they'd tangle with Willoughby, as heavily armed as you all are." He nods to the slender roll of bandages. "Could you help me with that?"

I quickly grab it and stand next to his shoulder, his words echoing in my ears. *Raiding unprotected homesteads.* Like the Liegs. I start to ask him about it, but the soft glow from the fireplace hits the bow of his mouth, and he quickly glances down at his shoulder to avoid my gaze.

Now isn't the time.

Resting my knee on the mattress beside him, I circle my arms around, pressing the end of the fabric to his flesh. He holds it in place as I wind it around his shoulder, pulling it tight so it doesn't slip. "Will that be enough?"

"It's shallow."

I lean down over him and bite down on the bandage, pulling one way with my head and the opposite with my hand until it rips. Carefully, I tuck it in.

"And the other one?"

"It won't bleed much more."

I gnaw on my lip to keep from asking how he knows that. The last time I asked him about the curse, he disappeared for a handful of days and only came back when he was maimed. "Lay back, I'll get this one."

He stiffens but leans back, resting his arm over his face.

My hands shake. I need a distraction. "Tell me about Buckenloe."

"Buckroe?"

"Yes, that one." I find some more of the cloth and dip it into the water.

"It's not much different than Willoughby." He grunts and pulls away as I swipe at the dark blotches of drying blood. "They walled themselves in a few generations ago. To keep the animals out or the people in, I don't know which. Only hunting parties leave, and they're almost always after polar bears. They'll track them for miles, but if they come across another opportunity, they will almost always take it."

An opportunity like a small family living on the edge of the shore? One with little but their winter stores and a warm fire? "What do they take?" The Liegs didn't have much, but the animals were noticeably absent when I went to empty it of its hay.

"Guns, ammunition, knives, mostly. Things easily carried, weapons used against them."

"Livestock?"

"Maybe, I don't know."

"Hmm." I toss the soiled fabric into the cooling pot of water and readjust, sinking down into the mattress, my hip next to his. I don't want to think about that night anymore. "Tell me about other places," I whisper as I lay the bandages over the second wound. "Where did you grow up?"

"Nowhere—" He draws in a sharp of breath as my hand glances over the injury. "Nowhere near here."

"You know everything about where I'm from. Tell me about your place. It'll—it'll take your mind off this." Or better yet, mine. I want the distraction, even though my heart rate slows, my hands no longer shake, and my voice sounds far steadier than it should.

He lets out a long sigh. "It was by the water, but not the—ahh—not the ocean. It rained all the time except in summer, and then the skies were empty and the air hot. My parents both worked at the base, and my sister and I—"

"You have a sister?" Imagining Valemon as anyone but a loner isn't an easy task. Imagining him as a child is an even more difficult one.

"I did. Once." Sadness creeps into his voice.

They must have been close. Like Linka and me. "Tell me about her."

"I thought you wanted me to tell you about Lakewood." He chuckles, but it turns into a soft moan.

"Lakewood. That's a nice name." I pass the last length of the bandage around his midsection and tuck the end under before sinking down to rest my head on his uninjured shoulder. "I just want to know everything about you."

"There's surprisingly little to tell."

I don't expect him to shift, to wrap his arm around my shoulders and turn me into him. His fingers play along my bicep, caressing down and then up.

"I should clean up," I protest. "And you're hurt."

His arm tightens around me. "No, stay. Just for a few moments.

It's… nice not to be alone."

I close my eyes and curl into him. He's right.

"My sister was older. She joined the military first, and I wanted to be like her, so… I did, too."

"What was her name?"

"Juniper. She'd gotten out—found another job teaching children—and when things got worse, I convinced her to rejoin. She didn't want to. She was happy and living in… well, she was living in the south, in a warm place. But I wore her down. She was running evacuation missions, getting people from the north down to warmer climates, when her ship went down in a storm. It was during the second wave."

"Wave?"

"Of catastrophic events. The storms came first. And then the clouds. And then the cold. I was still in school when that happened. But later, they got worse still. A second wave. I was already on this side of the country when it happened. I lost my parents three weeks later. They were going to try to make the drive and come to me, but I convinced them to take a transporter. It never made it out of the northwest, and neither did they."

I swallow, but I don't know what to say. He lost everyone in such a short time. And then again when he settled here. My chest constricts.

How long has he been here alone? And how long was he alone before?

"I'm sorry," I finally say, my voice sounding as young as I feel next to him. Is that why he pushed me away? Because I have no concept of time or his life? Because I have existed for no more than a blink of it? I want to ask him about the world before and where we fit into it now. I want to know how it was different and how it never changed. But it seems like only an opportunity to push our experiences farther apart, and I just want to be closer to him.

"If it weren't for me, well… it doesn't matter. They'd all be dead by now, anyway."

I breathe in his scent of snow and firewood and warmth. For a flash of a moment, I am back on the beach between him and Mella. If it wasn't for me, she wouldn't have died. And if it wasn't for him, I would have. "It seems we have something in common." A yawn escapes, and I burrow farther into him.

"I think we have far more in common than you think."

CHAPTER 24

The only furs wrapped around me when I wake up are thick and brown and splattered with blood.

I kick them aside and sit up as I scan the room.

I'm not alone. Not like I thought.

Sprawled across the floor on his back, Valemon sleeps in his polar bear form. A heavy paw covers his eyes, and he snores softly. The bandages we applied last night lay in a heap on the wood, the blood staining them now a dark, ugly brown. The same nasty color tinges his fur, crusty and dried along one side. Hopefully, we cleaned the wounds well enough they have already begun to heal. Red blood would mean it still flowed, but from my vantage point, I can't be sure it doesn't.

I shift to stand but sink back down. To get around, I would have to step over him. And what are the rules about waking polar bears? Are there any? Or does Valemon not count?

Best to be careful.

I crawl down the bed, lifting myself over the footboard and climbing atop the footlocker before my feet hit the ground. Thankfully, the floorboards hush as I cross over to the ugly, newly constructed hearth.

From a new angle, I consider the wounds. The one on the side still oozes, just along the edges. No pool of blood drips to the floor, but it also can't be comfortable. He won't be hunting today, not with wounds like those. Probably not tomorrow, either. And if he doesn't hunt, he doesn't eat.

If he doesn't hunt, *I* don't eat.

Little heat warms my bare skin when I hold my hand out over the ashes. I should stoke the fire back to life, even if he doesn't need it with his natural insulation. I gnaw my lip. I don't want him to get too hot. But I also want to come back to a comfortable room, not a frozen box. It will take all evening to reheat everything, especially with these temperatures.

My stomach rumbles as it twists with hunger.

Sighing, I stand. These were not the circumstances in which I expected to learn how to hunt. But we need to eat. And I'm a good shot.

Outside, the winds no longer race across the ice like scared hares, and the skies shine an empty blue. If I'm going to venture out, now would be the time. I'll stick close. Maybe find easy prey.

My stomach turns. I don't want to do this.

Bundled up in everything I can use for warmth, I trudge down the stairs to the storage room, rifle in hand. I loaded it with a single shot, but I'll need more ammunition to line my pockets if I'm going to not only protect myself, but feed us both.

I left the papery boxes in the hole where I found the rifle. Dozens of them, if not more, line the underside of the storage room, and the golden bullets are far more clean and pristine than the ones our gunsmith makes. Each the same, a copy of the one before it.

I ease a box from the hole and sit back on my haunches. A quick breath sends the dust flying. Inside, the bullets shine unsoiled, and I shove a handful into my pocket before closing the box and putting it on the opposite side of my outer coat. The rifle was in a similar state when I lifted it from the ground, but a thorough cleaning had it gleaming, a layer of oil helping the mechanisms to slide. The few practice rounds I shot off into a tree outside proved it jerked to the right, but I figured out how to compensate.

All right. Rifle. Ammunition. Binoculars. I stand and paw through the other supplies on the shelves. There has to be something else I can use.

I shoulder a length of bright yellow rope, the threads slick, unlike the fibers we use in Willoughby. A large length of thickly woven cloth in a sandy mud color rests behind some of the other supplies, and I ease it out. The hunters usually bring their hauls back on sleds. I may not have one of those, but maybe I can pull my find back on this.

Why did I never take Dunnal up on his offer to show me how to hunt on the ice? Or Moore?

Because you don't want to do this.

Tough shit.

I sling the rifle over my shoulder, so it bumps against the rope, and tuck the canvas under the opposite arm.

I'm as ready as I'll ever be.

Outside, stillness stretches over the white wilderness. The deep quiet of winter. Silence.

Snow reaches over my knees in the shallow areas, up to my thighs in the deeper drifts, and I lift my legs high to ease the journey to the wall. At home, I have a pair of snowshoes I'd strap to my boots whenever I leave the house. I miss them with each pull of my thigh muscles. If I am successful today, tomorrow I will fashion a new pair. With the hide of my kill, I'll be able to make strings. And wood is readily available for the frames.

But today I'll have to make do.

On the outer side of the wall, the wind picks up, sending wisps of snow skittering off the ice.

Valemon prefers seal. At least, that's all he's brought home to me with the exception of the ptarmigan and fish. He probably likes it for the same reason we in Willoughby like it: the thick layer of fat lining the meat. That fat keeps us warm in the winter months. The fat is prized, the most important part of the animal, though all of it is used. For both of us, I should find a seal.

Bearded seals are most abundant around Willoughby, and they laze on the ice near air holes, gaining their strength before fishing for their own food. Dunnal and some of the other patrollers go seal hunting in the winter months when the patrol portions are smaller. Only Dad, as chief, gets his full pay the year round. When I was training, I often heard the others talk about stalking the holes where seals come up, but I committed little of their process to memory. It's all on instinct from here.

And I don't have a practiced eye.

Or a clue as to what I am doing.

But I trudge forward.

If I don't find food, we don't eat.

If he doesn't eat, he won't keep up his strength.

I repeat those simple facts as my muscles strain and ache with each step. I'm not used to all of this walking, especially after so many weeks holed up inside the fortress. I'm not used to pulling my knees up to my chest just to move forward, of sliding down embankments I can't see beneath the cover of snow.

"Hike! Hike!"

My head snaps up, searching out the voice's source. It came from the south, distantly, echoing across the void. A musher's call.

Dark spots mar the horizon, growing larger as they near. I fumble for the binoculars, but the mushers race into view quickly, pulled by the bushy, hearty dogs used on the sleds when the ice and snow cover the land.

I swing the rifle off my shoulder and pull the socks covering my fingers off with my teeth. Hefting the barrel up, I rest my finger against the trigger. Turning into the lazy wind, the frosty air pulls my hood off my hair, so it flies around me in loose waves.

What appears to be a single team splits into two, the first one racing toward me, the other only a length behind.

"Whoa! Whoa!" the first musher calls as he approaches. "These are our hunting lands—Oh!"

The driver of the first sled pulls the dogs up short, holding his arm out in warning to the others.

"You're—you're the dead Cloon girl."

I recognize that voice, though. It belongs to Abel Wence, a hunter who lives on the bay side of town with his four sons. Swinging my gaze over to the other sled, I account for one of them. Rober is only a year older than I am. We took our lessons together up until he aged out and his father needed his help with the kills.

The dogs whine and settle into the snow, some sitting, others laying, all panting from their race across the ice. I recognize some. I helped socialize them when they were born into one of Mom's litters a few years back.

This could be it. This could be how I let everyone at home know I am alive. That they don't have to mourn me. But I shrink back. Will they come for me, drag me home before I can do what I set out to do, and then put me through a council trial? And what if they don't put me through a trial? Will I spend the rest of my days on funeral duty while my father blames me for each death?

I don't want to be dead to them, but continuing to be the disappointment they think me to be might actually be worse.

"And you're Abel Wence. Rober." I nod to the other. I remove my finger from the trigger and shoulder the rifle strap, swinging it to my back as I step forward. "You're rather far from Willoughby, aren't you?" I glance around the plains of ice. Maybe five miles isn't that far to hunt on the backs of sleds. I suppose I've always had the luxury of never having to ask.

"How—how are you here? You were mauled by that bear. Swallowed whole." Abel's voice shakes and he steps back, thick black brows pulling together warily over his dark eyes. "You—you're a ghost."

"Ghost," Rober mutters skeptically from behind his father.

My father is probably feeling pretty smug right about now. I bet if it was him standing before my ghost, he'd be chiding me with an I-told-you-so.

"Is that what they think?" I raise an eyebrow to hide the annoyance boiling just under the surface. My father is probably using that bit of fiction to control a whole village. I grit my teeth.

"It—it's not?" Rober asks.

I shake my head and sigh heavily. I can play this part up for them, even if it means sealing my own fate. I chose the polar bears once—it seems I'll choose them again. "Nope, not even a little. I fell through a seal hole. Stepped into it after too many brandies and slipped right under the ice. The current carried me away—you know how it is." No one would even try to catch someone who fell through the ice into the current. It would be a death sentence for more than just the one who fell. "Now, I'm forced to wander the floes for the rest of my days."

I turn my attention to Rober. We were once friendly. I hold out a finger. "Let that be a lesson to you." I wag it. "Never go out on the ice alone."

The pair stares at me.

How can I blame them? I would stare at me, too.

"Well, if you don't mind, I must go hunting for a seal I will never capture." Please don't let that be an omen. "My soul never resting, wandering the ice for eternity." I press the back of my hand to my forehead dramatically and start to turn from the pair.

"Wait!" Rober steps off his sled, a fox-fur-lined mitten held up.

I cross my arms as he jogs across the ice toward me.

"You aren't really a ghost, are you?" He leans forward so only I can hear him, tilting his chin up to try to match my height. I have at least three inches on him.

"What? Pfft." I wave a hand toward him. "Of course I am."

His eyes narrow on the puffs of breath rising from my mouth. "Most of the village may believe in that superstitious crap, but I know better. You never would have died looking so…"

My eyebrows shoot up. "Looking so what?"

"Run down."

Ouch. I grimace. I may not have been as diligent about the pots of oil and special creams my sisters smothered their faces with, but I also took care of myself. But Rober's right. I may not have always made sure I looked my best, especially when I was just going to spend the day tromping around the dunes with a notebook in hand, but since being with Valemon, the best I've had are a handful of baths in heated snow, salt my only cleanser. "What's your point?"

Rober leans in close enough I can smell the smoked fish on his breath. "Your brother, Linka, has insisted the whole time you weren't dead. Even after the funeral pyre was lit, he gathered search parties to go looking for you. He's certain you are alive; he said you're too ornery to die so easily."

I snort. He's probably right. And a part of me warms knowing I wasn't written off by my twin. The tense part of me that hasn't relaxed in weeks takes a breath and slackens. The part of me still angry and hurting from the secret he kept remains, even though I know it shouldn't. I miss my brother. Even when he's an idiot.

"Should I tell him?"

My mouth opens, but I quickly snap it shut again as a memory of Linka and Beren locked in an embrace resurfaces.

And with it, the pain. If Linka knew for certain where I was, he would come for me immediately. And I would want to return with him. Linka would wear me down, find the piece of my soul that needs Willoughby. The piece that loves my family, even if they don't love me quite the same way.

But how can I leave Valemon? Especially now that he's hurt. Especially now that... now that I...

I shake my head. "I am but a wayward spirit wandering the icy plains."

227

Sadness pulls his eyes down as he nods once. "Well, wayward spirit"—he raises his voice — "let us give you an offering so you may find peace." He nods, his lips tipped into a grim smile, and trots back to his sled. He throws back an oiled skin and rolls a heavy gray lump off the load.

A protest hangs from my lips as I recognize a seal. It's already been gutted and cleaned. I slide my gaze away before I catch its sightless stare. My stomach sinks and eyes water. It's already dead. And I won't have to kill it.

But bringing back food is his family's livelihood, and he's offering it to me. Giving it away while asking for nothing in return. I shouldn't accept, yet…

My stomach growls. I might never come across another seal; this is a sure thing.

I tip my head. "Many thanks," I call softly and reach with my naked hand for the tarp under my arm.

The dogs bark as they stand, and the two mushers call a chorus of "All right" and "Hike, hike!"

They leave me behind in a sprinkling of snow, and as I watch them disappear, I wonder if I can trust Rober to keep my lie.

CHAPTER 25

Dragging a hundred pounds of deadweight across the ice as daylight fades leaves my arms screaming louder than my legs. Shouldering it to get it inside nearly does me in.

The carcass flops onto the prep surface, and I lean over, panting for breath, my cheek pressed to the cold surface.

"Where the hell have you been?" Valemon demands hoarsely from the doorway.

My eyes drift closed, and I sigh before straightening. "Getting. Food," I huff.

"Are you crazy? You could have been hurt. Killed. The ice is dangerous and—"

"And we need to eat. You, especially. You can't heal if you're starving." I lean against the metal countertops and lift my eyes to where I imagine his face might be. I should start cooking, but I would rather crawl into bed and sleep for a day.

No, I can't sleep yet. I want to bathe first. A nice long soak in a real tub, scented oils for my hair and soft, creamy soap for my skin. I want to douse myself in rich moisturizers and comb my hair until it shines. Maybe then I won't look so run down. Maybe I will transform into a

believable ghost.

Then I want to sleep.

But it'll just have to wait. I reach into the sink for a knife before fishing the whetstone I found in the storage closet from my pocket. Small and jagged, it fits snugly in the palm of my hand, but it helps somewhat. Making small circles, I sharpen the half-rusty blade. No matter how many times I sharpen the knives here, they don't cut like the crescent-shaped one Mom wields.

"You are dead on your feet. We could both use the sleep and eat in the morning." Valemon's usual strength doesn't ring in his voice. Instead, each word is punctuated by a heavy breath.

I lower both knife and stone to the counter, slide them away, and lean my hands flat against the top.

"I shouldn't be. All I did was walk. I didn't even kill it," I toss over my shoulder. "I've never killed anything. I probably couldn't even if I wanted to." I swallow and shake my head. "But I was going to try for you. Because I was worried about you and—and you need to eat."

His boots shuffle on the smooth floors as he crosses to join me at the counter. His uninjured hand lands on my hip. Hesitantly at first, and then with more confidence, he slips it around to rest on my belly. Gently, he presses me into him, lowering his nose to the top of my head.

His warm breath flutters in my hair. "Thank you," he murmurs and plants a kiss to my crown.

Why is such a simple gesture, one so familiar it could be between anyone—a mother and child, an old married couple—so intimate? The fluttery feelings return, the softness of kissing in the dark, of sleeping beside one another, and I melt back into him, leaning my head to rest on his shoulder. He is warmth and comfort. Safety and… something more. Having him touch me has my insides quaking. Shaking. Quivering like a pinecone ready to fall from a branch.

I pull away to face him. But the last time I gave in to the temptation of kissing him, he left me for nearly a week. I throw up a wall the easiest way I know how. "You don't want to know how I came back with a full-grown seal?"

"I'm afraid to ask." He props himself up against the prep surface with his forearm, a hum of pain escaping his throat as he leans down.

"I went out onto the ice, and some hunters from Willoughby came across me. They thought I was a ghost." My laugh lacks mirth. "My father told them I was eaten by a polar bear. Can you believe it?" I reach for the knife and brush past him, movements jerky and tight. "I knew one of them well when I was a kid. He didn't believe I was dead. He told me Linka doesn't believe it, either, and that he's been arranging search parties to look for me. Then he gave me the seal—so I wouldn't haunt the ice forever, and my soul could rest. Or something. So, I must have been convincing enough for *someone*."

Anger at my father vibrates through me, and in a single motion, I slice through the seal's side. The rage lessens, the violence freeing some of my pent-up fury. The emptiness left is unsteadying.

Tears instantly well up in my eyes, and I sniff them away.

"You could have told him to let them know you aren't… trapped? They could send someone for you. Or you could have gone back with them. Why didn't you?"

"Why didn't I?" My voice rises. "Why didn't I? Because my father is using my death as some sort of scare tactic to control the town. I never thought he would be hungry for power, but there it is." I raise the knife up toward the ceiling. "He told everyone a polar bear killed me. It's the most ridiculous thing I've ever heard, and he knows it isn't true."

He reaches up to lower my hand and the knife I wield back to the metal surface. "Why? Why wouldn't it be true? Humans are just as much a threat to a bear's well-being as anything; they won't think twice before attacking if it means their safety. They aren't puppies, Dira. They're predators, and they will kill you given the opportunity."

I cut a glance at him before working the knife through the next section of meat. I want to argue with him—any other time I would. But... what if he's right? I reach for the only argument I have against someone who knows the bears better than I do or ever could. "You wouldn't."

"No, I wouldn't, but... but I could. And I've seen it, Dira. I lived through the worst of it. I watched, helpless, as a bear ripped the face off a girl. I've seen them tear through buildings to get to food. I've seen them desperate enough to approach a man holding a gun."

Unease settles between my shoulder blades. Continuing my bad butchering job isn't an option, and I set the knife down to turn to him. "But we can't go kill everything just because it *might* someday hurt someone."

"I know that. Don't you think I know that now? I've been forced to see the error of my ways, in the cruelest way possible. As much as I want to wipe every last one of them off the face of the planet, I know I can't."

My brows come together. "What do you mean?"

"You think being one of them has suddenly made me come to love them?" he whispers with a malice I've never heard from him before. "I'm forced to be the very thing I hate more than anything because I thought killing them was the only way to keep people safe. To survive. But what I failed to see was that they were dying too. They had been pushed to the brink of starvation because *of us*. If Peregrine hadn't betrayed me the way she did… I never would have seen that people weren't worth saving, either. We destroy everything we touch, and I'm the worst of all."

"If we're so bad, why don't you take us all out? Why didn't you let that mother bear take me? Why didn't you leave me to freeze to death on the ice?"

"Because that isn't my job, either."

"Job?" My eyebrows shoot up. "You have a job now?"

He straightens and backs away slowly, his movements stiff from the pain. "When I asked Peregrine for help ending the struggle between man and polar bear, I thought she would help me wipe them out. Instead, she turned me into one." He puts the prep surface between us, but the distance is much farther than the counter's surface. "It took me a long time to understand, but I finally did. I'm not supposed to end the struggle by destroying one side or the other. I'm supposed to help them—us—learn to live together."

"Then why won't you help me? Why won't you let me help *you?*" I angrily slam the pan down on the stove. "If we want the same thing, why do you want to keep me cooped up in here?"

My vision shimmers with hot tears, and I quickly blink them away. At least in the dark, he won't be able to see them. I bend down to the cylinder, turn the knob, and with the back of my hand, dash the tears away before standing to light the stove.

"It's not that simple," he murmurs.

I sniff and bounce on my leg to keep the emotion at bay. "Then why?"

"You shot at me. And missed on purpose."

"That isn't an explanation, Valemon."

"It is. It's the only explanation. I've found myself on the wrong end of a barrel many times. You were just the first one to miss on purpose."

"How often have you been shot?"

"Enough."

An immortal bear-man stuck here for a hundred years can only mean one thing. I've heard enough of Granny's tales to know how these things work. "And so, what? You brought me here so I could help you break your curse? And that's why you don't want me risking it out in the wilds? Me, the only one who loved you as a beast, ready to set you free? Fine. I'm game. Tell me what I have to do and I'll do it. Do you want a kiss? For me to tell you I lo—"

"No, Dira. Stop." He turns from me and the darkness swallows us both. "I thought I could let you do this, but it'll only destroy you, too."

CHAPTER 26

The wind screams my name.

It slips through the double-paned glass, wailing in a false soprano.

It gives me pause, but only for a moment, and then I swing my hammer harder, taking extreme satisfaction in the next hit. In the vibrations that run through the wood, up through the floorboards.

I swing again.

Crack.

And again.

Crack.

The hammer hits the nail squarely each time, the punctuation of well-practiced progress.

But the wind only calls my name louder. And louder.

I drop the hammer and wipe my hands free of sawdust. The shutters are a sight less sloppy than the hearth. I made sure to measure several times before taking the dull serrated blade to the wood of a door from a downstairs room. Fixing the window frames may have cut down on the draft, but an added barrier against the darkest, coldest nights of winter will be necessary.

Lifting my new creation, I balance it against the wall to test the fit.

"Dira!"

I drop the wood squarely on my foot. "Dammit." With a grunt, I fall to the floor and massage the spot where it will bruise, rocking as a wave of excruciating pain washes over me.

"Dira."

It isn't the wind.

Scrambling onto my knees, I peer out the window.

Just outside the wall, a dark form traipses around the snow.

I squeeze my eyes closed until black spots speckle the backs of my lids.

But when I open them again, she's still there.

My mother.

Here.

In Monroe.

Ignoring my throbbing toe, I race out of the room and down the hall. Three rooms away, the glass lies on the floor in small beads and dust and slivers. My boots crush it as I sling myself toward the window. "Mom!"

"Dira?" She's far away, on the other side of the wall, but she swings toward me.

"Mom. Wait. I'll be right there."

I'm down the stairs, racing through the snow, my heartbeat pounding and my skin immune to the cold. I don't remember any of the trip as I sprint toward the hole in the wall, erupting on the other side.

"Mama!" It rips through my throat, hoarse and breaking on the second syllable. I haven't called her by that name since I went off to lessons for the first time. I turn the curve of the wall, and there she is, balanced on the footboards of her dog sled as it races toward me.

"Whoa, whoa," she calls them to a stop. The sled barely comes to a halt before she jumps off the back, and we clash, her arms wrapping around me in a fierce, crushing hug. Despite her much smaller frame, I fall into her, letting her take my weight.

"I should have listened to Linka. I should have known," she sobs, her voice cracking. Her palms run down the sloppy braid falling down my back, one over the other.

I sniff and pull away from her snow and rosewater embrace, the cold I was able to ignore moments ago suddenly hitting me as her warmth disappears. "Is he here?" I scan the ice behind her for any sign of my brother, his lanky build and dopey grin.

She shakes her head and runs her hands over my arms until our hands clasp. "No, it's only me. I didn't—I didn't say anything to anyone."

Reluctantly, I step back. Would she really have come just for me? "Then what are you doing here?"

Her smile falters, and her lower lip wobbles. "I needed to see—I needed to see that you were okay. When Abel said he had seen your ghost, I—I had to see for myself."

My eyes flutter closed. Of course, Abel would have said something. The people of Willoughby may be a superstitious lot when it suits them and telling my family my spirit was wandering the ice would have played right into that. But no one would have come rushing out across the ice ahead of a storm to confront a ghost. "Rober told you, didn't he?" I sigh as I open my eyes again.

"And I will be forever thankful," she whispers. "Not just that he told me, but that he fed you as well."

I lift an eyebrow. He couldn't help but sing his own praises, could he? Or was it merely an insult to my own lack of skill?

She steps closer, her eyebrows coming together. "Dira, we thought we lost you. What happened? How did you get all the way out here? How have you been staying alive? This place isn't safe."

I pinch the bridge of my nose between my thumb and forefinger. Where do I start? On that day when I first saw a giant bear—Valemon—and refused to shoot him? As I built a pyre for a family I was blamed for killing? Or does my woeful tale not start until Beren and Linka showed me I had no way out of the hole I was in? Maybe all of this started when I was a small thing, seeing a polar bear up close for the first time. Wanting to touch. To follow. To be near it. "I was upset. And I went for a walk. And Valemon—"

"Valemon?" Her slender eyebrows snap together. "The king from those old stories Granny likes to tell?"

I blink. "Wait—what? What stories?" My mother has heard them? Granny told them to her too? I'm not sure if I am surprised or a bit jealous that Granny Grin didn't hold it close just for me until I needed it.

"The one about the polar bear king who offers the young beauty a golden crown of holly and whisks her off to his castle, where they live happily ever after. Granny Grin used to tell one every year around the summer solstice. She has since your father and I were children. It's one of her favorites."

I stare at her. I don't remember Granny ever telling it before the night of the ball. And she never mentioned a crown. Not one of gold or holly. She didn't say anything about a princess and a happy ending. My hand raises, fingers playing along my temple. I can almost feel the scratch of the thick, waxy leaves as they dragged at my braids all those weeks ago. Fisting my shaking hand, I lower it and shove it into a pocket.

Mom peers up at me thoughtfully. "They are just stories, Dira. But please, tell me of your Valemon."

Can I bear to see the disappointment on her face? Watch as her shoulders droop in defeat as I tell her Valemon is my polar bear king, but not like any fairy-tale prince she might imagine? No gleaming castle, no charming smile. Or if there is a charming smile, I have yet to see it. Dad never hides his displeasure as well as she, but I'm afraid the moment she learns Valemon wanders the ice on all fours, the enemy of our people, that's exactly what I'll see. "Well… I found him when I… couldn't go home. Or rather, he found me. And gave me shelter, food."

She crosses her arms as her eyebrows come together. Not disappointment. Worry. "And what does he expect in return?"

"What?" My head snaps up. "No. Nothing. It isn't like that."

"Then why haven't you come home?"

Why haven't I come home? *Why haven't I come home?* Is she really that unaware? For years I have begged them both to see me, to *really* see me, and all I got were scolds. Exasperated sighs and clipped anger. They wanted me to be more like my brothers or more like my sisters or both.

No, neither of those things is true. They wish they weren't saddled with me at all. I was the surprise. The odd girl no one planned for. The extra. I destroyed the perfect family my parents wanted… Two strong boys and two talented girls. I am their burden of surprise. The butt of jokes. And that was before Mella and the Leigs died.

My lips tighten around the edges, barely opening as I speak through clenched teeth. "In case you haven't noticed, it's quite a walk.

And across the ice. I didn't bring a rifle with me, my supplies are few, and…" And I won't be going back. Not until I've done what I set out to do.

My eyes wander over her, and I swallow around the painful lump in my throat.

"And you don't want to leave him," she finishes for me.

How did she know? I didn't think anyone but Linka saw me. I can't seem to look at her anymore, and I cut my eyes away as the cold seizes my muscles, a spasm rocking through my center.

"It's too cold for you to be out here in nothing but these old rags." She reaches forward and squeezes my arms. I left the heavy coat back in my new home, strewn across the bed. The lighter jackets and shirt beneath are no match for the cold, and the convulsions crescendo at her touch. "Come. I brought you supplies."

I stop to stare down at her. "Supplies? You mean you didn't come to force me home?"

She loops her arm through mine again, tugging me back toward the sled. "Dira, I would never try to force you to do anything."

I let her drag me along, my mind tangled up with confusion. Did I want her to want me to come home? Or accept that I could make my own decisions?

As we approach, the dogs hop up, their tongues lolling, feet prancing in the snow.

Disentangling from Mom, I drop down next to Dingle, the last dog I was given to socialize. He pulls on his lead to lap me in the face, his tongue hot, body wriggling with excitement. I wrap my arms around him as he pushes me back into the snow, and in that moment, I wish I was home. I wish I could smell Mom's cooking and hear Linka racing up the stairs two at a time. I want to find Dad at the table, but instead of a frown of consternation pointed my way, pleasure. Like the look he gives Landry or the smiles he offers to Dara.

Mom comes back to stand over me. "You rile them up," she says, but there is fondness in her voice, no scolding.

I stare at her, confused.

She holds out my thick parka, lined in fox fur. "Having you home with me is my greatest wish. But I'll bring these back for you before I go on my way, if that's what you want."

She doesn't say anything as I lead her into the front door and up the stairs, but curiosity oozes from her pores. Her steps tap slowly behind me, and as I reach the top floor, I find she lags, her gaze on the ceiling and the cobwebs there.

"You've been living here?"

I glance up, seeing the dirt and decay through her eyes. "Yes."

With a nudge of my hip, the door at the top of the stairwell swings open. We each carry an armload of supplies, the heavier of the two crates my burden.

"It's awfully…"

Rundown? Ugly? Filthy?

"Bare."

"It's fine," I say as I step through the door to our little habitat. The fire still burns bright in the hearth, and the ceiling is clear of dust, but my tools lay over the table, atop the bed. I step over a hammer and lower the crate onto the floor beneath one of the windows.

She stumbles over a screwdriver I dropped in the middle of the floor.

"Sorry," I mumble. "I was working when I heard you calling."

She shifts the weight of her load onto the chair in the corner, turning.

I should defend it. Explain what it looked like before. How the snow fell through a now-repaired hole, that I built the hearth all by myself with no help or plans or directions. But I can't. Not seeing it how she sees it. With sawdust sprinkling the scarred floorboards and stone jutting out at odd angles. A rumpled mess of a bed and a rickety table. It's nothing like the perfect home she keeps.

"I'm impressed. I never thought I'd see…" She offers me a soft smile. "You'll be warm enough?" Mom pointedly studies the hearth.

"Yes."

She scans the room again, gaze landing on the footlocker. "And you have food?"

"Valemon is hunting now."

She nods absently and then clears her throat. "I should get back to the dogs. If I leave now, I can make it before nightfall." She points to the crate I carried inside. "I brought some of your favorites from the stores. Smoked fish and dried mushrooms. The flatbread you like. A pot of jam, one with butter. Eggs." She rubs her palms together. "I couldn't bring too much without your father noticing, and I didn't want to say anything until I knew… Until I knew."

My heart jumps. "He doesn't know you're here? That I—"

She shakes her head. "I couldn't give him hope if there was none." A sigh heaves from her chest, and she clears her throat. "I couldn't watch his heart break again. So I had to be sure first, and if I did find you, I knew you would have left for a reason. I should have respected that more, but I'm your mother, and I had to see for myself. But if he knew where I was going or why, he would have insisted on coming, and I had to respect…" she sniffs. "You've always been the most stubborn of my children, you know."

A grimace pulls my lips downward. My father doesn't know I'm alive. He thinks I'm dead. "And the others? Do they know?"

"I didn't tell a soul. If this is what you want, I won't fight you."

I just nod numbly.

She places a hand on my cheek, cradling it, her skin soft yet cold. "I hope… I want you come back to us. But I want you happy more." She pulls away. "You know that, right? I just want you happy."

"Mom, I…" Am I happy? Do I even know what happiness feels like?

She smiles again and runs her hand over my hair just as Granny Grin does. "You being happy here is no slight to me."

I don't correct her.

"And your young man? He's treating you well? Respectful? Handsome?"

"Yes, of course," I say in a rush. "I mean, no."

Why did I add that? I should have left it. But her question unnerves me. There's so much I know about him, but his appearance… I can't answer that. And it niggles at the back of my mind like a hunger I push away until later.

"Only?"

I scratch the back of my neck absently, my fingernails brushing up against the wisps too short to be tamed into the braid. "It's so dark here, and he sticks to the shadows. I don't know what he looks like."

"You've never seen him?" Her understanding smile folds into a confused frown.

Slowly, I shake my head. "I don't think... I think he doesn't want me to see him."

"Is he scarred? Deformed?"

"I don't know. He could be, but it doesn't matter, does it? He's never said..."

"Would you accept him if he was? Would you stay here with him?" Judgement doesn't sift through her questions, only curiosity.

The scar running across his cheek. Visible as a bear. Rigid to the touch. Does it keep him in the dark, hidden? Or is there something more?

"Of—of course." And why wouldn't I? I've accepted him as a polar bear—what's a few scars? A deformity?

But I never considered that how he looks might be why he clings to the darkness.

Mom's eyes soften, and she tilts her head to the side as a sigh escapes her nose. "There are some candles at the bottom of that crate. They're old. Ones left from when my mother passed. But they should be enough to light the dreary winter nights." She motions to the crate she propped on the chair. "If you need one. I understand either way. I know what it's like to be young and in love. But love changes, sweetheart. And if you want to make it last a lifetime, you have to know for sure. It isn't fair for either of you to drag it along. Don't dwell in the in between too long; that's no way to live a life."

I swallow down a shock of panic.

Love.

I don't think I even know what that word means. People throw it around on the good days, or when they have to. Hollow words forced out for family because it's expected. Used as a platitude between friends. It comes with a mystery and confusion about it. And sometimes the people who are supposed to say it—to *feel it*—don't.

How close was I to throwing out that word in an attempt to free him of the curse?

We haven't spoken since, both settling down for the night silently, clinging to the edges of the bed so we didn't come within even a breath of one another.

And he was gone when I awoke.

Just like he always is.

But what if she's right, and I do love him? Will it all fade away when I see him in the light? Can it?

My stomach twists.

I don't want to lose what I feel for him.

Love or not.

"I'll… I'll remember that."

Mom folds me into her embrace again, her arms tightening. "I love you, sweetheart."

My heart aches. Does she mean it? Or does she only say it because she has to?

"And you are always welcome home. No matter what. Your father and I—we miss you. *He* misses you. I hope you know that. He only wanted—wants—you to be safe."

I step away. "Just not happy."

"Oh, honey." She brushes a lock of hair from my forehead. "He does. Of course he does. He would give anything to have you home, but as long as he knows you are happy, I think his heart would be at peace."

Tell him I'm all right, my mind whispers. But the words never make it to my mouth. Just like none of the other ones I want to say: They make me feel like I can't do anything right. What I want doesn't matter. The only way to do things is their way. They stick inside my throat like a clump of honey-soaked oat cake because as much as I want her to know every hurt churning inside me, I am afraid if I do, she'll be angry with me and take it all back. Or she'll apologize and I won't have the strength to stay.

So I only nod.

Arm-in-arm, we leave the room and walk back down the stairs. I give each of the dogs the love and attention I failed to show back out on the ice, and when they leave, I stand at the bottom of the icy steps and watch as they disappear around the corner of the wall. Caught in the in between.

CHAPTER 27

"Dira! Dira!" The door flies open.

On the other side, a silhouette darkens the hallway.

"What?" I lean backward to see around the open door. The second box of goods my mother brought is strewn across the floor, grouped together by item type. Boots and extra clothes, mittens and my snowshoes on one end, a rifle next to them. Ammunition and cleaning supplies next and then two quilts from my bed at home. The tallow candles rest perfectly folded inside the crease, hidden from view.

His sigh of relief echoes in the quiet of the room. "I saw sled tracks outside, and I thought—" He stops himself from rushing toward me and steps back into the shadows before the warm firelight can reach his chin.

"You thought I left?"

Don't dwell in the in between.

My mother's advice twists around my heart and squeezes. I don't want things to change, but isn't that just a fear to have our friendship stumble backwards, to trip and fall into a place where it doesn't exist at all? No, I want things to pedal forward, to leap into something more. But someone has to take the first step.

It's now or never. "Would that be so bad?" I hold my breath.

He hesitates beside the door, but ultimately decides to step in, pulling the door shut softly behind him. He angles his chin down, the fiery glow playing along the square cut of his jaw, but no farther. "I wouldn't—couldn't—keep you here, but I'd want to say goodbye."

Not the answer I hoped for. The air I held in my lungs escapes through my nose. I nod and turn back to the organized spread of goods. "Rober told my mother he saw me. She came out to see for herself."

"And you didn't go back with her?"

Shaking my head, I don't turn to him. How does he not see I stayed as much for him as myself?

Behind me, the wood bedframe murmurs under his weight as he sits on the mattress. Close enough, I could lean forward over the crate and touch him. But still leagues away.

"I… I didn't want… I wasn't ready… I don't think I can go back. Not yet." I bow my head and pull the edge of the blanket up into my lap. It has always been my favorite. A bright star spreads out from the center, creating four large points and four smaller ones. Each of the smaller ones points to a picture. On one side, two suns shine. The top over a sparkling summer sea, the bottom over a frozen tundra. On the other, a moon beams. The top over a snowscape, the bottom over waving dune grass. And in the middle, a polar bear stands on its hind legs. Granny Grin gave it to me when I was young, I think.

I always covered it with another one, one that wasn't included in the small crate. Mama must have kept the far less ornate one patched together with faded light blue squares.

"Why?"

I should tell him the truth. I should tell him I don't want to leave, not unless he comes with me. And it's stupid to think he could come with me. Or that he would.

I am weak. I can't make the leap. I need him to step toward me. Offer a hand. Let me know he's there to catch me should I stumble. So, I only shrug. "It's a long story."

"Though you seem to assume otherwise, I know surprisingly little about your life. Tell me."

I snort. How modest of him. I suspect he knows far more than he wants me to believe. "I don't know much about yours, either." I finally spin around to face him. Head bent down, he pulls at the boot laces. "Care to make a trade? A question for a question? Answer for an answer?"

His fingers falter and he pauses. "All right." They tug at the laces once more. "But I get to go first."

I draw my legs up and rest my chin on my knee. "All right."

He moves to the next boot. "Tell me about your mother."

"That isn't a question." I grin. "You're not very good at games, are you?"

He ignores my jab. "Why was your mother here?"

"To give me all this." I hold out an arm to encompass the little piles and stacks. As I look over my shoulder, I nearly lose my balance from the lack of support from my hand.

"She didn't come to take you home?" he asks gruffly.

I settle both arms behind me and lean back on flat hands. "That's two questions."

"You can ask me two."

Bobbing my head from side to side, I shrug. "Fair enough. She says she just had to see for herself if it was really me and if I was okay.

She didn't even really press me for why I left but didn't demand I go back, either."

"But you didn't go back."

"I didn't go back." I clap my hands and then rub them together. "Now, it's my turn."

But what do I ask him? All the things I want to know are so personal. Was he ever married? Almost married? Was he in love with someone before?

Is he in love now?

I lose whatever courage I had and ask instead, "Do you age?"

The hood shakes from one side to the other, and when the light hits it just right, I catch a slight cleft in his chin. "No. I don't think so. My life has been very monotonous. I've learned to appreciate it, though. I've seen so much, and though I struggled with the loneliness in the beginning, I've learned to live with it. For better, for worse."

"Alone? This whole time?"

"I'm counting that as your second question. And no, not the whole time, but… no one has ever stayed here as long as you."

Jealousy overwhelms me, and I duck my head. I didn't realize how much I hoped he would say no, that I was the only one. I want him to say more, to explain, to tell me none of them meant anything, but he remains silent. My question answered.

"Why did you really run away?"

The question of all questions. I knew it would come up; I just didn't think he would ask it so quickly.

"It's a long story."

"Are you in a hurry to get somewhere?"

I chuckle. "No. It's just… You probably know most of this, but—"

He waves a hand to speed me on.

I take a deep breath and let it out with a huff. "I don't fit in. I don't belong at all. I've been searching for the bear who saved me—you—ever since I was eight years old. I would watch for you from my bedroom window and jot down any sighting I saw in a notebook. When I figured out how to sneak away from the house without anyone catching me, I would go hide in the trees or the willow shrubs to observe the bears and do the same. At first it was just so I could make sure that bear—you—were okay. It seemed unfair that my father punished the one thing that saved me from being a stupid kid that day. And maybe I was a little obsessed, but it eventually changed and became... I don't know, I loved all of them. Not just the one that saved me, but each and every bear I observed. I hated that the patrol wouldn't find a way to keep the bears out of our food stores without killing them. I even made a suggestion to my father once about other options, but he refused to listen. He just told me to stay away from the wilds—that I was putting myself in danger." I roll my eyes.

"When I was eighteen, I wanted to apprentice to Granny Grin. She makes all the herbal teas and remedies for the town, and though it interests me far less than the polar bears, at least she never made me feel wrong for loving them. But my father refused. Told me I needed the discipline of the patrol. That it was expected of me as a Cloon. I hated it. Every second of it, and so I made sure they thought I was the worst shot. I only patrolled during the afternoon shift when it was too hot for the polar bears to do more than laze on the beach or wallow in the water.

"That morning you were on the beach—what did you say? Testing me?" I give a mock glare. "I wasn't supposed to be there. I mean, I was, but I didn't want to. My brother, Linka, just asked his girlfriend to marry him, and he wanted my shift so he could go out with the hunters in the mornings and earn more to build them their own home. My father gave it to him without even asking me if I minded the change." Bitterness creeps in, and my throat goes raw. I swallow painfully.

"It's almost funny that something so small can change everything else, isn't it? But I guess it's for the better. If it had been Linka out there with Landry, you probably would have gotten shot. I would still be at home, waiting to find out, and everything would be exactly as it was. I would be frustratingly unfulfilled, frustratingly infuriating to my father." I crack a wry smile. "But I wouldn't have been punished for letting you get away that day.

"And that's why I ran away. My father saw the death of the family in the wilds as my fault. He said if I had killed the bear on the beach, he wouldn't have been alive to kill the Leigs. That I had to clean up my mess. He thought I might as well have killed them myself, and the council would probably have felt the same." A sinking feeling fills my stomach. At the time, I grappled with a way to explain the deaths of the Leigs that didn't involve the bears, but I never asked Valemon about it. He had been there, hadn't he? At least long enough to tempt me away.

"I didn't attack them, if that's what you're thinking."

"Sorry. I know. Or I didn't know, but I suspected. I don't have a better explanation. Even now I wonder if it was something—*someone* else. But it wasn't just that. I am a disappointment to him. He doesn't treat any of my brothers or sisters that way. Just me. I'm the only one he has to tolerate. And on top of that, earlier that night..." I sniff and run my fingers through my hair. They catch on the snags and snarls, and I work them through to the ends as I collect my thoughts.

"Beren? My best friend? I thought he was going to propose to me that night. He needed me to take care of him and I... well, who else was there for me? He was the only one who seemed to like me in the whole town. And not just liked me, but *knew* me. Told me every... told me everything."

I can't seem to choke the words out. They stick in the back of my throat like a spoonful of fresh honey. I swallow and swallow to loosen them, but my tongue remains thick and heavy. "I went to go find him at the party, and he was with my brother. Linka. They were arguing and kissing. Linka didn't want to break off his engagement with Liddet, but if he didn't, Beren said he was going to marry me."

Why does that hurt so much? It shouldn't. I could have been happy with Beren. And he might have been happy with me, too. Barely. "I should have been happy. Ecstatic. But he wasn't in love with me. And even though I wasn't in love with him, I didn't want to be... I didn't want to be a punishment for my brother." My eyes water, vision swaying as the light shimmers.

"And my brother. I thought I knew him. Everything about him. But I didn't know that. So there on that beach, watching the pyre consume the Leigs while everyone else stood away from me, I realized I was alone. No one really wanted me; there wasn't anything left for me in Willoughby. My best friend didn't want me, only to use me. My twin kept secrets from me. My dad hated me and thought I was a danger to everyone. The council would be after my neck and... And I ran. Better to go on my own when no one would miss me than let them kick me out. And maybe then I would have a chance to fix everything."

I shrug helplessly and turn my gaze up to him. His silence spreads out like a blanket of snow, stretching endlessly and unmoving.

Maybe he waits for me. My turn. My question. Reaching deep for my last dregs of bravery, I ask, "Have you ever been in love?" The tears dry up, but my throat still aches. Asking about love might be my real punishment. Another log to the fire of my own pyre. Love seems like something I don't deserve, but now I want it. Desperately. If only to prove someone could want me, even just a little.

"I'm old, Dira."

"I know. I do," I add as he starts to protest. "But you don't seem old."

"You know what I mean."

"I know you haven't answered the question."

"Yes. I was. A few times."

A few times. Not once. And not in the present. My stomach tightens. I can't help but prod, though, to encourage him to twist the knife further. "And?"

"And you wanted an answer. I gave it to you," he says, tone clipped.

I scoff. "You gave me a non-answer after I poured my most embarrassing moments out to you."

"Fine. In high school, there was Madilyn Hawkins. But when we went off to college, she dumped me for a fraternity guy named Todd."

I narrow my eyes on him. "You're using words I don't understand."

"I dated other girls—"

"More explanation needed."

"But there wasn't anyone else until I met Alex."

"The one who was injured?"

"Mm. Alex would have done anything for me, but dying shouldn't have been one of them."

Anything I say will be another jab at the wound. I let the silence pass between us, and when he makes no move to fill it, I finally ask, "What of the others? The ones you brought here? Did you love them?"

"You're asking more questions than agreed upon."

"Then ask me one so we can get back to it."

"When will you be ready to go back to your family?"

"I don't know. Your turn."

He sighs. "No. Love is a liability, and we're doomed to destroy the ones we love most. So, no, I didn't love any of the ones who came before you. I didn't want to."

My heartbeat falters, and I bite my lower lip to keep from asking what I long to ask. If he didn't love any of them, could he love me? Am I the one who is different?

Will that break the spell?

It must.

CHAPTER 28

I rise before both the sun and Valemon.

Clothed in what my mother brought, the new rifle hooked over my shoulder, I ease the door open.

And hesitate.

Glancing over my shoulder, I rake my gaze over the bed. Valemon's silhouette sprawls beneath the quilts, my favorite now on top, slipping down his chest.

Wetting my lips, I cast a look in the direction of the rest of Mom's gifts. Buried under a packet of smoked fish and the seed bread I liked best as a child, the candles rest. It would be nothing to quickly light one in the embers of the fire and shine its light over his face. To know for certain.

My eyes squeeze shut, and I shake my head to clear it.

No. He'll show me when he's ready.

Slipping out into the dark hallway, I hold my breath so I can hear him if he wakes.

Only silence.

I scurry down the hall and skip down the stairs.

Outside, the snow sparkles under the moonlight, not even a thin ribbon of sun shining along the horizon. Nothing moves this early in the morning, and if it does, it does so silently enough to go undetected. I could stare out at it for hours, the perfect silvery landscape. Watch as the sun plays over the edges of the ruins to paint it gold. It wouldn't be so terrible to look out over it for a lifetime.

But I'm here for one thing and one thing only: the polar bears.

And I am not going to find them stuck inside the ruins of Monroe. I didn't leave to hide away forever, and if I ever want to go home, I need something to take with me. To prove I'm not wrong, that we can live with the bears without killing them. It's time to stop dwelling in the in between.

If I can put enough distance between me and Valemon before the sun comes up, I can cover a fair amount of ground before he catches up to me. Because as surely as I breathe, he will follow my tracks.

I don't know what I expect to find. But the book I can't read presses against my midsection. An old pencil pushed into the pages so they no longer lay flat. I may never know what those words say, what their passages mean. But the paper inside it is far more valuable to me than its story ever could be.

I hook my boots into the snowshoes Mom smuggled to me.

I'll find the polar bears. And learn everything there is to know about them. Then, somehow, I'll help fulfill Valemon's dream. And mine.

Perhaps then we'll find what's on the other side of failure and curses. And I'll know what it's like to make someone proud.

The north has little to distinguish it from the south.

Endless stretches of white. They break off into steep faces of pure blue, the edge of the glacier falling into a frozen sea. From a precipice high above, kilometers spread out before me, and one wrong step could break the ice shelf, send me falling to my death. And yet, I don't back away.

This must be what the top of the world feels like.

The wind a howling monster, the ice her willing conspirator.

And below, a polar bear.

Only with the binoculars can I clearly make out the female, smaller than the males by several hundred pounds, as she strolls amongst great jutting spikes of packed ice. She travels parallel to the cliff, nose held to the sky.

I dig the book out from under my parka and kneel in the shallow snow. Using my mouth, I adjust the pencil between the thumb and finger pocket of my mitten and start to make notes.

A size estimate. The direction in which she travels. Her movements.

She looks to be rather robust, not as skinny as some who summer around Willoughby, and her fur, thick and full, shines a bright white.

The pressure on my neck from the binoculars eases as I pick them up to trail her again.

I don't see any others.

No pack or herd, I write.

In the summer, most of the bears we come across are male. The females are far cagier, usually because they have cubs in tow. I always thought they might travel together to have safety in numbers, and I just caught the stragglers trying to convince their young to keep up.

Maybe I was wrong.

I lift the binoculars again. But just as I focus on her, she jerks to the side and collapses.

And then the loud crack of a gunshot reverberates off the walls of ice.

My chest squeezes as my mind catches up to my eyes. "No!" The cry crescendos, the note holds, splitting through my ears and chest.

I drop the binoculars as bright red blood stains the snow, my chest heaving with each painfully dry breath.

The wind still plasters the fox fur lining my hood against my face, and the clouds open to allow slender rays of sunlight to play along the ice.

But everything is still. Dead. Unmoving.

A sob escapes my throat, and I stifle it against my mittens.

Someone came all the way to the edge of the world to shoot a polar bear. One who did nothing but walk along the ice. And now she's gone.

Someone shot her.

Someone shot her.

I scramble up from the snow and swing my gaze around.

I'm not alone. Someone else is out here.

Fumbling for the binoculars, I hold them up to my eyes to find the bear once more. More white figures move to surround her.

Was I wrong? Do they move in packs?

No. I focus on one of them. The long barrel of a rifle hangs down their back.

And all of them move on two feet. Not four.

I adjust the lenses again.

Those are no bears.

They are men. In bear clothing.

Something darker moves between us, blocking out my view, and I gasp, falling back as I drop the binoculars.

"Who are you?"

I stare up at a pack of five standing between me and the edge of the cliff. They, too, wear white parkas, the fur unmistakably polar bear.

"I—I'm Dira Cloon. Of—of Willoughby."

The center figure shifts forward, dark piercing eyes glare down into mine as he stops just a foot before me. "Willoughby," he growls from behind a white cloth wrapped around the bottom half of his face.

I nod. "To the south."

"Why have you trespassed on our land, Willoughbier?"

I stand awkwardly, brushing off the snow that clings to me as I straighten. "Your land?" A quick scan of the landscape reveals no markers. No sign of a town or even a hut. "And who exactly are you? I see no boundary lines."

"*We* are the boundary lines."

I can't help it. I raise a single eyebrow. "I don't think you understand how lines work."

Two of the others standing behind him move forward menacingly.

But I stand my ground.

"What are you doing here, Willoughbier?" the first demands, his chin jutting forward.

"I'm here studying the polar bears."

His silent companions exchange glances, a few soft chuckles making their way to my ears.

"And why in hell would you want to do that?" their leader asks, his eyes creasing at the corners in a half-hidden smile.

"I don't know. Knowledge? A better understanding?"

"The only good polar bear is a dead one, girl. You'd be smart to remember that."

Of course, they share similarities with my father. I should have suspected. I nod behind them. "Friends of yours?" The others begin their journey back across the ice, a slender thread of red blood streaming behind them. My throat constricts.

I drag my gaze away and find the dark eyes again.

Don't cry. Don't show them weakness.

"The rest of our hunting party."

That they would hunt a bear while it strolls along the frozen sea, nowhere near civilization, turns my stomach and prickles my ire. "You don't find it dishonorable?"

"Dishonorable?" he echoes.

"Killing off your only competitor for food? Doesn't that hurt your pride?"

In a blink, he draws a hunting knife, pointing it straight at my throat.

My hands instantly raise, and I step back involuntarily. "Whoa."

"Say it again, girl."

My mouth works, but my focus is so drawn to the point of the blade, no words come out.

"Say it again."

I flick my gaze to meet his. A toxicity I don't recognize burns brightly there.

"That's what I thought." He sheaths the knife in his belt, but steps forward to wrap his hand around my arm. I have at least an inch on him, but he's broad and his grip strong.

"Hey!" I try to yank it away, but he holds tight. "What are you doing? Let me go."

His grip only hardens, and we turn toward the other party, who are dragging the dead polar bear.

Throwing a glance over my shoulder, I spot the book where it fell, the cover a bright spot in the snow. But no one else notices it. The last thing I want to do is draw attention to it, especially since the rifle still jostles against my back. I don't want them wrestling it away from me, either.

My snowshoes kick up powdery dust as I lengthen my strides to keep from falling behind. Despite our similar heights, my captor strides over far more land with each step than I do, his unencumbered arm swinging purposefully.

The others trail us, the one on my right staying just within my peripheral vision.

"What did you find me?" a woman's voice calls as we near the others.

The leader of the little gang takes two more giant steps before answering. "She claims she comes from Willoughby. Thought you'd want to question her."

Two halves of the same party clash, and I avert my eyes to the soft daylight glow of the moon in the sky. If I look at them, the bear will surely be in view, and I don't think I can stand to see her like that.

Their leader cants her head to grab my attention, and I lower my gaze just enough to stare at the top of her forehead. Faded gray hair springs from a pointed peak, hovering above her hawk-like eyebrows. Fine lines and steady wrinkles punctuate her face, and her thin-lipped smirk is as far as I allow myself to peer.

Dark eyes narrow as my own jump back to clash with them. "Willoughby," she murmurs through barely moving lips. "I haven't seen that place since I was a child." She chuckles. "It still stands, then? Not yet been burned to the ground?"

My heart jumps, and I lick my lips, even though I know I shouldn't. Already chapped and peeling, it will only make them worse. "Of course." I clear my dry throat. "Willoughby doesn't just exist. It thrives."

"Mmph. Our elders always predicted they would be devoured by the polar bears. Everyone to the south is weak and soft. Easy prey."

I really shouldn't antagonize her. Wasn't opening my big mouth what got me dragged in front of her in the first place? I jerk my arm away from her companion once more, and this time, he lets go. With the tips of my fingers, I dig into the bruises, massaging them away. And then quickly drop them when her eyebrows rise as if to tell me I prove her point. "I'd say you are the ones who barely exist. Hunting bears for what? Sport? Are you really so inept at feeding yourselves, you have to kill off the competition to be able to get food?

Every inch of her face pinches. "Why are you here? On our land?"

I bare my teeth and suck in a breath. "I'm pretty sure you can't call a giant block of ice land."

"Don't play stupid, girl. Who sent you to spy on us?"

"Spy on you? Why would anyone want to spy on you? I'm merely out here to observe the bears. Thanks, by the way, for making it that much more difficult. At the very least, I guess that answers the question of how your people have come to live with them." I mumble the last bit to myself, but not softly enough.

"Live with them? *Live* with them?" She throws her head back and laughs, a deep, echoing cackle. "We don't live with them. We put them down."

"I don't think—"

"Maybe that's your problem, girl. You don't think. To survive this place, you don't want to live with the polar bears. You want to destroy them. The fewer of them there are, the better off your people will be. They've learned to steer clear of Buckroe because they have no chance to even get near; we shoot to kill. Take that back to your people." She tosses her chin toward the south with a sneer. "Now get off our land. And the next time I see you, it will be with a bullet between your eyes."

My lips part. Eyes shifting, I glance at the others surrounding her. But their faces remain unreadable, their stares just as cold and unblinking.

But before I back away, an angry roar rises up from behind me.

I don't have to see the animal to know Valemon has followed me here.

Mitten held between my teeth, I get off one shot before a giant paw swipes me to the side.

I crash into the snow, the reverberations from the kickback still buzzing through my shoulder. My ass lands hard, my wrist screaming as I reach backward to catch myself.

Bright red blood spurts from the Buckroe hunter's shoulder, and he drops his gun. It lands in the snow and he follows it, painting the thin layer red.

Finding my knees, I fumble to reload, the pain in my wrist not stopping my fingers from the movements as familiar as tying my boot strings.

But before I can get off another shot, Valemon backs into me, and I go sprawling into the snow again. My head bounces back, smashing against the hard ice beneath, and I scramble up to my feet just as Valemon lunges forward, large jaws separated and sharp teeth gleaming. His body blocks my view as a feminine scream splits the air.

It rings high and long, like the call of summer seagulls as they whine above the waves.

But her cry cuts off short.

And as I scramble back up, the body of the woman crumples to the ground, blood pouring down her face, gray hair clumped over it.

My eyes clash with hers, neither of us blinking.

And she never blinks. And never will again. She doesn't move.

Whatever anger lit her eyes before has gone dark.

The wind whips between our two factions. Valemon and me. And the Buckroers. No one says anything. No one twitches a muscle.

Loose hair flutters across my face as the temperature drops, and shadows fall all around us as thick, heavy clouds blanket the sun.

The others shift uneasily as we square one another up. Only a second has passed, maybe three, since the old woman fell, but it could be minutes the way no one moves. Hours.

A stance repositions, just a bending of the knees and the raising of a hand.

My fingers react before my mind. It trails behind my movements, pulled along with whatever my muscles and bones perform. Almost from another body, I watch as my hands ready my rifle, and when the butt presses into my shoulder, I take aim. My enemy's body, only a few meters away, jerks to the side before falling to the ground, and yet it all seems so disconnected. When did I make the decision to move? When did I pull the trigger?

Valemon lunges forward in the same breath, moving through them like a knife through freshly churned butter. Blood clings to his paws, and as they stamp down against the glacier, it mixes with the snow to turn summer sunset pink.

My own movements are slow and clumsy as I take aim again, the shot hitting my mark but with less speed than his claws, his teeth.

The binoculars bang against my chest as I swing my sights to another Buckroer, and time catches up. The yells of the men as they fall converge into a collective cacophony of inhuman pain, their guns useless against the slicing claws and fifteen hundred pounds of bear flesh and bone.

My own yells sing like a siren in my ears, high-pitched scratches whining with every indrawn breath. Each shot.

The knife that had been pointing at me moments ago flashes, and his name rips through my throat in a wail. "Valemon!" Harder the wind wails, threading icy fingers through my hair and dragging it out from under the cover of my hood. And on its lips, my cry grows.

The man falters at my outburst, his dark gaze swinging to me and eyes blowing wide before Valemon moves between us. He rises onto his hind legs, towering over his victims.

A single scream rents the air.

And then silence.

The snow crunches as Valemon falls back to all fours.

Buckroe's hunting party lies ruined on the ice, broken and bloody.

Valemon turns black eyes to me, but I can only hold his gaze for a moment.

I straighten, peering down at the twisted, battered hunters, checking for signs of life.

Breath still belongs to most. An arm twitches.

We didn't kill them. Not all of them, anyway.

I avoid the body of the other polar bear, and my hands tighten around the rifle. It wouldn't take much to change that. To wipe them all out so they can't hurt another bear.

My finger falls against the trigger.

Valemon chuffs softly and lumbers toward me. His eyes flash. Warning me down. Yelling me away.

Will he take me out, too, if I point the barrel down at one of them?

His nose nods upward, nostrils flaring.

Not blinking away from his stare, I shoulder the rifle strap and turn. Snow falls into the wrist of my mitten, but I shove it over my hand anyway.

CHAPTER 29

"What were you thinking?" Valemon demands as he throws the door open. It swings on the hinges, bouncing off the wall behind it, only to round back on him. He catches the edge with the palm of his hand and stalks inside.

I pull the quilt over my head, dousing myself in darkness. I've been asking myself the same question since he left me at the bottom of the stairs and stalked off into the wilderness. I just wanted to find the bears. The *real* bears. But I should never have gone alone, not when I didn't know what I would find.

But I can't tell him that. Admitting I was wrong is like admitting others may have been right. Maybe not about the bears, but other things. Was I wrong when I snuck off to watch them from the trees? When I crept closer and closer? Was there really a danger that one would take my head in his mouth and crunch down?

Valemon crushed that woman's head between his teeth in an instant. And he may not be a *real* polar bear, but he certainly has the strength of one.

Once the adrenaline from the meeting wore off, the horror snuck in.

I've seen him fight. I've seen him attack. But they were other bears. But this time, it was people. Humans. And not the accident that claimed Mella. They may have been unnecessarily cruel, but how easily could it have been someone from Willoughby that he came upon? What if my brother and father followed Mom's sled tracks back here and tried to pry me away? Would I see their broken bones and blood littering the ground every time I closed my eyes? Was my father right, and he killed the Leigs in a fit of rage?

I bite down on my lip until it fills with a hot, metallic taste. I don't really think that's possible, but… what if?

"Dira?" he demands.

I grunt in response and curl up even tighter. My eyes ache from squeezing them, and white bursts dance along the backsides of my lids.

"Dira?" His voice drops an octave, so worry trims it, not the harsh stain of anger.

Will answering help anything? No, probably not.

I want Linka.

The thought comes from nowhere, along with a memory of our grandfather just after he died. He was laid out on the pyre, most of his body wrapped in long strips of gray cloth. Only his face remained uncovered, his eyes closed, as if asleep. But a puncture mark marred his wide cheekbone and something about his face was no longer as straight as it once was, thanks to the tusk of a narwhal.

I clung to Linka as Dad stepped forward with the torch. But he clung to me, too. Our heartbeats matched, just as they always did, and when the fire closed in on the birch and dried grasses laid out beneath our father's father, I turned into Linka and he turned into me. Two sides of the same mirror.

And as loss left a gaping hole that day for the man who showed me how to use the sharp side of a knife to carve a bar of soap, who taught me the steps to the reel, who always gave me a hug first, Linka eased it away.

But that gaping hole returned. Not today. Not yesterday, either. Not even the day of the Night Magic Ball. For some time, something has chipped away at whatever filled it, and now it is empty once more.

The back of my throat burns, and I resist the urge to sniff and give myself away from under the pile of blankets.

Why didn't I ask Mama about Linka? Why didn't it even occur to me? I could have easily inquired about wedding preparations or the patrol or just asked. Is the wedding still happening? Or are he and Beren now living in the small house on the beach?

The thought doesn't hurt like I thought it would. In fact, it almost feels... welcome.

Was Beren why he was so angry those last weeks we had together? Was he just scared? Alone? Trying to find himself and failing? Why didn't he come to me? Why didn't he just say something?

I try to picture them there, but all I can see is Linka, just as upset and lonely as I am. If he had disappeared off into the ice, I would turn into a wreck. I wouldn't sleep or eat, and the last thing on my mind would be a wedding or a broken engagement or moving in with Beren.

How could I not consider him when I left? How was I so wrapped up in myself?

Have I always been this way?

Misery washes over me, and I succumb to the urge to sniffle. "I want to go home."

The mattress shifts as Valemon sinks down next to me, his hip pressing into my folded legs.

I draw them in closer to my chest.

"I'll take you back. If that's what you want," he murmurs with the quiet of defeat.

Is it what I want?

Do I want Valemon here without me? No. I would have Linka, but I wouldn't have him. And that feels nearly as impossible.

I throw back the quilts and sit up. The glow of the fire outlines the edge of his cheekbones, the jut of his jaw, the soft cleft in his chin, but the rest of his features remain dark and flat. Frustration bubbles out of the melancholy, and a growl tickles the back of my throat. "It doesn't matter what I want." Because I want both. I want my brother in my life, fully, all the way. And I want Valemon—the Valemon I know, not the one I fear might lurk below the surface.

But I can't have both. I don't get *both.* People and polar bears don't mix, and if I want one, I don't get the other.

One of the boards cracks in the hearth, and a spray of bright yellow light flares with a sprinkle of sparks before settling down into the deep, golden glow. His jaw bounces down before popping back up, yet he says nothing.

"You do want me here, don't you?" My voice sounds weak and mewling, and I hate myself for it.

"Yes."

A single syllable. It's all I need to stoke the courage lurking somewhere in the back of my mind. I can't have both. But I can have him. I *have* him.

I lean forward, my lips parted, and my breath hitches as my nose brushes his. I draw in a steadying breath and fist my hand in his coat but keep my lips a whisper away from brushing his.

"Kiss me?"

He draws in a sharp intake of breath, but rather than pressing our mouths together, he draws a single fingertip down my cheek. The pad barely ruffles the soft, invisible hairs, and his skin doesn't skim mine.

I shiver in anticipation. Or maybe it's fear. Sadness. Longing.

The movement causes my lower lip to touch his, and he draws away just a bit.

"Why do you want to stay?" he murmurs.

The question is like the chilly splash of the autumn tide just before the ice takes over. "I—"

I don't want to leave you.

I want what's certain.

I'm tired of being stuck.

I'm ready to choose between the bears and the people.

I could say any of them. Should say them. But what part is most true? And which will hurt him the least? Hurt *me* the least? He has to find the common ground, to make it so we can all live together. But then he ripped through those people today. Calm, controlled Valemon lost control. And he *killed.*

Just like they killed.

It is a never-ending cycle, isn't it?

"We… I want there to be a way. I want to make it so what happened today—make it so it doesn't happen again." It isn't a lie, but it isn't exactly the truth. I want everyone to experience what he and I have when he's in bear form.

But that can never be.

He shifts away, leaving me leaning toward him awkwardly.

I slouch back into the pillows and press my feet into the mattress, sinking into the headboard.

"Why were you in Buckroe territory?"

"I didn't know it was their territory."

"That's beside the point. Why were you there? Alone? Anything could have gotten you."

"*Anything* almost did," I mutter.

"Dira."

I sigh. "I left Willoughby so I could study the polar bears and find a way to convince Willoughby there is no reason to kill them, Valemon."

"So why—"

"Will you let me finish?" I don't mean to snap, but anger now simmers below my surface. Anger at him, at the world. Maybe even myself.

He clams up.

"I can't study them from here. And I can't live like this forever. It's nice to have something to do, but I don't want to fix hearths and make shutters for the rest of my life while I wait for you to come back every evening. If I wanted that, I could have stayed in Willoughby. I could have gotten married to any of the ten bachelors my age and been bored for the next seventy years of my life without freezing my ass off in this ruin."

"You don't need to do any of those things here—it's been fine for a hundred years—"

I shake my head. "I know that. But what am I supposed to do? I have been hiding here, Valemon. Hiding from my family and refusing to move on."

"Fine. You want to study the bears. But to the north, if you look for bears, you'll find them. And those people—the ones from Buckroe—they are dangerous. You shouldn't have gone without at least letting me know first."

I pick at a piece of lint on a light edge of a quilt. "I thought you would try to dissuade me from going."

"And you would have been right. It's—"

"Dangerous. Yes. I know. I've been hearing that all my life. What is it about everyone that they can't trust me?" I hold up my hands before letting them flop back down on my lap.

"I do trust you."

I shake my head minutely. "No, you don't. You just told me you would have tried to keep me from going. And when I did go, you swooped in to save me and made it all worse. Don't you see that? I had it under control. It may not have been my finest hour, but they were letting me leave with a warning when you showed up."

"You don't understand, Dira—"

"But I do. They are terrible people, but you had no reason to be worried. I can handle myself."

"Haven't you ever been scared for someone? Scared that the risks they take will be enough to take them away from you forever?" His voice breaks, and he finishes in a whisper. "I was afraid I would lose you. Just like I lost my sister, and my parents, and Alex. If not to one of those sadistic bastards, then to the ice. Or another animal. But you throw yourself into the most dangerous situations without a second thought. They *kill* people, Dira. And they don't care."

I nearly snort. He sounds like Calla. A day doesn't go by where she doesn't worry that something will happen to Landry. He could be attacked or shot or fall into a hole and hit his head. It's never ending.

274

And exhausting. Yet my brother indulges her. He no longer scales the cliffs for barnacle geese eggs or joins the boar hunt. And he certainly doesn't stand up for me when he should.

"Do you know how it felt to watch you dangling from the ceiling? Or seeing that bear sniff you out on the ice?"

"No."

"Well, it felt impossible. And then today—"

Today I learned it is impossible. Everything I want to do. Willoughby may not be Buckroe, but they are one step away. If they had seen what Valemon did…

"It's impossible. We have an impossible task." I drop my face onto my knees and sigh heavily. Any anger, any fight, leaves me. I just want to curl back under my covers and go back into the darkness.

"No, I have an impossible task."

"I'm now as much a part of this as you are." I lean my temple down on his shoulder and close my eyes. He smells of snow and warmth. "You don't see any others coming to stand up for the bears, do you?"

His hand settles over mine, and I turn my own over so our palms rest against one another.

"No, I don't suppose I do."

"Then it's settled." I turn my nose into his shoulder and breathe in deep. His scent pushes away the memory of blood and gunpowder until all that's left is the snow and ice. "We are in this together…. Unless you have your eyes on someone else." My lips curve into a smile.

"There is no one else, Dira."

"Good, that's good."

We settle into each other like that for minutes. An hour. I don't know how long, just that calm rests every horrible thought, every muscle, every bone. I breathe him in, and he leans his cheek onto my crown, his breath ruffling my wildly unkempt hair. I could fall asleep like this, I think.

And then he ever so lightly presses a kiss to the corner of my forehead.

My head snaps up in an instant, and I seek his eyes out in the dark. Only the faint glow of the fire reflects back at me. "I thought you were mad at me," I whisper.

"Not mad." His thumb runs across my cheek. It bumps against the corner of my lips and lingers there. "Scared."

"I don't think I'm mad at you anymore, either. Just… scared, too."

"Fear always brings out the worst in us all."

I lean forward, finding his lips and let mine hover there like a bird waiting for a wave to pass before landing in the surf.

His hand dives into my hair as he draws me to him, his lips enthusiastically nipping mine open.

I melt into him, humming with contentment as I taste my first sip of him. The taste turns into a long, full drink. An intoxicating introduction to just how much I need him.

Leaning forward, I ask for more.

He curls back onto the mattress until he lays flat, and I stretch out over him. Beneath the heavy garments, his muscles flex and knit, his heart beating just as fast as mine.

Our mouths dance, flittering together and then apart like a pair of moths at a flame. His hands venture over my body. They start at my shoulders and move down my sleeves, over my wrists, and then find the hem of my jacket. Slowly, his fingers push the heavy fabric away from my midsection, and the heat of his hands warms my belly.

I moan.

He shifts his weight, and I slip down him, and we face each other in the darkness.

"I wish I could see you," I murmur against his temple as he lays a kiss just below my ear.

"Would it change anything?"

Yes, my curiosity screams. *Yes,* cry fear and anxiety. What if I see him and everything I feel melts away? What if, in an instant, this home I have created no longer feels welcoming?

I can go back to Willoughby. He even said he would take me himself. I could go back and…

"No, it wouldn't change anything," I murmur. The image of a life without him, even a life in the dark, forms an empty ache in my chest. It claws at my throat, pulling at my heart.

"Good." He nuzzles my cheek, and our lips lock into place, pulled together by some invisible longing connecting us together.

I nestle into him and close my eyes.

No, it wouldn't change anything. I could stay with him forever.

I just wish there was some way I could keep my family, too.

CHAPTER 30

"You're sure you're ready?"

I cinch my parka belt tighter around my waist and nod stiffly. Only my face is exposed, but once we leave the now-stuffy room, I'll pull a length of torn cloth over my cheeks to protect them from the wind and cold.

It's been three days since I left the room. I didn't want to. And Valemon didn't question it when he found me in the same position, curled up on the mattress, as he left me the first day. The second he only asked if I had gone outside. To which I shook my head and pressed my face into the pillow he uses, breathing in the warm, winter scent. But yesterday he prodded more. And when I just shrugged, he asked if I wanted to go looking for other bears.

With my mittened hands, I take inventory of everything I might need. The rifle lays across my back already, extra ammunition in my pocket. Binoculars hang from my neck, and my snowshoes wait beside the door, leaning against the wall where he propped them last night. I have everything but a notebook. "I guess."

"You guess?"

"I was using an old book to take notes, but… I lost it the other day when the Buckroe… I lost it."

"Mm." He leans against the wall next to the door and crosses one boot over the other. "Go look in the footlocker. I might have something in there you can use."

I shake my head. I've looked through the footlocker dozens of times, and there has never been anything suited for note taking. But I humor him, stiffly sinking down in my many layers to turn up the lid.

And there, on the top of his few belongings, is the book I dropped in the snow.

The pages wave slightly, and a large blotch on the cover is a darker color than the rest, but the flower symbol is the same. The thickness. Even the bump where a pencil rests between two pages.

I lift it out, and the pencil falls to roll a few inches across the floor toward my boot. "You found it."

But when I turn, questions of how and where and why on my lips, he no longer stands in the shadows a man.

His wide, black nose lifts insistently.

And though he's right there, no different from any other day, a deep sense of loneliness closes over me. He may be in my company, but there will be no conversation. No deeply uttered words, no snorts of amusement at my expense. I won't feel his hand on my cheek or his lips against mine for hours yet.

I slip the book under my parka so it rests against my heart. "Thank you," I murmur unconvincingly.

He snorts and turns to squeeze his overly large frame through the doorway.

Feet dragging, I follow, stooping only to gather my snowshoes and tuck them under my arm.

I should be excited to go out onto the ice with him. The notion did perk me up when he made the invitation, but I didn't really explore what it meant when I accepted. *The ice, the polar bears. This is what you want,* my mind sang.

But maybe my heart wasn't in it.

I follow him past the kitchen I no longer use and out the side door.

Little sun shines today. Heavy, dark clouds loom close enough I can almost reach up and touch them.

He waits patiently for me to climb onto his back as we discussed, and once my hands fist in the thick fur over his neck, he takes off, racing toward the tunnel. I lower myself into him, becoming as flat as possible as the winds sneak into every opening and crevice of my parka.

Will this be my life for the rest of the winter? Riding atop his back as he takes me to the far corners of the ice to observe his kind? Or holed up in the top of his frigid, crumbling ruin? It's everything I could have ever asked for only a few days ago. But if it's all hopeless, what's even the point?

He slows to a stop, and I lift my head.

Across the ice, a hundred meters away, three bears turn to stare at us.

The largest, a female, stands motionless, but her two cubs, smaller though still plump with fat and extra fur, step curiously forward.

I inch forward, but Valemon chuffs softly and steps between us, cutting me off from the young family.

Who does he protect? Me or them?

It doesn't matter.

Fumbling for the book, I pull it out, adjusting the pencil between my thumb and palm before finding a new page.

Glancing up, I stare at the twin bears.

One is larger than the other. It hangs back as the smaller steps forward.

The mother lifts her head and snorts a stream of steam into the air, but neither turn from me.

I wait, pencil poised, heart beating in anticipation.

Come on. Do something.

The wind sweeps snow between us, fading them from view for a breath. And when it dies down, the snow falling on the ice, the bears move. The smaller rounds on the larger cub, knocking him over, and they wrestle for a moment.

So soft. So sweet. So innocent.

How could anyone see them as bloodthirsty killers? They are beautiful, magnificent, as pure as any other animal. If only my father could see them like this. Would he see something worth killing?

Or would he see Linka in the larger one, holding back some of his strength to keep from knocking down a slightly smaller, more aggressive twin?

Does he ever look back on my childhood fondly like this mama bear stares after her cubs? Are there moments he thinks of me and smiles? Or does disappointment lurk there every time? Stab him with every thought of what he could have had with Linka if not for me?

I close my eyes. But it's my father's eyes crinkling into a smile I see hovering on the backs of my eyelids, not a cold stare of disappointment. It's his hand reaching up to pull on one of the braids hanging over my shoulder, his beard tickling my cheek as he presses a quick kiss to my temple. It's his arms wrapping around my waist as he hefts me against his wide barrel chest to point out toward the sea.

A spray of water rises over the waves as a whale surfaces.

It was just the two of us that day. And I remember no anger, no exasperation. Just his strength as he held me up to see one of the things he loved most: watching the whales as they came in to summer in Willoughby.

And when I hugged him to me, my arms wrapped around his head, my shirt drank up his tears.

How many other memories do I have like that one? How many lurk somewhere, overshadowed by a resentment growing as I did? Moments of tenderness or happiness or grief?

When my eyes open, they find the bear cubs trotting after their mother as she leaves us, back hips swaying.

I drop the pencil back into the crease of the book and shut it before laying my hand on Valemon. I wrote no words today, and I have no need to. I will remember every moment on the ice with those bear cubs and their mother.

And the way it made me feel.

My father may not understand why I love the bears, and I am not even sure I understand it myself. But maybe if I can remind him of the way he loves the whales, I can change the memories I keep of him.

And that's worth fighting for.

No more wallowing, Dira.

It's time to break out from the in between.

For good.

Valemon cranes his neck to look back at me.

He knows. He knows I am ready to work.

The margins are full.

Not all of them, but the first three chapters of the book are darkened by my quickly scratched notes, the pencil marks fattening and fading as the point dulled.

Above, what light filtered through the clouds darkens, and the exposed skin around my eyes burns from the wind and cold.

It's enough. For today, it's enough.

My stomach growls loudly, and I search out the other bear in the distance once more with the binoculars. But he's already loped away. I drop them to my chest and turn back to Valemon.

But he's gone, too.

I turn as I scan the flats, snow beginning to flurry around me. The wind barely whispers, and each drop of a flat flake comes with a soft tap as it lands on the ice.

Valemon's tracks turn in circles, mingled with mine and the other bear's. No clear trajectory points to where he went, and my breath puffs faster through the thin cloth protecting my face from the frost. It's still too soon for sunset, though not much time remains.

Movement catches my eye and I turn.

Not Valemon.

A seal.

I squint.

Against the white ice floe it perches upon, a slender ribbon of dark ice on either side, the seal is vaguely visible. Only slightly darker than the white-blue surface it rests upon, the silver sheen of its wet coat hides it. If not for the quick, heavy breathing and twitching of its head from side to side, I never would have noticed it.

I step forward and raise the binoculars.

But they don't make it to my face before something springs from behind the seal. The large, cumbersome creature perks up instantly and sprints to the edge of the floe, its nose and whiskers bobbing as its flippers drag it forward.

The hulking beast behind it is quick, only inches behind the seal as it dives below the surface.

In an instant, both are gone, and the water is calm.

I drop the binoculars and scan the small opening.

Not even a ripple breaks the surface.

"Valemon?" I call softly, nerves catching up to me. He's protected me all day, setting himself between me and the other bears we've crossed at a distance. I back farther away from the edge of the ice. Firm and thick here, it won't be breaking, but the closer to the edge I remain, the more likely I might become someone's snack. The less time I have to react with the rifle.

With my book and notes held close to my heart, I reach for the rifle, dropping the strap from over my shoulder. My hand shakes as I remove the mitten and fit my finger over the trigger.

"Valemon?"

A white head breaks through the water near the seal's ice floe, black nose pointed toward the ice. With far more grace than I have ever possessed, the bear pushes itself onto the ice, its kill grasped tightly in white jaws. Back feet join the front, and once all four feet touch ground, the bear drags the large, fat seal from the water, a gash in its side and no movement to its muscles.

"Valemon?" I whisper.

The bear turns to me and lifts its nose to the sky, the scar winking.

We stare at each other for a long moment, my mouth hanging

open and his fur dripping.

And then he lowers his head to feast.

CHAPTER 31

I pick at the meal on my plate. I hate to waste what Valemon left for me, but seeing the way the poor thing died has dulled my appetite.

"You have what you need, then?" Valemon nods to the book sitting next to my feet.

I lean my head to the side to stare down at it. "Need for what?"

"To take back to your father. Your observations. Is it enough to convince him?"

I frown. "It's only a day's worth. And what do you think I am trying to convince him of, exactly?"

"That you've been diligent. And you've studied them in a way he never could. What more do you need?"

We saw a mother and her cubs. A female on her own, a male chasing her in what I can only assume is some bizarre mating game. We watched a male stalk another, only to spar for a few wild moments and then break away, each to lick his own wounds. And at the end of it all, I saw a bear hunt. Saw him take down a seal with a quick, silent attack that resulted in my dinner.

It's only a day's worth of notes, but what more could I need? I can say I went out onto the ice. I can tell them I was never charged, that

no bear stalked me or sought me for dinner. But Valemon was with me every step of the way. Do any of my notes count? Or are they a larger body of proof that I might not know what I am talking about?

"I guess it's fine. Why?"

"I think it's time for you to go back to Willoughby."

The small piece of seal fat in my mouth loses all its flavor. I shove the plate across the table, all pretense of eating gone. "Is that what today was about? You're ready to be rid of me?"

"I don't want 'to be rid of you.' But you aren't happy here. I can take you back. In the morning."

My throat constricts. "What do you mean, I'm not happy?"

"Dira, you barely moved from the bed for two days."

"I'm… I was just trying to figure things out." Even if I do desperately want to go home. To eat food I never saw when it was alive, to be warm. The winter solstice has to be close, the candlelight dinners and town feasts not far away. "I do want to stay…I'm not ready to leave you."

"But?"

"I miss my family. I miss Granny Grin and Beren and Willoughby." I could give them all up for him, but I would always long for them. For the taste of Granny's fish stew and the teasing kindness in Beren's voice. "And Linka's supposed to be married soon and… I thought it would be different. I thought I could live without the way they made me feel…"

"But it's not all the time."

I bite my lip as a frown puckers my brow. "I thought I could fix everything. It all made so much sense back in Willoughby, but here, with you, with all of it… Nothing makes sense anymore. Nothing but you and… and the way you make me feel."

There. I said it. I said it in the best way I could without putting him on the spot and begging for the same. But it still rubs bitterly.

"I won't keep you here," he grumbles gruffly.

Regret instantly pierces my heart. He's been here so long, alone. I can't leave him. Pain rips from both sides. I can't have him and Willoughby. Can't have Willoughby and him. I have to choose.

Don't dwell in the in between.

The candlesticks are only on the other side of the room, tucked away where he won't find them.

Can I leave without having a face to remember?

"I'm not ready to leave you."

He stands and stalks toward the darkest corner of the room before turning back to me. "Why?"

"What do you mean 'why?'" I swallow. I know what he's asking. Does he want the words after so much denial?

"You came here for one thing. And I needed you for one thing. We've achieved that as best we can with what's available to us, haven't we? I gave you what you needed, and now—now it's time for you to take it back. Work with them, make the difference we both want."

"But I want you too."

"You can't have us both until we fix this."

I have to fix it. He showed me the way, but he can't do it all on his own.

I think I understand now.

It wars inside him, too.

My insides quaking, I cross to stand in front of him, the warmth of the hearth hot at my side as my toes hover just behind the precipice of darkness. "You deserve happiness, too."

And I step into the dark with him.

With a surprisingly steady hand, I pull the white-fur hood from over his face. My eyes adjust to the shadows, and I close them as I reach up with my lips, finding his.

"Dira." He turns his mouth to whisper against my cheek.

I lean into him, the scratchy stubble on his jaw rough against my soft skin. "If I don't go back, we'll never change anything, will we?"

"No."

"Then I'll go back. I'll try. For both of us." I pull back only slightly and search out his eyes. Not even firelight can reach them. "But only if you'll give me tonight."

The backs of his fingers trace the side of my face, a gentle touch reaching from temple to chin before he slips them beneath my hair to tuck it behind my ear. And then he leans his forehead into mine, both hands in the loose waves unbound from their usual braids. His thumbs cradle my chin, and he breathes deep, his swallow audible.

When his lips press to mine, soft and hesitant, I barely move. My eyes flutter closed, no longer trying to see anything of him. Our breaths mingle between parted lips, trembling ever so slightly as the most chaste of kisses pass between us.

He breaks away first, leaving a tingle on my lips, and I lean forward, begging for him to come back. To not leave it at that. To stay. With only a moment of hesitation, he returns, pressing his mouth to mine more firmly, tasting of snow and warmth and spice and *Valemon*.

Every inch of me warms for him, the room and the darkness and everything but touching him and him touching me fading to the background.

Fear he'll think I'm too young or inexperienced creeps in, but maybe if he sees this is what I want, he won't stop, so I rock away and raise my hands to his wrists, circling them and dragging them down to my hips. As their weight rests there, I loop my own arms around his neck and rise to my toes to kiss him again, cradling his lower lip between both of mine.

With a soft nuzzle, he opens me to him more, and I press my chest into his, every inch of me meeting every inch of him.

His fingers play along the waistband of my pants, pressing the soft fabric of the shirt into my flesh as he pushes and tugs it away enough to find my bare skin beneath.

A shiver rushes through me at the brush of his cool hands on my skin as he wraps them around the back of my waist, fingertips meeting along the lower dip of my spine. No one else has ever touched me like this. Part of me wants to giggle, to pull away and hide my face in embarrassment. Instead, I open up more to him. My tongue dances along the edge of his lips and he presses back.

The softness between thumb and forefinger slides up my waist, over ribs, and I tighten my arms around him, a gasp escaping as he drags his fingers back down. Everything is hot, my skin burning from the inside.

I pull away, my breath panting between us. My chest heaves, dragging in air I didn't know I lacked, and my fingers fumble with the closures of his jacket. They pull apart easily, and I drag the heavy fabric from over broad shoulders, fumbling and failing to yank it over his wrists.

He shakes it away, the material rumpling like a sheet flailing as it dries in the wind, before reaching for me again. He cradles the back of my head with one hand as his mouth dances across mine.

His shirt, the same soft material as mine, yanks from his own waistband easily, and my callused fingers find hot skin beneath. Both hands diving in, I run them up his flat stomach the same way he dragged his over my back, finding the soft hair and tense muscles foreign and exhilarating and delicious. Wandering across them tempts my fingers to inch for more, my body to beg for his. My mind muddles.

"I want," I gasp around his mouth as I tug upward on the hem of the shirt.

He leans away long enough to drag it over his head, and then his skin, warm and hard and *him,* is all mine. But it isn't enough. I can't feel enough. I need more. Want more.

I pluck at my own shirt until he helps it over my head, my skin instantly constricting in the chilly shadows of the room.

But even as my skin prickles, the cold becomes inconsequential against his heat.

We banish the space between us, every inch of my nakedness pressed against his. He caresses parts of me I have never shared with another, urgency humming in each flick of a digit and the scrape of a palm, patience overcoming his movements. I welcome his hands as they explore every inch, my own seeing him through the tips of my fingers.

Our mouths clash again, but only for a brief, hungry moment before his lips find the spot where neck meets shoulder.

I gasp and squirm, pressing in and pulling away at the same time, wanting more. Not sure I will survive it.

His arm tightens around my waist, and lifting me from my feet, he thrusts me into the darkness. The cool plaster wall presses between my shoulder blades as he trails hot lips downward, touching places I didn't know I wanted touched so badly, igniting fires I didn't know could be ignited.

My body rocks into him, craving more, demanding more, my fingernails digging into the hard muscle of his shoulders.

"Please, Valemon. Please," I whimper, knowing exactly what I beg for, but having no idea how to grasp it.

His lips find mine once more, ours mouths dancing, taking, needing, pleading.

"Are you sure?" He breaks away, his forehead rolling against mine, his arm tightening around me.

I cradle his cheeks in the palms of my hands, my lips a breath from touching his. "Please. You are all I want."

"I don't have to go right away," I whisper into the darkness.

Our legs still tangle beneath the bed coverings, the cold seeping between us after the heat wore off. I pull the quilt tighter over my shoulder and turn to him.

Light hair falls over his shoulders like moonlight, the rest of him hidden in shadow. I will my eyes to adjust to the dark, to take him in, see without the need of daylight, a candle, the glow of a fire. Left untended, the hearth darkened to little more than an orange smolder between blackened husks of wood. It's a lousy light.

And only the silhouettes and contours and penumbra of his face stare back.

Valemon's hand lifts between us, his thumb resting on my chin. The pad strokes down once lazily before moving to lie between us, the back of his hand resting against mine. But he makes no move to grab it, to hold on. "If you stay here, you'll never go back. And it will never end."

I swallow. "I could leave, and it would never end, anyway. What if my father doesn't care? Or doesn't believe me? I could fail. And then—"

"Don't let what we had tonight keep you from reaching your goals."

His words are like a punch straight to my gut. My lungs don't seem to fill completely, each breath shallow and unfulfilling. Was this only a goodbye for him? A way to place it all on me? I knew that's how it would work, but his words make it sound so final.

Does he not want me anymore? Want me to come back? Want me to *stay?*

I fight for something to say, a way to clarify. But as my mind trips over itself, his breathing evens out, long and low.

I've never felt closer to anyone before, and yet we might not be inches away. It feels farther. An arm's length. A kilometer. A whole handful of lifetimes. By refusing to touch me again, he forces me to become a victim to the exquisite agony of our circumstances. I want him to beg me to stay. To never want to be apart. And I could give it up, that slip of an impossible dream I can make Willoughby change. I could give it up easily for the sure thing. So many others have done it. Will do it. How many village girls marry men from the south and go to live in lands I've never seen? How many men follow their loves back to Willoughby after the summer trading season?

More than I can count. They've left their families and futures and dreams for the adventure of life, of love.

I could do it too.

I could give up on my family once and for all and pledge to be happy here with him forever. It's easy. Risk free. I could let go of

Willoughby and follow him out onto the ice to watch the polar bears every morning. And every evening, we could return and have nights like this one. Nights that leave me sore and aching and wanting all at the same time. We could have a lifetime of days like today. I could do it for him.

I could leave things like this, gripping the three words I so desperately want to release, to wake him with, behind tight lips. A broken curse would be as good as a broken heart to the man who wants this double life.

I stare into the darkness, finding the shadow of his chest moving beneath my quilt.

We could have a lifetime together.

My throat constricts.

I could have a lifetime with him. But then mine would be over, and he would be left without me.

Is that why I have to go? Why I have to try?

If this doesn't work, he curses me as well.

Because the loss of Valemon will be more than my heart can take.

Don't dwell in the in between.

I have to leave him, don't I?

And I've never even seen his face.

I deserve to know what I'm giving up, don't I? I've respected the boundary he erected, but I don't want a life of mourning fantasies. I want to own every aspect of my heartbreak, including the memory of his face.

The candles are still hidden between the mattress and the wall.

Shifting slowly, I reach under the pillow and inch my fingers between the plaster and bedframe until they brush soft tallow. My breath held, I slip from the bed, my treasure gripped in my fist.

The chime candles are barely longer than my palm. I hold one out over the dying glow of the fire and stare at the wick until it takes flame. The light is small, and it flickers as a shaky breath whispers through my nostrils. But it will be enough to reveal him. Enough for me to see each of his features before I go.

Breath held, I step forward.

The flame's halo brushes against his chest first. Plays along the sprinkling of chest hair I ran my fingers through earlier. The hard muscle beneath, sculpted and broad. Red marks run down them, exactly the same distance apart as my nails. Scratches I put there when I was half out of my mind for him. I raise my arm, and the lick of fire dances, twisting and twitching to its own silent song.

I hesitate. But just for the briefest of moments.

He is perfection.

A strong jaw. A square cleft chin. Thick, dark lashes spread across high cheekbones. Hair the color of freshly fallen snow, just like the bear he becomes. Lips I know as well as I know my own, soft and curved down in a bit of a frown.

I lean over him, my eyes roving over every exposed inch. The strong column of his neck, the well-defined muscles I've glimpsed in the *V* of the shirt collar before he stepped back into darkness. His cheek wears the only fault, a long, slashing scar just below his eye.

But even it is perfection.

I thought I would find a scarred man desperate to hide himself.

Instead, I find a fairy-tale prince.

A king.

A lone tear escapes, rolling down my face. Why would he hide from me?

I hastily swipe it away.

But the movement is enough to shake the candle held in my other hand, and a drip of molten wax plunges down.

Horror grips me and the world momentarily stops as I helplessly watch it leap toward his cheek. It lands, marksmanship perfect. The wax hits just below the scar, and I hold my breath.

Maybe he didn't notice it. Maybe he's deep enough asleep, I can wipe it away.

But that scenario abandons me as his eyes fly open.

The flicker of light glows in his dark eyes as the pupils narrow to pinpoints.

"What have you done?" he whispers, pain breaking his voice. He swipes at the drop of cooled tallow as he swings his legs off the bed and tosses my quilt to the ground.

I stumble away as he pushes past. But he whirls around, towering over me, his chest nearly pressed into mine.

Hot wax splashes onto my hand as I flinch, a wince pulling my lips back. Words don't work their way up my throat, and I can only stare into his eyes, my focus bouncing from one to the other.

"How could you, Dira? We were so close. How could you?"

What does he mean? Why is he so angry? It doesn't change anything. "Valemon, I—"

He backs away, stooping to snatch up his boots and the white fur coat laying in a heap next to them.

Without a backwards glance, he leaves me.

"Wait," I say, but it slips out as barely a murmur. "Wait!" I choke, scrambling for my own clothes. My pants lie in a heap beside the footlocker, my shirt and jacket in the far corner. My hands tremble as they pull on thick socks, as a second layer of pants covers the lighter ones I wore during the unsatisfactory dinner. I drop the lace to my boot twice before I am able to thread it through its other end. I dress the rest of the way as I sprint down the stairs.

His tracks are easy to follow in the snow. New hasn't fallen in days, and what is left has grown crunchy and brittle. I fit my feet into his boot tracks, the snowshoes forgotten in the room, following the long strides with an awkward hop. Was he running?

Out through the wall and onto the ice, I follow. A jagged landscape of ice and snow spreads out before me, a world glowing with a brightness that comes just before daybreak. Valemon's tracks lope between sculptures hewn by wind and flakes, and I cut and swerve to follow them. My breath puffs heavily, drying my throat. I run until my muscles won't run anymore, my lungs too tired to drag in an ounce more of the frigid air. My legs ache and my throat burns, but I force myself forward. If I don't catch up to him, will I ever see him again? I have to tell him. I have to explain. I just wanted to see him once before I returned home.

I wanted to remember him.

As the first ribbon of light settles over the horizon, I can make out the building in the distance. A high roof with twin windmills balanced on its apex. It's little more than a dot that bounces as I trudge forward on unsteady feet.

Granny Grin's house.

Willoughby.

Home.

The pain and cold melt away, and I run faster and faster, no longer seeing Valemon's footprints as I speed past. After all this time, I'm home.

Granny Grin will be inside. And she'll know how to fix this, how to fix all of it.

I skid to a stop in front of her door.

His footsteps lead right inside, the pattern of his boot soles still visible. Why would he come here? Why Granny Grin's?

I glance over my shoulder at the beaming sunset.

He came to Granny Grin's as a man.

My heart thumps a rapid tattoo of elation.

The curse is broken.

I broke the curse.

CHAPTER 32

My heart pounds.

I lift my hand to the door, but…

Something isn't right. Weight drags my arm down, and my muscles pull oddly. I can't raise it.

I glance down, but instead of my ice-covered boots staring up at me, I find large, white paws, turned slightly inward, tipped with sharp black claws.

My gasp comes out a growl and I stumble backwards. Bones bend and muscles flex in ways I don't recognize, heavy and clunky and not mine. Because they aren't mine. How did this happen?

What have you done?

The words ring through my mind like a bell. And ring and ring and ring.

With a controlled yank, the door opens, and Granny Grin hobbles outside, Sparrow perched on her shoulder. He bobs as she places knobby fists on her hips. "It's going to be a tight squeeze, but we'd best get you inside before anyone sees you, girlie."

I blink at her.

She doesn't seem surprised by my shape, the sheer size of me. But then, when has Granny ever been surprised by anything?

With astounding ease, I balance myself on the four wide paws and amble for the door. She backs away, giving me access.

Candles dimly light the inside, and hunched over the table, hands fisted in pure white hair, sits Valemon. He doesn't turn to acknowledge me and defeat drips off his edges like melt from icicles.

"Make yourself as comfortable as you can," Granny says as she pushes the door closed. She bustles around me to the hearth and uses the edge of her apron to cover her hand as she lifts a kettle from over the flames. Not a glance is tossed my way as she pours the bubbling water into two cups on the table.

She pushes one toward Valemon and sits down heavily.

"You have to give it back to me, Peregrine," he says.

Peregrine. A name he mentioned before. Peregrine. Granny Grin. I should have put the two together. But why would I? She's old, old as dirt, but *that* old? No, she couldn't be.

"I can't do that. You knew the price of someone discovering your true identity, Val. I never thought we'd still be working through this all these years later, but…" She shrugs and wags a finger at him. "Should have been more careful."

"More careful? More careful?" he demands. "She caught me while I was sleeping."

"Should have kept your distance, then." Sparrow hops off her shoulder and gallops across the table for the honey pot. Butting it squarely with the top of his head, he nudges it back to her with loud scratches and scrapes, his nails tapping on the table.

"You told me I couldn't do it on my own. You told me I had to work with someone else, that bearing it on my own would doom me.

Well, Peregrine, you can't work with others from a distance."

Granny Grin doesn't look at him. Instead, she tracks her hand as the honey spoon dips into the small pot and then releases a stream of golden syrup into her stone mug. "There's no sense arguing over it now. It's done. You're released. Go live out your days." She turns to me. Soft regret paints her wrinkled face. "It's Dira's turn to take up the cause."

The cause? What cause? I open my mouth, but all that comes out is a sneeze-like snuff.

Valemon shoves his chair back. The legs scrape against the wood floor, and it nearly tips over before it rocks back on all fours. "You know I can't do that, Peregrine."

She sips her steaming tea slowly. "And why not?"

"You. Know. Why," he says through gritted teeth. But he still won't look at me.

He avoids my eyes, his own locked on her. Is he afraid to look at me? Disgusted? Or just too angry?

"It was a bargain you welcomed."

"Until I really understood it! I lost everything once. And now that I finally found it, I'm losing it all over again."

Am I it? Am I everything?

Why is this happening to me?

"Magic always comes with a price, Valemon." But her eyes meet mine, not his.

I sink down onto the floor. I didn't ask for any of this. I didn't want it. And yet here I am, caught between the polar bear king and the witch who cursed him.

I shouldn't be the price. And yet, it seems to be what I have to pay for everything I've done.

I can't leave, but I don't want to be here anymore.

This place is a cage.

Granny Grin's cottage was always my refuge, but now the ceiling looms too low, the walls closing in. The heat from the hearth clogs my throat, sticking in my nose, and makes my skin crawl. Each whir of the windmills above is like nails dragging down tightly pulled fabric.

And after hours, Valemon still won't look at me. He drinks himself into a quiet, brooding stupor, finishing off a jug of berry brandy from Granny Grin's stores, placed in front of him when talking no longer came, and only silence fell over her home.

Granny putters around the hearth and her worktable, grinding the herbs hanging from the rafters with her mortar and pestle before shaking them into glass jars. The scents waft strong and pungent my way, far stronger than I remember them ever smelling before. My nose twitches.

"It's almost time," she croons softly when the silence grows so thick it hurts.

I turn my eyes to her, but she isn't looking at me. Her gaze bores onto Valemon's back, still hunched over the table. A hand curls around a stone cup, the cup's lip stained red.

"I'll leave you two alone." She plods over to the door of her bedroom with her uneven gait, casting a glance over her shoulder. Our gazes meet, and her expression turns to one of sadness and worry. "Come, Sparrow."

The raven slips through the open door on spread wings, and she closes the door, clicking it shut.

A few moments pass before the tingling starts, rushing over my skin like a foamy wave, and then it's gone.

The intense smells dull, the heat cools. I sigh with relief, and my own voice echoes in my ears. "I'm sorry," I murmur as I push myself up off the floor. Dropping a hand onto the back of one of the chairs, I hover there, waiting for some indication that he would welcome me sitting with him. Or allow it, at least.

Valemon stiffens at the sound and slowly turns. Red burns the rims of his eyes, and they sparkle blearily in the dreary light.

His white-gold brows come together, and his head dips to one side. "Why are you sorry? It's my fault you're… like this."

Hollowness spreads through my chest, and I shake my head. "No. I can't let you blame yourself when it was me. It was all me. I flout the rules all the time, and this time…" I swallow. "This is just the first time it caught up to me." My lungs fill, and I let the breath out slowly, shakily. "I asked, and you told me no. I should have respected that. I knew I should have, but I was scared… I was scared of what I was feeling for you and I thought…" I can't find the words now, even though they take up most of the space on my tongue. They hang heavy off the end of it, but I can't shake them loose. "I just wanted to see you before you left. I wanted to be able to remember you as you."

"We were so close, Dira. Why couldn't you just let things be?" Emotion thickens his voice.

"You didn't tell me I couldn't!" It comes out an accusation. Regret instantly consumes me.

"How could I? You're so obsessed with the bears and getting close to them. The moment I told you it could be yours, you would have fought to take it from me. It would have driven you mad until you could possess it, and you wouldn't have listened to any of the consequences. Dira, you are the most stubborn and forceful—you wouldn't have let it go and—and it isn't your burden, shouldn't *be* your burden to bear. It should still be mine." His voice breaks.

I open my mouth, but then shut it again. Arguing would be pointless because he's right. When I first came to him, I would have been desperate to see the world as one of the bears. To know firsthand where they went, how they think, fight, dream, feel. I would have taken it for myself without a second thought and…

"Then take it back," I whisper. "You can have it if it means so much to you. You can go back to living like a recluse and—and I'll leave you alone." My heart aches just suggesting it.

He spins his empty cup on the tabletop, the stone whirring softly against the wood. "I can never have it back. And to break it, people who don't know about the curse have to spare you, but they can never know it's you—"

Hope sparks. "But I already did that. I spared you!" Something was wrong with the spell. Granny Grin will have to try to fix it.

"No, you didn't shoot. But the others didn't follow. It can't be one person, Dira. It has to be more. Minds have to be changed. It's all well and good to have one person show a little sympathy for a fellow living being. One person can change the world, but not alone."

He leans back in the chair, slumping down against the wood backing. "Can't you see? It's a delicate balance. *She*" —he waves his hand toward Granny Grin's closed door— "made sure there was no easy way out for me. She gave me exactly what I deserved and ensured there was no opportunity for me to get out of it unscathed. She knew me well enough to know exactly how to turn the knife, to gut me when it really mattered. And now she's done just that."

A sneer lifts his top lip, but it doesn't last long. He threads his hands through his hair and bows over the table, shoulders hunching.

The ache in my chest spreads and my vision wavers. "I thought being a bear was what you wanted—" My breath catches.

He shakes his head. "I wanted the punishment. And she knew I would never let anyone else take over my burden. She knew I couldn't get close to anyone without running this risk—and she was right. The first time I let my guard down, this happened."

"But you said there were others."

He laughs bitterly. "I didn't want you to believe I was a lonely asshole. There were others. But barely. An hour on the ice. A day in a hunting lodge. None of them got to know me, got close enough to see more than an animal they simply didn't want to kill. You were the first to show more than a glimpse of that, and I let you get too close because I got too hopeful."

He grips the cup in his hand, winds his arm back, and lets it fly into the hearth. The logs crack into one another, sparks flying as alcohol hits flame, and the vessel bounces out onto the stone floor, scattering ash with it. And then he sinks back into the chair, melting into it like warmed wax.

"How do we fix it?" I murmur as I slide into a chair as far away from him as I can get. Not because I don't want to be right there, my hand wrapped around his palm, my heartbeat calming his. But because I don't think he wants me anywhere near him. He needs me to stay away, to let his heart break.

Mine only feels numb. Lifeless. None of this feels real, a strange, heavy dream that I can still wake from.

"How do we fix it?" He snorts. "I don't know. I don't know how we make any of this right. I spent more than a hundred years looking for the answer, and I only just found it. Now you… you have to start all over. And there is nothing I can do to help you."

Is that a tear that slides down his cheek, dripping into the shadow of his scar?

My chest squeezes. "Why? You could—"

His head snaps up to nail me with an icy stare. "I could what? Walk into the center of Willoughby, a stranger, and ask them not to shoot the bears anymore? We were grasping at straws that you, one of their own, would be able to change a few minds. They have no reason to listen to me."

"But—"

"It could take me years to build up their trust, and that's if Peregrine doesn't sabotage my efforts. And what will you do until that can happen? Hide out in front of her hearth all day? Starve while you wait for the moon to rise so you can seek out a few pitiful hours with her as your only companion? You have to forget about me and move on. Find someone else who has the power to make the changes you need."

"But I love you."

The words hit the floor, heavy. Uncatchable. He shifts his gaze away and presses his fingers into his eyes.

"We—we can just go back to Monroe. We'll pretend nothing's changed. I'll—" I swallow painfully. I sound every bit like the child I feel myself to be. Like my words can fix everything, even though my actions have made it so I can't. "I'll hunt as you did. Come back to you every night. We'll have each other and—"

"For a blip. A second of your long, miserable, lonely life. I will die, Dira. Don't you understand that? I will shrivel up right before your eyes and die. You'll watch as I become a husk of a man. And then you will be alone. For how long? Decades? A century like I was? No one will remember you except for Peregrine and that musty old brush she calls a bird. You will lose your family forever. I destroy everything I love, Dira, and I've already done enough to destroy you. But if you find someone else, if you play this game smarter than I did, you might find a way to have everything I just lost."

CHAPTER 33

He left me.

He left my words like stones on the floor, heavy and burdensome.

And he walked out of Granny Grin's cottage.

Now I stare at the door standing open, the breeze off the sea tempting it into a sorrowful sway. It swings back and forth with eerie creaks, none strong enough to close it or open it forward. Instead, it whines pitifully.

He thought he destroyed me before, but it isn't until he leaves me behind that I break completely.

Granny Grin returns after a few moments—or was it longer?—Sparrow perched on her shoulder. She stands before me and cups my tear-streaked cheeks with her papery hands, the bones as slender and brittle as her bird's. "I always knew this would be where we ended up some day," she murmurs. "When your parents sought balance and there you were, I knew you were destined for this."

She leans forward and presses a kiss to my forehead, the heavy scent of the herbs still clinging to her.

Sparrow gracefully hops from her shoulder as she backs away, taking up his favorite perch on the back of a chair.

"My parents?"

She puttered away to her prep space, an old, worn table on long legs, a shelf cluttered with bottles and pots below.

"Which will it be? Nice warm tea? Or something stronger?"

I only stare at her numbly.

"Oh, fine, fine. Yes, they came to me begging for balance. They already had one son and two daughters. They had some vision in their mind about the way family should be. Oh, don't look at me like that. All parents do it—they conjure up the perfect image based on their own wants. Anyway." She waves a hand over her head as she bends down to look at her stock of leaves. "I told them that was easy enough. Nature always prefers balance. I gave them a candle, some words to mutter, and sent them on their way. They were surprised when you came along, that's for sure. But I knew."

A finger taps her temple, and she turns a twinkling eye to me. "You were brought to us for something more."

Did she suspect this would be my fate all along? And she let it happen? A frown pulls at the muscles in my face. She pushed me toward this, didn't she? The night of the ball?

She chuckles softly at my expression and goes about filling the kettle with ice melt. But before she sits down to wait for it to boil, she grabs a bottle by the neck and a stone cup from a cupboard. "We have some rules to discuss."

"Valemon told me," I grumble and slump back in my chair. I want to hurl something at her, but there isn't anything close enough.

"Yes, well, I am sure he did. But I should make them perfectly clear. The magic will only wear off when the town stands in defense of you. But they can't know it's you. I suppose they can have… What do you call it? Thoughts? Inklings? But they can't know for sure. Your true form, your identity, who you *really* are, must be hidden just as Valemon hid his from you. I honestly thought that big oaf would have it all worked out *years* ago; I couldn't have him convincing all the girls who followed him around like puppies to do it for him. But he went brooding out in the old military installation, instead, so it was a stupid safeguard, wasn't it? Well, it was rather brilliant, but it backfired just a bit, don't you think?" She barked a laugh. "*But* since you're here, among people who all know you so well… I would venture a guess that you should keep that voice of yours under wraps, too. Unless you want to pass the curse around all willy-nilly. In that case, I suggest revealing yourself only to your worst enemy. Although, I don't think Landry will take too kindly to you turning his wife into a polar bear."

"So I can't even talk to anyone?" I demand, fresh indignation bubbling up.

"You can talk to anyone you want. But if they know it's you by your voice, they won't be able to help you out of this little predicament you threw yourself into. If they tell anyone else? Those become exempt, as well. And if they see your face as both human and bear as you saw him, well… Poof. You're free. But they won't be."

"You think—you think I got myself into this? You have to be joking. This is all your fault. Why did you have to put a curse on anyone? What kind of monster does that?" I stand whirling on her. My granny, the one person I thought I could always trust. Fair and kind and wise. A witch who turns people into bears for a hundred years.

Her lips purse, a thousand lines deepening around it. "I was young. Headstrong. In love. And heartbroken. At least I thought I was." Her eyes soften around the edges as her lips tilt up. "He looks just as I remember him. Except for the hair, of course." She nods up at me. "It used to be dark, you know. Almost black."

I thread my hand through my own hair, pulling a few strands from my braid in front of my eyes.

It shines just as white as his. My dark hair, stark as snow. I drop it.

"You were in love with Valemon?" Something like disgust or maybe jealousy settles in the pit of my stomach.

"Yes, of course, Valemon." She sputters. "Is that so hard to believe? I had hoped he would take to me in the same way. But he never saw me, *really* saw me. He was too blinded by his need for control, for power. When he showed up outside my cottage—this cottage—all of my dreams seemed to be falling into place. There he was; he finally wanted me for more than—Well. I thought he came to me to settle down. To start a life. But no, he was too focused on the bears. On being the exalted leader. I thought I was getting a proposal, and instead, I got asked for help in ending a perceived struggle with wild animals.

"So, I cursed him." She shrugs. "An impossible curse. One I instantly regretted. There was no way for me to reverse it; I'd made sure of it. But regret followed. Swift and harsh. And I bound myself to it, so I have to see it to its bitter end." She visibly deflates.

"I was cruel, making him into a thing he hated. When I finally saw that, it was too late. Let it be a lesson to you when I am finally gone from this place and you take up my work."

My eyebrows shoot up. "Take up your work?"

"Yes, all of this." She raises her hands and her gaze to the ceiling. "Someone has to take care of all those nitwits in the village. You don't think they can brew their own teas or mix their medicines themselves, do you?" Her eyes twinkle when they fall back on me. "Don't worry,

I've kept excellent notes. My grimoires are quite extensive."

"That's what you think? That I'll somehow be your successor?" I know she wants me to feel sympathy for her, but I can't. And the last thing I want is to take up where she left off.

"You're a bright girl, Dira. Not as soft or disciplined as your sisters. But you have the heart. And the smarts." She leans forward. "I've always known you would outlive me. Let's just get it done soon, eh?"

Dawn is nearly on the horizon, and I've watched the door, eyes bleary and refusing sleep, but it never opens. Not even the wind knocked it open after I latched it. I thought he would be back. Be by my side when the change happened again. My whole chest hurts from the pain of wanting him and his complete abandonment.

I slump across the table, my cheek pressed against the wood. "What am I supposed to do, Granny?"

She rocks slowly in the chair next to the hearth, her eyes drooping and the knitting folded across her lap no further along than when she sat down.

"If I stay in Willoughby, the patrol will know. There's no hiding bear tracks in the snow. So where am I supposed to go? How do I figure this out if I have to stay away?"

Granny Grin's eyes drift closed, but her lips fall apart. "You're a clever thing. You stay here with me, just know your surroundings and take the proper precautions. That brother of yours still comes around often. More often now that you up and died." Her eyelids slit open as she cackles, a twinkle lighting in her eyes. "You best be on your way. The curse won't break if you sit here all day moping."

I don't want to stay with her, but what choice do I have? So I nod and take to my feet, but stop at the door to look back at her. She smiles reassuringly, and the tingling starts running up my fingers, into my shoulder, and down to my toes. Like a limb regaining its lost feeling, the sensation sweeps over me, nearly painful, yet not, and then it's gone, the front room of the cottage unbearably hot and full of pungent scents.

Granny Grin waves me on, balancing her hands on either side of the rocker to hoist herself to a stand. And as I step out into the first grey cast of morning light on four legs, the door shuts soundly behind me.

Few will be up this early, especially at this time of year. As the longest day nears, the people of Willoughby become shut-ins. They don't travel out onto the ice unless it's critical to hunt. As the cold harshens further, Mom will trade whatever reserves we have for those we don't. She'll promise puppies from her spring litters in exchange for fresh meat, training for material goods. And Dad will continue to collect his stipend as long as he keeps the office fire burning for emergencies.

I stare toward the pointed roofs, brightly colored walls, and churning windmills. It's doubtful I will run into anyone. I keep to the edge of the ice, heading southeast where the spit thickens and the dunes rise over the frozen ocean waters.

Of everyone in town, I can only think of one person who will hesitate to shoot anything—even a polar bear.

Beren's house lays the farthest from anyone, and delicious smells waft from it on the wind. Fish. The remnants of crabs. Are those clams? Oysters? I follow my nose despite having no desire to eat.

The little house sits atop the snow-covered dunes, the windows dark and the boat pulled up onto the deck. White encrusts every surface, and the wind shoves the snow right up under the windows in heavy drifts, and a lone, shallow set of snowshoe tracks winds around to the door.

Is Linka there? Are those his footsteps leading up to the lone entrance? Or did Linka choose Liddet? I scan the seams of the house, looking for signs of my twin's workmanship. It's there in the even wooden grooves, the careful symmetry of the windows. Was it while they toiled to construct the cabin that he and our best friend drew close? Or was it before and construction was just an excuse to spend more time together? Why the secrecy? Why from me? There may never be an opportunity to ask.

I settle in the snow and stare up at the deck, looking for some sign of Beren. Imagining him walking out onto the wood planks and catching sight of me is an easy fantasy to construct. His hair would be sticking out wildly and his face scruffy from not shaving in a few days. Bleary eyes would grow wide as his gaze fell on me and he would just stare. Unmoving.

Beren would never reach for a rifle and never take aim because of everyone. He is the only one who believed me about the day his mother died. He accepted my tale of a bear who came to save me and a tragic accident. And maybe not because he wanted to, but because he loved me and knew how hurt I was that no one else believed me. He might not have ever been in love with me in a way we could have made each other happy, but he loves me nonetheless, and he'd never cross the line.

Loved.

I have to remember they all think me dead. It could change things. Change them.

But if anyone will stay his hand against me, it's Beren.

Sinking down, I rest my head on my paws. My eyes drift closed.

I'll just wait here for a few moments. Just until the sun warms my back. And then I'll go. I shouldn't risk it. Not yet.

A change in scent wakes me.

I lift my head and turn it into the wind.

Familiar. Like gun oil and wood smoke.

Like Linka.

Scrambling to my feet, I lift my nose to the sky and sniff again. There's also sweat and honey ale and old socks.

No doubt about it. Linka. And based on the direction the wind blows, he's close.

I'm exposed out here on the beach, but if I can get to the willow shrubs, they will offer some protection, if not as much as they do in the summer when their leaves are fat and full. Swiftly, I put as much distance as I can between myself and the cabin, and duck down behind the spindly branches. Snow covers most of the sand, and I lay against it, flattening down and taking long, steady breaths.

Seconds later, Linka's fur-lined parka appears, and he bounds up the steps. A knock on the door follows, and then only murmurs I can't make out.

"What do you mean there was a polar bear out here?" Linka's booming voice carries.

"…there on the beach." Beren's words grow louder, and a second pair of boots thump on the wood. He must have exited to point out my sleeping spot.

"It just slept?"

"Yeah. It took off into the willow reeds a few minutes ago. Must have heard you coming."

Heavy footsteps thud against the wooden stairs before crunching into the snow. Through the branches, I can make out Linka's legs, his large, scuffed boots, but the sticks obscure most of him. But, oh, do I smell him.

"I should let Dad know—" Those large boots turn in the snow, but abruptly stop, Beren's much smaller boots on the other side of him.

"Why? What does that help?" Beren asks sharply.

"There's a bear on the loose. It could be the same one that got Dira."

"I thought we agreed Dira's still out there, Linka." His voice softens on my brother's name. "You can't let yourself believe a bear killed her; she never would have allowed it."

"It's been more than a month, Beren. If she were still alive, we would have seen some sign. She would have made her presence known. My father's right. I have to… I have to believe she's gone, Beren. So I can move on."

"Fine. Do what you need to do to move on. But I still believe she's out there. Because I know her. And so do you." His voice softens with tenderness. "But even if you did kill another bear, what good would it do? Nothing can bring her back."

"It couldn't hurt anyone else," Linka grumbles and then sniffs loudly. "It couldn't hurt you."

"I'm fine, Linka. You need to stop coming out here to check on me. Now dry your tears. We'll find her… She's stubborn. She probably just wants to teach us all a lesson. When spring awakens, she'll be back.

She'll come roaring in here and set your dad and Landry to shame."

A smile tugs at my heart, but the silence stretches. I wish I could see them.

"I mean it, Linka. You can't keep doing this." Beren's comment ends on a sigh, and his feet peddle backward.

"I needed to see you," Linka says, bashfulness present in his voice.

So they still hide? Linka still plans a wedding, and Beren huddles on the edge of town? Alone?

"Why?" Beren asks, steel in his voice. "Why keep torturing both of us?"

"I love you."

"If you loved me, you would break it off with Liddet." Each word is clipped, exasperated. Anger flies off him. Soft-spoken, quiet Beren.

"But I love her too. And with her parents gone, she's already lost so much—" Whatever Linka was going to say remains unsaid. "I'm sorry, I didn't mean—"

Beren's boots turn away, carrying him from where I rest in the willow shrub branches. "It's fine, Linka. I'm used to being alone. Now stop coming around." His voice carries back to me as he walks away.

Linka stays, boots pointed away as Beren's footsteps fade.

Sand and ice crunch beneath his feet as he shuffles his toes back to me. I can just make out the scruff of his beard as he stoops to look into the tangled brambles, but I don't catch his eyes. Does he see me? Stare right back?

Quietly, he leaves.

I guess I'll never know.

Chapter 34

Walking the streets of Willoughby is easy when you know the patrols.

When you know their patterns, their schedule.

It's easy when winter comes in and the other polar bears leave, most of the men abandoning their posts for the warmth of their homes and a chance to fill their stores with whatever meat their rifles find. I stick to the shadows nonetheless, glancing around corners before stepping into the next snowdrift or slushy puddle of mud.

Most lamps in the windows were extinguished long before, but a few still offer enough light to peek inside. I stop outside my parents' house the longest, peering in through the open shutters.

Everything is exactly as I remember it, yet the warmth doesn't remain. Sure, there is a fire roaring in the fireplace and blankets draped across the couch. But Mom sits at the table in the back, alone, polishing the knives, and Dad stares off into the distance from his chair. Age droops from his once ruddy features. Expression vacant and cheeks gaunt under his beard.

The only other time I remember him looking so defeated was when his father died. For days, no light shone in his eyes, and his face

crumpled as he held the torch to the pyre. And the only one recently dead is me.

Did I do that? Did I turn my father into a husk of himself? Snuff out the light?

No, he would never mourn for me, not like that. Maybe there would be a tear for show. But he's strong. And resilient. I'm only exasperating and extra. A drain on his time and patience. Now that I know they sought balance from Granny Grin, the ache of it all doubles.

But part of me still wants to barge in and show him I'm alive. To beg his forgiveness and never leave.

My fingers go to the necklace around my throat, and I worry the tiny beads. Morning will eventually come, though, and then I will no longer be me. Will the heartbreak disappear as he sees nothing but the monster he's hated all his life? Or will his heart break all over again?

Banging on the door won't fix anything. Marching through it even less. And if Granny Grin is right, revealing myself will only complicate things. I'd have no way of undoing this thing then.

But would that be so bad? I could go back to Monroe and find Valemon. I can make him believe I would rather have him than anything else. Even if it means spending a thousand years alone afterward. I crave our little room, the ugly hearth that somehow manages to carry the smoke outside. Living each day like the one he took me to find the polar bears out on the ice would be the best kind of life. We would be happy. I know we would.

Footsteps crunch behind me, and I quickly sidestep into the darkness and leap for cover. The necklace comes loose and falls out of my hand, bouncing off the front of my parka, and dropping into the snow. I bolt into the shadows and peek around the corner as Linka sidles up to the front door. But he stops abruptly and stares down at the spot I just occupied. Kneeling, he inspects the darkened footprint I left in the icy snow, tracing it with his finger.

I hold my breath as he glances over his shoulder, stands with the necklace in hand, and then swivels around. But the darkness covers my tracks, and he stares off in the wrong direction.

"I expected you back ages ago," Granny Grin says from her rocking chair. Wooden needles clack as they weave together thick, springy, musk ox yarn.

"I'm sorry."

The rocking chair creaks forward and groans as she tilts back. "No need to apologize to me. I just want to ensure you're being careful. You always act first and think later."

"What? No, I don't."

A soft chuckle erupts from her chest, growing louder and more forceful as she throws back her head. "Oh, Dira." She sighs, but a few more laughs escape. "I know you mean well, but your penchant for danger is well-known and widely accepted. Well, maybe not accepted." Her head bobs from side to side. "Expected, maybe. How do you think you always end up in these troublesome situations? Chased by a mother bear? Letting bears run loose through the town? Turned into a *bear?*"

I cross my arms over my chest and glare down at her. "I don't—" My mouth snaps closed.

She drops her hands and knitting to her lap as she offers up a withering stare. "Where were you?"

"I came from my parents' house." I give her my back and search for a clean bowl in the cabinet as an image of Linka examining my boot print next to the window and collecting the beads replays in my mind. "But don't worry, no one saw me."

"And before that?"

"Beren's. He saw me… the bear, but that was it. He doesn't know… He doesn't know I'm me." Steaming clam stew spills into the bowl from the ladle, the broth heavily scented with thyme and onion.

She breathes in deeply, her chest puffing out, and then lets it out in a huff. "That's good. That's very good. That boy could be the one, Dira. Just don't do anything stupid. Our young man's hopes are riding on you breaking this thing, after all. And more importantly, so are mine. These bones weren't made to last more than a hundred years."

I drop down into one of the dining chairs and sprawl out across the top of the table, my head propped in one hand, the other lazily stirring my dinner. "Why are you so eager to die? In half of your fairy tales, the characters wanted immortal life."

"The villains, you mean. Like me?" She makes a disgusted noise. "I stopped wanting to be one of those generations ago. I'm tired. Ready to put these old bones to rest."

"I'm tired too." The soup doesn't remedy that, and despite the appealing aroma, once it's in my mouth, the flavor turns to nothingness. I shove the bowl away and cast a look up into the loft. Mostly used for storage. Last time I was up there it was covered in dust and mouse nests. But there were also piles of old quilts, a dozen knit blankets, even the odd pillow. If I burrow under them all, maybe this will all go away.

"Oh, no, you can't be going up there. When you turn, you'll bring the whole place crashing down under all that weight." She drops her knitting into the basket at her feet and heaves herself out of the chair.

It rocks heavily backward, the wood knocking into the wall behind it, and Sparrow spreads his wings to keep his balance atop his armrest perch. "We'll have to make you a pallet on the floor."

I follow her into the back room where her own bed sits, hovering in the doorway as she throws open a chest and rifles through its depths. She passes me a flat feather pillow, and then a bundle of blankets.

"You'll probably be warmest by the fire."

I nod. "Do you want me to clean your cottage for you, too? See to all of your cooking?"

She lifts a thin eyebrow in question.

"Like your tale of the little cinder girl?"

She throws back her head and cackles. "She was kind and generous, timid and quiet."

"So?"

"You are none of those things."

My jaw drops. "You don't think I am kind? Or generous?"

"I think you've learned to be. Some time away has done you good, Dira Cloon." She reaches up to pat my cheek. "It's good to see what was lurking beneath all that pent-up frustration and ambition."

Defensiveness settles in and I stiffen. "What's wrong with those things?"

"Nothing, girl. Nothing at all. So long as the wearer knows her true self without them. It took you a while to find yours, but I do believe you've got it now. Don't hide who you are. And don't try to be something you aren't just for the attention of others. Embrace what makes you you. What makes you happy."

She shuffles back to her bedroom door, and once Sparrow flaps through, she pulls the door shut with a click.

What would make me happy? What kind of question is that?

And yet...

I don't know.

I spread one of the blankets out across the floor and toss the pillow down on top of it. My brow knits as I toe off my boots, and as I pull the second blanket over my shoulders, an ache sets in.

Because even now, after all of this, what I want is days on the ice.

And nights with Valemon.

CHAPTER 35

Watching Beren feels like a lie. And I've been living that lie for a week.

I once thought we would spend all of our lives together, and now I wait here hoping he can give me something far more: my life with someone else.

Why do I always find myself asking so much of him? When he asks so little of me?

I should feel far worse than I do. I should leave. Bother someone else. But curses must end and who else is there to do it? Granny Grin is right. He's the way in. The key to getting others to follow.

Linka might follow.

I sit atop the swell of the dunes so he sees me when he exits his house.

The first morning, he didn't take two steps outside before ducking back in.

The second, he moved slowly past.

By the third, we are old friends again. He nodded to me before turning toward town.

And I remain, perched among the waving grasses, watching him

as he leaves.

Every day I move closer.

Every day he watches me, cautious, but he never shows any signs of fear.

Is this what life was like for Valemon? Sitting around, waiting for an opportunity to present itself? Waiting for me?

How did he not expire from boredom?

Yet I'm afraid to leave. What if I miss an opportunity? My chance?

In this form, hunger weighs on me. It's no wonder he spent so much time on the ice, killing. But I can't drag myself away, becoming weaker by the day, by the hour. Every night I gorge myself on Granny Grin's fish and seafood stews, though they taste of ash in my mouth. And then, after a fitful night of sleep, I slink back to the dunes.

What else is there to do? If I am ever to get back to Monroe, back to my simple little life, Beren has to end this for me.

And once he does, I can help him too. I don't know how. But I will make it up to him. All of it, everything I did, everything I said without using words. Because he believed in me when no one else did.

But when the door cracks open and I sit up to greet my friend, my twin steps out.

How was I to know he would be there? Last night the winds were wild, the snow falling in sheets. It must have covered his tracks.

And his scent.

Our eyes meet and for one long moment, I think he sees me. He sees straight into my soul and he knows.

He knows it's me standing on the shore. He has to.

I stand and step forward.

But he reaches for his rifle.

No.

My feet stop.

Please.

He lifts the firearm, fitting the butt into his shoulder.

"Linka, you—" Beren stumbles out onto the wooden porch.

Linka hesitates.

And I use my opportunity.

I disappear into the ice.

Footprints.

The scent of snow and warmth.

Of a winter night wrapped up together next to the fire.

I lift my nose up.

He was here.

While I was on the ice, he was here.

I burst into Granny Grin's house, but she doesn't even turn around from her cooking, and the only sign of him is a golden ivy crown like the one he gave me all those nights ago at the Night Magic Ball.

I nudge it with my nose and then turn, my eyes sweeping over every visible inch of the cottage.

"He isn't here."

What do you mean, he isn't here? I want to demand. But an exasperated chuff is all I can manage as I back away. With this nose, I might be able to track him. I caught his scent so easily, and once the sun sets—

"Don't even think about it, Dira. There's already talk of a bear spending time on the outskirts of town. Do you want to get yourself shot? Because I can tell you, it won't feel good." She turns and waves a wooden spoon at me. "And with this eyesight, you don't want me digging out a bullet and sewing you back up."

I groan.

"Have *patience.*"

With so little room in her house, pacing is relegated to a small corner. As the tingling starts, I barely take a second to stop, whirling back for the door once I balance on two feet again.

"He's probably long gone by now," Granny yells after me as I grab up the crown and race out of her cottage. I speed down the spit, my heart pounding and mind envisioning him there, in Willoughby, slowly striding down the street. I'll call his name, and he'll turn. We'll clash into each other, and I'll bury my nose in the crook of his neck. His arms will crush me to him…

Or he won't be there at all. There won't be any sign of him, not a footprint in the snow.

I glance down to be sure I follow his tracks. Purposeful. Large. His feet might be nearly as big as Landry's, though that would be quite a feat.

But I should avoid the main street in town. Veering around the outskirts would be smarter. Reduce my chances of being seen.

Reaching up, I yank the hood of my parka down to my nose and hope it's similar enough to others' that no one will recognize it as mine. Sun may have set on Willoughby, but there will be stragglers not yet inside. Work still has to be done, even with less sunlight.

Hunching into myself, I shorten my gait and shove my hands in the pockets.

Of course, he walked into the center of town. Of course, he kept to the center of the thoroughfare.

I slink into a shadowed alley as the healer steps out from inside the gunsmith's workshop. She whisks right past me on churning feet, her own head bent as her pack of supplies bumps heavily against her hip. Once I can no longer hear her shuffle, I lean out and glance around the corner.

The street is empty. But for how long?

I hone in on Valemon's tracks once more, jogging across the muddy, wet lane as they turn the corner. Dashing across the street, I duck into the next ribbon of shadow and follow them up onto the wooden walkway.

And draw up short.

Valemon's tracks are scattered and obscured, but I can't mistake their trajectory.

Right into the patrol office.

My breath warms the windowpane as I peek inside, two white clouds forming under my nose.

Dad sits alone, only the soft lamplight shining across his desk.

And on the flat, well-organized surface, sits the book from Monroe.

The stained cover, a flower in its center, stares back at him, even as he glares at it.

My notes are on those pages. Every observation from my day on the ice. My handwriting was sloppy with my own excitement, shoved in empty margins and blank expanses of paper.

Atop the table, Dad's hands grip into tight fists, thick and meaty. They clench and unclench.

And then he presses one into each eye, rocking forward over the book, a sob escaping.

Before my eyes, through a pane of wavy, thick glass, my father breaks.

Great, gulping wails shake his shoulders as he rocks first over the book and then back.

Frozen, I watch as he quiets. As he brushes away the tears in his eyes. As he opens the book.

I can't make out any of the words, just the dark marks blotting out the yellowed pages.

He reaches for his own piece of paper, drawing it near.

And begins to write.

I step away.

It's everything I have ever wanted. My father to hear out my words, my thoughts. To see my observations as worthy of consideration.

Maybe it will make a difference. Maybe when he sees a polar bear the next time, his instinct won't be to kill. Perhaps he will warn it away and tell the others to do the same.

Perhaps as he reads it, sees my heart inside of it, he'll find a reason to be proud.

The wind won't have swept away all of Valemon's tracks, not yet. And though fresh snow falls lightly around me, I might still have time to find him before he disappears forever.

Perhaps one last thank you will be enough to make him stay. That book was our last hope, and he didn't give up on it. So maybe he isn't ready to give up on me either.

I glance down at the golden crown in my hand. I don't know if it's the same one I tossed onto the beach what feels like a lifetime ago or not. But now it is a symbol of something more. Of bathtubs and steaming water. Binoculars. Of magic and freedom. And a man who chose me.

I bite my lip and tighten my grip on the waxy leaves until the spines bite into my flesh.

I drop it onto the patrol doorstep and back away.

The crown was the greatest gift of all. Because without it, I could never let them know I am coming back. That I am here and I am strong. That I was right. And I am going to change things for Willoughby.

With a final glance toward the front window, the dark shadow of my father just beyond it, I swallow around my parched throat.

I will be back. And everything will change.

For the better.

Whirling, I jog back toward Granny Grin's house, my head held high—but only because the streets are deserted. My feet don't stumble as I race past Granny Grin's, the silence of the bay on one side, the aching creak of ice to the sea side. But I don't see either, the trek gone in a blink of the eye until I stand on the narrow spit.

The ice glitters and glows on both sides, the moon full and white.

I don't look back as I step back onto the ice. Only forward now. There is work to do.

I step out onto the ice, thick and unmoving after weeks of frozen temperatures and snows.

And I head home.

For Monroe.

CHAPTER 36

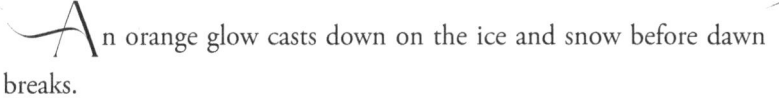

n orange glow casts down on the ice and snow before dawn breaks.

It shouldn't look like that. Not on such a clear night, with the stars sprinkled across the black sky like grains of sand. Not with the moon full and the wilds spreading out in all directions.

A gust of wind ruffles my hair, and on it plays the heavy, acrid scent of smoke.

I drag my gaze from the toes up my boots and come to a sharp standstill.

In the distance, the unmistakable glow of fire lights the horizon, a thick, dark cloud rising to blot the starlight in a column.

Monroe is burning.

Just like my cousin Merritt said the Leig homestead burned.

"Valemon," I whisper. One foot lifts, and then the other. "Valemon!" I scream, though there is no chance he can hear me. Is he even there? In the home I built for us? I'm too far away, and dawn approaches.

Cold, dry air pours down my throat in gulps, scraping like needles with every breath. Without snowshoes, my feet sink heavily into the snow, and though the ice has carried me most of the way, it cracks under my feet. Thin, too thin for me. I race faster, desperate to reach Monroe. To reach Valemon.

A sharp fracture rents through the air, and the ice jolts beneath my feet. I pitch to the side, steadying myself, but with the next step, my foot sinks, plunging below the surface. A cold so deep it burns surrounds me, sucks me in. It closes over my face, pouring into my mouth, my ears. My nerves scream out even as my muscles refuse to move.

To fall below the ice is a death sentence. It won't be long. I'll be gone in seconds.

A tingle rushes over me.

Cold is no longer cold, my lungs no longer burn.

With ease, I shoot back toward the surface, white paws balancing on the broken ice and pulling me up onto the floe. A single kick below the water sees it tipping and me back on solid ground, even if it threatens to knock me back off. Water drips through my fur, pooling at my feet, but the cold that was there moments before, the cold of death, it's gone.

Following my nose, I turn my attention to the smoke, to the burning fortress.

The roof flickers with bright orange flames, huge curtains of black smoke waving from them like tattered banners. As I near it, the tiny specks around the broken bridge take shape, growing larger and more solid. White-clad warriors with rifles in one hand and spears in the other.

I recognize those parkas.

Buckroe.

Only one doesn't wear their colors, and I would recognize his white-blonde hair anywhere. It haunts my dreams and my every waking moment. He is here. He didn't run. He stayed. Waiting.

For me.

"Valemon!" I scream as I run from the water, but it erupts as only a roar.

They all whirl, but only he loses his balance, falling down to his knees in the thick blanket of snow. Hands stuck behind his back, he is only able to regain his footing as one of the intruders grabs him by the arm, hauling him up.

I charge as they ready their rifles, speed I never knew existed sending me shooting toward the banks and the wall. My breath huffs out in a steamy fog. The ice cracks and breaks around me, splintering loudly, and I lose my balance only to plunge under water again. But this time I am ready, jumping back onto the next floe.

He's there and they have him.

I have to get to him.

They already advance forward, and no amount of speed will get me to dry land before they box me onto the ice floes. They step out onto the ice in lines, shoulder to shoulder, rifles pointed forward. Valemon is at their center, a rifle to his back.

"Run, Dira!"

I skid to a stop.

"Run!"

But they have him. I can't run while they have him. He came for me, and I won't give him anything less.

The first shot hits the ice a meter away. The second only centimeters from my paw.

More shots come close; I'm just in range.

He's right.

I have to run.

But to coax them forward, not as a coward. Onto the broken ice, the thin, unsteady sheets.

With one last glance toward him, I hope he sees my warning.

Get away, Valemon. Get away before they drag you under.

The shots continue to echo behind me as I spring to the south, back toward Willoughby. My paws glide and slide on the ice as I avoid the ribbons of open water. They can't see me falter or they'll know.

To the east, the sky lightens into a clear cerulean, fading into the darker sky, sweeping away the stars.

Only a few lone rifles fire now, most saving their ammunition for a better shot.

I leap to the left, avoiding more water and changing my trajectory. Beneath my feet, the ice hardens into a thick slab. Unyielding, unmovable.

Each leap takes me farther away, the sounds of Buckroe's hunters dulling.

And then a dog barks.

Another. And another.

No, not any dogs.

Sled dogs.

My back legs skid out from behind me as I try to stop.

Sleds race toward me from the south.

I turn.

Buckroe isn't as far behind me as I thought.

I'm caught between the two.

Heavy breaths wrack my whole body. After more than a week of not feeding the bear side, exhaustion pulls down on my bones as the adrenaline spurring me forward no longer courses through my body. It's too much. They're coming at me from both sides. And both sides will want me dead.

And my only ally is held captive by one of them.

Both close in, and the smoke from Monroe burns my nose, the back of my throat.

Rallying the strength I have left, I stand and turn to Buckroe.

Most changed their trajectory, but a few on the edges misstep, plunging through the ice where it weakened. The water quickly swallows their screams, none of their comrades turning to help them.

It wouldn't do any good, anyway. The ice releases no one.

The first Buckroe hunter skids to a stop, going down on one knee.

I won't be able to get to him before he pulls the trigger, and bears move fast.

The ice clicks and snaps around me. There are too many of them, their weight pressing down, causing fractures.

If they come any farther, they'll snap into floes, plunging everyone to their death.

Buckroe.

Willoughby.

Valemon.

I should rush the Buckroe hunter before he shoots me. I could take them all out. With these claws and teeth, this speed and strength, they will all fall.

It's exactly what I want to do. What I would do before.

Granny Grin was right. I always run headfirst into whatever I am doing. I never stop to think of the consequences. Of who could get hurt.

But what happens to Valemon if I fight back? Does he get caught in the crosshairs? They've already dragged him out on the ice in pursuit of me. If I had just given myself to them on the shore, he would be safe.

If I just gave up back there, the ice wouldn't break beneath their weight, putting my people in jeopardy.

Everyone I care about is seconds from disaster.

And it's all my fault.

I sit back on my haunches and stare at the barrel.

The hunter positions the rifle, steadying it against his shoulder.

And squeezes the trigger.

CHAPTER 37

Nothing happens.

No click. No crack. No shot.

The hunter lowers the rifle and jiggles one of the mechanisms.

At this temperature out on the ice, it probably jammed. In the winter, most hunters turn to the old ways. To knives and spears and harpoons. Because guns can sometimes freeze.

Another hunter falls to her knees, raising her rifle as well.

Nothing.

I glance to the south.

The dog barks grow louder, closer. They're nearly to me.

Please hold, I beg the ice.

Please don't come any farther, I beg them.

One of the Buckroe spears rises. Launches. And flies for me.

But I don't move.

"No!" Valemon cries, his voice close, recognizable, burned into my heart. It cuts through my flesh just as the edge of the spear slices through my front leg. The searing comes seconds after the impact as the spear clatters onto the ice, dripping bright red blood with it.

One of the Buckroe hunters laughs only a few meters from me.

"Does that bother you?" she croons over her shoulder as she approaches. "We'll take your bear just like we took your home. You can't save them from us. You can't even save yourself."

"Don't," Valemon yells as she pulls a hunting knife from her belt.

Her feet crunch in the snow, purposeful, even steps, and she stops just in front of me. Through the pain, I manage to focus on her boots. Soft, light leather with thick soles and spikes for gripping the ice. Through the haze, I glance up as she tosses the field knife from one hand to the other. The slap of the grip in her palm rings in my ears.

And then the sun catches the blade, and it flashes as the tip plunges toward me.

"Fight!" Valemon screams as I roll to the side. "Fight back," he begs.

The butt of a rifle slams into the back of his head and he crumples.

And I see red.

Not the red of his blood. Not the red of mine.

But an anger hotter than the pain slicing through my leg.

I dodge the blade, and the knife embeds in the ice beneath. I raise a paw. Swipe. The woman screams as my claws rip into her skin, laying open her face. Ribbons of flesh stain red with fresh blood, and she howls, hands warding me off. With another swipe, I send her tumbling into the snow, the ground turning as pink as the sunrise.

Valemon's captor takes a cautious step back but raises his rifle.

Polar bears have speed. And stealth. For such large animals, they are able to cover a lot of ground quickly.

And I use it. I knock the rifle from one man's hand before going for his jugular. I want to make him pay. Want to make all of them pay. And like this, I can.

A bullet lodges itself in my back leg and I cry out. Another slams into my side. I was shot. Twice.

The pain overwhelms, throbbing, burning. I twist away from it, landing on the cold, hard ground and stare back toward Willoughby. My father stands, feet spread, my brothers flanking him on either side. Mom hangs back with the dogs, her face puckered with worry. Beren steps forward, his hair flying wildly around him, balancing over the ice as he puts distance between himself and the patrol.

But only one rifle points at me. Only one.

Liddet.

The rest set their sights on Buckroe.

But not Liddet.

I stare at her, but all I can feel is… thankfulness. It should have been any one of them that killed me. Any one of them that took the final shot. But she saved them from it.

And for that, I am grateful.

Liddet steps forward as she reloads the rifle.

No fear shines in her eyes as she comes within striking distance. The rifle held aloft. She points it squarely at my head, and—

"Stop!"

Linka rushes forward, falling to his knees and skidding across the ice on bent legs. He stops centimeters from me, his hands held up. My blood seeps toward his boots, circling the toes where they press against the ice. "Stop, Liddet."

"Move, Linka," she says coldly, motioning him aside with a tilt of the head.

"I won't."

"You have to," she snaps, tears shimmering in her eyes.

"No, I don't. Put the gun down."

"We have to kill it," she whispers. Her hands tremble, the nose of the firearm swaying. "We have to avenge Dira."

"No, we don't," he says softly. He reaches out a hand, and it lands on my head. Black beads in the shape of polar bears hang loosely from it. Wound around twice. My necklace. My beads. His hand shakes violently, fear pouring off him so pungently I can smell it.

"She wouldn't want this. She would never want this."

Tears stream down Liddet's face, mixing with a string of snot dripping from her nose. "But we have to, Linka. So you can move on. So everything can go back to the way it—it was. Before that—that bear came—that bear came to Willoughby." Her lower lip wobbles and she sniffs.

"Liddet, it will never be the same. I'm—I'm sorry. But it won't go back to the way things were… because I don't want them to."

Whatever fight holds Liddet together abandons her. She melts into a puddle on the ice, her lips pulled down and her eyes squeezing shut as tears flow heavily.

Beren steps closer, his Adam's apple bobbing. Hope shines in his eyes.

"This is all really touching, but we're going to take the bear and go now," one of the Buckroe hunters says as he steps forward.

"No!" Dad jumps forward, raising his own gun. He puts himself between me and their guns, his big form casting a shadow on me.

The others move with him.

They place themselves between me and Buckroe. Between a bear and the guns.

The rest of my people move in front of me, obscuring the hunters of Buckroe from view. But the last thing I see as a rush of tingles washes over my body is Valemon's face, covered with blood as he leans down and kisses my lips. "Stay with me, Dira," he murmurs desperately. "Stay with me."

CHAPTER 38

"We're going to be late."

Sparrow chortles and hops across the worktable to peck at Valemon's hand.

"Ouch!" He pulls it away. "Overgrown boot brush," he grumbles as he rubs the offending digit.

"He doesn't like it when you stop," I say as I shove the last sprig of spring flowers into the holly circle. My lips quirk up into a smile as our gazes meet in the little mirror. His white hair pulls back from his face, but otherwise hangs long over his shoulders. And mine, the same snowy shade of a polar bear, twists around my head, the first blossoms of spring woven into the plaits.

Valemon leaves the book open, my notes still scribbled in the margins, a clean spoon laid across the pages to keep it open. I haven't overcome the struggle to read the script, but he's been penciling in over the faded letters and reading me the words as he does. I enjoy listening to his voice as he reads me the tales of the March sisters. I've found the one called Jo and I have much in common.

But he doesn't tease me about my fondness for Sparrow like he usually does, only taps a finger impatiently. "I promised your mother I

would have you there on time."

The pull he seems to feel in keeping Mother happy at all times would be charming if it wasn't so consistent. "I know, I know. Help me get this on straight." I hold up the crown in both hands.

He shakes his head and takes the crown, dropping it on top of my head with the same finesse he would use to dump out a bucket of water. "There. Now let's go."

"Ugh, fine." I loop my arm through his. "Sparrow, you're in charge."

The old raven caws once and takes up his favorite spot next to the windowsill overlooking the water.

When Dad carried me back over the ice cradled against his chest to Granny Grin's house, the last thing anyone expected was to find the old woman gone, her beloved Sparrow alone next to the hearth.

Well, perhaps the last thing anyone expected was for the polar bear they fought over to turn into a young woman, but it happened, and I needed medical attention. The healer was called as I was gently laid in Granny's rocking chair, and my father sobbed in my arms, my hand held so tightly in his it's a wonder the healer didn't have to mend crushed finger bones as well.

Maybe it seems strange that I was the one comforting him instead of the other way around, but it isn't every day one's child comes back from the dead, is it? It isn't every day a second chance can be had, one to change the exasperated sighs and shouts.

Once color came back to my cheeks and I could stand for more than five minutes, he offered me my position on the patrol back. I told him I wouldn't shoot a bear.

He told me he wouldn't, either. Unless it meant life and death right then and there.

But still I hesitated. He assured me they would be taking a new approach. A softer approach. One that focused on keeping the polar bears safe as well as the people.

It was then he pulled the book out of his parka, where it lay nestled against his heart.

He had read my observations.

Every last one.

We've spent the last several weeks training everyone on scare tactics to move the bears out of town on their own. And with the help of Granny Grin's recipes and the artisans in town, we have a small supply of darts that will put an aggressive bear to sleep long enough that we can move them outside the town limits.

But I haven't given him my answer if the position will be permanent, not yet. Not when there are teas to make for the townspeople. And books and journals to read through. Granny Grin made her final wishes very plain, and drying leaves offers lots of time for other things. It requires a lot of gathering, too. And I can't think of any place I would rather be than along the shores in the willow shrubs.

Besides, the bears will be returning soon. To not be with them almost feels like a bit of a punishment.

I pull the door to Granny's cottage shut behind me and lean into Valemon as we walk the slender path between the bay and sea toward Willoughby.

"See? We're late." He points toward Beren's house where a large crowd already assembles.

"I'll let you make the excuses. Everyone loves you way more than they love me."

"Hey, none of that." The exasperation at our tardiness instantly disappears and his voice softens. "You know it isn't true."

He's right. I do. It took me a while to understand. But almost losing Valemon, feeling my heart stop when he was a second from death put a lot of things into a sharp perspective. My family always loved me. "I know."

They simply feared for me.

There's been a lot of hurt we've been working through on both sides. But I think we're getting there.

I lean my head against his shoulder. "But they have a harder time getting mad at you. You're still fresh and new."

As we sift through the small crowd huddled on the beach, Calla sends me a sour look across the attendees as she drums her fingers impatiently over her swollen belly. Some things never change.

Landry stares pointedly at me before moving in front of the townspeople. For once, he trimmed his straggly beard around the edges. "Now that we're all here, we'd like to begin." He lifts his eyebrows and motions forward with his fingers.

Valemon and I round the crowd, coming to stand on the porch opposite Landry, Dara, and Dasha. My sisters are dressed the same as me in long-sleeved, brightly colored dresses the same color as a sunrise, their flower crowns perfectly even and uncrushed. Sharp contrasts to my wild one.

Valemon drops a hand to my waist as Linka and Beren emerge from inside the cabin, my parents each taking up a side. His thumb rubs the small of my back. A silent message. This could be us soon.

It probably will be.

I turn to grin up at him.

The couple joins hands, surrounded by their family, witnessed by their friends, and join themselves together. The ceremony is a sweet one, presided over by no one but themselves. I want the same.

Just maybe not with quite so many people looking on.

And as they lean in to share their first kiss as a married couple, Valemon leans down and whispers, "I love you, Dira Cloon."

I clasp his hand. Tears blur my vision. Not for him, but for my brother. For my best friend. That by dying and coming back, I had a part in finally bringing two of the best men I know together. "I love you, too."

And for the first time in my life, the pressure to be something—someone—I'm not doesn't exist. Because I already changed Willoughby.

For the better.

ACKNOWLEDGEMENTS

I don't know how to start thanking everyone who made this book possible or real. I also don't know who to start with. Or which order to go in from there. All of my decisions from here on our are probably horribly wrong, and for that, I apologize. David. You may not be here any longer to read this book, and I am fully aware reading romance novels penned by your sister were far from your idea of fun, but not a day goes by that I don't credit its publication with you. I don't know who or what you whispered to when you left us, but whatever you said… thank you. Thank you, Laynie and MB, for seeing something in "Polar Bears" and giving it life. I am truly grateful you took a chance on us and I hope we make you proud. And to the rest of the S&S team, thank you for welcoming me and making me a part of your little family. I have truly felt honored to "meet" and get to know each of you. I have immense amounts of gratitude to my parents for their support. Dad, if you hadn't watched thirty documentaries about polar bears, the northern passage, and the arctic with me, I never would have written this book. Mom, when I did write it, you read it more times than anyone else, and you've only ever had nice things to say. Thank you for always being encouraging, even when I was ready to set the manuscript on fire. Tracy, you have always been my biggest inspiration. You're not only my book best friend, you're my best friend, and even if I could do this writing thing without you, I wouldn't want to. To my Write Squad! Christy, Audrey, Kelly O, Rachael and Brett, Shannon, Joel, Kelly K, thank you for being some of the first people to pick Polar Bears apart and then help me put it back together. Even when I sobbed and cried and despaired. There is a piece of each of you in this book! To my Wolfpack! Thank you for always being there and being supportive. When we first met each other more than ten years ago, I had no idea what a fantastic group of women I was joining. To my Army family. You prove the world is very, very small, but that distance doesn't mean we can't be there for each other. A special thank you to Rebecca Jaycox for your help in making this book the book it is today. Endelyn, Alistair, Ferelith, and Tegwen, you are all my favorite young people, and I hope that when you are ready to read this, you see some of yourselves in these characters. Thank you, Eugene, for volunteering as a writing desk even when I didn't want one, and Flynn for never insisting on a turn with that honor. And, as always, thank you Steve for always being supportive and encouraging, for believing in me even when I don't, and forever being an optimist when I can't be one for myself.

Author Bio

Kyra grew up outside of Atlanta, thriving on a steady diet of heavy traffic, Coca-Cola, and fairy tales. An unabashed hopeless romantic, she has been penning her own magical love stories to share with her friends since she was eight, though A Burden of Ice and Bone is the first to take place in a frozen tundra, perhaps as a bit of wistfulness over the hot and humid weather of the South. She currently lives among the coastal marshes in Fort Stewart, GA with her Army officer husband, their four children, two basset hounds, and cat named after a sandwich.

Other Books By

Into the Otherworld, July 2018,
The Wild Rose Press (https://catalog.wildrosepress.com/bookpage.
php?TitleID=12194)

Through the Veil, November 2019,
The Wild Rose Press (https://catalog.wildrosepress.com/bookpage.
php?TitleID=13240)

www.ingramcontent.com/pod-product-compliance
Lightning Source LLC
Chambersburg PA
CBHW060936030726
47503CB00003B/610